Gang Land

Gang Land

Chuck Hogan

GRAND CENTRAL
PUBLISHING

NEW YORK   BOSTON

Grand Central Publishing
Hachette Book Group
1290 Avenue of the Americas, New York, NY 10104
grandcentralpublishing.com
twitter.com/grandcentralpub

First Edition: August 2022

Grand Central Publishing is a division of Hachette Book Group, Inc. The Grand Central Publishing name and logo is a trademark of Hachette Book Group, Inc.

The publisher is not responsible for websites (or their content) that are not owned by the publisher.

The Hachette Speakers Bureau provides a wide range of authors for speaking events. To find out more, go to www.hachettespeakersbureau.com or call (866) 376-6591.

Library of Congress Cataloging-in-Publication Data

Names: Hogan, Chuck, author.
Title: Gangland / Chuck Hogan.
Description: New York : Grand Central Publishing, 2022.
Identifiers: LCCN 2021053874 | ISBN 9781538751756 (hardcover) | ISBN
    9781538751749 (ebook)
Subjects: LCSH: Organized crime—Fiction. | LCGFT: Thrillers (Fiction) |
    Novels.
Classification: LCC PS3558.O34723 G36 2022 | DDC 813/.54—dc23/eng/20211116
LC record available at https://lccn.loc.gov/2021053874

ISBNs: 9781538751756 (hardcover), 9781538751749 (ebook)

Printed in the United States of America

LSC-C

Printing 1, 2022

To my father,
who would have loved this book

Gang Land

1975

Cop detail's watching the house—I shoulda warned you," Sam Giancana said.

Balding, paper-skinned, and sickly, the sixty-seven-year-old former boss of the Chicago Outfit picked his way down the basement stairs ahead of Nicky.

"No shit," said Nicky. "I didn't see it."

The tan Coronet sedan had been parked on the opposite side of South Wenonah Avenue, two houses back from Giancana's brick bungalow. Nicky had been sitting low in his '74 Plymouth Satellite, parked four houses down from the unmarked Coronet. Long enough to see Giancana's daughter and her husband leave with two Outfit guys Nicky knew but not well, Butch Blasi, a longtime Giancana confidant, and Chuckie English. The wine must have flowed at dinner, because everyone looked happy as they paired off into their cars and drove away. Ten minutes later, the Coronet came to life, swinging around in a U-turn and leaving its post well before the end of its midnight shift. Nicky'd ducked down onto his right shoulder when the Coronet rolled past him, then sat back up, waited ten minutes to be sure, and carried his shopping bag up the street to Giancana's side entrance. It was June 19, 1975.

"Anyways," said Nicky, "my plate number's nothing new to them."

Giancana had Nicky's bag in his hands as they descended. Two steps in front of and below Nicky, Giancana's ashen scalp showed blemishes of aging through his wispy hair. "You're bringing food to a sick friend! So fuck 'em. This from Caputo's?"

His real name was Gilormo Giangana, also known as Momo, also known as Mooney, Outfit boss from 1957 to 1966, early supporter of and later antagonist of John F. Kennedy, sometime companion to famous popular songstresses. Sam G. was world famous, but at age sixty-seven he'd hit a rough patch. After almost a decade in exile in Mexico, he'd been unceremoniously deported back to the States. Then his gallbladder went. Blood clots followed, and it was touch and go for a while. All this had aged him.

Nicky came off the stairs into a basement apartment redolent of tobacco smoke and the woolly essence of old man. Giancana owned the house, set on the corner of Wenonah and Fillmore in suburban Oak Park, but chose to live only in the part that was underground. Nicky knew other old-timers who lived the same, guys who had spent most of their lives avoiding being watched. Guys who didn't want to feel any eyes on them.

Giancana had made a fortune during his exile in Mexico, something to do with casinos overseas. At least that was what everyone said, him most prominently among them. Or else it was a nut of truth wrapped in a caramel of bullshit, like Sam G.'s CIA tales. Globe-trotting multimillionaires with CIA connections rarely live in their basements.

That said, he had it furnished with everything he needed. Nicky never got farther than the kitchen, which was complete. Through one doorway he saw a television and a humidor, some framed golf tee flags on the wall. A coatrack on which hung a fedora like the ones he wore when he was the boss. The other way, Nicky saw the foot of a bed and the back of another TV, the open door to a bathroom with a stand-up shower. Caretakers lived in the main part of the house upstairs, an older couple who would come down in the morning and make the dirty dishes in the sink go away. And he had three grown daughters to take him out to places now and then. There were worse ways to play out your string.

Some people—not Nicky—wondered why a guy with money like that would return to the city he *used* to run, rather than anywhere else in this beautiful land. Some people thought it strange, even suspicious. But Nicky understood. Home was home. It was the streets and the language and the people you knew. It was the markets and the food. It was the familiar. But it was still some questionable decision-making.

Giancana unpacked the grocery bag on the counter next to the sink full of dinner dishes. "Sausage. Escarole. You take orders good, Nicky. A lost art."

Nicky pulled out a chair with a soft backrest and sat at a table for four, upon which stood a porcelain creamer and glass shakers of pepper and salt. Nicky wore a short-sleeve white cotton button-up under a light jacket with a navy nylon outer shell, which he did not remove. The .22 sat snugly against the small of his back in the waistband of his slacks, the suppressor weighing down his left jacket pocket like a long roll of quarters. He sat with his right forearm resting on the table, his hands touching nothing.

"Getting your strength back," said Nicky. "Having people over and still hungry afterwards. A good sign."

"Blasi and English. My Francine and her husband. I'm up to here with the concern, but they insisted." Giancana splashed what was left of an open bottle of red wine into a juice glass, brought it over to Nicky. "This is good red."

Nicky accepted the glass and placed it on the table.

Giancana opened his refrigerator, showing Nicky. "Look at this. Francine, my youngest, she went through and took away anything and everything with the littlest bit of taste. She wiped me out."

"She's concerned," said Nicky. "I don't know—maybe you should eat bland."

"Eat bland," said Giancana with a sneer. "I should live bland and be bland. This was your idea!"

"I know it. But I don't wanna be responsible for no health setbacks."

"A snack, a *tastari*," said Giancana, slicing open the package of sausage with a tomato knife. "Look at me."

"You did drop a lot of weight. I thought maybe it was all a gambit, you know? A ploy. Get out of the grand jury thing and put the crime commission off your back."

"It was as real as it fucking gets, my friend. Hand to God, I had one foot in Mount Carmel. My doctor in Houston looking at me like there was gonna be a free bed in about five minutes." He was rinsing out a fry pan. "I don't need no health ruse to keep my mouth shut. I did a long fucking year for not talking. And the thanks I got? A one-way ticket outta town." He turned on the hissing gas burner and ignited it with a match—*bwomph*. The tile backsplash near the oven burner was tanned from spattered grease. "No, I stood up. Unlike some." He wiped his hands on a damp dishrag. "A little late-night snack, Nicky, huh? This is gonna be good."

Nicky heard a smattering of laughter from a television somewhere above him. The caretakers must be hard of hearing. No movement.

Nicky said, "Unlike who?"

Giancana turned halfway around. "Huh?"

"You said unlike some. Who?"

Giancana said, "Not you, Nicky. You did your bid. I'll tell you a story—you like stories. Capone, right? He goes away for his tax thing in '32. Frank Nitti too, same time. Capone gets something like eleven years, he's gone. Nitti, only eighteen months. Year and a half, not bad at all. And when Nitti gets out, he's made boss—it's waiting for him. All good, right? But—what happened in there? Prison went to Nitti's head, and he's got—what is it? He's a claustrophobe. Tight spots—he gets anxious. He sweats. Hides it. It was never talked about, but we knew. It was known. So he's careful like a nun, a sister takes a vow of silence, because he doesn't wanna go back—he can't. Puts everyone else on edge around him, tightens things up. But guess what? A matter of time, he gets tangled up in a thing. Projectionists' union, extorting movie studios—a great racket until the indictments came down. He's on the hook. But he knows—he can't go back in the box. Can't do it. Just the thought of it . . ."

Giancana laid two fat sausages in the pan, then returned to chopping up the escarole next to the rinsed ceci beans, working mostly with his back to Nicky.

"Day before the grand jury, he sends his wife—his new wife, his other one died, Anna or Annette, this was the new one. Anyway, sends her to church, say a novena, say the rosary. And so she goes. He drops something like a pint of the good stuff, just blotto, stumbles outta the house, over to a rail yard in North Riverside—and shoots himself in the face three times. Three fucking times, Nicky! In his own fucking face!"

Nicky pictured it, a 1940s crime boss, dapper and spit shined, tripping across the rail yard—maybe a childhood spot of his, or he just couldn't think of a better place to go out—stopping, turning his gun on himself, looking at that muzzle, wanting it, blasting away at his face—once—twice—and again—until his trigger finger stopped squeezing.

Nicky said, "Three does seem a little extreme."

"I mean, look at me," Giancana said over his shoulder. "I'm a fuckin' psychopath. Why army doctors kept me out of the war. A documented fuckin' psychopath who army doctors are afraid of— and I couldn't do that to myself!"

It made Nicky smile to think of this man in loafers and an oxford shirt, dishrag over his shoulder, as a scary fucking recruit grown men didn't want to be in the same room with, but Nicky believed it just the same. He was glad not to have known Sam Giancana in his prime—or Capone, or target-practice Nitti for that matter—back in the Wild West days.

"Now, Capone, different story, but the same result. They let him out earlier than his eleven years because the syphilis had eaten away his brain like a rat on a wheel of cheese. Fonzo was fucking gonzo. He was like a kid again, couldn't care for himself. A fat, angry, syphilitic kid. They took him down to Florida after he got out, and never once did he come back home. Not once." Giancana knocked on the side of his head, working the spatula with his other hand. "Loony bird. What I'm saying is, heavy sits the crown—where was I going with all this? Accardo—right. You don't know Joe Batters the way I do."

Nicky said, "I know him not at all."

"Now, Tony Accardo, see, I was his wheelman when he took over soon after Nitti. After the Kefauver hearings in '51, he got heat for the mansion he was living in, with a bowling alley and billiard rooms and these fucking parties he'd throw, forget it—and he thinks I lived too big in my day? But he had an IRS scare, same as Capone, who he learned from, and knew not to play with that. Next man up is me. 'Cause I earned—I earned so much, Nicky. The fifties, it was all wide open if you had the nuts, if you had the cheese up here, and boy, I had both. But Accardo, he never really stepped aside—only stepped back. I still hadda go to him and Ricca"—Giancana crossed himself out of respect for Paul "the Waiter," who had dropped dead two and a half years before—"for all the major moves. So they got all the sway, and I'm out front taking bullets for them. And when the heat came down, and I did the right thing and kept my fuckin' trap shut—I do my year for contempt—I'm thrown over. I'm out, exiled. Then who? Battaglia. And Milwaukee Phil, remember him?

To a man, every one of them, prison. See the pattern here? Now do me a favor. Guess how many nights Tony Accardo's spent in jail. You guess. I'll give you a hint."

"None."

"None is the answer. Never spent one night in jail. Think on that. Not once. What's it telling you?"

"That he's got this city buttoned up tight. Police chiefs to judges and aldermen—"

"The butcher, baker, the candlestick maker—sure, but all for him." Giancana waved his spatula like a magic wand. "All for him. I feel for you, and worse for the young guys coming up like you. Because Tony Accardo is not risking nothing for nobody. For the simple reason, he's got too much to lose. Go to prison *now*? Do eighteen months *now*, like a boss's supposed to? Nicky, he's seventy. Never broke his fuckin' cherry. And now it's a burden. Now he's just runnin' out the clock."

Nicky shrugged. "I wouldn't know. But you would."

"You bet I would. I ever take winters off, go to Palm Springs? Do you? He's a fuckin' banker now or something, I dunno. What a life he's got."

"He's the Chairman. But I'm saying, with all he owns and controls, what's there for him to worry about?"

"For him? Weakness from within. Somebody who's seen enough and maybe had enough. Or gets tagged on another thing and can't take the pinch. The only real danger."

"You mean—a snitch."

"It's what the whole thing is built on. Trust. You're as strong as your weakest man. All it takes to knock down the top boss is one fuckin' fink." Giancana turned the heat down to a simmer. "Get me two plates, will ya? You want more wine, I can open up a—"

The pistol, front-heavy now from the suppressor Nicky had quietly screwed on, jerked in Nicky's hand as he fired a round into the back of Sam Giancana's head from three feet away.

Giancana's head snapped forward, chin to chest, and all at once his body dropped to the floor with no attempt to break its fall.

Nicky stood in the center of the kitchen, his gun arm dropping to his side. In his ears and in his mind the report was loud and still reverberating. The sound of the body dropping to the linoleum—dead before it hit the floor—was the kind of complicated noise that makes people take notice.

He listened for television laughter, which he did not hear. Only a crackling, popping noise, like the aftereffects of an electrical explosion, voltage sizzling, but it was just the sausages cooking on the stovetop.

Nicky moved quickly even as he told himself to go slow. Giancana lay on his front with one arm under his chest and his legs crossed at the ankles, blood dampening the only real hair he had, on the back of his head. Wedging a scuffed leather shoe under Giancana's ribs, Nicky rolled him off the arm, laying him out flat on his back. Giancana's swollen eyes stared upward, lips parted, blood filling in the linoleum grooves of the floor. The .22 round had not exited the front of his skull.

The next part, Nicky wasn't proud of. Six shots, fired into Sam Giancana's mouth and face. It was over fast, sound and smoke hanging in the kitchen with the food smell, Nicky's hand thrumming from the energy emitted by the .22.

He looked up at the low ceiling, listening, unable to trust the pounding in his head.

Television laughter. He was good.

Nicky dumped the wine into the sink and used Giancana's damp dishrag to wipe the juice glass clean, adding it to the dirty dishes. He wiped down the .22 and its suppressor, dropping the towel and the target pistol into the paper bag from Caputo's, which he took with him, leaving the food simmering on the stove.

* * *

He didn't run. It was a short distance back to his car, but a long walk. The keys dropped down out of the visor, and the engine turned over and he drove away. With the shopping bag in the passenger seat next to him, Nicky turned left on Lexington and got on Harlem, crossing the Eisenhower, a straight shot north into River Forest, another plush suburb, about a fifteen-minute drive.

He replayed everything, every step of it, and couldn't see any slipups. He had gamed everything out ahead of time, many times, including ways it could go wrong. He alternated between reliving the job and making sure to focus on the road so he could get where he was going. This wasn't over yet.

He parked two blocks away on Lathrop, to be safe, getting out without the bag or the gun, walking the rest of the way to Ashland Avenue along a sidewalk set back from the curb by a lane of grass twice as wide, trees planted every ten yards or so. A cool, clear night. Number 1407 was a low-slung modern home, another corner lot, this one with a wide crescent-shaped driveway and an attached three-car garage. Nicky had driven past a few times out of curiosity but had never been inside. It always struck him that you wouldn't think the boss of bosses would live on a suburban street like and among normal people.

The doorbell chimed inside. Nicky's right hand still felt a little juiced from the gunshots, his mouth dry.

The man who answered the door was tall and silver haired, maybe seventy, looking at Nicky through owl-like eyeglasses with extra-wide lenses. He wore a light sweater with a cowl collar.

"Yes?" he said.

"Mr. Accardo?" said Nicky. "He's expecting me."

"Yes, and-a you are?"

Nicky's mouth opened, but he wasn't sure if he should give his real name. "I'm Nicky Passero."

"Mr. Passero, come right in."

The door opened fully, and Nicky stepped into the foyer. A hall-way went straight ahead, with coral-colored carpeted stairs rising to the right. A tiny wooden table near the door held a small bronze elephant with trunk curled back like it was full of water, next to a crystal dish of soft pastel dinner mints. The houseman closed the door, and Nicky saw himself reflected directly to his right in a wall of mirrored panels framed in chrome.

Nicky's eyes looked a little larger than usual, as though he'd just had a close call out on the road. He swiped back a forelock of dark hair and relaxed his shoulders. His face, too long and too broad at the same time, his mouth thick and wide, looked like a mask to him, reflected so starkly in this ornate mirror. He thought his jacket made him look like a gas station attendant or an automobile valet. He pulled in his gut. With this all behind him now, all the stress, he should eat smarter.

"My name is Michael, Michael Volpe," said the houseman. "May I take-a your jacket?" he said, perhaps reading Nicky's lingering self-appraisal.

"No, I'm okay. Oh—or do you...?" Nicky lifted up the hem all the way around to show his waistband was clear, no weapon. But Volpe quickly shook his head; there was no need. He led the way to the first doorway on the left.

"Mr. Passero is here," he announced.

Still solid at almost seventy, Tony Accardo wore an after-dinner robe—scarlet satin, though on him it somehow looked neither fancy nor quaint—over his daytime dress shirt and suit pants. Up close, Nicky saw that the silvering hair ran back from an untroubled forehead, the long ears drooped. Deep lines slanted below the broad nose, framing his colorless lips. His arms hung a little too long for his stout torso; his legs stood a little too short. His broad shoulders stooped in a grandfatherly way. Accardo was always shorter than Nicky expected, each time they met, looking like any pit boss or haberdasher Nicky had ever come across. He was pouring two rocks glasses on a sideboard bar.

"Nicky Pins," he said. "Scotch good?"

It was already poured, so it wasn't a choice. Volpe exited the room behind Nicky, silently. Nicky wanted the drink, but first he stepped up to Accardo, not wanting to make any mistakes.

"I hadda give him my real name," Nicky said quietly.

"Who, Michael?" Accardo waved it off with a thick, mitt-like hand. "Michael's been with me since he stepped off the boat from Palermo forty years ago. Part of the family. Here."

Accardo handed Nicky his drink. They exchanged a half salute, glasses raised, and Nicky threw back a sneaky large gulp, exhaling softly through gritted teeth after. Accardo took a smaller bite, nodding after swallowing. "There it is," he said. "The first one's always the roughest goin' down."

Nicky nodded. "Thank you," he said, and drank again.

"Let's take these out back," said the boss of bosses. "Come with."

The backyard was more expansive than Nicky had guessed from the street, its perimeter marked off by trees inside and outside a six-foot-tall iron fence. An in-ground swimming pool was lit from below, the surface shimmering, ripples being put forth by a squirrel paddling for its life along the deep-end wall, pointy head and tiny paws struggling to stay above water.

"Every morning," said Accardo, who had lit a cigar, sitting in a mesh-backed lawn chair on the other side of the glass-topped table from Nicky, facing the pool and the yard, "a drowned squirrel. This is why, right here. Evening swim. Michael!"

Nicky watched as the old houseman retrieved a long-handled mesh skimmer from a rack on the side of a small pool shed. He scooped up the squirrel, which spread its limbs on the mesh as if it were in free fall. Volpe rotated the long arm over the grass and laid it down. The exhausted rodent hopped off, slick with water. It shook off a bit, then scampered away in tiny, leaping arcs.

"No thank you, nothin'," grumbled Accardo, watching it go. "Typical."

Volpe returned the skimmer pole to the shed rack and made his way back to the patio. Nicky took another sip, finishing his drink, having declined the boss's offer of a cigar. Accardo picked up a fly swatter off the table.

"I think Mr. Passero here could use another," said Accardo, and Nicky gratefully handed Volpe his glass, the houseman stepping inside, leaving them alone.

Accardo looked at the sky. "Not too humid tonight," he said. "I like this."

"No," said Nicky, "it's nice."

The fly swatter switched back and forth on his leg. Smoke drew bugs.

Accardo said, "Nice and quiet back here, summers."

"Private," said Nicky, nodding. "Real nice."

Volpe reappeared, this time with a double. Nicky thanked him and set the drink down on the table glass. He felt as if he were in a state of suspended animation. He wanted to do well here, and he also wanted it to be over so he could leave. He and Accardo knew each other but not well.

Volpe went back inside and slid the door closed.

"So," Accardo said. "No problems?"

"None. None at all."

"Nothing?"

"I did like you said exactly. Six times in the face. Message sent."

Accardo took another puff. He didn't inhale; he just took the smoke in his mouth for the flavor, then expelled it, watching it float away into the night.

"He say anything?"

"Not really," said Nicky.

"About me?"

Nicky shook his head. It seemed better not to report what Giancana had said to him, better than the boss knowing Nicky knew something he maybe shouldn't. "He talked a lot. But didn't say much."

"Sounds like him," said Accardo. "Nothing about going down to Washington tomorrow on a flight chartered by the government, testifying?"

"Not specifically. Not even generally. No."

Accardo nodded. "But nothing he said about me?"

Accardo expected Nicky to say something, but the play here was ignorance. "He told me a story about Frank Nitti."

"About Frank? What story?"

"Him getting stir crazy from prison, shooting himself in the face."

"Why would that be on his mind, I wonder?"

Nicky nodded. "Fair point."

Accardo blew more smoke. Flies buzzed near, but he was waiting to pick out one he liked.

"Why come back to Chicago?" said Accardo. "Right? Lotta places Mooney could've gone. Year-round sun. He comes here? For what? To tell me he decided he don't need to pay his split from his casino doings? And then—then the FBI gives him grand jury immunity? Immunity from prosecution? After getting him deported outta Mexico? On top of which—a health scare? See, that's the trickiest one. Staring eternity in the face, Nicky Pins, it makes a man think."

"Him it just made hungry."

Accardo looked sideways at Nicky. The drink had loosened Nicky considerably. He had been tense before; now he was going the other way. But Accardo didn't seem to mind.

"Good, then," said the boss, which seemed to be the final word on the subject. "What's done is done. You know what Capone called me, why he made me his wheelman when he saw what I could do? Capable. That's what he said I was. You're capable, Nicky. That's a very good thing to be. *Capable* is how you move up."

This was all Nicky wanted to hear. Still, he wasn't quite ready for it. "Thank you," he said.

"You did good, and won't nobody connect it up. Because this here"—he pointed the fly swatter at each of them, back and forth— "don't exist. A good thing we got, you and me. Nobody knows. Better that way. No ties."

"No ties."

"But you know that *I* know. How capable you can be."

"I appreciate that."

The door slid open behind them, Volpe stepping out with the decanter of scotch in his hands. Accardo said, "Very good, yes, Michael. Michael stayed late on account of you. How about one more for Mr. Passero here. He don't live far. Where's home, Nicky Pins?"

"Over by the basilica. Avondale."

"Right, right," said Accardo, remembering. "How we met."

"Polish wives."

"I don't wish it on my enemies," said Accardo, a smile in his voice. "Strong willed, my Clarice. Takes a strong man."

Accardo's wife, Clarice, a showgirl when they'd met, never forgot her Polish heritage, and liked to go to Sunday mass at the basilica now and then and occasionally drag along her husband. Nicky's wife, Helena, a department store clerk in ladies' wear when they'd met, sang in the basilica choir at high mass and usually dragged along her husband. Nicky would see the boss of bosses sitting in the pew with his hat in his lap and, despite the fact that Nicky was several rungs down the ladder and basically unknown to him, conspired one day to make a move.

The basilica held a street fair after a mass during Lent, a few tents and tables out front selling smoked cheeses, baked goods, toys, and such. Helena was at the jewelry table, and it happened almost naturally, without Nicky having to get cute. The women got to talking, and Accardo, looking bored as all hell, perked up when Nicky let slip that they had numerous associates in common, and a polite church friendship was struck.

The seed that was planted that day took several months to bloom. Nicky had since done some little things for Accardo, nothing anywhere near as heavy as this, just things Accardo didn't want to involve others in. Like leaning on a neighbor of his daughter's who was giving her family a hard time. An arson to clear out some property he owned. Almost nobody knew they had ever even exchanged words, so the arrangement was a tight one. Via Nicky, Accardo was able to push buttons he needed pushed quietly or quickly and Nicky got to make himself known to the boss. All thanks to their wives.

Volpe returned inside. Accardo said, "You grew up where?"

"Archer Heights," said Nicky. "My father was a brother, Local 743."

"Driver?"

"Yes."

Accardo nodded, but he was thinking. "Passero, huh? Not ringing a bell."

"I doubt you ever dealt with him directly. But he had a lot of respect for you, I remember. He would tell stories. When that big blue Nash Statesman would roll by us on Pulaski? 'That's Tony Accardo,' he'd tell me and all the neighborhood kids."

Accardo smiled broadly. "Good man."

"Yeah. Only—I really don't know, actually. He drove away for good when I was ten."

"Drove away? Took off on the family?"

Nicky nodded, wondering why he was telling Accardo this. "For good."

"That's not easy. I mean, for you."

Nicky took another good swig. No tight exhale followed, not

anymore; it was going down smooth. His brain lay back in a warm bath.

Accardo stubbed out his cigar, tossing the fly swatter next to the ashtray, getting to his feet. "I don't have to tell you nothing, I know. Tomorrow is a normal day, and you'll read the news in the newspaper like anyone, either tomorrow or the next day."

Nicky stood, glass in hand. Feeling it. Accardo walked through the open sliding door, where Michael Volpe was waiting.

"See Nicky out, Michael, and set the alarms." With that, Accardo walked out of the room.

Nicky finished the last of his drink because he thought he should. Didn't need it but couldn't leave it. He handed the rocks glass to Volpe, who took it to the sink. Nicky nodded.

Volpe closed and locked the sliding door, and Nicky followed him down the hallway to the front. Volpe produced a ring of three keys and inserted one into an alarm panel built flush into the wall near the door, turning it, a green light going out under another light blinking red. Volpe opened the door and Nicky exited first, moving off the front step into the driveway.

Volpe checked the door handle after he closed it. Locked tight. He pocketed his keys and said, "Good night, Mr. Passero."

"Thank you, yourself," said Nicky, drunkenly fighting back giddiness. It was over; he was free. He walked with the studied posture of a man who knew the booze was hitting him, down the broad sidewalk in the direction of his car.

Linda Ronstadt's "You're No Good" played on the radio, and Nicky didn't know many of the lyrics beyond those in the title, but that didn't stop him from singing along, badly, with his window down. This thing he'd been dreading for weeks—dreading doing it, but more so dreading something going wrong—he was on the other side now. All behind him.

Nicky's mind was organized like a switchboard. Compartmental-ized. Nicky was proud of it. This was his secret weapon. He was nowhere near a genius, but he was smart and organized. And he was patient. His brain didn't take any evenings off. It wasn't often he sang along with the radio. But this was his step-up day. He had been tasked to act as the right hand of Tony Accardo, and he had come through. He was married to Accardo now, in the way of known-guy talk, and in the best way: nobody else knew it.

Of course, Sam Giancana had trusted him too. And he was lying on the floor of his kitchen now, six rounds in his face.

Nicky had made a neighborhood name for himself young, in the early 1960s, when Giancana was sitting on top of the world, or at least Chicago. Made a name not for violence, because that really wasn't his thing, nor thieving or making book, which would become his thing, but for bowling. Nicky, who never grew out of a childhood affection for games, was one of the best bowlers in Chicagoland for most of his twenties. No small feat, because bowling was even bigger and more popular then. It played on TV every weekend, local matches and the *Pro Bowlers Tour*, and everyone watched, more than they did now. When people started coming to him, looking for tips on improving their scores, he was amused. Bowling was something that came easy to him, along with being a game he liked, so playing good was natural. In side bets, he made some short money, but he was too well known to hustle. He tried teaching friends, offering his advice, but over time became convinced that nobody ever improved much. He wasn't good at teaching bowling. It was just something he did and how he earned his nickname, Nicky Pins.

Giancana went away in '65, so Nicky's bowling prowess was frozen in the mobster's mind, how he remembered this kid around town. Nicky hadn't tossed a ball down a bowling alley—remarkable because he owned and operated a bowling alley now—since he rolled his perfect game in 1967.

First time he ever came face-to-face with Giancana was at the track, around 1960 or so. Running bets for made guys for tips, it beat working. Nicky's draft number had come out low, and his mother was worried, because he was all she had at home. Somebody introduced him to Sam Giancana, sitting in a private box, wearing his fedora and sunglasses in the shade, looking as if he were taking in the Grand Prix in Monaco instead of the fourth heat at Arlington. "You the bowler?" he said. Just like that. Sam Giancana knew of him. "I heard you drew a low number—what was it?"

"Eighty-eight."

"Lucky number, but not for you. Thinkin' of enlisting?"

Nicky said, "I'd rather do two years than four."

"It's not a prison sentence, you know. The army, you learn things."

"I'm okay with learning."

"Discipline and bed-making. How to get yelled at and take it."

Nicky said, "I also can learn those things here."

"Could you?" Giancana smiled and flicked ash on the floor, glancing back at the guys with him.

"I think I could," said Nicky.

"Eighty-eight, huh?" He summoned over someone behind him. "We can fix that."

And he did. It was favors such as that—removing obstacles that seemed impossible, set in stone—that made a boss a boss. Opening doors, moving people up in line—or back, like Nicky. The boss was a politician but ten times more powerful.

One day some months ago Sam Giancana walked into Ten Pin Lanes with his daughter and granddaughter. He came to sit and watch them bowl. One look at Nicky and he said, like he was reading it off a sign, "Nicky Pins. Lucky number eighty-eight."

A decade removed, after the prison sentence and a longer sojourn in Mexico and parts unknown, Giancana remembered him. A lot of the older-generation guys had a sweet spot for Nicky, who knew why.

Giancana was no different. His daughters took care of him, doing his shopping and taking him places, but every now and then he phoned Nicky at Ten Pin and asked him to come by with some things. Sweets, usually. *Get two Danish from a certain bakery, but don't go in after eleven a.m.—it's gotta be fresh. Get raspberry, not lemon. And pick up one for yourself.* And Nicky would get himself one, and Giancana, who was maybe lonely or nostalgic or both, would sit him down and spill a little Frangelico into his coffee and tell him stories from the old, old days.

"Baby, you're no goooood..."

Nicky sang it loud—loud enough to block out the static-like sound of the beans and sausage simmering in the fry pan, and the burble of blood emptying from Sam G.'s head like something spilling from a fallen carton.

Nicky had straight-up betrayed Sam G., and he couldn't run away from that. But Giancana was not a nice guy to everyone; he was a hard guy to most, and he had burned bridges, which, despite his black-and-white account of it, contributed to him being unwelcome in Chicago after his bid for contempt. Why was he back in town now, and why did he refuse to pay his kick to Accardo if only to keep the peace, and why was the government offering him immunity and flying him down to testify like a star witness? Accardo was dead right, in that it didn't add up. Giancana had been back a year. That was a lot of runway, a lot of rope. There were several simple steps he could have taken along the way that would have saved him from what he got.

"I'm gonna SAY it again..."

Nicky, in midnote, happened to glance down a side street as he passed it, spotting a vehicle parked half a block down, all dark, with the telltale roof rack of a Chicago Police patrol car. A glimpse and it was gone, Nicky driving on.

It could be nothing. A pair of cops catching a nap. Or it could be something.

Nicky stopped singing. At the next intersection, he turned right. He reached inside the paper shopping bag, his hand finding the damp dishrag first. Using it, he grabbed the .22 pistol, pulling it out, switching it to his left hand. With no headlights coming toward him, nobody looking, Nicky hung his arm out his open window, the wind flapping at the rag—and with all his might catapulted the murder weapon over the roof of his Satellite, hurling it high and deep into a grove of trees to his right, an empty lot of undeveloped land between houses.

He pulled his arm back in and turned down the radio, watching his rearview. Just as he was starting to think maybe he had ditched the weapon for nothing, headlights swung around the corner behind him—bright rectangles, gaining on him. The patrol car's roof rack lit up, blue-and-whites twirling, bringing the trees lining the neighborhood street to life.

Nicky stayed cool, both hands on the steering wheel. Nothing else in the car, trunk clean—Nicky always kept things neat. Nothing on his person, he was sure of that. Just an empty shopping bag from Caputo's on the seat next to him.

He signaled right and eased over to the curb. The cop lights came up on him fast, like they meant business, not slowing, and Nicky watched as the patrol car zoomed past him on his left. Nicky could see the officer speaking into his radio as he drove. The revolving blues flashed a nimbus of light onto the curbside trees that moved with the unit as it sped away.

False alarm. Nicky sat there a moment, hands hanging from the steering wheel. It was the kind of close call that sobers you—and, momentarily clearheaded, Nicky realized how fucked up he was right now. He had been chauffeuring around a murder weapon while barking Linda Ronstadt out his open windows. His recklessness chilled him.

Nicky checked his rearview mirror again and considered going back for the pistol. He had a flashlight in the glove; he could maybe recover it, give the stolen weapon a proper burial, off South Canal Street into the South Branch of the river.

But it was stupid to be hunting around in the trees with a flashlight and no legitimate excuse. He'd wiped the gun down good. Probably it would be found someday, but so what? Not worth going back for.

His turn signal clicked like a ticking clock. Nicky's eyes went from checking out the street behind him in the rearview to looking directly at the reflection of his own face, eyes staring back. He looked at this other Nicky in the glass. This fucked-up Nicky. This reckless, irresponsible Nicky.

Go home, Nicky.

That was what the voice said. Only, home wasn't really home anymore. He was heading back to a squeaky cot in the side office of his darkened bowling alley. With nothing and nobody there for him.

He looked himself in the eye, knowing his mind was already made up. It was late, he was wired and wasted, and this was the charade he went through, reminding himself what he should do—then doing the other thing.

Rain spat at his windshield as he cruised under the neon sign, a martini glass with a glowing green olive and a candy-red toothpick. He eyed the cars parked on both sides of Merle's—due diligence, because really, what did he expect to see? If it didn't feel right, he would roll on home. Simple.

But nothing jumped out at him, and he wanted it to feel right, so he did another loop and parked in sight of the lounge, across the street. He switched off the ignition and sat and listened to the engine cooling as thin drops of rain landed on the hood and evaporated into steam. He watched the door to Merle's through the windshield until the soft rain blurred the neon sign, getting up his nerve. There was danger here. He felt it in his chest. But that was why he was here—to feel something. To have an adventure. When the lounge-sign colors started to bleed with the runoff, Nicky got out of his car. He locked the door, shoved his keys in his pocket, turned up his jacket collar, and crossed the wet street.

Down two steps, through the door, no bouncer. He felt an immediate change in atmosphere, the outside world gone, replaced by soft music and low lighting, the smell of sweet cologne rivaling the fresh-sliced oranges and limes that garnished the cocktails.

The bar that swept along the right side was nearly empty, one or two lonely souls turning their heads toward him. Nicky dropped his chin and kept his eyes forward, making straight for one of the vinyl booths along the left side, red, high backed, and safe. He sat deep in the second empty one, tucked away nicely, his first objective achieved.

He got his bearings, looking across the lounge from his vantage point, taking in a section of the bar. He was so self-conscious, he felt like he was outside his own body, watching himself here. Playing it cool. A man on a mission.

Light laughter two booths over—not directed at him. Nicky recognized, over the soft crackle and popping of the well-worn record, the singer's voice. It was Lena Horne singing "Mad About the Boy."

Nicky pulled his hand back from the table so his sweaty palm wouldn't leave a damp smear. He rested his forearm sleeve on the scored wood in the same manner in which he had positioned himself at Sam Giancana's kitchen table. But he was nervous here in a way he hadn't been there.

In the center of the round table were an almost-clean glass ashtray and a small plastic caddy of sugar packets and gold-colored matchbooks with *Merle's* printed in black script. A door opened somewhere nearby, on squeaking hinges, not the front door but the men's room.

The bartender came over, young and skinny, shirt unbuttoned to midchest. Dirty blond hair parted artlessly in the middle, falling down and flipped back on each side. Tight tuxedo pants.

His eyes took in Nicky's face but did not recognize a regular. "Welcome to Merle's," he said, laying a gold-colored cocktail napkin on the table.

"Scotch mist, water back."

"Lemon twist?" he asked.

"Good," said Nicky, his voice sounding steady to him, in control. "No straw."

"You got it. Know where the men's is?"

Nicky nodded. "I do."

The young bartender glided over to another booth, the one where the laughter had come from. Nicky couldn't hear the order there, but as the bartender started back to the bar, two men rose from the booth and walked to a cleared space on the floor at the back end of the lounge. Nicky leaned out sideways a few inches, just far enough to glimpse them slow-dancing in each other's arms. The two men at the bar looked like business travelers hoping for a late night. High hopes and low expectations at the same time. Nicky sat back deeply in the booth.

The young bartender mixed Nicky's drink, making conversation with one of the men at the bar as he did. The kid looked barely old enough to drink himself, but he handled the bottles like he knew what he was doing. He didn't look especially fragile, only rather plain, and cheaply made, like the kind you see outside bus stations watching men go in and out.

Places like Merle's had their own mood, their own cadence, Nicky had found. Foreign to him, but similar to each other. So different from everywhere else he went, it was difficult to get used to. Like driving on the wrong side of the road. Strange currency, different language. Nothing coming easy to him.

The front door opened on the sound of swishing wet tires from passing cars, and the door fell back and sealed out the night again. Nicky heard the heel of a boot before he saw the man descend the two steps and pause just inside the entrance. The rain must have picked up, because the new arrival finger-combed wetness back from his amber hair, pinching the fabric of each flared pant leg, shaking out his cuffs.

Tan denim suit with vest. A coastal look, trendy elsewhere but a standout in Illinois. Fair skin, full mustache.

The skinny bartender arrived with Nicky's drink and a glass of ice water, obstructing his view.

"Two ninety-five," he said.

"Start a tab," said Nicky. "There'll be more."

The bartender nodded and said, "My name is Randy."

Randy walked back across to the bar, stopping on the customer side to engage with the new arrival, taking his drink order. The guy stood with his hip against the bar, not sitting, taking in the selection of spirits.

Nicky reached for his drink. The crushed ice was firm, and he sipped the scotch right through it, his top lip going cold. A hint of lemon, cool and bracing.

Randy laughed and pointed and said, "You're so right," just loud enough for Nicky to hear, the bartender enlivened by the new customer. The hinges of the men's-room door squeaked again, drawing the new arrival's attention. He looked down the length of the bar, seemingly unimpressed, then scanned the room.

Eye contact. Nicky felt it like a bolt. He glanced away self-consciously, guiltily, then looked back again. But the man in the tan denim suit had turned back to the bar to watch Randy mix his drink.

Nicky swallowed hard. He reached for his drink, sucking more scotch out of the ice to keep from cursing himself. He was a lost cause. A fucking head case—and what was he doing here anyway, flirting with fucking danger? If the police came in and raided the place right now, it would be over for Nicky. *I wanted a drink, I stopped in, I didn't know.* Nobody would buy that. It wouldn't go away. He would be marked. Forever.

He set down the glass and made a soft fist of his hand and felt his wedding band at the base of his finger. Stupid. Reckless. He knew what he had to do now. He fished some cash out of his pocket to leave on the table so he could get out of there.

And then the man in the tan denim suit was standing before his table. "Sorry," he said, smiling warmly under his mustache, deep lines parenthesizing his lips. He held a drink in each hand. "Oh, were you leaving?"

Nicky said, "I was, uh . . ."

"I didn't know if you were expecting someone?"

Nicky stared dumbly. He felt breath go in and out of his open mouth.

The man appeared friendly in a rugged way, maybe a few years Nicky's junior. He smiled again. "I'm intruding, aren't I?"

"Sure," said Nicky. "I mean—no. It's fine. Hi there."

"Randy said you were drinking scotch mist." He shrugged without spilling a drop of the two cocktails, each glass with a lemon peel looped neatly over the rim. "I thought you looked thirsty."

"Randy's right, and so are you," said Nicky. "Sorry, you . . . you almost scared me."

"Snuck up on you," said the guy, still smiling. "Is this your first time? First time here?"

"First time in a long while. Sit down, sit."

"Thanks." He placed Nicky's drink down and slid into the other side, across from Nicky. "Gerry," he said.

Nicky nodded. "I'm Nick." He pulled his new drink closer. "This looks good, real good. Thanks."

Gerry tugged down on his vest, getting comfortable, both arms resting atop the table, hands around his glass. No rings on his fingers. Gerry was trim, but not skinny like Randy. Not anxious like Nicky. His eyes were blue and remarkably, icily pale.

"What brings you out tonight, Nick?" Gerry asked. "Celebrating something?"

Nicky floundered a moment, thinking about Giancana again.

Standing over him in the basement kitchen.

Rolling him onto his back and watching him settle onto the floor.

Leaning in and firing six times into his staring face.

"I closed a deal tonight," said Nicky, nodding away the intrusive images. "A big deal, good for me. But the other guy? The other guy got screwed."

"I see. Are you okay? You looked a little sick there for a moment."

"Nope, no," insisted Nicky, wanting to be present, wanting to forget. "I just…I'm lucky. I feel lucky tonight. Don't ask me why."

Gerry said "Good" and held forward his drink. "Feeling lucky is good. Here's to the other guy."

Nicky picked up his drink, and their glasses clinked. Nicky sucked scotch through the crushed ice and focused on amber-haired Gerry's confident smile.

1977

S aturday night in late December in Chicago, and thirty-one-year-old thief Johnny Salita was up near the top of a telephone pole set back from the street in an alley off West Superior, around the corner from North Clark Street. Roughly ten blocks west of Lake Michigan, and he felt it, an arctic wind knifing through the three layers he wore, including a three-quarters length black windbreaker shell.

The icy cold was brutal on his hands but good for robbing. Freezing temperatures kept people home at night, or if they had to go out, they went bundled up, hunched over, head down. The problem for Johnny Salita was that he was losing feeling in his exposed fingertips, and this was close and careful work. But he could not afford to hurry.

Below him, looking out at West Superior to make sure nobody stumbled into the narrow lot, Vin Labotta kept watch. Labotta was in his midfifties, ancient for this line of work, which was why he was on the ground. He was an ex-cop from a family of ex-cops—two older brothers had been kicked off the force, same as him—but he looked like he was still on the job, with the hardened face and the doubting eyes. Labotta heard happy voices and watched from the shadows as a foursome approached, two couples talking excitedly from deep within their coats. One of their group jumped out in front of the others and did some fancy dance moves, rolling his arms around in front of him, strutting along the sidewalk. Good and drunk, thought Labotta. One of the women caught up to the dancing man, linking her arm in his, calling him her John Travolta. Labotta knew what they were talking about. It was the new movie he had given his kid five bucks to see that night, just opened the day before, *Saturday Night Fever*. This was more like *Saturday Night Freezing*, thought Labotta, watching the young people walk away into the night. He looked up the pole to Salita, hoping to Christ he was almost there.

Salita's boot spikes dug into the wood, a line worker's strap looped around the pole, supporting his hips. The pole was a special connection point for five dedicated phone cables as well as an electric line and a second wire leading to a backup battery box. Salita had run his own wire up the pole, sourced from a spool stashed at the other end of the alleyway, drawing juice from the cracked-open base of a public utility lamppost—stolen city power feeding his work-around.

By the light of a small flashlight covered with a red gel lens, Salita worked out of the unlocked exchange box, applying clamps to wires connected to a smaller bypass box, which he had made himself in his workshop and which included a voltage meter. If he couldn't maintain a continuous electrical circuit, the alarms would trip, running directly to the Central District headquarters of the Chicago Police Department, setting their bells ringing less than two blocks away.

The alarm rig was an expensive setup, state of the art. Installing a dedicated pole for consumer use was almost unheard of. The system was guaranteed burglar proof—which was just the sort of claim a wire guy like Johnny Salita needed to hear.

Tell me I can't. Watch as I do.

He double-checked his work, scanning the wiring by the red light, making sure. This was the ball game right here. His breath steamed red in the flashlight beam. He readied the alligator clips in his nearly frozen fingers—and clamped down on the final connection.

The voltage gauge jumped a hair, a flicker of movement. But the needle stayed within the green zone.

Good to go.

Salita unpeeled the filter over the flashlight lens, aiming the now-white beam skyward, flashing it twice at the roof of the six-story building of faded brick.

Up top, Dom Guarino saw the signal he had been waiting for. "Fucking finally," said the man known as Rhino, unhugging himself, crossing to where he and Carl Pino, a.k.a. Cue Stick, had strung up the wind-whipped black tarpaulin, obscuring the roof access door from the sight of the higher buildings along Chicagoland's skyline.

"We're on," Rhino said, ducking under the loose flap, cinching the bungee cord tight, switching on the hurricane lamp. Cue Stick had precut into the door over the lock plate and now set his brace drill and continued cranking to push through. Rhino went at the frame with a pry bar when he was done. Neither Rhino nor Cue Stick had any special talents; they were muscle guys who were good only at doing what they were told. It was artless breaking and entering.

Salita and Labotta met around the rear of the building, where Joey "the Jew" Lemmelman and Gonzo Forte waited with heavy acetylene tanks on hand racks, Didi Paré behind them hauling a peach crate full of torches and tools. Rhino opened the door from the inside, and they loaded in.

It was a four-flight hump, since Salita didn't like the cage elevator for all the weight they had to carry. The building was empty on weekends, with no night watchman, but still they went up making as little noise as possible—because Salita said to, and because Labotta had made it clear that what Salita said, they did.

Salita's flashlight beam led them to the door. The glass read, *Harry A. Levinson's Jewelers*. Below that: *Loans*.

Salita used his flashlight to find a door wire painted the same beige as the wall. He followed it up to the top seam where the wall met the ceiling, and tracked it along the hallway to the corner where the painted wire ended at a metal box. Its hinge door was not locked, and Salita pulled it open, revealing an eight-inch gray school-type dome bell.

There was no tamper switch. Salita cut the wire as easy as snipping baker's twine.

Rhino and Cue Stick were already jimmying open multiple door locks along the reinforced doorjamb. Their lack of finesse and the ruckus they made didn't annoy Salita now. His delicacy and strategy separated him from the rest.

When the door opened, the others waited for him to be the first to step through.

Johnny Salita, whose real first name was Artyom, was the son of Ukrainian immigrants who had settled in South Dakota on the advice of people from their home village who had gone before them. Johnny was a boy with an eye for bigger things and a drive to get them. Reruns of *The Untouchables* told him Chicago was the place to go. He started driving for a Ukrainian-owned taxi company, and on his fourth day he was waiting for a fare outside a bank when the alarm bell went off. Two guys in pantyhose masks came running out of the doors, holding guns. Maybe Salita's cab was blocking their getaway car, or maybe they just panicked, but they jumped in the back of his cab and yelled at him to start driving.

Salita drove them three blocks away at their direction, leaving them off at a playground and watching them run in separate directions. They had quickly divided up the cash in the back seat, leaving behind a few twenties by mistake. Salita pocketed those and returned to the bank after the police arrived, picking up his fare. Nothing about this incident upset him, but he returned to the taxi company at the end of his shift and told them he was quitting. He looked up alarm companies in the phone book and picked one that didn't use the letter *A* in its name to get listed first. He apprenticed as an electrician but never attended school or pursued becoming licensed. Illinois was different from most states in that you didn't need a license so long as you worked under a supervising electrician.

This was how he learned his trade, bouncing from alarm company to alarm company, understanding the systems from the inside out, never staying long enough to attract too much attention. Nights, he was working the other side of alarm systems, starting small, avoiding banks, breaking and entering retail stores and private homes. He had never lacked for nerve. He had decided he was going to be the best, and so far as he knew, now he was the best.

This was his score, his take. He'd put it together. Vin Labotta was a guy with an eye for talent that could make him money, using his cop antenna to suss out good thieves from bad. He had no problem giving Salita the reins, and so Salita left it to him to assemble the crew. It wasn't an all-star team—that was for sure—but Salita didn't need lockpicks and cat burglars. He needed humps who were good enough at following directions to do what he needed to get done. Vin had vouched that these guys were loyal and hungry, and that was plenty for now. Salita's next job would be bigger, the next team better.

Inside, Salita quickly scanned the interior doorframe with his flashlight beam for backup alarms. Just as he'd assumed, there were none. The owner of the store, a minor local celebrity named Mr. Harry A. Levinson, had gone out and bought himself the best alarm system in the state and figured that was that. He never realized that an alarm system that could be installed could be uninstalled too.

Salita turned on all six light switches on the panel beside the door, and the jewelry store came to life. The display cases glowed, gems twinkling in showcase lights. Gaudy chandeliers above, plush carpeting below. It was a jeweler's but also a pawnshop. Levinson's shtick was that he played it up like he was the epitome of class, but people on the street knew his bread and butter was actually second-hand signet rings and pawned furs. The lesser merchandise was on twin display racks to the left, along with some hi-fi equipment and a guitar signed by "Muddy Waters," complete with a certificate of authenticity filled out by Levinson himself, probably using the same Magic Marker.

But there was quality ice in the showcases, and when he saw the three safes in the back office, Salita smiled widely. What a glorious night and day of work lay ahead of him. He checked his wrist-watch, estimating they had roughly thirty hours to see how far they could get.

"Okay," said Salita, stepping back out into the showroom, where the others were setting up the heavy tanks and laying out tools. "Listen up. Gloves stay on at all times, even in the john. Don't filch. The pawned shit stays. It's easily traced—except the watch Pino gave him when he cased the place."

"And my coins," said Gonzo.

"And Gonzo's coins. Vin is downstairs on first watch. Hard part's over. We're in. Now the fun begins."

He pulled a pry bar out of Rhino's hand and brought it down with terrific force on the showcase of diamonds and gems next to him, its glass top shattering with the sound of Johnny Salita getting rich.

"Oh, I almost forgot," he said before they started moving. "Merry Christmas."

Ant," said Doves, shaking his head. "He's a big pain in the ass."

Inside the private back room at Chez Paul on the North Side, three men ate lunch. Napkins tucked into collars, they sliced their softly prepared meat and dragged it through sweet sauce. A server stood at the doorway, hands folded behind his back, facing away into the main room, where other midday business lunches hummed along. Christmas music played, lyrics sung in French.

Joseph "Joey Doves" Aiuppa, the official boss of the Outfit, was seventy, his face reflective of his early days as a boxer. Doves had fought professionally under the name "Joey O'Brien" because in the twenties better fights and therefore better purses came to Irish brawlers. In 1962, upon returning from a hunting trip in Kansas—Doves, like Accardo, enjoyed hunting game and sport fishing in the great outdoors, even going on African safaris with him—he was greeted by federal game authorities, whereupon a search of his van revealed 563 mourning doves, dead and frozen—well over the twenty-four-bird limit it was legal for one person to possess. Pure harassment, because they couldn't get him on anything real. Three years of legal wrangling and three months of prison time followed, and the end result was that Joey Doves had a nickname for life.

Tony Accardo said, "He is. Like the fire hose that gets away from the firemen holding it, whipping around on its own, spraying free. That's part of the beauty of sending him elsewheres."

"He's making everybody in Nevada fucking crazy," said Jackie Cerone.

At sixty-three, Jackie "the Lackey" Cerone was the baby of the bunch. A dapper gent, disarmingly genial, he had recently served three and a half years for interstate gambling. The onetime protégé of Sam Giancana and former driver for Tony Accardo was generally understood to be next in line after Doves.

Doves said, "He's getting a big head over there, that crazy fucking midget."

Tony Accardo sliced off another chunk of blood-rare chateaubriand. The son of an immigrant shoemaker, Accardo's tastes had become refined over the years, developing in inverse proportion to his propensity for violence. This was not the Joe Batters of old. He hadn't bashed anybody with a Louisville Slugger in years. Now he pushed buttons instead.

Accardo's shoulders held the broadness of youth but slumped sharply as though his suit jacket were made of lead. His eyes were sad and tired looking, downturned at the outer edges. His thick nose and hangdog face made him appear agreeable even when he was not—until and unless he got angry. Then the look came into his eyes. Nobody mistook that look. "The Ant is a fuckin' menace," he said, "and that is exactly what we need. Keep the casinos in line."

They were discussing Anthony "the Ant" Spilotro, whom they had sent to Las Vegas to protect the skim of illegal casino profits.

Jackie Cerone said, "He might turn out to be more trouble than he's worth, is what I'm saying. That dog's off its leash. Needs a watchful eye on him, else he acts out."

"Long as the percentage comes in," said Accardo—and then he shrugged, which tabled the matter for the time being.

Cerone, who sat facing the doorway, saw the white-haired jeweler standing outside, hat in hand. He pointed with his fork. "Harry the Jeweler."

Accardo glanced over, chewing. He glanced back. He said, "Yeah, sure."

Cerone looked up with a smile and waved over Harry Levinson, who entered gratefully and walked to the table.

"Tony," he said, greeting Accardo first. "Joey," to Doves. "Jackie."

Doves said, "You got hit hard, Harry."

Cerone said, "All weekend them thieves were in there?"

"The best burglar alarm system money can buy," said Harry. "The *best*. Direct line into Central District headquarters. A fortune, it cost me. And these, excuse my French, *cocksuckers* bypassed all of it."

Doves said, "It's a French restaurant," with a smile. "You can speak your mind."

Accardo and Cerone chuckled.

"They didn't get the big bauble, though," said Cerone. "Going by what the papers say."

"No, that vault held up," said Harry, looking to the ceiling and God in heaven beyond. "The only thing that did."

Some years earlier, Harry A. Levinson of Harry A. Levinson's Jewelers had made a big show of purchasing, at auction, the Idol's Eye, a 70.2-carat diamond, one of the largest stones in the world. He claimed to have bought it for his wife, but really it was for the press and the promotion. The Idol's Eye had an interesting provenance, some of which was even legitimate, but none of this was of any interest whatsoever to the three men at the table.

"They used these torches," said Harry, "water-cooled tanks. I've got water an inch thick in my showroom. A flood. The carpet's destroyed. *I'm* destroyed. They wiped me out."

Accardo said, "You called the cops."

"I didn't, Tony," said Harry Levinson. Very quickly, he added,

"They found the back door to the building open. Came to my house, got me out of bed. Drove me to the building in my morning robe and slippers. I am in a very bad place here, Tony."

"You got good insurance, though."

"The best, the *very* best. But how long until they pay out? And I can never be made whole. Never mind the quality of certain stones, but these animals shredded my pawn-ticket book, flushed it down the john. To be spiteful, I don't know? I keep good books, but... And now I'll have the insurance detectives up my ass for weeks."

Doves said, "There's that French again."

Harry smiled and nodded, unsure whether he was in on the joke or he was the joke.

"Tony," he said, "this is my Christmas—busiest week of the year. I'm losing money every hour my shop is closed."

"Other than being sympathetic," said Accardo, "what is it you would like us to do?"

"Well, I don't..." Harry fumbled for words. "I would never cast aspersions. I just wonder—was there something I did or didn't do? That would maybe make someone look the other way about a bold crime such as this?"

Accardo smiled at the other two. "Harry, this is a head-scratcher, because you should know, nobody in this room would okay anything like that done to a loyal friend of ours."

Harry Levinson's face collapsed in such relief he almost started crying. "Thank you, Tony. Thank you."

"Let's ask around, huh?" he said, turning to Cerone. "Jackie will make some calls."

"Thank you, I..." Harry Levinson wanted to embrace them but settled for mangling the hat held in his hands. "I was a little nervous coming here, coming to you, Tony. Because there is something else."

Accardo exhaled. "Yes?"

"One of the pieces taken from the safe in my personal office...where I keep my most important pieces, you can be sure of that, including special orders for my very best clients...well..."

Accardo set down his knife and fork and looked Harry Levinson in the face for the first time since the jeweler had walked into the private dining room.

Harry Levinson stammered, "Your Christmas present for Mrs. Accardo." He looked at Doves and Cerone in desperation, as though they might help him.

Accardo said, "Why didn't you tell me that first thing when you came in here?"

"I don't..."

"Or call me, as soon as you found out? Why am I hearing this only now?"

Harry Levinson said, "I thought you...I assumed you assumed..."

Cerone, reading Accardo, took a last swig of cabernet and plucked his linen napkin from his collar, swiping his mouth and setting it on the table next to his unfinished plate. "I'll make some calls," he said, standing to leave.

Doves side-eyed Harry Levinson. "Bad news first, always, Harry," he admonished.

Accardo stared at the table, his sad eyes narrowed in disgust. "Okay," he said. "Somebody's gonna get a talkin' to."

Doves said, "It was a big job. Somebody knows."

Accardo nodded, returning to his meal. Harry Levinson backed away to the door, making his escape with neither man noticing or caring.

Chuckie answered the phone with his only arm. "Ten Pin, this is Chuckie."

Rainy Mondays were usually great for business, but the freezing rain crashing down outside wasn't good for anybody or anything. A few senior citizens bowled, chatting the afternoon away, pensioners playing out their strings. School hadn't gotten out for the day yet, most of the thirty-six lanes dark, the arcade room empty. A handful of down-and-outers sipped beer at the bar, eyes on the television soap opera or marking up the racing form or idly catching up on the Sunday paper somebody had left behind.

Tinsel and garland gave the Lanes a little Christmas sheen. Monday was the day to go over the previous week's receipts, restock the candy and cigarette machines, clean out the popcorn maker. Good thing about managing a bowling alley was the ease of upkeep. Chuckie had lost his left arm at the shoulder in Quang Tri, the second battle, giving it to the North Vietnamese while taking back a heavily defended citadel there, but like a lot of those guys, he rarely talked about it. In terms of manual labor, there wasn't much he could do besides answer the phone, pour beer, run the carpet sweeper every now and then. But Nicky felt strongly about finding ways to carry guys like Chuckie, since every once in a while when he looked at him, Nicky remembered how his low draft number got swapped out. That was how life worked: you were connected and got the breaks, or you didn't. And Chuckie was a good soul and generally trustworthy and always on time, and he didn't ask a lot of questions. One night, late, after he had had more than his usual few, Chuckie asked Nicky why he kept him on there. Nicky explained that it was because one-armed guys have a tougher time stealing from the cash register.

"Yeah, he's here," said Chuckie, cigarette bouncing off his lips as he spoke. "Nicky!"

Nicky was on his stool at the shoe-rental counter, reading that day's *Tribune*. He had already received the Vegas line, the odds sheet handwritten on an index card under the rubber foot of the telephone. Maybe there had been a change. Better yet, maybe someone had received an inside tip. He set down the paper such that the headline—*Levinson's Looted of $1 Million in Jewels*—was facing up.

Nicky picked up his extension. "This is Nicky."

Nicky ducked out of the rain under the lean-to opening of the metal-sided coffee truck outside the construction project on South Wabash. He pulled back his hood and recognized the guy cleaning the grill but couldn't remember his name. It was something Greek. A transistor radio standing on the cooler played talk radio.

"Slow day today, huh?"

"Hey, Nicky," said the Greek guy, a grease-spattered apron protecting his wool coat. Nicky ran a half-dozen food trucks across town, set outside construction sites for breakfast, lunch, coffee. The Greek—middle aged, lost his restaurant, Nicky remembered, a good worker—was wary, wondering if maybe something had warranted a surprise inspection. "One of the slowest," he continued. "They blew the whistle about an hour ago. What brings you round in this storm?"

"Meeting someone nearby." He tried a smile to put the guy at ease. "At least the grill gives off heat, right?"

"You know. I get by. Get you something?"

"Anything left over from lunch?"

"Couple of cheese sandwiches. No takers."

"Put 'em all in a bag for me and then close out, take off. You don't need to be here. Oh, dump the rest of that coffee into two cups. Black."

Nicky heard a car pull up, the gutter sloshing. He put his hood back up and looked around the side of the truck and made the unmarked sedan. The Greek set out a white paper bag with the sandwiches in it and the two coffees in blue-and-white cardboard cups with the name of the fellow's Greek restaurant on them. Now Nicky remembered—he had bought the guy out at cost, throwing in the truck to get him back on his feet. Kosmo. Kozma? Kyros! Nicky stuffed a ten-dollar bill in the coffee can. "Appreciate you hanging in here today, Kyros, I really do. Clear skies tomorrow."

"Thanks, Nicky. Thanks a lot."

Nicky stacked the coffees and stepped out into the slapping rain. He crouched into the passenger-side door, knocking the window with his elbow. The driver leaned over and pushed open the door.

Nicky got in as fast as he could without dropping anything, pulling the door shut. "Goddamn," he said.

"I know, right?" said Detective Kevin Quiston. "Could be snow, though."

"Could be sunny and seventy, we were at all smart."

Quiston laughed. He was a round-faced Irishman, approaching his twenty years on the job, father of four. A plainclothes detective in property crimes, but not undercover. Quiston could never have passed for anyone other than a round-faced Irishman, approaching his twenty years on the job, father of four. And his clothes were in fact quite plain, several years out of date. Quiston looked at the coffees, the bag, and stubbed out his cigarette in the open, nearly full ashtray. "Buy that off a truck?"

Nicky handed him the wet bag. "For you and your friends."

Quiston opened it, curious, poking around. He pulled out a sandwich and unwrapped the thin foil. "Cheese, bread, butter," he said, biting in. "Perfect."

Nicky set both coffees on the dash, one closer to Quiston. In doing so he bumped the police radio underneath his side, the handset falling to the floor. "Dammit, sorry." Nicky didn't like being in a cop car under any circumstances, but rain was running the day. The wipers worked back and forth violently.

Quiston, mouth full, leaned over and replaced the handset in its cradle. He looked past Nicky to the building going up on the other side of the sidewalk fence, almost invisible in the rain. "What's this gonna be here?"

"Apartments, I think."

"Jesus, why?" he said. "I live in this city because I have to, the job. But good money on a rental? In this war zone? I don't get it."

"You'll be here to protect and serve them."

"Right. Hey, Nicky—Sunday's game. Twelve to nine, overtime, you believe that? You must have made out good. Good for you, shitty for me. And with Sweetness running."

"Payton can't do it all on his own."

"He sure can't. I thought they were a sure thing to make the spread."

"You always do."

"Even when they win, I lose. Why can't I catch a break?"

Nicky said, "Because you bet games, not winners, and you have a soft spot for Chicago teams, that's why. Because you like getting your heart broken, your wallet kicked into the street."

"I am down again, as you know."

"Way down," said Nicky.

"Okay, okay. Float me to the playoffs. I can get back. Not even, but—close the gap."

Nicky smiled. Quiston had a problem, but Nicky wasn't sure if it was stupidity or compulsion. Nicky told him, "One condition."

Quiston looked surprised. "What?"

"Do not take the fuckin' Bears."

Quiston laughed, too hard. Nicky knew he was going to take the Bears anyway. Quiston bet games like a ten-year-old kid in love with his home team.

Nicky said, "So what do you got for me?"

Quiston nodded, thumbing the plastic lid off his coffee, taking a hot sip. "Looks like it was a black box job, I'm told. Patched over the relay on the pole outside, ran wires to another place—I really don't know how this shit works. But they were up on the pole. Messing around with high voltages and whatnot. Went in through the roof. Used acetylene torches on the safes, burn bars. Real industrial."

Nicky nodded. "A high-line job, huh?"

"And no. They went through the door with a pry bar and a sledge-hammer, some such. This wasn't the Pink Panther, right? But they had alarm savvy, for sure. They shut it down good."

Nicky nodded again. That sealed it. He knew who it was. Only one thief that good, that bold, that crazy.

"They jacked up the safes," Quiston continued. "With actual car jacks. Tipped them over so they could burn in through the bottom, the softest spot. These were professionals, and they came prepared. They had all day and night."

"And yet they still didn't get the . . . what's it called."

"Yeah, the Idol's Eye. No. Ran outta time."

"Maybe," said Nicky. "Or they figured, why bother? Famous stone, massive diamond. The most traceable thing ever. Imagine the headlines then, you want the Pink Panther."

"Huh." Quiston went into the bag for another sandwich. "I suppose that's right too. Anyway—what's your interest?"

"Curious is all. This crew hit a jeweler's—I figure a bowling alley must be next."

Quiston's barking laugh followed Nicky out of the unmarked car and back into the harsh rain.

Nicky had a couple of things in his cart so that he blended in with the frenzy. A Six Million Dollar Man action figure with Bionic Grip, a Slime Monster Game with an extra plastic garbage can of green Slime, Mattel Electronics *Football*, a Kojak board game, an official Mark "the Bird" Fidrych glove. But this Child World in Forest Park was the absolute last place he wanted to be the week before Christmas.

That said, the store would be a good mark. No glory in taking down a toy store, but in the month of December, Child World was where the money was. Delivery entrance in the back, hidden from the street. Big intersection out front to split up after. Something to file away in case things got tough next year.

Nicky wheeled his cart around mothers and young families checking off their lists. Shelves that once held popular toys looked like a bomb had gone off there, everything cleared out or picked over. The toys that weren't selling sitting there unwanted and unloved. Apparently, cowboy stuff was out. One year Nicky got a six-shooter popgun in a brown plastic belt holster under his tree—wore that thing to sleep. Westerns were old hat now. The *Star Wars* movie that had come out in the summer—Nicky saw it twice with his Nicholas, who saw it maybe twice more on top of that, but for some reason they couldn't get the toys in stores by Christmas. To Nicky's eyes, it was a western with laser guns and an old-fashioned black-hat villain, but naturally the kids didn't see it that way.

Up ahead, he watched Johnny Salita pushing a cart while his wife— short, attractive in a cloth coat with a fake-fur collar—bounced their baby daughter on her hip. Nicky trailed them close enough to listen a bit to what they were saying as they chose between a child-sized plastic tea set and a pink doll stroller.

"Get 'em both," said Salita. "Anything she wants."

Their cart was filling up. A spending spree. The wife went up on her toes to kiss Salita on the cheek. Such financial freedom was new to her. "Best new daddy ever," she said.

Nicky rolled up on them as the baby pawed an Oscar the Grouch plush figure that came out of a soft toy trash can. He squeezed past, bumping up against Salita's three-quarter leather jacket, apologizing, and then making like he was trying to put a name to a face.

"Johnny Salita," he said. "Thought that was you."

Salita froze up.

Nicky said, "Nicky Passero. We know each other—I can't for the life of me remember where from."

Salita recovered, turning on the charm.

"Nicky, sure, yeah. Hey, how you doin'?"

"Good, but not better than you. Look at this cart."

"Sorry, yeah, I didn't recognize..."

Nicky said, "I do that all the time. You see a face you ain't expect-ing, out of context. Throws you. Who's this little bean here?"

"This?" he said, remembering his wife and child. "This is Stephanie."

"Stephanie Salita, hi, you. Adorable."

"And this is Angie. Angie, you met Nicky before...?"

Angie had a cherubic face like the baby daughter in her arms. She smiled at Nicky and wore fake eyelashes that fluttered.

"I don't think so," she said.

"A pleasure," said Nicky, making a play to get the baby's attention. "How old is she?"

"She's eight months," said Angie, first-time mother proud at her creation.

"She's a real bean," said Nicky, almost getting a smile. "That's nice, babies're usually afraid of me."

Salita was growing antsy, and Nicky ignored him, letting him squirm. The longer this went on, the less Salita believed it was a random meeting.

Angie said, with an accent somewhere west of Illinois, "You have children yourself, Nicky?"

"Me? I have one. He's a boy, just turned ten. Whole different ball game, ten, let me tell you. I got the Slime here, this electronic push-button game. Thirty dollars. What am I, crazy? You got Play-Doh Fun Factory, and what's this? Sunshine Family Farm. View-Master, Baby Come Back. That's so great, though. My God, spoil her. That face."

"Thank you," gushed Angie. "We just can't help ourselves."

Nicky nodded, taking a look at Salita, smiling through the pause.

"Anyway," said Nicky, "I don't wanna hold you up."

"Yeah," said Salita, nodding, wanting it to be over. "No problem, Nicky, real good runnin' into you."

"And a very merry to you, Angie, enjoy. You and Stephanie go on ahead here, I'm'a borrow Johnny just a minute longer."

Angie smiled and nodded, confused now, looking at her husband. Salita reassured her with a look. He didn't seem especially nervous. "Go ahead, I'll catch up."

Angie put one hand on the cart handle and pushed ahead, put off by her dismissal but appeased by her husband's mood. "So nice meeting you," she said to Nicky.

Nicky and Salita both watched her go.

"Special time," said Nicky. "Baby's first Christmas. Magical."

"Yeah, yeah," said Salita. "Gonna be good."

"*Real* good, judging by that cart."

"Ah, you know," said Salita. "Not all for her. Gifts."

"Sure, sure," said Nicky. "Let's pull over outta the way here, before we get trampled."

Nicky steered his cart over to a shelf of Cher Makeup Centers, and Salita followed. A $9.98 bust of Cher with a face you could paint and hair you could brush.

"What a racket, huh?" said Nicky.

Salita smiled, holding his own. "So, what's up, Nicky, you okay?"

"Me? Good, sure. Yeah, no, I wanted to check in with you about the Levinson's thing."

Salita played it confused. "The Levinson's thing?"

"Yeah, the jeweler."

"Sure, I know. It was in the paper."

Nicky smiled. "The line work, the bypasses. Knocking down multiple alarms." Nicky leaned in closer. "Soon as I heard that, I thought—only one guy could and would."

"Nicky," said Salita, raising his empty palms, "you flatter me. I was at my brother-in-law's all day Sunday."

"Sure, sure, I get it. Vin Labotta probably has a solid alibi too, right? And who else? Maybe Cue Stick? But Labotta—he shoulda known better. Cleared it beforehand."

"I . . ."

"That's the part I don't get. It's not on you, but did Vin think you guys wouldn't have to pay up? Anyhow, someday—not today—I'd love to know what the fuck you guys were thinking. Right now, you gotta figure this thing out."

"Nicky, look, I'm telling you—"

"I'm not anybody in this, you understand." Nicky put his hand to his heart. "Don't plead your case to me. Won't do nothin'. I'm here trying to help you."

Salita squinted, still riding his bluff. "Help me how?"

"You're getting called in for a meeting."

That was when the bluff slipped away. Salita's face fell as he swallowed and glanced around the store.

"You can fix this," Nicky reassured him. "If you couldn't, it wouldn't be me here with you—right? It'd be somebody else." Nicky let that implication set in. "You gotta come in. All of you. That's it. That's the message. Got it?"

Salita nodded. His eyes had become unfocused, as though he was thinking about what this meant for him.

"Tell Labotta—he'll understand," said Nicky, and he left Salita standing there by the Cher heads, pushing his cart away.

The venerable Calumet Country Club, founded in 1901, was closed for the season. The tables in the dining room overlooking the eighteenth green were pushed to the side, their chairs stacked eight high. A light snow was falling outside the latticed windows, tiny flakes swirled madly by occasional gusts, but the carpeted room inside was dead quiet.

Salita and his six fellow jewel thieves stood or paced around the banquet room. Salita had to be talked out of carrying a weapon to defend himself—but now Vin Labotta wasn't sure how much longer Salita would listen to him.

"We did it too good," said Vin. "We got so excited, we had dollar signs for eyes like in the funny papers. We fucked this up."

Salita said, "We fucked up nothing. It was a primo score, we took it square and didn't pop nobody. It was you, Vin. You, the guy said he was most surprised at. You who shoulda known better."

"We were gonna cut them in," argued Vin, warming up his defense for Joey Doves when he arrived. "It's all a big fucking misunderstanding."

"Cut them in when?" said Salita. "You never said nothing about a percentage to anyone else, and trust me, I woulda fuckin' remembered."

…ue Stick had a pockmarked face like he'd taken a load of …ckshot at some point in his teenaged years, when more likely he …uldn't keep himself from digging away at his pimples. "Who was it who came to you, Johnny?"

Salita watched a squall come up and take the snow sideways past the windows. "It was Nicky Passero. The bowling alley stooge."

Vin said, "Hold on. Nicky Pins ain't no stooge. Luckily he ain't no soldier neither."

Didi Paré wore a seaman's sweater under his coat, collar up to his chin. He rubbed his bare hands, the heat not turned on. "So tell me, why is the bowling alley owner coming to see Johnny about this?"

Vin said, "It's a good question, Didi. For which I don't have a good answer."

Salita turned on his heel and paced the other way. "What else is new?"

Gonzo Forte, hands tucked into the pockets of his soft-lined leather bomber jacket, said, "Good popcorn at Ten Pin. Maybe best in the city."

Joey the Jew looked over at Gonzo in amazement, lighting a cigarette with a disposable lighter and taking a deep pull. "Popcorn," he said.

"I'm telling you," said Gonzo.

"Jesus Christ," said Salita, shaking his head. "Forget about the fuckin' popcorn."

Vin crossed his arms, looking at his shoes. "We're gonna have to pay up. Just so you know. Double the street tax."

Everybody looked at Vin, but none of them turned on him faster than Salita. "What are you talking about, *double*? Street tax is fifty percent. Double is everything. All of it."

"Double is we get to go home, Johnny."

"Fuck that," said Salita, "and fuck him."

"Christ, Johnny, keep your voice down, they're due any fuckin' second here." Vin put his hands up apologetically. "All I'm doing here is telling you how it's gonna go. So you can be ready."

Salita looked at the other thieves in amazement. Rhino pulled off his knit cap like he'd just realized he was in church. He strangled it in his hand. He had plans for the money—they all did.

Salita's mind went back to being high up on that pole in the back alley, freezing his dick off, working the wires, everything going perfect. He recalled the feel of the jewels in his hands. Everything went aces on his end. Planned out and executed. He could have seen one of the other meatheads tripping them up somehow, but he never imagined he'd have to worry about old Vin fucking up.

"So Doves wants us to kneel," Salita said. "I ain't fucking kneeling, Vin."

"You're kneeling," said Vin. He turned in a semicircle, addressing the others. "Sorry and thank you, every fuckin' one of us."

"You fucked us, Vin," said Salita. "When you gonna admit it?"

Vin's ex-cop face tightened. "Like I said, we got carried away."

"I didn't get carried away," said Salita, poking his own chest with his forefinger. "I did everything right. Everybody else here, to a man, came through on their end, everybody except—"

The sound of doors opening and closing made Salita stop.

Vin exhaled and swallowed. The other thieves retreated so they formed a loose group, watching the hallway.

A driver entered first. Muscle, a big guy in a loose suit, midforties. The enforcer looked them over, then glanced at the doors to the kitchen, the empty bar. Putting everybody and everything on notice.

Then Doves walked in, removing his hat. He shrugged off his heavy overcoat and handed it to his driver with barely a look at the seven thieves.

Jackie Cerone followed with his driver, a guy in his twenties with not much of a build but wild eyes. Jackie handed the kid his wool cap but elected to keep his coat on.

Vin stepped forward, taking the initiative. "Doves, how are you? We're eager to get this thing straightened out. Hello, Jackie."

Jackie said, "Vin, long time. How are your brothers?"

"Ah, you know," said Vin. "Doing their time, getting by. Behaving."

"Behaving," chuckled Jackie.

Doves walked to the bar, which was bare, no glassware, napkins, nothing. Either he was curious or maybe he was looking for something. He turned and faced them. "Vin," he said. "Boys."

Some of the thieves nodded, mumbled. Salita said nothing.

"We'll get started in a minute," said Doves.

Vin nodded and stepped back like a funeral home worker giving the bereaved time alone with the corpse. Salita had never had an audience with Doves or Cerone or any of the old guys. Doves Aiuppa looked grumpy, watching them like a shopkeeper eyeing kids so they don't steal.

Jackie Cerone dragged a chair over from the wall, but nobody else did or said anything and it was silent again. The longer the silence went on, the more ominous the empty chair appeared.

Some of the guys looked to Salita, but he didn't know what the stall was about. He caught Vin's eye, Vin's expression telling him he didn't know what they were waiting for either.

Salita broke protocol by walking back to the windows. Let the others get wound up by this show. It was all cheap mind games, bullshit, trying to sweat them. He watched tiny, frozen flakes of snow skitter along the blacktop golf cart.

The front door was heard to open and close again. Somebody else had entered. Salita turned and listened to the soft footsteps approaching over the carpet.

Tony Accardo walked into the dining room. Salita thought he could see Vin going weak just standing there. Rhino, nearest Salita, looked stricken. One of the other guys swallowed audibly, and another of them said, under his breath, "Jesus, God."

Here he was. In the flesh. Shorter than Salita had thought, and older, but otherwise the same guy he recognized from newspaper photos.

Accardo removed his hat and his coat, which his driver accepted and laid across the nearest table. Accardo wore a loose wool suit, church shoes, a wide tie of black and cream stripes. He walked to the empty chair and pinched up the fabric over his thighs and sat.

Everybody in the room watched this. Some seemed to be holding their breath. After many more seconds of tense silence, Accardo made his raspy voice heard.

"Maybe I need to introduce myself," he said.

He looked at each face. Nobody said anything.

He said, "My name is Antonino Leonardo Accardo. Some know me as 'Joe Batters.' Other people just refer to me as 'the Man.' That is because I hold a position of responsibility in an organization of like-minded individuals. It's a thing we have, like a union, with structure, not written down nowheres, but rules anyone can follow. A regime. Orders go down, money goes up. Nod your head if you're following me—you all seem kinda slow."

The others nodded dutifully. Salita was on edge, keeping half an eye on the drivers flanking Accardo, no idea where this was going.

"Chicago is a big city," said Accardo, "but it's a small town too. 'The City That Works'—works for *us*. Some people think because a machine runs good, it's easy to run it, anybody can. Maybe that's what you all think."

To a man, they shook their heads. Accardo looked around at them, eyes only, his head still.

"You're good thieves," he said. "Good thieves can go far. Doves was a good thief in Cicero. Me, I did all right for myself. There's room for earners, always. There's room for loyalty. There ain't room for nothin' else."

He let that settle on them. Then he swiped at his nose.

"Which one of you is John Salita?"

Salita lowered his head, stepped forward. "That's my name," he said.

Accardo nodded as though he had guessed right as to which thief he was. "You're good with alarms, huh?"

"Good, yeah. Don't know anyone better."

"That's good," said Accardo, nodding. "Good talent to have. Good skill."

Salita nodded.

"You gotta give the jewels back," said Accardo. "All of it."

Salita turned his head as though he hadn't heard correctly.

Accardo's eyes left Salita, addressing everyone. "I don't think you could pull off a job like that and be stupid, but stupid is what you are. Especially you, Vin."

Vin stepped up, looking dizzy. "We got carried away, I know. We were gonna pay. We made mistakes, but we're not, you know— not crazy."

"I wanna stay outta the weeds here, so let's not quibble. If what you're saying is you fucked up, then I am saying I agree with your assessment one hundred percent. Guys are put in the barrel for less—much less."

Vin said, "We didn't know he was a friend of yours—"

Accardo stopped him with a hand wave. "Not the point, Vin. And in case you didn't know, this right here is a case of the more you keep talking, the worse it can get. I am everybody's friend until I'm not. So it's not about me, my friends. It's not about who. This ain't no special case needs to be figured out. You clear things first, you pay your whack, everyone's friends. You fuckin' freelance? Then who am I? What am I and what is this?"

Salita was breathing hard, trying to hold back. But he couldn't do it. He said, "We already fenced it."

Accardo's gaze swung back Salita's way. Without even considering all the other men who had been on the receiving end of those eyes—more than a few for the last time—Salita was shaken.

Vin held out an open hand toward Salita, speaking to Accardo. "Joe—we can get it back."

The two drivers stiffened. Salita didn't feel like he was looking or acting threatening. To him, it felt more like he was on the verge of a breakdown. All that work for nothing—less than nothing.

"And if we can't?" said Salita, more to Vin, though Accardo didn't hear it that way.

Salita had Doves Aiuppa's and Jackie Cerone's attention now too.

Accardo's eyes came off Salita, going to Vin, looking at him as one might a parent for allowing their child's temper tantrum. "Vin, you wanna tell him?"

Vin put his hands together flat, in prayer. "Joe, I promise you. We will get it back."

Accardo stood slowly. He looked at Doves behind him. Doves had no reaction. Accardo shrugged. "Maybe you were right," he said.

Vin reacted quickly. "No, no, Joe, you said it. We want a future here. Johnny here is very good at what he can do, the best, something few can. A talent through and through. Your patience will be rewarded—all you gentlemen—I think many, many times over."

Accardo accepted his coat and hat, then looked Salita over again. "All of it," he said, and then, followed by Doves and Jackie Cerone, he walked out of the room.

C lyde's, which Nicky owned a piece of, was three blocks from Ten Pin, a dark hole-in-the-wall place for reliable one-dollar drafts or a flat pizza baked out of the old stone oven in the back or to do some quiet day-drinking. Or, in Nicky's case, a spot for conducting business.

Crease Man—Frankie Santangelo, a lug with close-set eyes and three fingers total on his left hand—had a stool at the bar, sipping a ginger ale, watching the door. Brags—Salvatore Bragotti, shorter and smarter than Crease Man, and fully fingered—hung near Nicky at the back booths near the dartboard.

Sally Brags and Crease Man were Nicky's guys, friends since third grade. Part of a larger group of kids who used to hang around after school without anywhere better to go, finding trouble where they could. But the three of them hadn't become tight until seventh grade, when one of the popular kids, named Floodie, whose dad was connected—Brags's and Crease Man's fathers steered clear of the rackets, and Nicky's dad was long gone by then—decided he was going to take on Crease Man in a fistfight after school. It was the most talked-about event that week, Floodie riling up every boy in their grade as well as some girls, promoting the brawl. Crease

Man was an odd target for fighting. Most kids steered clear because he was quiet, lumbering, and looked slower than he was. Also, he had grown quite a bit that year, and his size alone was intimidating, despite his generally oblivious demeanor.

The fight was to take place behind the baseball field backstop at four thirty, a half hour before sundown. Their entire seventh-grade class of boys on one side, an audience of girls watching from the other side of the fence, and Crease Man (then known simply as Frankie) with Nicky and Sally Brags behind him. Three against the whole grade. Nicky couldn't remember now what had made him choose the underdog side. Part of it was some of his other friends immediately jumping over to the cool kids' side against Crease Man. Sally Brags—then simply Salvatore—sided more with Nicky than with Crease Man. And so lines had been drawn. Frankie enjoyed the attention, despite the fact that everyone else in their grade was rooting for his opponent to beat him to a pulp. They all just wanted a good show. Frankie was ready to throw down—but it was Floodie who paced nervously. Incredibly, he had shown up for the fight wearing a forearm pad from his older brother's old football uniform, elbow-to-palm on his right hand. Either he or his brother had sewn a taped roll of quarters into the hand grip. It turned out that the kid who had instigated the fight was now shitting his pants at the thought of going toe to toe with Frankie Santangelo in a match that wouldn't be graded on points. Even his buddies in the cool crowd were telling him to take off the pad, trying to shame him into fighting fair, but Floodie somewhat hysterically insisted he was allowed to wear this seventh-grade version of brass knuckles. After a lot of back and forth, it reached a point where Floodie refused to fight without his loaded forearm pad, and everybody but him saw that under those circumstances, this fight was never going to happen. His buddies gave up, and everybody else went their separate ways, the air gone from the balloon, leaving Nicky, Salvatore, and Frankie alone behind the backstop. It wasn't a victory for them, but it sure was a loss for Floodie. Incredibly, the kid didn't suffer at all for his actions, remaining just as popular when everybody got back to school the next week, even after that wildly public show of cowardice. Kids were too afraid of his father to call him on his pants-shitting.

Two weeks later Crease Man was playing around with cherry bombs in a vacant lot near his house and blew off the pinkie and ring finger of his left hand.

After Nicky did his nineteen months for race fixing, he came out of prison looking to tighten up his circle, putting trust ahead of everything, even talent, even connections. Nicky swore he would never let anybody else's screwup sink him again, and neither Sally Brags nor Crease Man had the wattage or the gumption to screw him over for their own benefit. Nicky never lost sleep over their ambition. He controlled them, though that wasn't how he liked to think of it. He wanted loyalty from them, not responsibility for them. They looked to him for everything, trusting his instincts, and he delivered. No huge swings or major gambles, no home runs, because Nicky was interested in hitting singles and doubles and the occasional stand-up triple. Staying out on the street, living well enough, looking to the future. Being smart.

Two other patrons sat inside Clyde's that afternoon, daytimers getting blitzed. The old man sitting three stools down from Crease Man at the bar mumbled to himself every few minutes and shook his head. The other guy abruptly stood up and walked stiff-legged to the front door, letting in a spear of daylight.

Vin Labotta caught the door before it closed, entering ahead of Johnny Salita. After a few moments allowing their eyes to adjust to the darkness, Vin led the way to the rear. He carried a small, familiarly shaped bag with short handles, which Nicky recognized to be a vinyl AMF bowling ball bag.

"That's a nice touch," said Nicky. "The bag."

"It was handy," said Vin. "And the right size."

Salita stood behind, looking at Nicky and Brags over Vin's shoulder.

"You're twenty minutes late—I was about to leave," said Nicky. "Sit."

Nicky slid into one side of the booth, Vin sitting across from him, Salita next to Vin. Vin set the bag on the table.

"No disrespect," said Vin, "but just out of curiosity, how did you become the guy on this, Nicky?"

"My usual bad luck," said Nicky, selling it with a smile. "Being the bag man ain't glamorous, that's for sure. Must be a relief to you two, getting it all back for the Man."

"It's the opposite," said Salita.

Vin pushed the bag across the table. "It's all there. Take a look."

"Not on your life," said Nicky. "I don't want to see it, I don't want to know it. You say it's good, it's good. He'll be the judge. The sooner this is out of my hands, the better."

"It's good," said Vin.

Salita said, "But what's to keep you from dipping your hand in once we're out of here?"

"Nothing," said Nicky, "except I like my hand, I like it wearing skin. Sounds like you're inviting yourself along. Come with me. You can put it in the Man's hands yourself."

Salita frowned, not interested in taking Nicky up on his offer.

Vin said to Salita, playing peacekeeper, "Nicky is good people, Johnny."

"Nicky," said Nicky, "didn't ask for this. Nicky doesn't need this."

Vin said, "I told Johnny we went down on a thing together."

Nicky said, "Yeah, don't remind me."

To Salita, Vin went on, "He stood up, I stood up. He did, what, almost two? I did a little more than three. Nobody got more than that."

"Ancient history," said Nicky.

And it was that, but still. Vin Labotta was one of the reasons Nicky and the other three guys went down—and why Nicky stuck to people he trusted now, exclusively. Vin wasn't a beefer, and he wasn't reckless by design, but he wasn't foxhole material either. John Salita was learning this now. If Vin hadn't wound up doing a year more than Nicky, Nicky might have thought differently of him.

Salita kept looking at Nicky, who didn't flinch. "I don't think he likes me anymore," Nicky said to Vin.

Vin put out an open hand to both men. "He's just upset, rightly so."

"But he's looking at me like I'm the one making him give it all back."

Salita's eyes narrowed, then he looked away. "Let's get out of here, Vin."

Vin said, "Nicky, we're here. We came through. Our fence hadn't moved anything yet—we got a full accounting. I'd like to think all's well that ends well, but I know it's not up to you."

"Nothing's up to me. I think you're very, very lucky, but what do I know?"

"Okay," said Vin, turning to Salita. "Let's go."

Salita stood out of the booth, still with the attitude. He put Nicky in the mind of seventh-grade Floodie, who postured and grandstanded until he found out the fight wouldn't be rigged in his favor. Salita's arrogance was too much.

"Hey, Johnny," said Nicky. "Merry Christmas to you and Angie and little Stephanie."

Salita shot him a look back, clearly stung that Nicky remembered his family's names and, in doing so, brought them into this. But Vin stood out of the booth and pushed Salita along to the door before he could make a stand or say anything.

Another spear of intrusive daylight and they were gone.

Sally Brags drifted over from the dartboard, having heard all of it. "Somebody ain't learned his lesson," he said.

Nicky picked up the bowling ball bag and stood. "Not my problem, but yeah."

Crease Man walked over from his barstool. "Good?"

"Good enough," said Nicky, holding a bag of jewelry.

"What do you think?" said Crease Man. "A million?"

Nicky shrugged, having no idea. "I wasn't kidding. The sooner it's out of my hands, the better."

"We going with you?" asked Sally Brags.

They knew about the heist, and they knew vaguely that Nicky was doing this bag work for Accardo, which impressed them, but they didn't know any more than that. They didn't need to.

"Walk me to my car," he told them, the sit-down with Salita having left a sour taste in his mouth. "I'm good to go from there."

Michael Volpe answered the door wearing his owl-eyed glasses, a little short of breath.

"Mr. Passero," he said. "Come in."

The foyer was crowded with more than a dozen matching suitcases and a pair of garment bags packed full and laid out on the floor. This explained why Michael was out of breath.

"Looks like I just caught him," said Nicky.

Volpe nodded, checking his wristwatch before resuming attaching the luggage tags. "They should leave in forty-five minutes if they don't want to miss the plane."

Mrs. Clarice Accardo came down the stairs, a woman in her sixties wearing a cardigan over another sweater above a pleated skirt. Full-faced and just on this side of grandmotherly, the former showgirl, still a true beauty, carried a white fox fur stole in her hands. "Michael, find room for this, will you? Hello, Nick."

"Hello, Mrs. Accardo."

"*Clarice*, Nick," she said, counting bags with her forefinger as though conducting music. "I've told you."

"Clarice," said Nicky. "Ready for your trip, looks like?"

"Almost," she said. "I love the holidays, but the hassle..." She

66

looked at the bowling bag in his hand with a slight tightening of her eyebrows but didn't ask. "How is your lovely wife?"

"Helena is terrific, thanks. My boy is doing cartwheels, he's so excited for Christmas."

"Wonderful age," she said, then turned her head toward the rear of the house. "Joe!"

It made Nicky smile that Joe Batters's wife called her husband by the same nickname as his friends and foes did.

Accardo came walking down the main hall from the kitchen, chewing something, while Volpe went around opening suitcases, looking for room for the fur stole. "Nicky Pins," Accardo said.

"Forty-five minutes," said Volpe.

"I know, I know." Accardo was in a good mood.

"Are you taking up bowling, Joe?" asked Clarice.

"Thinking about it, my love. Are you bringing a mink to Palm Springs?"

"It's fox, dear. My shoulders get cold at night."

"Your shoulders. Of course. Can't have that. Right, Nicky?"

"No, definitely not," said Nicky.

"No cold shoulders from the wife," said Accardo.

"I'm going to take one more look around," said Clarice, gripping the handrail and starting back up the stairs. "Merry Christmas, Nick."

"Have a great trip," he said.

Accardo waited until she was up the stairs and out of sight before shaking his head at Nicky. "Fifteen suitcases," he said. "We'll come back with twenty. It's in the bowling bag? That one yours?"

Nicky shook his head. "What they gave me."

Accardo worked something out of his teeth with his tongue as he looked at the bag in Nicky's hand. "Awright," he said. "We need a safe spot for this." Accardo walked through the luggage to the side wall of the foyer. Nicky stepped aside for him, wondering if he needed to check his teeth in the mirrored panel or something. Instead, Accardo tugged on the panel frame, the entire section swinging open—revealing an interior door with a push-button lock.

Accardo punched in the combination and opened that door, revealing steps leading down.

"Nicky, c'mon. Michael, you too."

Accardo started down. Nicky moved through the two secret doors onto wooden stairs, which hooked left immediately. The air felt cooler as he descended but also different somehow. At the bottom, Nicky saw a long, central hallway ahead. He was shocked and a little confused by the size of the basement, which was vast, maybe the same dimensions as the house itself. An underground lair that was carpeted, climate controlled, everything.

Nicky got only partway down the hallway, glimpsing a darkened office on the right but following Accardo left through a door into a conference room with a boardroom-style table and more than a dozen leather chairs.

Nicky could not believe he was being shown this. How many meetings had been held in this room? How many lives discussed?

"Let's see now," said Accardo.

Accardo unzipped the bag and overturned it, the contents spilling out onto the lacquered mahogany table. Diamonds, rubies, emeralds, and other baubles Nicky couldn't put a name to, all in a pile. Some in little plastic bags, but most loose. Also rings, earrings, necklaces—all dumped onto the table like a candy haul at Halloween.

As a pile of stones, the jewels didn't impress that much. Nicky understood why they needed to be displayed on velvet under quality lighting.

Nicky said, "They say it's all here. They took it right back from the fence."

"You believe them?"

"Well, I think they'd be exceedingly stupid to steal something now, after going through all this."

Accardo separated out some tangled chains with his thick finger-tip, moving around hundreds of thousands of dollars in jewels. He opened a couple of velvet pouches holding bigger pieces, rings and bracelets with tiny string tags on them, special orders. He stopped when he found a ladies' gold-and-diamond bracelet about a half inch wide. He held it up to a ceiling light to inspect the inside of the band.

"Yup," he said, holding it out at arm's length, admiring it. "Whaddayou think?"

Nicky nodded. "It's nice."

"Here." Accardo handed Nicky the bracelet. "The inscription."

Nicky made out fine cursive engraving on the inside. *For Clarice, My Love, Christmas, 1977.*

Nicky smiled. Accardo's impatience with this caper finally made sense to him. Why he wanted Nicky personally involved. This cheered Nicky, who had been concerned he was becoming Accardo's errand boy—just another bag man. This was special. He'd wanted somebody he could trust.

"That's beautiful," said Nicky, handing it back.

"Michael, put this in a nice box, right?" said Accardo. "Tuck it inside my carry-on. Don't let Clarice see it."

"Of course," said Volpe, accepting the bracelet in his cupped hands as if it were a fragile baby bird and carrying it out of the room.

Nicky was distracted by a photograph on the wall of Accardo and Clarice smiling with Frank Sinatra at a reception somewhere. And another picture of Accardo seated with Mayor Daley and His Eminence Cardinal Cody.

"So what do you think?" said Accardo, frowning at the recovered jewels. "About Salita and his crew there?"

"He's definitely, you know, a hothead."

Accardo nodded. "Hotheads are okay. I was a hothead. I was young once and brash myself. But I knew how to fuckin' behave, Nicky."

Nicky nodded. "Right."

"Since when did impatience become a fuckin' virtue?"

"What surprises me most is Labotta. There's a guy old enough to know."

"Vin's never been what I would call prudent. Him, nor his brothers."

"Salita," said Nicky, still bothered by the look the thief was giving him at Clyde's earlier, like a ringing in his ear. "He's good at what he does. Not so good at being who he is."

Accardo glanced at Nicky over his eyeglasses, then sifted through the treasure on his table again. "I should be done with him. That's what you're sayin'?"

"Me?" said Nicky, with a start. "No. What do I know? I'm just sayin'."

"Teach him some manners, someone. Make sure he gets the lesson."

Nicky put up both palms. "Somebody else's department."

"You don't like him."

"He don't like *me*." Nicky indicated the jewels. "He learned a hard lesson here. Maybe it'll take."

"It fuckin' better."

Accardo slid out a thin gold bracelet with sapphire and diamond stones, pinching it between thumb and forefinger, lifting it off the table in his fingertips like a strand of cooked spaghetti. "This one is nice. The blue, the diamonds, the gold. Very nice."

"Nice indeed," said Nicky.

Accardo held it out to Nicky. "Merry Christmas, Nicky Pins."

Nicky looked at him like this was a test. "What do you mean?"

"Take it."

"Take it?" Nicky laughed once. Then he got serious. "No, thank you."

Accardo said, "Take it."

Nicky wasn't sure. "Me?"

"Not for you—I was thinking of your wife, actually."

Nicky held out his hand. Accardo laid the fine strand of gems in his palm.

A true gift from the boss of bosses. Nicky was struck dumb. He had to say something. "What do I say here?"

"Say 'Merry Christmas.' Levinson owes you anyway. We got his stones back, right?"

Nicky was fighting emotion, overwhelmed by gratitude. Just nodding.

Accardo said, "Look, if that thing don't get you laid on Christmas Day, nothing will. Help me with all this. I got a plane to catch."

Nicky slid the bracelet into his pants pocket where he carried his coins, then took the AMF bag and held it open at the edge of the table—Accardo sweeping a fortune in jewels into it.

Nicholas Jr., at ten, sweating through his footed pajamas, was on Christmas morning the happiest Nicky had ever seen him. Nicky's son was a tough read most of the time, but not this morning. So many toys. So much wrapping paper and so many cardboard boxes cast aside. His fat stocking lying on its side on the floor, Hershey's Miniatures and Smarties candy spilling out.

He was down to the last few gifts. The harmonica intrigued but did not excite him. The new comb and toothbrush, a nudge from Santa Claus to improve his personal grooming, were tossed behind him. His disappointment and near revulsion at unwrapping new underwear and undershirts was genuine.

The official NFL football, easy to tell from the shape it made inside the wrapping paper, was a winner.

"Let me see it," said his mother, Helena, bringing her instant camera to her eye. "Big smile." She pressed the side button and a rectangle of film tongued out, carefully set aside on the fireplace mantel to develop. Nicky grabbed another gift to open.

Helena set down her camera and sat on the firm green hassock with her black hair still mussed from bed, but otherwise prim and pretty in a white terry-cloth robe decorated with stitched flowers. She might have felt Nicky looking at her admiringly but did not look his way, instead picking up her ceramic coffee mug, making that her focus.

"Slime!"

Nicholas held the garbage-can container triumphantly aloft.

"To go with the game, right?" said Nicky. "I tell you, Santa Claus thinks of everything."

Nicholas was at the age where the questions had matured into full-blown doubts but you continued to play the game as a hedge bet, because nobody wants to be wrong about Santa Claus and his reindeer actually existing and then miss out on a huge Christmas-morning haul.

"Make sure that's it, look around," said Nicky. The boy rummaged under the crumpled paper, pushing his pile together. Nicky figured now was the time. Out of the bag at his side, he lifted the small box wrapped in gold paper, secured with a ribbon of pine green with gold edging. He held it out to Helena.

She accepted the gift, no idea what it could be. Nicky caught Nicholas's attention, and the boy walked over on his knees on the rug to watch his mother undo the bow and carefully slide a finger beneath the adhesive tape to separate the paper wrapping. She lifted the lid off the box. Nicky watched her eyes widen. She lifted the bracelet off the square of tissue paper, letting it hang from her fingers, shocked by its quality and beauty.

"Wow," said Nicholas.

"'Wow' is exactly right," said Nicky.

The boy returned to his presents. Helena seemed to be trying to figure out what to say. When she looked at him, her eyes showed more suspicion than happiness.

"Nope," he told her, "bought and paid for."

"Paid for how?" Said with a mix of confusion and distrust.

"I worked a deal with a jeweler I know. Forget about all that— what do you think?"

She was bewildered by the gesture. "Nicky, it's...Where will I wear it?"

"On your wrist? I'm kidding—you'll wear it whenever you want. Special occasions. It's technically a tennis bracelet. You can wear it playing volleyball if you like."

All his jokes were wasted on her at the moment. "It's real?" she said.

"It sure better be. You should at least maybe try it on."

She pushed back the sleeve of her robe and laid the bracelet over her wrist. "It's really beautiful, but…"

"No buts. Can I clasp it?"

He reached over and worked the tiny clasp, hooking it on the second try. She let her arm hang, feeling the gold against her skin, shaking her hand to make sure it wouldn't fall off.

"It's too much," she said.

"Good," said Nicky, smiling. "Just right, then."

Nicholas sat between them in church, squirming in a new wool sweater with an itchy collar. Helena reached for the boy's arm to settle him down, and Nicky saw her bare wrist, saw that she hadn't worn the bracelet. Christmas mass was the most special occasion she went to, year to year. He didn't take offense, knowing that she was genuinely embarrassed by such nice things. She wasn't trying to spite him. But he had hoped she might wear it, and that if so, maybe that would mean something. That the gesture had worked, that she had responded to the gift. That she was ready to resume, to forget, to move ahead.

They stood to sing. Nicky thought about the boy standing between them. Nicky had grown up without his father around and knew that for him, it had meant growing up a lot faster and a bit wilder than most. This separation had gone on too long; it was setting in. He needed to find a way to put himself and Helena back together, to make this work.

The arrival of Sally Brags and Crease Man before dinner gave the evening the shot of excitement it needed. Crease Man's girlfriend, Debra, flashed her engagement ring before the coats even came off, all the ladies screaming and hugging in delight. Then Sally Brags's wife, Trixie, shed her maternity coat, and the ladies marveled at the firmness of her round belly. Nicky enjoyed watching Helena gush over her girl-friends, but it was bittersweet too. Nicky and Helena had gotten way out ahead of their friends, in marrying, having Nicholas, buying a house. But now the other two were catching up and even poised to move ahead of them soon, with Nicky and Helena going sideways at best.

The ladies chatted in the kitchen after dinner, while the men drank Michelob in the living room and scooped onion dip out of a glass bowl with the remaining Wise chips. "I got her alone in her parents' parlor, finally," said Crease Man, "and I gave her the ring, then got down on one knee."

"It's usually the other way around," said Nicky.

"And she calls in in her mother, her aunts, second cousins. Every-body's happy, everybody's crying. I don't know what the big surprise was. You couldn't hint any more than she did. If I *didn't* get her a ring, then it would be something."

"It's better than a bullet in the back of the head," said Sally Brags, "but only a little."

"She's a good girl," said Crease Man. "I know I can trust her. I mean—she works with a buncha fags at the salon all day. She ain't gonna mess around."

Nicky looked at Nicholas, who was sitting deeply in the chair before the television with his Six Million Dollar Man action figure next to him, watching *The Six Million Dollar Man* on TV. He didn't look like he was paying any attention to them, but kids were always listening.

The show went to commercial, and Nicholas picked up his Mattel Electronics *Football* game again, started playing. "Hey, Nicholas, c'mere," said Nicky.

Nicholas dutifully stood, game in hand.

"Listen," said Nicky, "I got a special mission for you. You see these

Michelobs here? There's three more of these brown bottles in the fridge, but the women are in there gossiping and stuff, and the three of us are too terrified to go in."

Nicholas grinned and rolled his eyes.

Sally Brags said, "The truth is, Nicholas, they don't want us near them anyways."

"There's that too," said Nicky. "Now, I can't promise you might not get a cheek pinched or your hair messed up a bit. But you're the guy for the job. Can you slip in behind enemy lines and return with three cold ones?"

Nicky got a smile out of his son, like blood from a stone. The boy handed him his new game and went to the kitchen.

Sally Brags finished his beer as he watched Nicholas go. "He looks just like you did when you was his age. It's like I'm looking at an old home movie when I see him now."

"Yeah?" said Nicky. He'd have to pull out the old photos he had somewhere in the house. Of his old man too. Maybe there was a triple resemblance. He looked at the electronic game in his hand, which Nicholas had left turned on. The magic machine was just a couple of blinking diodes, a calculator circuit, and a nine-volt battery inside plastic casing. Which reminded Nicky of something.

"Hey, listen up," he said. "I don't wanna get into it too much now, but I got a thing I'm working on, something good for us. Maybe our thing for the new year. After the first we'll huddle up at the Lanes."

"Hold on," said Sally Brags. "You can't lay that out there and not give us a hint or somethin'."

Nicky shook the football game at them. "Trust me," he said.

Brags and Crease Man looked at each other, exchanging shrugs. Sally Brags said, "I guess we gotta trust him."

Crease Man said, "I got a wedding and a honeymoon comin' up. I need it, whatever the hell it is. I'm in."

Crease Man worked as a longshoreman on the docks, a good union job for a screw-off like him. Sally Brags worked maintenance for the Chicago Transit Authority, keeping the L trains running. Good steady jobs Nicky had helped set them up in, but forty-hour weeks were not going to get them where they wanted to go.

"First of the year, we'll talk," said Nicky. "Don't get too giddy on me."

But Nicky was feeling very good about it. Hope was what kept him going; it carried him through. Which was why he liked this holiday week especially. A new year was coming, a new opportunity—1978 would be Nicky's year. All signs pointed in that direction. There was only one obstacle in his way—one thing he had to deal with, one thing he couldn't figure his way around.

Nicholas came back in, hugging three cold beers, and Nicky helped him set them safely on the coffee table. "Look at that," he said, his jokey tone belying true pride. "Thank you, soldier. Good job. Here's your reward."

Nicholas accepted his game back and returned to the deep chair in front of the television.

Nicky and his guys uncapped beers and toasted. "To the future."

After everyone was gone and he had stuffed the trash into the metal barrel in the backyard and locked the back door, Nicky walked softly upstairs to Nicholas's bedroom. The boy was asleep, his new baseball mitt jammed under his mattress with a new baseball in it to break it in. On his night table was the first thing he'd opened that morning, a red plastic egg-shaped container of Silly Putty from his stocking, set next to his nightly glass of water.

This kid, thought Nicky. He missed seeing him on a daily basis, but they had big plans this school vacation, and a model to build and paint: Krypto, Superman's dog, a Labrador retriever in a cape who could fly through space, but whatever, it was something they could do together.

Nicky switched on the night-light, and as he was retreating, Nicholas spoke. "Why don't you live here with us?"

Nicky froze, half startled, half caught. "I thought you were asleep."

"Almost," he said.

The boy had been fighting sleep so he could wait up and ask him this. Nicky guessed it meant Nicholas had had a great day and wanted more. He pulled the covers up tighter under the boy's arms, looking into his drowsy eyes.

"I don't know why," Nicky said. "It starts with a cross word, then a disagreement, and next thing you know, it goes too far. And I see your face when your mother and I fight. I know what it does to you. I even remember what that was like. You don't want that. I don't want that."

The boy swallowed dryly, sleepily. "What do you fight about?"

Nicky rubbed his son's hair gently, his rough, soft hair. "We fight over who loves you more. Always ends in a tie."

Nicholas's mouth opened once or twice more, but he was slipping away. Nicky watched him go under and stood there a minute more, then went downstairs.

The house still smelled like the roast. The chairs had been put back, the table cleared. The tree was lit in the corner, with the toys beneath. It should have been the perfect time to wind down together, to reflect on the day.

Helena was still doing the dishes when Nicky stepped into the kitchen. It seemed to him that she had been doing them for some time. Anything to avoid having to speak with him one-on-one.

Her back was to him. A plate of leftovers was already on the table, wrapped in tinfoil, ready to go. The message was clear.

Still, Nicky lingered, hoping she'd turn, knowing she knew he was there. Hoping she'd give him some kind word, anything.

"I guess I'm gonna take off," he said.

She nodded, half turning her head his way. "I made you a plate—"

"Yeah, I see it. Thanks."

He waited a moment longer, watching her rinse out a bowl, taking her time. He nodded, unseen by her.

"All right, then," he said, and got his plate and left.

The sign out in front—TEN PIN LANES across the middle in blue, under a bowling pin reading 36 LANES and over a smaller, kayak-shaped sign reading COCKTAILS above a rectangular movie-theater-style marquee with replaceable letters spelling out OPEN BOWLING BEFORE 5PM WEEK-DAYS AND ALL DAY SAT & SUN and PINBALL ARCADE—was dark as Nicky pulled into the first parking spot near the entrance.

Inside, he flipped on one of the light switches on a bank of eight, illuminating only the bar, leaving the lanes dark. He carried his duffel bag and the plate of leftovers to his office, unlocking the door, passing his desk on the way to the second room. He dumped his bag on the floor, next to the cot, and went into the adjoining bathroom to take a quick piss, crowded by the standing shower he had installed there.

Out at the bar, he switched on the white, twinkling Christmas lights strung along the top shelf, a failed attempt to improve his sour mood. He left his plate there and walked into the darkness alongside lane thirty-six to the very rear, where he unlocked the fire-exit door with his master key. Then he returned to the bar and peeled back the foil from his food.

The roast and potatoes were warm enough. He pulled a Miller High Life from the under-bar refrigerator, found a plastic fork, and started to eat. He heard himself chewing and so went to the end of the bar where the hi-fi tuner was and switched on the radio for company.

He wondered about Palm Springs. He had never been, of course, but associated it with the Bing Crosbys and Frank Sinatras of the world. It was where Tony Accardo and the other top guys, not only from Chicago but from Newark and New York too, spent part of their winters now. Accardo had a house on a golf course, Nicky had heard. Golfing in December. As he chewed, he tried to imagine life in the resort city built on the edge of a desert.

A house with wide glass doors front and back. Accardo sitting in the minty-green backyard with his face turned toward the sun. Taking it all in. Carting around the golf course in goofy-looking golf pants, short-arming his strokes, putting badly. Eating lunch out on the clubhouse patio with the ever-patient Clarice.

Nicky pictured Accardo watching his family open presents on Christmas morning before an artificial white Christmas tree. Daughters Marie and Linda, adopted sons Anthony and Joe, sons-in-law and daughters-in-law, the grandchildren—all gathered. The last present given would be from him to Clarice, in a neatly wrapped box, the bracelet, the inscription read aloud, Clarice tearing up, the gift passed around the room, its craftsmanship admired by all. Accardo and Clarice sharing a puckered kiss on the lips. As the rest of his family went along mixing happily amid breakfast and eggnog, Accardo fed the discarded wrapping paper into the fireplace, watching the flames, content.

It was a particularly vivid series of images, and Nicky wondered why. He was jealous, sure, though not resentful. Could he, one day, have a place in the sun himself, and his own extended family, like Accardo? Or was he looking at something he knew somehow was not in the cards?

Headlights shone in through the glass front doors, a car entering the lot and not parking in front but rolling around the side, to the back, breaking the spell.

Nicky put down his fork, getting that sick feeling in his gut, the one that never really went away, that had nothing to do with the food, that had been eating at him like an ulcer over the past two and a half years. And with the sick feeling came anger.

The heavy, never-used fire-exit door scraped against the floor as it was pushed open from outside. Nicky watched the shadowy figure shut the door and walk up from the lanes out of the darkness. Nicky took a drink of beer but couldn't taste it. The figure reached the raised, carpeted lobby, coming around the rental counter, into view.

Gerald Roy wore an apricot sports jacket with tiger-orange oval elbow patches over a bee-yellow shirt with a flared collar, no necktie, and fawn-colored polyester pants. His amber hair was shorter than it had been when he and Nicky had first met, swept back, more mod. For some reason Nicky always expected him to look exactly the same as he had that night he walked out of the rain and into Merle's.

"Strange, seeing the sign dark," said Roy. "How many days a year you closed?"

Nicky knocked once on the bar. "This is it."

"Even Easter?"

"Jews bowl."

Roy smiled, stepping up to the bar, stopping one chair away from Nicky. "I don't know if we have any Jewish agents," Roy said. "Married agents get Christmas off, I know that. I worked." He removed his jacket, draping it over the back of a bar chair, and something fell out of it, slapping against the floor. Roy bent over and picked it up, tossing it onto the bar. His FBI credentials, badge and photo identification card in a billfold. "Mind if I . . . ?" He stretched, nodding at the bottles behind the bar.

Nicky said nothing. Roy went around him, behind the bar, selecting a clean glass tumbler, pouring some Canadian Club into it.

"You didn't eat dinner at home?" he asked, looking at Nicky's plate.

Nicky looked at the FBI agent standing behind his bar, drinking his whiskey. "Can we just get to it?" said Nicky.

"Yeah," said Roy, "we can get to it." He took a drink, wincing, exhaling. "The Levinson jewelry-store heist. What do you hear?"

Nicky gave him an open-armed shrug. "I read the same papers you do."

"Big job, total silence. No street recriminations, that's what sticks out to me. Nothing. I thought Levinson was a friend of the Outfit? Or did they get tired of his shtick?"

"I wouldn't know," said Nicky. "Jewel heists are a little above my station here."

Roy grinned. "Right," he said. "I know you play that way to the rank and file." Roy waved at the lounge, the lanes. "Nicky Pins, humble bowling alley proprietor. I'm not saying this is the crossroads of organized crime in Chicago, but it'll do in a pinch. Every day but Christmas, Outfit guys move through here. Payoffs and gossip. Your bullshit, it galls me. And," Roy added, pointing at the bar telephone, "we can't bug it because of the bowling noise."

Nicky saw now that the drink in Roy's hand was not his first of the evening. "All you'd get would be the same nonsense bullshit anywhere when guys get together. You really do overrate me."

"Yeah," said Roy, not believing him but tired of calling him on the lie. "So. Levinson's. A million-dollar-plus heist and nobody in here has even brought it up with you. Not interesting to anyone."

"Again, people talk about the weather and bitch about their lives, but nobody, and I mean nobody, walks in the door and announces they did a felony. You think somebody would come in here and brag about sitting on real money? You wouldn't live too long afterward, you did that."

Roy nodded, accepting that much. "So nothing you've heard."

Nicky said, "Wait here, I'll go get the jewels from my other pair of shoes."

"Your sense of humor is also overrated."

"Now ask me who killed Hoffa."

Roy ignored that. "Whoever did Levinson's, they've got to clear it first, right? Then find a fence who could handle it. A lot of this doesn't add up."

Nicky said, "Makes more sense that it could be somebody from outta town. There's a crew out of Buffalo I heard's good. Coulda been them."

Roy looked at him. "Buffalo."

"Buffalo, that's right. What's wrong with Buffalo?"

Roy looked around the bar, the bottles and glassware. He took another slurp of whiskey. Getting loose. "Fucking Christmas," he said. "What'd Santa bring you? Anything good?"

"Electric razor," said Nicky. "But I'm a straight-edge guy."

Roy shook his head. "Make the switch," he said, swiping at his own cheek and chin. "Give it a few weeks, trust me. Half the time, half the mess." Roy found and held up a porcelain punch bowl in the shape of a tenpin ball, with holes for straws. "This is quality," he said.

"Careful putting it back."

Roy returned it to the shelf under the bar. He came back toward Nicky. "You wanna know what I asked for?"

"From Santa Claus?" said Nicky.

"A homicide conviction. Just one. That's all." He casually un-screwed the cap of the Canadian Club and poured himself half as much more. "I'm not greedy. Doesn't have to be Giancana, right? Though that would pretty much make my career." He took another drink. "As I recall, Giancana was iced the night we first met, it turned out."

Nicky had a pretty good poker face, but he didn't like being reminded of that night. For either reason.

"But as I said," Roy went on, "I'm not greedy. Any Outfit conviction would do. Do you know that in the thirty months since somebody popped Sam G., there have been thirty-one gangland slayings? More than one a month in the city of Chicago, on average. And not one single conviction."

"I like that term, 'gangland slayings,'" said Nicky, goofing on the parlance. "Sounds like an amusement park or something. *Gangland.* Is that where we live here?"

Roy said, "That's where we live."

"A guy crosses another guy—or is *perceived* to cross another guy. *Pop-pop*, somebody falls down dead. Your 'gangland slayings'—there's no rhyme or reason to it. I'm saying, thirty-one murders? Adds up to nothing, except thirty-one murders."

"That's just it," said Roy. "Why people shrug. Because it's internecine. It's the Outfit turning on each other, gangster shooting gangster, killing their own. Jimmy the fucking... 'Jimmy Cheekbones,' whatever, make up a stupid nickname. And it gets covered in the papers like sports and entertainment."

"You're half-right," said Nicky. "But then everybody turns the page and goes on with their day."

Roy shook his head. "Not me. Because what you shrug away as housecleaning hits? I think it's more than that. I think there's a generational power struggle going on. Maybe you see it too, though you don't want to say. Or maybe you think it doesn't affect you, because you're what, thirty-five? Right in the middle. Young on this end, old up here. A bunch of old men deciding things, who won't step down. Tony Accardo won't, that's for sure. It's not who he is. You said to me once, the only way you go out—"

"Is feetfirst, yeah. That was just a comment, that don't mean—"

"Tony Accardo has had a good, long run. Too good, and too long." Roy smiled widely and crept up close to Nicky, real familiar. "That's my take."

Nicky had thus far succeeded in walling off Accardo from Roy's prodding. Serving Roy chum rather than bait. Offering as little as possible, enough to get by. It was tiring and infuriating, this dance. Nicky had nightmares he was getting pulled in two different directions, torn apart, while simultaneously being crushed in the middle.

Roy had him. Roy knew. It sickened Nicky, having to play along with him.

Nicky's countenance must have changed, darkened due to his

negative thoughts, because Roy's attitude went from argumentative to wary. "Anyway," he said. "Now you know what I want to know." He finished his drink.

"I'll ask around about Levinson," said Nicky. "Good enough?"

"Less than I'd hoped for," said Roy. "Then again, it usually is."

Nicky said, "You want something I don't have."

Roy smiled. "And you want something I do."

Nicky's face burned. "Fuck you," he said.

"Yeah," said Roy, then sighed. "Yeah." He set down his glass, starting out from behind the bar. "Listen, sweetheart," he said. "A new year approaches. I want more from you, that's how it is. You need to produce for me. Or else." He reached for his jacket, searching its pockets, finding and pulling out a business card. "This number. New secure line. Use it."

He held out the card to Nicky, his hand unsteady. After a moment, Nicky took it, set it down on the bar.

Roy said, "You do for me so I don't do to you. Got it?"

Nicky didn't answer.

Roy pulled on his jacket, not looking at Nicky. "It doesn't have to be this hard, you know," he said. "This could be mutually beneficial. You help me, I help you. Think about how this could be good for you, why don't you? Instead of acting like it's a trip to the fucking dentist." He tugged down on his lapels, fixing his open shirt collar. "Produce, and keep your hands clean doing it. Simple. Are we clear?"

Nicky said nothing.

"I'll take your silence as a yes," he said. "Thanks for the drink." He started off, then turned back, remembering his credentials still on the bar. "Merry Christmas, Nicky Pins." He walked off toward the rear door, addressing the empty lanes. "And to all, a good night!"

ome of you know I was three years undercover in Vegas before coming here."

Chicago Police detective Feliks Banka arrived late to the strike force meeting. He'd had trouble locating the conference room on the ninth floor of the Dirksen Federal Building. Eight men looked over at him, four of them FBI agents, four from other federal agencies. Banka was the only city cop. The FBI didn't invite him there very often.

Rather than make any more of a distraction of himself, he drifted to the rear of the room and leaned against the wall of painted cement. The agent holding court at the front of the room, Gerald Roy, was the one who had invited him. Roy was the youngest man in the room, and the most casually dressed, though Banka supposed the cream-colored jacket and matching pants technically composed a suit. Banka had not updated his wardrobe since about 1971.

Roy went on speaking.

"I put away some street-level guys, flipped a few others. Tough to get a seat at that table without already being somebody's cousin. But months in, after putting in my time at every shitty lounge and every off-Strip casino, I connected with a guy who I turned, who then turned a guy himself, who got me to somebody real. Not big, not top level, but real. An older guy—and I *had* him. Jersey George Galizi, if that name rings any bells. Not 'jersey' as in 'New Jersey.' 'Jersey' as in 'shirt.' Jersey George had never even been east of the Mississippi, as far as I know. Even he didn't know how he got the nickname. But I hooked him, and I flipped him. He was mine. He served his purpose, got me into some things, ratted some of his friends. But I'd reached the ceiling with him and was already looking to springboard off him to the next level, when something went wrong. Word came down—from here, from Chicago. It wasn't about me, it was something else—what exactly, I never knew. But Jersey George ended up with his throat cut in the desert fifty miles north of town. Now, don't misunderstand me. Jersey George wasn't a sweetheart. He wasn't a good guy at all. Outside of me and a couple of guys he owed, no one except some underage prostitutes marked his passing. So he wasn't undeserving. What struck me was how top-down it was. The word came out and he got snapped in two. Done. I guess that was my introduction to Chicago, how things worked. How much of Vegas is controlled by the Outfit, and that it's been that way since the fifties. Specifically, and largely, by one man. Pat?"

The agent nearest the film projector turned it on with his cigarette hand, while Roy switched off the room lights. The shades were already lowered.

A square of light with rounded corners appeared on the wall. After a header listing some FBI indexing numbers, Banka watched blurry, badly shot home-movie footage of a foursome of retirees on a golf course. The focus was improved manually—fingers momentarily obscuring the view, which Banka surmised was filmed from a Super 8 camera hidden inside a golf bag on the back of a cart on an adjoining green—and Banka smiled when he recognized the golfer in the checkered pants and pickle-green polyester shirt to be none other than Tony Accardo.

Accardo chomped on a cigar as he hastily lined up a putt, which he then hit with the stiffness of a man of his age. The ball rolled out of frame, the camera recording Accardo's evident disappointment.

The agents snickered at the miss, and maybe the pants, which looked like patches sewn together. Banka removed his eyeglasses and cleaned them with his waffle-knit necktie.

Roy narrated. "This is two days ago. Christmas in Palm Springs. Not too bad, right? The notorious 'Joe Batters' here looks more like 'Grandpa Joe,' doesn't he?"

Accardo had walked back to his cart, where, without warning, he used a two-handed swing to club one of the roof supports with his putter, hammering it again and again, stopping only after his putter snapped.

Roy stepped into the image, which went white. The agent with the cigarette switched off the projector motor, but the lamp remained lit.

"Tony Accardo is taking a few weeks in the sun to fish and golf and beat the hell out of inanimate objects. He's still got a temper. You may know, we're looking at north of fifty organized crime figures in Palm Springs, right now, this week. Chicago, New York, Newark. Like Switzerland for gangsters, their playground since fleeing Miami when they changed the wiretap laws down there. Give these old geezers credit for adapting. Anyway. We're still here working while Accardo is basking in the Southern California sun. Is that clear enough for you? We're not laughing at him. He's laughing at us."

The young agent showed a flash of anger, of passion. Rare for an FBI agent, and Banka was impressed.

Roy ended by saying, "This coming year, 1978, is going to be our year. The year that we in this room introduce Tony Accardo to the inside of a prison cell for the very first time."

After the lights came on and the class was dismissed, the others left the room quickly. Banka walked forward to chat with Roy, just the two of them.

"Sorry I was a little late," said Banka. "Glad I didn't miss the movie."

Roy smiled, shaking Banka's hand. "Palm Springs, Detective Banka. You believe it? Like movie stars, like royalty."

Banka said, "Is that what's gotten under your skin? The privilege? Because there's plenty of that for them here in Chicago."

"No, no—the whole dirty thing. But, sure, that? Let's call it the cream on top. I thought it might be useful here today for the others as fuel. Considering how it's about eight degrees outside."

Banka nodded, sizing up the young agent. Most of the FBI agents he came across were diligent, true believers, committed to the law and almost religious about carrying it out. But few were truly ambitious. Gerald Roy had ambition wafting off him. It was interesting.

"Okay," said Banka. "So why am I here?"

"I thought that was obvious. I think it's critical to have a local on this task force. Anyone can look at an org chart of Italian gangsters. You have true historical knowledge of the players and the streets."

"I see," said Banka, nodding. "Nice to be invited to the big dance. I thought they frowned on opening these task forces up to municipals."

Roy shrugged. "Probably they do. I've been given more say in this. I'm able to do things my way. Additionally—well, here in Chicago it's not easy finding people to trust. From judges on down to meter maids, everybody's hooked up to the Outfit. You come strongly recommended."

Banka smiled. "Maybe we've both got an independent streak. I never moved up too far, because I saw what came along with it. It's a tricky game. Guys who are not bad guys, by the way—they're good guys—they just got a little corrupted, and that's all it takes. It's a claw trap. Nobody's gonna eat their own leg off to get away. So they figure out a way to get along instead."

"Not you."

"I like to sleep at night."

Roy nodded. "What did you think about what I said? About who I'm targeting."

"Tony Accardo?" said Banka. "You dream big. "

"I'm not a supercop. We'll go steady, if not slow, but we'll build a case. And if we miss the top guy? Good chances we'll take down some others. But truly I don't plan on missing."

"Just let me say, and don't take this the wrong way, but you're not the first to try."

Roy grinned, not afraid of hearing the truth. "It's my turn to take a swing. My ax will cut true. Regimes do get toppled, Detective Banka. Find a weak point and exploit it. One little crack, one little opening, one little stumble—all it takes."

"Sounds to me like you already have a weak point all picked out."

Roy smiled tellingly. "Weighing my options, put it that way. How about I buy you a coffee from the machine down the hall, tell you what I *can* tell you."

V in Labotta looked back from the bar at Johnny Salita sitting at the table with his leg bouncing like it had a twitch and realized it might take a full afternoon of drinking to settle the guy down.

The hiss and clink of bottles being uncapped turned him back. Down at the far end of the bar, a bored dancer with a B+ chest— quality rating, not cup size—shimmied in a G-string, watched but not ogled by day-drinking dead-enders. Pegasus Lounge wasn't much more than a dark cave, the kind of dive you slipped into when you wanted to disappear from the world for a few hours, and it still played go-go music when every other joint had changed over to disco.

Labotta carried the bottles back to Salita, gearing up for another session of hand-holding. Salita accepted his Schlitz and brought it right to his lips, tipping it upside down, draining half of it at once.

"Good, right?" said Labotta with a smile. "Coldest beer in town. Glass bottles as cold as ice."

"The jeweler is getting an insurance payout."

Labotta almost coughed up his beer. One-track mind. "What're you talking about, insurance payout?"

"Levinson. Accardo is gonna fence the ice himself. Our pocket to his."

Labotta glanced around. Salita wasn't even keeping his voice down. "That can't be right, Johnny. That's bullshit. Who told you this?"

Salita didn't answer. Labotta could tell his mind was racing. "Everybody's getting rich except us, the guys who did the thing. I'm tired of it, Vin. Fucking tired of getting fucked."

"Johnny. Where the hell is this coming from?"

"He's in fucking Palm Springs! Living the life. Because of guys like us funding him. He sits us down, oh, he talks about how it's an organization and we're all in this together, la-la-la. It's all for one, Vin. Open your fuckin' eyes—I have."

"Look, Johnny, you pay up the ladder, you make your bones, you earn and produce and you make your way. It's how it's done. How it's always been done. I know you think you're special—"

"How was your Christmas, Vin? Huh? Was it perfect and beautiful? Let me tell you about mine. A dinky fuckin' tree with a handful of presents under it, another cloth coat for Angie, Raggedy Ann doll for my baby girl. And me singing 'Deck the Halls,' top of my voice. No, actually, it was me with an empty smile pasted on my fuckin' face, thinking about how it *should* have been."

"I know, Johnny, it's rough, seeing a good thing snatched back like that—"

"It was a fucking humiliation, Vin. We got played. Thieves who got their take taken from them. *We* was robbed. Only a punk could see it any other way."

"Now hold on. Is that what I am, you're saying?"

Salita looked away, staring at the wall like something was written there that made sense to him. Whatever his eyes were seeing instead, it wasn't good. "Accardo flew outta town the same day we gave him back the goods. That means the ice is still in his house, over on Ashland Ave."

"And so?" said Labotta.

"And so it's right there, in his fuckin' house, sittin' there."

"His...?" Labotta waited for some further detail that would pull this conversation out of the tailspin it was in, but it didn't come. "Wait a fucking minute, Johnny."

"That's *my* money, Vin. Yours too, if that matters to you, which it doesn't seem like it does."

"It's our money, mine and yours and all the other guys—*and it's gone*. Gone, Johnny. Jesus. Look at me. Maybe I'm the one who's confused."

"My family's fuckin' Christmas they didn't get."

"Johnny. Lower your fuckin' voice and look at me."

Salita looked at him. "You worried about these fuckin' people hearing me? You worry too much about the little things and not enough about the big. Look at us here, Vin. Look where we are. This shithole you brung me to. This is Loserville. Can't you see? Accardo's taking food from our mouths!"

He was practically yelling, and throwing Tony Accardo's name around that loudly was like taking the Lord's name in vain. "Get up," said Labotta.

"I'm not getting up."

"Get up."

"I'm finishing my Schlitz—"

Labotta grabbed Salita and yanked him up, his chair scraping back over the warped wooden floor. Labotta pushed Salita past the tables to the back door, exactly the way he used to rush drunks when he was in uniform. Outside, the cold air was shocking, an alley of filthy, trampled snow. Labotta gave Salita one last angry shove, and the younger man stumbled sideways into a skid, almost falling.

"What the fuck, Vin!"

Labotta shut the door behind him. He wanted to hit Salita in the face. But that would have ended things between them forever, and Labotta had plans. "Wise up. You hear me? Wise the fuck up, Johnny. This is over. Get over it. You're pissed still, and that's a problem. *Let it go!* Plenty of other scores. A city *full* of them."

"Plenty of other scores," said Salita, mockingly. "That I gotta *beg* permission for."

"Jesus," said Labotta. "I thought you were smart."

"Want to know how smart I am, Vin?"

"No, I don't, Johnny."

"Here's how smart I am," said Salita, practically spitting the words into Labotta's face. "Accardo's houseman is gone every day by five. Old guy sets the alarm, locks the door, drives his fuckin' Cressida home. It's an Ademco bell box, triple zone. Converter relay with a latching circuit. No dialer. One tamper switch, which is a joke—why the fuck bother?"

Labotta stared at him, his own breath coming out in heavy gusts, pushing out steam that was almost too thick to see through.

"Stop," said Labotta, much more quietly than he expected. "Stop fucking talking. What you're saying, just uttering these words, putting them into the air, could get you clipped. And me with you." Labotta looked skyward. The Sears Tower, a corner of it, was high in the distance. "Tell you what. Let's rip off Sears Tower, how about that? The entire thing, we'll take it floor by floor. Let's take down Fort Knox. There's a plan, Goldfinger. Get a flatbed for all our gold bars. You could convince me of that." He got up in Salita's face to keep himself from yelling. "But get your mind straight, and *stay the fuck away from the Man's house.*"

Salita's face soured, his mustache curling up over his lip. Labotta was ready to walk away right then. Walk away from Salita and never look back. End it. Despite the fact that this guy was his meal ticket. Labotta's obvious poor judgment had put him in this position with this wild man who couldn't see more than five feet in front of him.

Labotta kept himself in check. Labotta wasn't any less broke than Salita, but he had twenty-five more years on him, and nowhere near as much horizon left. This was his racehorse, his one and only shot.

Salita's eyes finally relaxed. Maybe seeing Labotta's rage here broke the spell. Maybe this was all Salita needed, some discipline. He needed to feel fear.

"Okay," said Salita, taking a step back. "Fine. Okay."

Labotta did not let up. "Not *fine*. Not *okay*. You got a problem, Johnny. You got a big fucking attitude problem. And that means *I* got a problem—*and I don't want no problems.*"

"Vin—I said okay."

"You are looking at me like you wish you'd never met me. How do I know this? Because I'm thinking the exact same thing. We gotta move past this, Johnny. We can do it, we can do big things. Did I screw up? I screwed up. But part of my screwup was letting you run the thing all your own. You wanted five guys who wouldn't think for themselves, I got you them. We can do better next time. Put in guys who are a little smarter. You wanna do it all on your own and you can't. You need me. The sky's the limit if we trust each other. We'll look back on this moment right here, this alley behind the Pegasus Lounge, and we'll laugh our asses off. Let's start fresh. Clean slate. Fuck those other guys, short-timers. Me and you, all the way. Just gimme your word. Your *word*, that you'll stay away from the Man's house, you'll steer clear. Your word."

Salita's stare remained hot. Labotta couldn't read him, had no idea what his answer would be. The only thing that was clear was that Salita didn't like getting a talking-to.

"Your word," Labotta said again. "Say it."

"Okay, Vin," said Salita, his mouth tight like the words tasted like poison. "Okay."

1978

nside the arcade room at Ten Pin Lanes, teenagers bunched up around the game cabinets, cheering on their friends and even cheering for kids from other schools whom they didn't know, who ever had the hot hand playing *Breakout*, trying to beat the high score.

Over at *Pong*, you would think it was the finals at Wimbledon, Connors taking on Björn Borg. Kids stacked their quarters on the game panel to hold a spot in line for the next game.

Little lights careening around an electric screen, rectangles versus squares, and the kids followed every beep and bounce like they were standing at the rail of the final turn at Arlington.

Mostly boys played, but there were girls watching too—watching both the game screens and also the body English of the blue-jeaned behinds of the boys playing them.

It was a scene. At the same time, Nicky's lineup of pinball machines with their traditional bulb-light displays and actual bells stood mostly silent, unused. One kid flailed away at the Elton John pinball game, probably because he had already invested so much time and money in getting good at it. But nobody was watching him. That wasn't where the action was anymore.

"You see it right here," said Nicky, standing back by the glass doors with Sally Brags and Crease Man. "Pinball is black-and-white television to these kids. It's the stagecoach. The plunger launch, *clang-clang*, flipper-flipper, bad ricochet, game over. That's their fathers' game. Push-button stuff, video arcade cabinets, this is the hottest thing going. And if you didn't notice, this is Monday. Not Saturday or Sunday. Every afternoon, straight out of school, they play until they run outta money or they gotta get home for dinner— and the weekends are busier. I get more kids coming in to hang out in here weekends, checking out this scene, than show up to bowl. I can't get more machines fast enough, because there's a backlog. And it's a quarter to play. What kid can't get a couple of quarters from their parents?"

Nicky faced them.

"My thinking is, we could get in on this. The way the Cicero guys did vending and cigarette machines, back in the day. Passive revenue source. These quarters add up fast. Think about us getting a piece of every blinking, beeping kiddie slot machine in all of Cook County."

Crease Man unfolded his arms, nodding. Brags said, "I like the sound of that."

Crease Man said, "Fuckin' genius, Nicky. When do we start?"

Nicky said, "I'm already talking to my game guy, not letting on anything, just how's it all work, what's the wait for new games? They license these things from Japan, can't make 'em fast enough. I'm getting trade magazines, finding out who the distributors are, and we'll do it like the vending guys. You two will go in and convince them, with a little arm-twisting, that it's better for them too, we pave the way. Better for everyone. We'll put them in every store, every restaurant and pizza parlor in the county, the state. They pay us to put it in, kick back a percentage of the take. You see what I'm saying?"

Sally Brags said, "You were always ahead of things with games, since we were kids."

"Well," said Nicky, "it's time to put that to good use."

A fun groan from the teenagers as somebody's turn ended and the machine played a little tune. Nicky turned the guys around and took them back outside the arcade room, into the lanes proper. Crease Man said, over his shoulder, "What about all the pinball machines?"

"Put 'em on a truck," said Nicky. "Put 'em in a museum."

"You clear this with anyone?"

"Too soon for that. You move too early, you get partners and you're the percentage guy, or it's taken away from you altogether. We're keeping this close, the three of us. I'll take care of bringing in who we gotta bring in when the time is right."

"Accardo?" said Crease Man.

Nicky threw him a look. "What you just did is the opposite of keeping it quiet."

"Okay, okay," said Crease Man.

Chuckie was beckoning to Nicky from the counter, with the phone receiver held aloft in his one hand.

Nicky said, "Awright, back to work. You guys too. More to come."

Crease Man and Sally Brags, tall and short, headed for the door. Nicky was intercepted on his way to the counter by a fat city commissioner whose job title he couldn't remember but whose name was Ruben. "Nicky, how are ya?" said Ruben the commissioner, a sealed white envelope in hand.

"Hey, good, good," said Nicky, seeing the payoff coming. "My one-armed bandit, Chuckie, he can take that for you right there."

"Oh, sure thing," said fat Ruben, pulling back the envelope, walking with him. "How you keeping?"

"Ah, you know, it's a Monday. Chuckie'll make sure that gets where it's going."

Nicky reached the phone, nodding Chuckie to the commissioner's intent, letting them do the exchange, not wanting his hand on it. Nicky pulled the receiver to his ear. "Ten Pin, this is Nicky."

Nicky hurriedly crossed Ashland Avenue, eyes scanning the street for surveillance. He had never visited Accardo's home during daylight hours.

He didn't like the houseman's voice on the telephone. The old man sounded shaken, and he had never called Nicky before.

Nicky rang the bell and waited. He didn't expect Tony Accardo to open the door instead of Michael Volpe, but that was what happened.

Accardo's eyes were no longer beagle-sad. They assessed him with a quick up-and-down, then looked past Nicky to the street. Nicky wondered for a moment: Was it him who was in trouble?

Nicky said, "What are you doing back so soon?"

"Get in here," said Accardo.

Accardo stepped aside, motioning him inside with a slight sideways nod. Nicky stepped onto the polished tile as Accardo shut the door. Accardo didn't say anything, facing Nicky in the mirrored foyer as though watching for a reaction other than confusion.

Nicky said, "Michael said to come quick. I came quick—what is it? What?"

Accardo said, "You don't know?"

"Don't know what? What happened? Why are you home?"

Accardo's evident paranoia ebbed, the spell broken. "Come with," he said, jabbing at the carpeted stairs with his thumb.

Nicky followed him up. He'd never been to the second floor. Accardo walked him around a corner into the master bedroom, big with a sitting area and a television, double doors open to a walk-in closet, and a bathroom furnished in black marble and silver.

Clothes lay strewn on the floor outside the closet, Clarice's things, tossed there. As though the closet had been searched. The padded chair to her makeup table was on its side, drawers open, powders spilled to the floor.

A fight? Nicky was confused. He looked at Accardo—and in doing so, noticed that the bedcovers behind him, done in oriental-style crimson and cream, were rumpled and indented, as though somebody had walked across the king-sized bed.

Had Accardo torn up his own bedroom? "Is Mrs. A. okay?" said Nicky.

Accardo was seething and did not answer. He exited the room, Nicky following, perplexed.

Back downstairs, down the hallway to the kitchen. A half-eaten sandwich sat on the counter. Drawers and cabinets were pulled out and opened. A smear of mustard stained the countertop like a streak of animal shit.

It couldn't be a break-in. That made no sense.

"Over here," said Accardo, moving stiffly, tension apparent. He led Nicky back to the foyer and opened the mirrored panel near the front door.

The punch-lock on the door inside was busted.

Nicky said, "What the fuck...?"

Down the narrow, hooking stairs to the basement they went. Past the conference room door, nothing to see in there. Accardo turned right, into an office.

His office. The locked door had been forced, the wood around the handle scored and chipped with a sharp tool.

Inside Tony Accardo's private office was a desk that looked like it was for show rather than regular work. Framed photographs stood on the shelf behind it, Accardo with caught fish, shot zebra. Under the shelf was a wide wood-faced file cabinet.

The cabinets had been yanked open, papers lying on the floor. Some appeared to be invoices, others newspaper clippings. A few stock certificates.

Nicky got it now. It didn't make any sense, but at least he understood. He visualized an intruder busting through the locked office door, sifting through files, cavalierly scattering papers on the floor.

"Shit," said Nicky. He looked at Accardo. "Holy shit." Then Nicky remembered the one and only time he had been down there. "The jewels?"

Accardo shook his head. That surprised Nicky.

"No? Still here?"

Accardo, too furious to explain things, turned and abruptly walked out of the room.

Nicky walked back upstairs. Accardo stood in the living room, which was conservatively furnished, the sofas and chairs all upholstered in tough, woven honey-colored fabric stitched as tight as a pincushion. Michael Volpe was on his hands and knees on the plush rug, an apron over his suit, scrubbing out a wide, stubborn stain.

Nicky held back on his gasp. Accardo's rage needed an outlet, and if Nicky wasn't careful here, it could be him. So he didn't say aloud what he was thinking.

Somebody took a piss on Tony Accardo's living room floor.

The houseman looked up at Nicky through his owl-like eyeglasses with an expression that said a sad hello. Then he resumed his scrubbing.

Nicky looked around at everything except Accardo. "The house alarm?"

Accardo said "Tell him, Michael" and walked out of the room.

Volpe reached for the arm of a chair, getting to one knee. Nicky helped the old man to his feet.

"What the hell happened?" Nicky asked him, quietly.

"I come in this-a morning," Volpe said, his accent made thicker by shortness of breath. "Same as always, I unlock door, I turn to alarm with key. No red light. Steady green."

"You set it the night before—"

104

"Sure, I always set it, Mr. Passero. But for a moment, yes, I think about it, I question myself. Then I see the panel to the basement. It's-a open. So then I think—somebody's here."

"Right," said Nicky. "And?"

"Nobody here. Thank God they were gone. But somebody been here."

"Jesus," breathed Nicky.

"I call his other home, he's not there. I reach him at the club. He say don't call nobody, no police. Wait until he gets here. That's-a what I did."

Nicky palmed his face, letting his fingers drag down on his cheeks while this all sank in. Nicky wondered if he had been Accardo's first call once he got back to Chicago and inside his home. Seemed like it. That meant the problem fell to him—and Accardo wanted it kept quiet.

The home alarm had gotten beat. Was it Salita? And what was Accardo expecting Nicky to do about it?

"Go slow, okay?" said Nicky, worried about Volpe's health but needing to go off and find Accardo. He walked back down the hall again, past the kitchen to the sliding door, which had been pulled open, out to the cold backyard patio.

Accardo stood next to the glass table. On it was an ashtray containing fresh cigar stubs.

Nicky pictured Johnny Salita sitting on the Man's patio in the frigid midnight air, savoring an expensive smoke like the lord of the manor. Nothing made sense.

"You see this?" said Accardo.

Nicky said, "I see it." But he didn't believe it.

Accardo was trembling with anger. His energy was scary.

"Are you okay?" said Nicky.

"Did you just ask me am I okay?"

"I don't mean it like that—"

"THIS IS MY FUCKING HOUSE!"

His voice rang in Nicky's ears, the angry steam of his breath whipped away by the wind. Nicky nodded fast and kept nodding. It was a stupid fucking question.

"Where is Mrs. Accardo?"

Accardo glared at Nicky until he had settled down enough to respond. "Still in Palm Springs."

"Okay. She know about this?"

Accardo shook his head no.

"Nobody knows?" said Nicky.

"*I* know," said Accardo. "The fucks who did this, *they* know."

Because Accardo wasn't speculating on who it was, Nicky knew he thought it was Salita too. "They were here awhile. What did they take?"

"Cuff links."

"Say again?"

"A pair of cuff links. From my nightstand. Stardust Hotel cuff links. A gift."

"Okay," said Nicky. "Cuff links. What else?"

"They drank my liquor."

Nicky nodded. That made some sense. "Had to be drunk to go on a rampage like this here."

Accardo pointed downward, indicating his house, but he might as well have been pointing all the way down at hell. *"My home."*

"I can't fucking believe it. There's no words. Who knows you're here? Knows you're back?"

"Who would know? No one."

"So just Michael. And me."

"Nobody finds out about this. Understand me, Nicky? *Nobody.*"

"Okay. Of course, sure."

"No one. On your boy's life. Say it."

Accardo faced Nicky, fever-hot in the arctic cold. Nicky met his eye, queasy but steady. "On my boy's life."

Accardo held his gaze, marking the moment. Then he nodded. "Nobody else," he said again.

Nicky grasped the man's embarrassment. The humiliation of this profane act. Pissing on the boss's carpet. But more than that, it was a clear shot across the bow. There was the actual power the boss had, and then there was the power the boss was perceived to have. Tony Accardo was only as invulnerable as people thought he was. This was part of the code of the Outfit and of organized crime in general, where perceived slights led to murder as often as actual slights. You were your reputation, the strength you projected. That was why Accardo didn't want anyone knowing, why he had come to Nicky with this. Nicky saw it through Accardo's eyes now and felt a sting of anger himself. Secrets needed to be kept at all costs.

"Okay," said Nicky. "What do you want me to do?"

"What do I want you to do?" Accardo looked up at the darkening sky. January nights were long; Nicky saw that they were about to get longer. "This needs to be handled quickly," said Accardo.

"Okay," said Nicky.

"*Definitively.* With a plan. And a list."

"A list," said Nicky, not understanding, not just yet.

Accardo nodded once, then stepped past Nicky, moving back inside the house to begin figuring things out. Nicky remained out in the cold a moment longer, looking at the backyard and the pool covered in canvas, a long, broad hole in the frozen earth like a mass grave. He turned and followed Accardo inside.

Hi-Quality Tile and Flooring was an outlet tile company off South Damen, one of a strip of low-rent manufacturing warehouses that had risen up on land once dominated by the meatpacking stockyards in the neighborhood still known as the Back of the Yards. The immigrant neighborhood was turning over again, going quickly Mexican now, businesses pulling out, the area in danger of slipping back into slums.

The showroom was awash in apricot- and avocado-colored linoleum and Formica along with other, random pastels. The laminate odor gave the store a chemical smell, and dust from the chipped edges of tile samples coated nearly every display. Behind the sales counter, a bunker fashioned out of stacked sample books, Vin Labotta slurped hot tomato soup out of the top cup of a tartan-patterned thermos. It was the same thermos he had carried with him into Harry A. Levinson Jewelers that frigid Saturday night before Christmas—a good memory turned bad.

The bell over the door jingled, a customer making his way to the counter. Labotta recognized the broad face and dark hair, and his heart sank a bit at the sight but he didn't let on.

"Nicky," he said, greeting the bowling alley owner, swiping soup from his chin and lips. "What brings you in?"

"Good," said Nicky, "you're on lunch."

"Ah—I am, sort of."

"A word? Maybe we could go in the back."

Labotta asked Carol to keep an eye on things and capped his soup thermos, carrying it with him through the store to the employees-only door to the warehouse. He opened the door on the high, whining sound of a wet saw cutting tile. Labotta steered Nicky away from the noise, toward the truck entrance near flat chunks of raw tile leaning against heavy wooden easels, opposite rolls of laminate flooring. Labotta was concerned by Nicky's presence but not afraid. Nicky didn't have that reputation. Labotta set his thermos down on a cutting table.

"This can't be good," said Labotta. "What's up?"

"Maybe nothing, I don't know." Nicky thrust his gloved hands deep into the pockets of his peacoat. "I keep thinking back to you and Johnny Salita sitting with me at Clyde's that day, when you brought the bowling ball bag."

"Sure, yeah?"

"I don't know, he just—it seemed like he had a problem with me."

"That's Johnny. He's got a problem in general, with most people, no question, but that was just him being brought to heel. He don't like it. Even if he's in the wrong, you can't tell him anything. He didn't mean to make it personal."

"Left me with a funny feeling, that's all. Bothering me. I wanted to get your two cents on it."

Labotta was relieved this was just some follow-up. Salita had a knack for getting under people's skin. "Johnny mouths off, he does that. To say the least—he does that. I got my hands full with that kid."

"Yeah, well," said Nicky, wincing like he wasn't buying it, "he ain't no kid anymore either. He still mouthing off about the job you two hadda give back?"

"Nicky, I'd be lying if I didn't say it's a little stuck in his craw, still. But look, I hashed it out with him. We screwed up on that thing—it won't happen again."

"You don't have to tell it to me," said Nicky, lifting his hands out of his pockets, showing his gloved palms in a grand shrug. "That's between you and, you know, Joe. I'm just—I don't know about that guy."

Nicky wasn't letting this go, and now Labotta saw that Nicky Pins's concern about Salita was outsized. "Is there something you're not telling me, or...what am I missing here?"

"Vin. We go back. The racetrack thing—that fiasco—all that. Old news. Salita, I'm not sold on. I'm telling you that right now. And I wonder, maybe, if you're not as clued in to him as you think."

Labotta sighed deeply. "He's a wild kid, Nicky. His brain's too fuckin' big. He's got an attitude, no doubt. But he's worth the trouble. If I didn't feel that, I would cut ties. But you don't have anything to be concerned about."

"Again, I'm not worried about me. And to tell the truth, I'm not all that worried for him. I'm worried for you, Vin. That's why I'm here. But if you say you can vouch for him..."

Labotta bristled at that word. This was getting heavy. "You mean, vouch?"

"It means what it means."

"Like—'vouch' vouch?"

Nicky Pins didn't nod, didn't shrug. He just waited, and in those few moments Labotta felt himself go pale and dry. He feared the worst. And he knew Nicky could see it on his face.

"Nicky," said Labotta, his voice lowering. "Nicky—tell me, what'd he do?"

After Nicky Pins left him, Labotta walked back to the showroom in a daze. He had things to do that afternoon, work was backed up, and it would all have to wait. He told Carol he wasn't feeling well and found his heavy coat, walking out to his Buick, making sure he had coins in his pocket.

Labotta drove two blocks. By the time he reached the phone booth they used, his anxiety was at an all-time high. Had anyone been inside talking on the phone, he would have pulled them out by their neck. But the booth was empty, and he went inside and closed the folding door on the whizzing cars, pumping a dime in the slot. He dialed seven numbers, one at a time, on the rotary.

He listened for the tone. When he heard it, he hung up and waited.

Johnny Salita was the first guy Labotta knew who had a beeper. Before he saw one on a doctor, that time he took his wife to get her hysterectomy, he saw Salita had one. Labotta still wasn't 100 percent clear on how it worked, but somehow when he called Johnny on this number, the little device told Salita to call him back, and this phone booth was the only number they used. Leave it to him to have the newest gadget.

Labotta set his head back against the cold plexiglass of the door and closed his eyes. Nicky Pins wouldn't tell him what Salita had done. But Labotta knew. And yet—there was just no way. Labotta shook his head, rattling the booth as he did so, opening his eyes and standing straight again. No fucking way. He stared at the telephone as though it could be intimidated into ringing.

It worked. The telephone rang. Labotta grabbed the receiver off the hook so fast, it was at his ear before the connection was completed.

"Johnny?" he said.

"Hey, Vin."

"Where are you, Johnny?" said Labotta. "Johnny, what the fuck's going on?"

A long pause. Then Salita said, "It got out of hand, Vin."

Labotta's body went cold inside his coat. "What got out of hand?"

Salita was standing in his own phone booth somewhere. Labotta could hear him breathing into the other end of the line, figuring out how to say what he had to say.

"He don't know it's me," said Salita. "I didn't touch the vault, the jewels. Didn't go near it. So there's no proof."

"No *proof*?" said Labotta, in disbelief.

"None, no."

"You don't think . . . ?" Labotta slowed himself down, looking up at the ceiling of the phone booth, a faded white wad of chewing gum stuck there. He was losing his cool and his mind at the same time. "Let me get this straight. You think that he don't know?"

"There's no proof—"

"I warned you, Johnny. I fuckin' . . . I *begged* you and . . . I FUCKIN' WARNED YOU!"

Silence on the other end. Labotta's voice seemed to echo in his booth.

"Yeah, so—Vin?" said Salita, his voice surprisingly level and calm. "Don't talk to me like that."

Labotta's eyes widened maniacally. He looked around the phone booth like he was surrounded by fools and idiots. "What did you say to me?" he said.

"Don't talk to me like that, Vin. Like you're the one bringing me along. I'm bringing *you* along. Get it straight in your mind."

Labotta's body grew even colder. He put his hand on top of the pay-phone box because he needed something to hold on to. His mouth was open awhile before he found words.

"I don't know," Labotta began, his voice dropping to a hush as if he were speaking to a terminally ill patient, "if I can make this right for you, Johnny. Or even if I should. Stick my neck out for you some more? Why am I wasting my breath?"

"*Fuck* Tony Accardo."

Labotta smiled then, almost laughed. He shook his head in

amazement. "Jesus, Johnny. How do you get to be your age and not know which way is up?"

"Fuck him, Vin. I've had it."

"You think you've had it?" said Labotta.

His mind raced. He was seeing things Salita evidently could not. He was nervous for himself, but even more than that, in this moment, he was scared for Johnny Salita.

"Listen to me, Johnny," he said. "Listen good. Where's Angie and your baby *right now?*"

Twenty minutes later, Labotta pulled in under the Ten Pin Lanes sign, parking two spaces over from Nicky's blue Plymouth Satellite. He was there to plead his case. It was his only hope. Labotta got out and walked quickly toward the entrance, so focused on the task at hand he didn't see the guy come up to intercept him.

Labotta jerked back like he was about to get popped. The guy wore an army jacket and baggy jeans. He wasn't tall, but he had big hands, and there was something about the quick way he moved that was implacable and intimidating. Labotta recognized the sandy-haired man's round face.

"Sal," he said. "Sally Brags. Jesus, you gave me a fright."

Sally Brags said, with a shake of his head, "Not here, Vin."

"No, no, you don't understand. I gotta see Nicky Pins about something—"

"Vin," said Sally Brags. "Not here."

Brags's thick hand was against Labotta's chest. Labotta spun around quickly and saw Frankie Santangelo behind the wheel of a green sedan in the parking lot—and he realized now, he had seen the same sedan near the phone booth.

Labotta turned back fast to Sally Brags. They were following him. This was dire.

Labotta had to make them understand. "Sally, listen—"

"Clyde's Lounge," said Brags. "Same as before. I'll tell Nicky you're there waiting for him."

Labotta backed away from Sally Brags's hand. This was a real thing that was happening. Labotta needed to pull himself together and navigate it.

"I'm going," said Labotta, and walked right to his Buick. He pulled out of the parking lot, past Santangelo's green sedan, Sally Brags still standing where Labotta had left him.

Labotta jumped off the barstool when Nicky Pins entered. Nicky nodded to the bartender but declined a drink. Nicky told him, "I'm gonna be down below a minute or two with him," meaning Labotta.

Sally Brags entered behind Nicky Pins and shook the bartender's hand. Santangelo must have been parking the car. Nicky wore the same peacoat and black pants and shoes he'd had on at the tile store earlier. Labotta remembered that Nicky owned a piece of this place, having helped out the owner or some such. Labotta followed him around to the end of the bar, where Nicky Pins bent over and pulled up an iron latch inlaid in the old wooden floor, yanking open a trapdoor over unfinished wooden stairs leading down.

Nicky went first, pulling on a string light, Labotta following. The stone cellar was dank and refrigerator cold. Cases of Budweiser and Old Style were stacked near untapped draft kegs; a rack of coats, some of them fur; and three twenty-five-inch Magnavox televisions in store boxes.

Labotta said, before Nicky Pins even turned around, "Why is Sally Brags following me?"

"He's worried," said Nicky, crossing his arms against the cold. "We're all worried. Worried about you."

Labotta took that both ways. He came clean fast. "I talked to him, Nicky. I don't know where he is. He did do something. He did it. That fuck."

"Something, what? He did what?"

Labotta shook his head, confused. Either Nicky was playing him, or else it was so forbidden even he didn't want to give it words. "Nicky, if you don't know...I'm not gonna be the one to tell you."

Nicky chewed his bottom lip, then nodded, reasoning it through. "Must be pretty bad."

"Just know, Nicky—I had *nothing* whatsoever to do with it. I tried to *stop* it. I told him no."

"So you knew."

"No! I knew he was talking, he was hot. I never thought...Oh, Jesus. I wasn't there, and I wasn't in on it, and it wasn't me. Look at me, I'm nauseous."

"Easy, easy. Wipe your mouth."

Labotta pulled out his handkerchief and swiped at his lips and mustache, unaware he'd been spitting.

Nicky Pins walked away with his arms crossed tight, then came back, thinking. "What do we do here, Vin?"

"Nicky," said Labotta, stuffing the handkerchief back in his pocket, reaching for his forearm, "Can you help me out here, Nicky?"

Nicky studied Labotta's face for sincerity, then nodded. "I'll try, Vin. I'll try. Let's try to figure this thing out together."

The baby was wailing, inconsolable, her teeth coming in. Angie Salita bounced her back and forth past the foot of the motel room double bed, from the window to the wooden crib. The teething ring in her mouth wasn't helping, even after chilling it in the ice bucket.

Salita couldn't hear shit, so he paid out the phone cord and withdrew into the bathroom, closing the door behind him. He sat on the edge of the tub with the base of the telephone on the closed lid of the hopper. The motel was in Ingalls Park, just east of Joliet, an hour southwest of the Loop.

"Stephanie's pitching a fit," he said into the phone. "Say that again?"

Labotta said, "I figured it out, Johnny. Come to the office, we'll talk."

Salita stared at the pattern of hexagonal tiles on the motel floor, varying in shade from dandelion to marmalade, frowning at the thought of Labotta's flooring shop. "How?"

"By me vouching you. To my own personal risk. Putting my neck out like I said I wouldn't do."

"And what do *I* gotta do?"

"Well, it starts by coming in. We'll figure it out."

"Figure it out? 'I'm sorry' isn't gonna cut it, Vin. Where is there to go?"

"I'm putting my ass on the line for you, Johnny. I answer for you now. I promised them you would do this. Do not let me down."

Salita ran his fingers vigorously through his hair, the muffled wailing on the other side of the door assailing his thinking. Through the phone he heard traffic, and he could see Labotta in a moth-bitten wool hat in the phone booth in Back of the Yards, giving him orders. Once upon a time, Salita had thought Vin Labotta was a good fit for him. He had contacts and seniority, a crook's mind with an ex-cop's experience, a potent combination, and Salita believed Labotta could show him things, usher him into the big time. That was the handshake. That was the deal. But every third step Labotta had taken since that moment had been some version of a fuckup. Labotta was just another small-time hustler who talked big, the only difference being he believed his own hustle; he mistakenly thought he was the real deal. This was how he hit his fifties and had little to show for it. And this was the guy now brokering Salita's survival.

Yes, Salita had fucked up too. Got shit faced on brandy and coke and broke into the boss's home while he was out of town   then got even more shit-faced inside and let his anger show. That was stupid, but what did they expect? He was gonna eat shit all winter long? If they were smart and at all enterprising, they would see the guts he had shown, the daring. Maybe they would give him a pass. Call it a wash. But more likely he was fooling himself with that. There had to be punishment. Maybe the ultimate.

The other option was to keep going. Start over. But where? Back to South Dakota? Angie wouldn't have it, any more than he would. Go to some other city, not too big, not too small, work his way in again? Try not to get hooked up with another Labotta, but a winner this time, a true player? And how long would that take, to make connections in a new city?

He was out of good options. If there was even a slim chance Labotta could indeed fix things for him—maybe it was worth a shot. And then cut the line on old Vin and let him fall away.

"How soon?" said Salita.

"Soon as you get here," said Labotta.

"Gimme two hours."

Salita hung up. He stared at the phone set atop the olive-green toilet. The call could be traced, but Salita didn't care; he would soon be long gone from this shithole motel. He wished he had a cigarette to smoke while he thought things through.

Angie was at her wits' end when he emerged. "What's going on, Johnny?" she said. "Who was that? Was that Vin?"

She still had faith in Labotta. Angie was close with her father, who ran a tool-and-die shop with a sideline making illegal gun suppressors, so she was built to trust older men.

"That was Vin," said Salita. He reached for his work duffel, lifting it onto the bed.

"What is it, Johnny? Is it good news? Tell me."

If he didn't tell her something, she was going to assume he had offed someone, and he couldn't have her thinking that. "I did something. Nothing really bad, but something I shouldn't have done. It might be all right now. I'm gonna go see. But until I know I'm in the clear, you and the baby need to go."

"Go? Go where? Johnny, we'll stay here—"

"You hate it here. But I can't bring you back with me, not just yet. So you're going. Here's the thing. Don't tell me where, even when you get there. I don't want to know. Pick a town a couple hours away, any place that looks good to you. Get a room and wait. Don't tell your dad where you are, no one, got it? Understand? Don't call anyone, and definitely don't go anywhere you might see someone you know."

"My God, Johnny. That sounds like—"

"It's not that bad. I just need to know you're safe. You and Steffie. And that means being careful."

"But why don't you want to know where we are?"

"If I don't know, nobody can make me tell them, okay? Here."

He dug out two elastic-banded rolls of cash, dropping them on the bedcovers like curlers. "More than you need, it's plenty," he said. He found one of his beepers and checked the number affixed to it.

He held it out to her. "You keep this with you at all times. When this beeps, call the service, this number here." He had punched the phone number onto red embossing tape and affixed it to the device. "They'll give you the number I give them, where I'm at, so you can call. That's how I don't need to know where you are. Got it?"

She took the device in her hand, looking it over. "Johnny, I...I guess."

Salita put his hand over hers holding the beeper. He rubbed the smooth edge of his fingernail against Stephanie's puffy cheek as she sucked on her pacifier. "It's tough now, I know, but it's gonna be okay, I promise you. I always come through for us, right? I'm gonna be fine. There's a decent chance I call you tonight and say, 'It's over, Ange, come on back home.'"

She studied his eyes intently. It warmed Salita, the trust she put in him.

"Why you smiling?" she said, near tears.

"Because you're beautiful. And you believe in me, almost as much as I believe in myself. You're gonna do fine. Just remember—talk to no one but me."

He kissed her, then kissed the baby. When she turned away to do something, Salita checked that his gun was in the duffel bag before zipping it shut.

Salita rolled past Hi-Quality Tile and Flooring twice. A few vehicles in the parking lot in the late afternoon, though not the usual contractor's trucks, just regular cars. Otherwise, not much to see. Third time, he pulled in. Backed into a space closest to the retail entrance. He sat there for a bit, watching the store windows, unsure what he was looking for. Signage and some hanging spider plants obscured much of the interior.

The CLOSED sign was turned out inside the door. Maybe Labotta had shut down early. Probably he did, he was so worked up. Salita exited his rental car and fixed his jacket over his midsection. Salita tried the door, which was locked. He banged on the glass. After a moment, Labotta came around, unlocking the door and admitting him.

"Johnny, hey," he said. "There you are. Right on time."

Salita let the door close behind him. "Just us?"

"Yeah, yeah. Let me get my things. We're going to a meeting."

Labotta started into the store. He seemed a little charged up but not hinky.

"A meeting?" said Salita.

"I made it public, so no worries."

"Just like that?"

"Well, it's a meeting. Nothing's done or over. It's a start, a good start." He turned toward the door to the warehouse. "Let me get my stuff. Come on back."

Labotta pushed through the employees-only door, and Salita followed him as far as the threshold, his hand on the door. No farther.

It wasn't any one thing. Or maybe it was: Labotta going in ahead of him like that.

Salita backed away a few steps. If it was nothing, he could wait there.

Labotta came back through the door, leaning, just his head and shoulders, looking for him. "C'mon. We'll go out this way."

"That way?" said Salita.

"Yeah, through here."

"Taking your car?"

"Why not?"

Salita nodded. "I'll follow you in mine instead."

Labotta stayed where he was, half in the store, half out. "Sure, fine, whatever you want. C'mon, let's go."

Now Salita really didn't like it. He backed away another few steps. "I'll go out this way."

"Johnny, what are you doing—?"

All at once Labotta fell forward, shoved from behind, running a few steps to keep his balance, catching himself on a display rack.

A guy came through the door behind him, round-faced and grimacing, wearing an army coat, a gun in his right hand.

Salita was running when he heard the first *crack* and *thunk*, the round missing. He ducked around a corner as he heard the second and third cracks, and window glass breaking.

He hit the front door while pulling his own handgun from the back of his waistband, knowing he was bound to encounter more trouble outside.

He sprinted the short distance to his car, looking back, seeing the army-coat guy running to the store door as it was closing.

Salita fired twice, *cap-cap*, squeezing the trigger too hard, the shots kicking wild but it was enough cover to get him to his car, where he'd left the keys waiting in the ignition.

Then louder cracks, and the sound of something chipping off the asphalt near him like a stone.

A second gunman, a bigger guy, had come lumbering out of the warehouse side of the building, shooting as he ran toward Salita's car.

Salita let go of one more wild shot, then jumped into his car, turning the key so hard he nearly broke it off. The engine turned over and Salita let out the clutch, flooring the gas pedal.

His windshield took a round in the near corner, and cracks webbed through the glass. Salita ducked to his right as he spun the wheel toward the street. The cracked windshield made it tough to see oncoming traffic from his left.

He bounced hard off the curb, suspension springing. He cut the steering wheel hard right, his back end fishtailing, Salita briefly losing control of the vehicle before it righted itself.

He heard a *plink* as another round struck the body of the car, which scraped a parked van before the tires grabbed the road. Peeking over the dash, Salita saw the road ahead of him clear, and he floored the gas again, speeding down South Damen toward Garfield and away.

Fifteen minutes after closing, Nicky put another 7 and 7 in front of Vin Labotta. The thief's darkly lined face became looser and more expressive with each sip.

"Gettin' better?" said Nicky.

"Oh, much," said Labotta, wiping away the wet ring on the bar with his palm. "What a fuckin' day. Unbelievable."

"We all have 'em," said Nicky.

"Like this?" said Labotta, with an incredulous smile.

"Maybe not like that," said Nicky. "How's the eye?"

Labotta touched his forehead just above his right eyebrow, which he had cut falling into the display rack when Sally Brags shoved him through the door from the warehouse. "It's nothin'," he said. "Nothin'."

"I didn't even think I pushed you that hard, Vin," said Sally Brags, sitting three empty seats away. "In the moment, I guess."

"No, no, don't worry about it." Labotta sipped the fresh drink, carbonation from the cold soda still popping above the glass rim. "I'm lucky I didn't get plunked in the cross fire. Goddamn." He sat back, straightening his shoulders like he was going to stand and leave, only to crack his neck left and right, then lean forward against the bar again. "Best alarm man in the three-one-two."

"Hey," said Nicky. "You tried."

"I fuckin' tried, I did. A month ago, Nicky, I was all set. I mean, I was *set*. The future looked good. Now...?"

"Best-laid plans, Vin."

"He's got a little girl. A baby girl, young. Pretty wife. Stupid fuckin' son of a bitch."

Labotta let his head dip, mourning the impending demise of Johnny Salita. Nicky saw Crease Man emerge from the office, clicking off the light. Crease Man looked at Nicky, then at Sally Brags. All three men exchanged glances. Then Labotta raised his head again, looking at Nicky.

"How'd you get started in this place anyway?"

"Me, here?" said Nicky. "You remember Stu? Not Stew the Jew. Stu the candy-store guy, owned this. One milky eye?"

"Oh, yeah."

"Diabetes, and he owned candy stores. Anyway, he owed. He remembered me from back in the day when I was in my bowling prime. Brought me in to help smooth things over, a little protection for him, a small piece for me. His health kept going downhill, losing toes, he wouldn't eat right. At the same time, he took bigger risks gambling too, now that he could go out to Vegas for a weekend with me here to run things. It went really wrong for him out there, buffets and roulette, and he had no family, and suddenly he's spending more time in the hospital than here. I had to take on more of the business. Anyway, he passed, and I didn't want to give the place up. Part of me getting hooked into our racetrack misadventure was working to keep the lights on here. Funny thing is, while I was away, business picked up. So it all worked out. For me anyway."

The story held Labotta rapt. He found an inspirational message in it for him. "This is gonna work out for me too," he decided. "Whatever I hafta do to make this up, I'll do." He pressed the meat of his left fist against the edge of the bar, making a pledge. "I don't think

Johnny'll listen to me no more, but...you tell them, Nicky, to tell me what to do, and I'll do it. Tell Joe Batters. Whatever it takes."

Nicky said, "Good, Vin. Good."

Labotta's head drooped again. He hadn't noticed that Sally Brags was up off his stool. Or that Crease Man stood near him now—both men looking at Nicky like they were certain Nicky was going to call this off.

Nicky looked at Vin before him, sitting head down. He said, "I know you didn't want any of this, Vin."

"I appreciate that, Nicky. I do."

"And I want you to know, the racetrack thing, I did hold you responsible for it, partly. Fucking us all up. But I forgive it. I forgive you, Vin."

Labotta looked up at Nicky, appreciation in his eyes, and for a second saw, reflected in the mirror behind the bottles at the back of the bar, Sally Brags and Crease Man moving behind him.

He never had a chance. Sally Brags dropped a cloth sack over Labotta's head. Labotta's right hand flailed out, knocking over his glass and spilling the remains of his drink over the bar as Crease Man looped a wire cord under Labotta's chin and yanked him back off the stool.

Labotta's legs kicked out. He gurgled something, a choked cry, before landing hard on his shoulders on the floor, flailing as Crease Man's knee dropped hard onto his chest.

Sally Brags reared back and kicked at the hood over Labotta's face, blood from Labotta's nose exploding into the cotton fabric, soaking through, none of it leaking onto the carpet.

Labotta's legs relaxed then. He kicked a little, gently, then his body lay still.

Sally Brags and Crease Man looked down at what they'd done. Nicky wiped up the spill on the bar.

"I'll get the lights," said Nicky. "You two carry him down to the fire exit in back."

Sally Brags used to run a chop shop on the Far Northwest Side of the city before giving it up when he got his city job with the transit authority. He had held on to the double-bay garage in Dunning, not far from where the notorious mental hospital had been, where all their mothers had threatened to send the boys whenever they got into trouble.

Now with the sign taken down and "CLOSED" permanently written in soap on the front window, the body shop was a part-time clubhouse for them, with a fridge and a working bathroom nobody ever cleaned and a TV on a rolling tool cart. They could work on their cars if they needed to or store weapons and tools—things they wouldn't want to keep at home—or just sit around and drink beer and play hearts. It was their place. Nobody else ever came in there.

Nicky sat in his Satellite out front, engine off, shivering in the cold but also because of his nerves. It was late, and getting later. He wanted to be done with all this. The distinctive rectangular Cadillac headlamps swung into the parking lot—and Nicky's gut tightened, and suddenly he was wishing this could wait a few hours more.

Nicky got out of his car. Tony Accardo got out of his black Caddy, wearing a camel topcoat with a flat fur collar, a tweed-wool fedora, wing-tip shoes. He looked like a square-shouldered insurance ad-juster responding to a claim in the middle of the night. The big, sleek Cadillac would stand out in the memory of anybody who noticed, but the lot was dark, unlit. Still, they needed to make this fast.

Nicky, arms crossed against the freezing cold, said, "I don't like you here."

Accardo said, "I'm here."

They went in through the office door, which Nicky locked behind them, then another door, into the dual-bay garage. The only light was from a work lamp in the corner, but it was bright. Shadows were stark and long.

In the center of the garage, a chair was set on a twelve-by-twelve square of thick plastic. Tied to the chair with thin cord by his elbows, wrists, and ankles was Vin Labotta.

The bloody hood covered his bowed head. Sally Brags and Crease Man stood back from the plastic, watching. They had never had an audience with the Outfit boss before, never even been in a room with Tony Accardo. Accardo didn't look at them, didn't talk to them, his polished wing tips stepping onto the crinkling plastic, his attention on the bound thief.

With a leather-gloved hand, he plucked the hood off Labotta's head. The thief's nose was busted, blood and snot caked over his mustache and a kerchief gagging his mouth.

His eyes came to life when he saw Accardo. Fear first, then hope. He tried to speak through the gag. *"Mrm-hirm-rrm—!"* He was trying to tell Accardo that he had nothing to do with the break-in.

Accardo watched him squirm. "Hello, Vin," he said.

More noises from Labotta. He looked at Nicky, trying to get him to speak on his behalf.

Accardo said, "I was too forgiving. Too soft. I see my mistake now."

Labotta's head bucked. *"MMM-HMM-RRMM—!"*

"Of all of them, Vin, you knew better. You let this happen."

Accardo pointed at Crease Man, startling him. After a moment, Crease Man realized what Accardo was asking for.

He wheeled over the acetylene tank.

Labotta's eyes went as wide as they could go when he saw the tank with the burn bar attached.

Accardo watched him, taking in Labotta's panic. It was fascination more than out-and-out pleasure. Accardo was drinking in the peak experience of another. Certifying his victim's terror.

Accardo said, "You know how these tanks work, Vin, right?" Accardo moved next to the red cylinder. "Burglar tools. I'm told this'll burn through anything if you give it enough time. Steel, cement—anything. Flesh and bone should be easy." Accardo pointed at Crease Man. "Let's see it."

Crease Man understood the request. He turned the valve on the top of the tank with his three-fingered left hand, then ignited the torch with his right. Flame roared out of the nozzle.

Labotta was shaking his head, whipping it side to side, rocking the chair. Accardo stepped up to him suddenly and gripped Labotta's throat with such force, it stopped Labotta's thrashing fit.

"One hour from now," said Accardo, just loud enough to be heard over the dragon's hiss of the flame, "I'm gonna be cutting into a nice, thick steak—at exactly the same time these two are cutting into *you*."

Labotta's eyes bulged, lit by the flame, staring into Accardo's face. Accardo held him a few moments more, strangling him, then released Labotta's throat, turning and walking abruptly off the plastic, back out to the office.

Crease Man looked at Nicky, the torch in his hand. Sally Brags gave Nicky a slight shrug, as if to say, *An hour we have to wait?*

Nicky made the mistake of looking at Labotta one more time—Labotta's eyes pleading, imploring him.

Crease Man turned off the flame. The garage was extra silent.

Sally Brags said, "Nicky—you sure?"

He didn't have a choice, so neither did they. "Wait an hour," he said, starting away. "Then get it done."

Nicky went to the office. The Man was waiting for him to unlock the door. Nicky did so.

"Let's go," said Accardo. "Leave this for them."

Nicky looked back to the garage. While he didn't want to stay there, he wasn't sure he wanted to go anywhere else with Accardo at that hour. "Where are we going?" Nicky asked.

"Where else?" said Accardo.

By the time Michael Volpe served Accardo and Nicky, seated across from each other at Accardo's dining table, it was well after midnight. On each plate was a twelve-ounce sirloin steak hot off the grill. No starch, no vegetable. Just the meat.

Accardo checked his wristwatch before snapping open a napkin and laying it across one knee. "Thank you, Michael. Right on time."

Volpe slid Nicky's plate in front of him, smoke swirling off the seared meat. Nicky had no idea if Volpe knew what the occasion was.

"Anything else?" asked Volpe.

"No," said Accardo, and Volpe departed.

Accardo shook pepper onto the center of his steak, forming a tiny pile, which he then spread out with his knife. He put the knife down and checked his watch again.

"Give it another two minutes."

Nicky felt crazy. He had the privilege of sitting with the boss at his dinner table, but his mind and his conscience were back in the garage with Sally Brags and Crease Man. Feeling responsible for what they had to do—but also anxious that they do it right.

"You do know," said, Nicky, "that Vin wasn't one of the ones who..."

He didn't finish the sentence, instead indicating the house he was in with a shrug.

Accardo looked across the table at him. "And?"

"He's Salita's guy, don't get me wrong."

"And did you get me Salita?"

"Uh...no."

"Okay, then." Accardo checked his watch again. Nicky studied his face, the tanned skin, the soft bags under the eyes, his television-screen-shaped eyeglass frames, the long-lobed ears. His thin gray hair, swept back from the top of his head and his temples. Lips the same color as his flesh. Nicky remembered that Accardo's father had been a shoemaker. It wasn't a stretch to say that the Chairman looked like a kindly old cobbler.

"Your guys," said Accardo. "They're reliable? Punctual?"

"Oh, yeah," said Nicky.

The old man was watching his second hand, the timing critical to him.

"Okay," he said, looking up. "Now we eat."

Accardo stabbed his steak with his fork and drew his knife through it. Juice escaped the pinkish red beef, sponging out onto the plate. He carved off a chunk and examined it before bringing it to his mouth, to his tongue. His pale lips closed around it and he chewed slowly, with satisfaction, savoring the beef.

Nicky's stomach turned. Accardo sliced off another hunk and ate this one faster than before, as though it were Vin Labotta's seared flesh itself.

Nicky made himself cut into his steak. Juice ran out immediately, blood-red with flecks of black in it. He sliced off a piece about the size of a casino die and got it onto his fork but just couldn't bring it to his mouth.

Queasy, he set down his fork and reached for the crystal goblet of wine. He tasted a bit before setting the goblet back down. Nicky started talking because he had to do something other than eat. "Can I ask you something?"

Accardo didn't look up from his carving. He shrugged.

Nicky said, "Is it true you never spent a night in jail?"

It was the first thing that came into his thoughts, something Nicky wanted to ask but a topic he never would have broached if he hadn't been dizzy with disgust and desperate for a complete change of subject.

Accardo stopped his cutting. He looked up. "Why you wanna know about that?"

Nicky had crossed a line, but it was too late, and still it was preferable to the blood feast going on in front of him. "I dunno, I guess... because it's incredible. If it's actually true."

Accardo tipped his head to one side. "Incredible?" he said. He took a drink of his wine. The body and blood. "I don't think so."

Nicky said, "I think it definitely is."

"That was the Kefauver Committee, started that never-spent-a-night shit. They tried to hang that around my neck, make it like I was flaunting. Kefauver was before your time. Twenty-five years ago now, I think it was in '51. This same time of year. A Senate special committee. They pull these things together once every decade or so when a sitting senator needs to make headlines. But this one, Kefauver, this happened to be the early days of television, it was still very new. And they were looking for things to put on, you know, fill the hours during the day, because these hearings played live coast to coast. You believe that?"

Nicky, grateful to have Accardo talking and not feasting, spurred him on. "Live TV?"

"I walk in, these big cameras with the network letters on the side filling the back of the room, and bright lights everywhere. I never took my sunglasses off, it was so bright. Anyway, they took their shot at me—and they missed." He forked another chunk of steak into his mouth, talking through the chewing. "Senator Estes Kefauver, suddenly he's more interested in interstate commerce crimes than communists. 'Mr. Accardo,' he says to me, 'do you have any connection whatsoever with gambling in the city of Chicago, the state of Illinois, or anywhere in the United States of America?' Makin' a speech. So I say, 'Senator, I refuse to answer.' We go back and forth. 'Do you have any connection to illegal narcotics?' I say, 'No, I don't.' 'Do you belong to the Mafia, Mr. Accardo?' I say, 'I don't even know what the Mafia is all about.' He didn't like that. 'What about an organization known as "the Outfit?"' I say, 'That, I refuse to answer.'

"See, back then, you could pick and choose. 'I'll answer this, but I won't answer this.' Take the fifth when you wanted to, answer the question when you don't. They wised up to that. Now it's gotta be all, 'I decline to answer on the grounds that it might incriminate me.'—right across the board. Or else you've opened the door or the gate or something, and you have to answer it all."

Nicky said, "I see."

"Anyway." Another slice. "They pull my record from when I'm sixteen up through then. 'Mr. Accardo, how is it you have been arrested twenty-three times in the past twenty-five years and always beat the rap?' He didn't say 'beat the rap,' but, you know. Now he thinks he's knocking me down, but really he's just building me up—only I don't want any of it. 'Are you the beneficiary of political influence in Chicago?' he says. I say, 'Mr. Kefauver, Senator, you political men know as well as I do that a good man cannot be negatively influenced.' He didn't like that answer neither."

Nicky smiled. He got some more wine into him, and this time it went down fast and made its presence known.

"So, after the hearings, which made me look like a smart aleck on television, they hadda get me for something. They cite me for contempt of Congress. Only, guess what? I beat that too." Another shrug. "But this other thing stuck to me like gum—the damage was done. It's what gets under do-gooders' skin, that I never did time.

People make like I got a phobia about it, after Capone went crazy in stir, and Nitti shot himself in the face rather than go back. But it's simple common sense. You did, what, two years in Joliet, Nicky? Tell me—is it something I should prefer to avoid?"

"Indeed, it is," answered Nicky. "I can't in good faith recommend it."

"I get that some guys make their bones doing time and doing it right. I also get that some guys who don't go...maybe are smart." Accardo shrugged. "I got brains. You, Nicky, you got brains."

"Still got me tripped up."

"True, but what'd you learn?"

Nicky nodded. "I did learn to be smarter about things."

Accardo pointed his knife at Nicky, punctuating his argument. "Maybe I didn't need that lesson. Something wrong with your steak?"

"Um..." Nicky looked at the cube on his fork. He put it in his mouth. Chewed it, got it down. He was better now. It was just steak again.

"Eat up," said Accardo. "You're gonna need your strength."

"My strength?"

Accardo nodded, finishing his wine. "This is just getting started."

Sally Brags and Crease Man sat across from Nicky in the diner booth with their heads down, tearing through the breakfast specials Nicky had bought them, ravenous and dazed.

The waitress came with a plastic carafe of coffee. "Yeah, everybody, please," said Nicky, and she topped off all three coffee mugs before moving along.

"You thinking about going in to work or what?" asked Nicky, keeping his voice low.

"I dunno," said Crease Man, biting into his toast. He looked blitzed. He held out his left hand, the one missing two fingers, checking it front and back. Nicky did not know why. "Is there a smell on me?"

"No," said Nicky.

"I smell it," said Sally Brags.

"Me too," Crease Man said. "I hope to Christ it goes away."

Sally Brags said, "Where did you go with him?"

Nicky said, "His house. He wanted me to make sure he got home."

Sally's voice got even softer. "He came to you with this?"

Nicky didn't want to get into it. He made a crazy face and paired it with a shrug. "Here we are," he said.

"Jesus, Nicky," said Sally Brags, more concerned for Nicky than himself.

"Look," said Nicky, framing it up for them. "I know this is a lot for you. But you have to see it for what it can get you, right? Think about it." He dropped his voice to a whisper. "Joe is a guy who remembers guys who do the hard work. The tough jobs, right? I know it's bad. But I'm telling you. This is a thing. You have a marker now. One you'll never have to cash in, don't worry, but—it's known. That's the payout here. Recognition. Being a part of the larger thing. You do for someone—he does for you."

Crease Man sat back, confused. Sally Brags nodded. Nicky wasn't sure he was getting through to them.

"As I said," said Nicky, "I know it's a lot."

"It's a fuckin' nightmare, Nicky," said Crease Man.

Nicky nodded. He could tell they wanted to talk about it. Nicky did not want to get into any details, but he had to ask something. "How's the garage?" he said. "Cleaned up and all, right?"

Sally Brags nodded. "I gotta sell the shop. I don't wanna go back there, ever. I can't."

Crease Man nodded in agreement.

Nicky nodded too, though not in agreement. He was trying to find a way to tell them. "That'll have to wait, I think."

"Why's that?" said Sally Brags.

"Because," said Nicky, "we might have to go back there a few more times."

The guys looked at him. Nicky watched as they slowly made sense of his words.

Sally Brags leaned over the table, closer. "Nicky—this is fucked up."

"I know," said Nicky quickly. "I know it is."

Crease Man said, "What's 'a few more times'?"

Nicky wasn't sure, but he could guess. Seven thieves did the job. One was down; that left six more to pay the price. Unless Accardo cooled off, which Nicky hoped was a possibility. Or maybe if they got to Salita quickly, that would be enough, and it would end there.

Nicky said, "If I knew for sure, I would tell you."

"What's it all about?" said Sally Brags. "Nicky, I gotta know."

"You don't want to know," said Nicky. "Believe me."

Sally Brags and Crease Man looked at each other.

Nicky said, "I'm telling you, just—you don't. Let me carry that part of it for now."

Crease Man picked up his mug of coffee, then set it back down again. "*Fuuuuck,*" he sighed.

"And you?" said Sally Brags, after a long look out the window. "You're okay with this?"

"First of all," said Nicky, "do I get a choice to be okay? No, I don't. Second—yes. I am okay with this. Because these guys crossed a line. I want you to imagine, like, the worst thing you can think of," he said.

"Kid touchers," said Crease Man.

Nicky exhaled. "Almost as bad as that. This is straight-up justice, and the less you know, the better off you are. We're on the right side of this, that much I can guarantee you. But you gotta tell me, can you do this?"

They looked at each other. Sally Brags said, "This isn't... This ain't gonna be our *thing*, you know, like what we *do*, for a living—is it?"

"No," said Nicky quickly. "We're a team here. We're a unit. And all's fair when it comes to war."

"*War?*" said Crease Man.

"Not if we do what needs to be done," said Nicky. "Not if we do this right."

Nicky knew Gonzo Forte through Dimes Forbstein, the shark. Nicky didn't put money out on the street anymore; he carried only a few people he had relationships with, so somebody's friend who came into Ten Pin looking for a sum to tide them over until the first of the month or whatever, Nicky put them with Dimes. So naturally Dimes spent a good deal of time in the afternoons loafing around the Lanes—loan sharks don't keep strict schedules—and sometimes Gonzo came around, ate free popcorn, and showed off his imported leather jacket, the type he was always selling on the cheap. That was how Nicky came to know he had a thing for coins.

Nicky ran into Gonzo outside a coffee shop on Racine Avenue in Pilsen, Gonzo emerging with cigarette in hand, smoke rising into the falling snow. He had close-set eyes that were wide and made him look shifty and a little crazy, which was how Gonzo got his name.

"Nicky, hey," he said.

Nicky said, "I recognized the jacket before I saw your face. 'One of Gonzo's,' I thought. And lo and behold."

"Quality stands out," said Gonzo. "Where you headed?"

"I'm actually headed to a thing. Did Dimes tell you I wanted to see you?"

"No. What's this now?"

Nicky took him aside, a few steps away from the door traffic. "It's coins, rare coins, a dealer. Your thing, no? I thought of you right off."

"Hell yeah. I even collect 'em." Gonzo lowered his voice, sharing a secret with Nicky. "Six certified-mint Double Eagles, I got stashed. My retirement." He looked up and down the street. "Lotta money in coins, if they're right. People underestimate 'em. But you gotta know what you're looking for. So what, you need advice, or is this something else?"

"This is something else. Guy's a dealer in Arlington Heights. You might even know of him. But you're gonna love the setup."

"I love it already."

Nicky said, "I can show you some things. My car's up here, I just got on snow chains. Sally Brags is with me."

Gonzo flicked his cigarette butt into a puddle of slush. "I got time. This is good."

Nicky pointed the way, crossing the street with Gonzo, not seeing anyone they knew. Nicky got in front, sliding behind the wheel, Gonzo climbing in back.

"Brags, how you doin'?" said Gonzo.

Sally Brags, sitting next to Nicky, barely turned his head. "I'm good, Gonzo," Sally Brags said. "I'm good."

Nicky ate a knish standing at the front window of Lev's deli in West Ridge, selling Joey "the Jew" Lemmelman on a scheme. "Gonzo recommended you for this."

"Really? That's nice, if unusual. Not like him to share."

"You know him. Small-timer."

Lemmelman smiled. "Always trying to sell me one of his jackets. I seen him sell one off his back. 'You like it? Here, forty bucks.' A walking flea market. Worth it to him to shiver the rest of the day."

Lemmelman wore a heavy wool overcoat with a scarf home-knitted out of yarn stuffed into one pocket. His shirt was made of soft cotton, sugar-cookie yellow, buttoned to his neck.

Nicky said, "I thought maybe you might be looking for something after the fiasco I heard about."

Lemmelman lowered his head and shook it side to side. "Calling it a fiasco is polite in the extreme. I still don't even know exactly what went wrong, but I don't want to. I know I'm better off."

"Smart."

"I know it. It was scary, though. Getting called in like that. I suppose Gonzo is going to expect a referral fee."

"Oh, I dunno. That's between you two."

"Well," said Lemmelman, looking around, making sure nobody was close enough to listen in, "maybe I'll hear you out and then make up my mind."

Nicky said, "I don't blame you being generally wary, once bitten. Tell me what you think about armored-truck depots."

Lemmelman blinked several times. "What I think? I think it's challenging, I think it's ambitious. I think it's jackpot fucking city."

"We got a guy on the inside. A guy who owes. Not me—owes somebody else. There's no connection. But he's trying to buy his way out. He's desperate. Now, this is a lot to bite off. Ambitious, as you say. I like to keep the manpower numbers low. I been burned before."

"The racetrack," said Lemmelman, remembering, wheels turning. "That was with Vin."

"Right. So not surprisingly, Vin's not in on this."

Lemmelman shrugged. "Fine by me."

"I got a strict no-fiasco policy."

Lemmelman nodded and said, "I like everything I'm hearing so far. Continue."

"This would go straight down the line. *Real* careful. We take our time, we tee it up. We clear it with who we have to clear it with. We take care of who we gotta take care of ahead of time and after. I's dotted, T's crossed. By the book."

"By the book," agreed Lemmelman. "This is a beautiful song you're singing."

"But here's the thing. We need Salita. I know it's problematic. Maybe he's moody I was the one who hadda go talk to him. But that wasn't me—I was sent. There's nobody better. What do you think?"

"He's the best, of course. That's why I got in on the other thing. He has talents. He also has, let's call them, flaws. I think there might be some personality issues with him and you, yes. But a depot? That doesn't come along but once or twice in a lifetime. I think he'd meet that challenge, yes. If you go to him like that, Nicky. Saying it's a long shot but it's got huge upside, and you're the only one who can make it happen. I think he just needs a stronger hand on his shoulder, more guidance."

"I don't know if I'm that guy, but maybe we approach him together, you and me. I want this to go right, but it has to go smooth too."

"You know what I think?" said Lemmelman. "I think we should go somewhere else with a bit more privacy and continue this conversation."

"Good, good," said Nicky, wiping his hands, wrapping up the knish in wax paper, dumping it in the trash. They moved together to the door. "Maybe we should talk to Salita sooner rather than later. But it wouldn't be right for me to get him on the phone. I don't know him that well either. Maybe you got better contacts for him than me?"

Didi Paré lovingly checked his face in the visor mirror, sitting next to Nicky in the front seat of the Satellite, driving through thick slush on Addison Street. Didi had an Italian name but dressed Irish and was built Irish too, all chest and head, stout, like a boxer. His wife was seen going around with a shiner or a mark on her face more than once, so there was that too. Nicky didn't know him much at all and didn't want to. He found Didi unpleasant to be with. He was strictly a strong-arm guy, a battering ram, a hump.

"Rare books," said Nicky. "'Don't waste my time'—right? Gimme diamonds, not books. Paintings, maybe, but not books. Copper piping—anything—no fuckin' books."

Didi smiled and nodded. "Books," he said. "Who needs books?"

"But this guy," said Nicky, "deals all in cash."

"Cash," said Didi, flipping up the visor. "Cash is nice."

"So cash, not books."

"Now I'm listenin'."

"Guy doesn't bank. Doesn't believe in it? I don't know, maybe. Too lazy to? Whatever. So he sits on it. Like a mother hen."

"How much?"

"I mean, I don't know how the fuck I would know how much— I'm not his bookkeeper. Rare books, I don't know. But they *cost*. He does a business. As I say—a cash business."

"Gotcha."

"I figure, a bookworm, he scares easy, right? And with all that money around, he must have a good alarm, probably. I think this has Johnny Salita written all over it. His magic touch."

"He's the guy," said Didi, nodding. "No question."

"You seen him recently? I haven't. We run in different circles."

"Have I seen Johnny?" said Didi.

"Right."

"Nicky, I thought he sent me you."

"What? No, no. I'm coming to you looking for *him*. For this thing."

"I ain't seen him since...It was before New Year's. You tried his house?"

"I went by, yeah. Nobody home."

"Maybe he's on a trip."

"Maybe he's on a trip? I guess. I hear he uses a beeper sometimes. You have his number on that?"

"A what?"

"A beeper. The thing you call, leave a number, calls you back."

Didi shook his head incuriously, like he didn't know and didn't care to find out. "Maybe he went on a vacation."

Nicky's spirits sank as he turned off the street into the body-shop parking lot. "Yeah, that must be it, then."

Didi looked up. "Hey. This is Sally Brags's old chop shop."

The right-side garage door was open, Crease Man standing just inside, his hand on the door chain. Nicky pulled right into the bay, and Crease Man yanked down the door behind him, slamming it shut on Didi Paré forever.

S o where the fuck is he?" Accardo said. "His family, something."

Nicky was farther down the central hallway of the hidden basement house underneath Accardo's actual house than he'd ever been, beyond the conference room and Accardo's office, past a room-sized pantry stocked with food and a walk-in freezer, all the way to a partially finished utility room. Accardo had installed a custom industrial heating and air-conditioning system downstairs, as well as some sort of air-filtration system. Nicky noticed that air was always moving through the rooms, dry and hospital-clean. There was an incinerator behind an exposed brick wall in the unfinished room, access to which was through a two-foot-square steel door set roughly at shoulder height.

Accardo stood before it with his shirtsleeve cuffs rolled back from his gray-haired forearms, a laundry basket of common household goods on a stool next to him. He was feeding them one by one into the harsh heat, items such as Mrs. Accardo's clothes, what looked like office files, the comforter from their bed. All things that Johnny Salita and his accomplices had touched. The oven blazed orange yellow, emitting undulating waves of intense heat.

Nicky told him, "His wife and baby are gone. Father-in-law runs a tool-and-die shop. I know him a bit—he makes suppressors. He and I had a talk. And—no."

"You think he's bullshitting? This is his daughter."

"I do not," said Nicky.

It was an answer Accardo didn't like. Accardo looked at the glass ashtray in his hand, the one from the patio table out back, cigar butts still in the dish, and thrust it into the raging heat. A few sparks and embers spit back out of the opening, settling on the cement floor, fizzling out.

"You gotta keep going," he said.

Nicky nodded, but he didn't know what that meant. He was exhausted, mentally. "So we've taken three swings and misses. Three thieves didn't know Salita any better'n I do, which is hardly at all. That leaves two other thieves in his crew, Rhino and Cue Stick—"

"These are stupid fucking names."

"Yup, and they've gone underground—I can't scare them up either. We moved fast, like you wanted, taking guys by surprise. But maybe they knew somehow, what's coming, maybe they heard...but I think, more likely, they were in on this"—Nicky indicated the house upstairs, the break-in—"directly, maybe. And so now they're running scared, and rightly so."

"Cocksuckers."

"Plus Salita, that makes seven. All seven from the Levinson job. That's everyone."

Accardo nodded. "Just keep going."

"I am," Nicky said, "but as I told you, they're hiding out some-where. We'll get them...but it's gonna take time."

"Nicky, you're not hearing me. Just keep fuckin' going."

Nicky went from wondering if Accardo had misunderstood him to realizing that Accardo had understood him too well.

"You don't mean...you don't mean their families?"

Accardo turned to Nicky impatiently, brow wet with perspiration, face red from the heat. "Other thieves! For Christ's sake! Keep going."

Nicky nodded but he was still confused. Accardo threw in some combs and lotions of his wife's that the intruding thieves may have touched. A crematory purge.

"Which ones?" asked Nicky.

"I don't care. Thieves. This is about teaching a lesson. Get me an assortment."

Nicky was pushing it here; Accardo was near rage, but Nicky had to know what the fuck he was talking about. "Just so I don't . . . I need you to be perfectly clear about this."

Accardo looked at him again, disappointed, exasperated. "Fucking Christ, Passero. An assortment. Of thieves. So the message goes out loud and clear."

"Right," said Nicky, still trying to make this understandable. Accardo was saying that innocent thieves—ones who had nothing to do with the break-in—were to be taken out too. And Nicky was supposed to choose?

Nicky tried to think of a way to talk him down—but really it was Nicky standing out on the wobbly tightrope. Having gone four steps already—Labotta, Gonzo, Lemmelman, and Didi Paré—he couldn't simply pivot and go back to the start. How do you do that? He had committed to the path. He had to toe it the whole way.

"Listen, Joe," Nicky said, calling Accardo what his wife and everybody else called him, "I'm here to do what you need done—"

"Yes, you are."

Nicky nodded. "And so I just want to put in some special consideration for my guys, who, they don't really do this sort of thing. I'm saying they don't enjoy it. Maybe some do—not them. But they're doing what you want. But it's taking a toll."

"It's like anything," said Accardo. "You get used to it."

"Maybe," said Nicky. "But you are sending a message—and it's the *right* message—about a thing, your home here, that nobody outside knows anything about."

Accardo tossed in a couple of ladies' slips, and the basket was empty. He closed the incinerator door on the searing heat, latching it shut with a metal-on-brick *clank*, shutting out the breathy noise.

"Nicky," he said, overheated, "what would you have me do?"

This was a trap. Nicky said, "I'm not suggesting you do or not do—"

"You just told me you can't find this fuck Salita."

Nicky nodded. "That's right."

"So what would you have me do? Should I let it go?"

Nicky shook his head.

"I shouldn't? Okay. So, then, I should what?"

Nicky nodded, and said quietly, "Keep going."

"Which I am relying on you for. Can you do what I need to get done?"

Nicky nodded.

"Can you bring me Salita?"

Nicky said, "I didn't say I couldn't. I said it was gonna take time."

That was the wrong answer. Anything other than *I got Johnny Salita in the trunk of my car* was the wrong answer.

Accardo said, "I'd hoped you could handle this."

Nicky looked away and nodded. "It's being handled."

Accardo started past him with his empty basket. "Then handle it, Nicky Pins."

A bustling Saturday afternoon at the Lanes, two nine-year-old birthday parties going on at once, plus a Senior League tourney. Nicky had hired the teenage son of one of his regulars to work weekends, Danny, a skinny kid who wore flared jeans with long stripes and sleeveless shirts in winter. Danny kept an eye on the kids in the arcade room and had already made one change run to the laundromat around the corner that afternoon to keep the quarters flowing. The kid was also on birthday-candle-lighting and stuck-ball duty.

Chuckie kept the popcorn popping, and Leo, Nicky's weekend bartender, uncapped beers and stirred out highballs and sours at the side lounge. Leo, borrowed from Clyde's, told anybody who'd listen tales of how he'd bootlegged cheap Canadian whiskey in the 1950s, and paid back most of his wages to the bar for drinks after his day shift was over. At the end of the bar nearest the lanes, a clot of made guys and hangers-on were shooting the shit and busting balls, smoking, drinking, laughing.

Dimes Forbstein broke away from the pack, seeing Nicky alone behind the counter sorting mail. Dimes ran about 350 pounds and carried it about as well as a man could, belt and suspenders. He wore a caterpillar mustache. When he smiled, he looked like a cartoon character falling in love with a chocolate cake.

"What say you, Nicky Pins?" He peeled cellophane off a pack of Winston Golds.

"Cold and snow's turned my bowling alley into a clubhouse for felons here, Dimes."

Dimes chuckled. He was balding and avuncular, but tough. However, like Nicky, he had others do his strong-arming for him. "You should consider charging them the birthday-party rate. Has Gonzo been by here lately?"

"Gonzo the thief?" said Nicky, not looking up from his bills and circulars.

"You know how he loves your popcorn."

"My free popcorn, yeah." Nicky shook his head. "Check with Chuckie—I don't think so. Any reason?"

"I've been looking for him." Dimes moved closer to the counter, as close as his girth would allow. "You don't happen to know anything about . . . what's been going on?"

Nicky set down the mail, playing intrigued. "Going on? I don't follow."

"Gonzo, regular as rain, he pays his juice. He's always good for it, just a little fuckin' flaky with his leather apparel and those crazy eyes. But it's not like him to duck me. I can let some things slide, but two weeks crosses the line. He and I've done business for years, and I was in the neighborhood anyway, so I make a courtesy call—just a courtesy—to his door. Lady Gonzo answers the door, and she's frantic for information. Has me come in. Says Gonzo hasn't called, nothing. His car's gone and nobody knows where he went, and do I know anything about him?"

"Shit," said Nicky.

"More than a week ago, this was."

"Huh."

"Last time she saw him, he said he had an appointment and went out early in the morning. No one's seen hide nor hair since."

"Appointment?"

"Her words."

"Nobody's seen him?"

"Gonzo comes and goes—like all of us—so I said to myself, what's to worry? I let it sit a few more days. I figured I'd check on him with Joey the Jew, a fellow Levantine, this morning at services. He likes to sit right up at the bema like me."

"Yeah?" said Nicky. "What'd he say?"

"He wasn't there. Joey's gone too."

Nicky made his eyes widen. "*Gone* gone?"

"Somebody there was friends with the wife. Same thing. Here one day, gone the next."

"Well," said Nicky, "it could be anything."

"And look, it's none of my business—except, of course, the piece that *is* my business—but it feels to me like something is in the air. And you are somebody who is generally in the know on these things."

"First I'm hearing it is right now, from you."

"Anecdotally, I'm hearing some other people are getting nervous. Paying up early, telling me they're getting out of town for a few days. Saying waiting for things to blow over is better than vanishing into thin air."

"And these are thieves?"

Dimes shrugged that it was so.

Nicky scratched his chin. "Well, you know thieves. Maybe something's cooking on out of town. Remember that pharmaceutical-warehouse thing in Aurora that time?"

Dimes said, "True, yes. I forgot about that."

"It was like a ghost town here. Nobody knew why. Then suddenly, guys are back in town, nobody's saying nothing, but miraculously they were all suddenly flush with cash. And high all the time."

Dimes smiled, his entire face curling up with the mirth. "That was an interesting week."

The counter phone rang. Chuckie wasn't around. Nicky showed Dimes a forefinger and picked up. "Ten Pin, this is Nicky."

Even with the cacophony of rolling balls and pin falls, Nicky heard that the call was different, an operator's voice droning over a hum of distortion. "Will you accept a collect call from Joliet Correctional Center?"

Nicky froze. Dimes was right there in front of him, lighting up one of his Winstons. Nicky glanced down at the betting lines scribbled out on a card under the phone, like it had to do with that. "Uh, sure. Yeah. Can you hold please?"

Nicky turned and looked everywhere for Chuckie. He spotted him talking to a couple of old guys in bowling shirts at the tourney. Nicky whistled through his teeth and Chuckie looked up, Nicky waving him over.

Nicky said to Dimes, "I gotta take this in the office."

Dimes blew out a plume of smoke and waved it away. "Sure thing," he said, walking back to join the bozos at the bar.

Chuckie climbed the two steps to the counter. "What's up?"

"I gotta take this private," said Nicky, setting the receiver down on the counter.

Chuckie watched him step out from behind, trading places with him. Nicky walked through the bowlers waiting for lane assignments and shoes, past the Lustre King ball-polishing machine, to his office door not far from the arcade room. Nicky grabbed the phone off his desk, holding it at his side as he stepped back to the open doorway and pointed to Chuckie, who hung up.

Nicky closed the door on the noise. He got into his chair, the phone pressed against his chest. He wheeled forward to the desk, pushing back his adding machine, AMF catalog, and time sheets. It was important that he be focused. He leaned over the Brunswick calendar blotter and put the cool receiver to his ear.

"Yeah, go ahead," he said.

"This call is monitored and recorded," said the operator.

A pair of clicks. The distortion lessened as a new connection was made.

"Hello, Nicky?"

Nicky clamped his free hand against the back of his neck, hunching over farther, his lips inches away from the blotter. "Christopher, hey," he said. "Long time."

"Nicky," Christopher said.

"Hey, how are you?"

"I didn't know if you'd take my call."

"What do you mean?" said Nicky. "What are you talking about? Of course I'd take—"

"Maybe you forgot about me."

Nicky focused on Christopher's voice, trying to decode it, hoping to divine his mood despite the dry pay-phone connection.

"No, I didn't forget," said Nicky. "Why are you saying that? Here I am, as always. You get the money in your account?"

"They got us on lockdown. Some unit infractions. Guys getting violent. And the weather—man, they won't even let us out in the yard now. Four walls here, Nicky, and I'm climbing 'em all."

"I know, I know." Nicky pictured it, vividly. The cell they'd once shared. "You gotta hang in there, right? Three more months, by my calendar. You're in the home stretch."

"I try to think like that," said Christopher. He interrupted himself, some raised voices in the background distracting him. Christopher would be in the common area, though on a Saturday afternoon, there probably wasn't too long a line for the pay phones.

"How's the cellmate?" asked Nicky, wary of the answer, treading carefully. "That okay?"

"He's okay," said Christopher. "He's whatever. He's not you."

Nicky looked up, checking his door as though somebody was going to barge in and take the phone from him, then put his head back down. "Ninety days," he said, trying to sound hopeful. "It's a handstand after what you been through."

"What's it gonna be like, Nicky? Me gettin' outta here?"

"You'll be fine, it'll be good. Real good. You'll be out."

"But what'll it be *like*?" Christopher's thin voice got quieter. "With us?"

Nicky felt his own breath coming back at him warmly from the blotter, he was so close. He did not want to have this conversation, now or ever. "I don't know," he said, choosing his words carefully. "Not the same."

A long silence on Christopher's end. "That's what I thought," said Christopher.

"How could it be?" said Nicky. "It's different on the outside. Everything's different. You'll be different."

"You're different?"

"I . . . Yeah, I'm different. I'm telling you, you're gonna be looking at a whole new world, a new existence. That place, Joliet, it goes away. Not overnight. But it goes away. You forget."

"Is that what you did? Forget?"

Jesus. "It's hard to explain. Just focus on getting out, on you, on being out on your own. I'll help how I can. Of course I will— you know that. Get you on your feet. But . . . it's just that there's life inside, and there's life out."

Christopher didn't comment.

Nicky went on, after his silence, "It's gonna be good for you, gonna be great. You just gotta be . . . I want you to be realistic."

"I am realistic."

"You'll see." Nicky winced. This was too painful. "Hey—for someone on their way outta there, you don't sound too great."

"I'm not, Nicky. By a long shot, I'm not."

Christopher's voice broke at the end. Nicky remained silent, waiting for him to pull it back.

"I'm not," Christopher said again.

"Okay," said Nicky.

"I should go."

"Hey, listen, don't take what I say too—"

Click.

"Christopher?"

When he realized the line was dead, Nicky hung up fast. He sat back from his desk and looked at the ceiling. He cursed.

Christopher was mentally frail, Nicky already knew. It was a real problem, one he'd been worried about for a few years. He cared for Christopher, and he didn't like what it might mean if Nicky felt the pull again, upon seeing him, which he feared. For both their sakes.

Now the bill was coming due. This poor kid out on the streets again. Getting his legs underneath him—who knew what he might say or try to do? Or how much he'd talk if he needed to...?

Blackmail was an option. There was emotional blackmail, as well as actual blackmail, both of which Christopher could resort to if things really went wrong for him. Of course, Christopher wouldn't call it blackmail, but if he got desperate—*more* desperate—who was to say he wouldn't hold their relationship over Nicky's head like a sword?

Just like Gerald Roy did.

Nicky cursed again and rubbed hard at his face. Himself to blame. Too much was going on to handle all at once. He jumped up and reached for his office door, going back out into the lanes and the happy noises of people having fun on a Saturday afternoon—determined to keep moving forward.

Detective Feliks Banka sat in his idling Oldsmobile Delta 88 with the heat on full blast. A foot of snow had fallen that week from a storm system that brought a blizzard to the Ohio Valley and Great Lakes. One of the all-time worst storms in the region, the news trumpeted, with Michigan taking the brunt. The temperature in Chicago hadn't risen above freezing for many days, and the weather reports were calling for much more of the same.

A tan Mercury Bobcat pulled around the tow truck, parking next to the medical examiner's van at an angle to the curb. Banka turned off his engine and tightened up his coat collar before climbing out to meet Roy. One thing about the cold was it kept the curiosity seekers away. Even the uniform cops stayed in their patrol cars.

Special Agent Gerald Roy saw Banka coming and hopped over a hump of plowed snow onto the shoveled sidewalk. He wore polished boots too nice for the snow and a heavy coat that wasn't nearly heavy enough. Banka was snug inside his trusty charcoal overcoat with faux-sheepskin lining.

"You need to work on your weather gear," Banka said.

Roy was already hug-rubbing his own arms. "I really never thought I'd miss Vegas."

"We can make this quick. I only thought you'd want to see this."

"Thanks. I owe you."

"Nonsense. Anyway, you might want to hold your appreciation." A coroner's-office employee came out to watch, making sure nobody touched anything. Banka shook out the key to the green Toronado, the vehicle not that different in body style from his own Delta 88. The frozen snow the cops had cleared off it lay in busted chunks around the tires.

He turned the key and the trunk sprang open. The corpse inside lay in the fetal position, naked but for a pair of shit-and-blood-stained underwear. It was trussed up like a Sunday bird with a thin nylon cord around its neck, the ligature marks sliced deep into the skin, the cord running down its back to the body's bound wrists and ankles. The head was bagged in opaque plastic, mouth gagged with thick rope, features black and distorted beyond recognition. And then there was the smell.

"Christ," said Roy, trying not to breathe in through his nose.

"I've never seen worse," said Banka. "Gonna be a bitch to identify."

"What's with the face?"

"Burned off again."

Roy stepped back from the trunk, seeking unfouled air to inhale. When he could, he said, "Again?"

Banka surrendered the keys and the scene to the coroner's men, taking Roy back to his car so they could talk. He turned on the engine and upped the defrost, Roy settling in next to him.

"This is from three days ago," said Banka, passing him the crime-scene photograph from the file on his dashboard. "Found in the trunk of a Lincoln Continental parked in a hotel lot near O'Hare. Lot ticket said it had been there about a week."

Next, he handed him an autopsy photo.

"Had to let the body thaw out before the M.E. could perform the autopsy. You believe that? This one was not only burned but also disemboweled. And castrated."

Roy scanned the report that came with the photos. "Vincent Labotta? He was a cop?"

"Ex-cop. One of a family of ex-cops. Labotta got bounced from the force two decades ago, get this, for taking a twenty-five-dollar bribe to fix a ticket. Twenty-five dollars. Different time then. Different *union* then. Made a hard U-turn into being a full-time thief. And a gambler—got turned around on a race-fixing thing six or so years ago. Leaning on jockeys to throw races, slant the betting odds. Not a *bad* bad guy, you understand, not a violent offender, like his brothers. More like a guy working the margins. Living the life."

Roy handed back the documents. "Okay. So who did he cheat or piss off?"

"What I thought. But now there's two."

Roy nodded. "Two guys with their faces burned off."

"The flesh on their hands too. No fingerprints. That's saying something. Between defrosting and pulling teeth, matching dental records, identifying Mr. Toronado here's gonna take days."

"Been parked out here for a while, huh?"

"Since before the big snow, so a week at least." Banka had been brooding on this as he waited for Roy's arrival. "I had a thought. You have an hour or so to try something out?"

"You taking me coat shopping?"

"Maybe some other time," said Banka, grabbing the handset of his under-dash radio, thinking of what to say to the dispatcher. "I have an idea."

Banka piloted his Olds through the Chicago city streets, narrower from encroaching snowbanks, treacherous for long, front-weighted cars, as he waited for his radio to talk.

"Question for you," he said to Roy. "Ever worry about running into guys from your undercover days in Vegas?"

Roy looked out the window and shrugged. "To be honest, I don't think I made enough inroads out there to be worth the effort. Worth the blowback going after an agent of the FBI, at least. I mean—

I *hope*. But you never know. I'm careful. I never go home the same way twice—ever. Part of how I live now, and who I am."

Banka nodded. "That's smart. I got curious, from your talk. I looked up Jersey George, asked around. There's a dark tale."

"Yeah," said Roy. "The underage girls?"

Banka nodded.

"You couldn't have been too surprised, Feliks. These are not good people."

"Of course not, but still. That how you flipped him?"

"What do you mean?"

"Implicating him. Setting him up in a situation or a sting. With these street girls. Make it for him that it's either prison or 'you help me'?"

Roy sighed before speaking. Banka didn't expect him to divulge everything, but the deep breath pretty much confirmed Banka's version. "I will tell you what I learned," said Roy. "I learned that a well-placed informant? Is worth the efforts of five undercover agents, easy. Undercover guys have limitations. We both know that. What you can do, how far you can go. But a guy who's already baked in, who doesn't have to earn his way up the ladder? Then you're drilling into the nerve. Then you got a live one."

"Huh," said Banka, surprised at his candor. "That leads me to think maybe you have somebody on the inside here now."

Roy smiled. "I didn't say that."

"No," said Banka. "No, you didn't."

Banka's radio crackled. He picked up the handset.

"This is Banka, go ahead."

"Detective Banka, we have one vehicle with four citations in the past seven days—5215 South Sangamon."

Banka and Roy crossed the street to a snow-covered Cadillac. Only one citation showed through the windshield snow. Banka had his scraper and went around to the trunk, while Roy moved to the driver's-side window, clawing away at the snow covering with his wool gloves.

Banka hadn't gotten very far on the trunk work when Roy said, "Feliks."

Banka went around to join him at the window. Roy had gotten down to an icy glaze coating the glass. It was opaque, but there was a figure inside, a body, slumped over the steering wheel.

Roy moved aside so Banka could go at the ice with his scraper blade, shaving away enough to see more clearly.

A naked male corpse.

Roy pointed to the inside lock, which was pulled up, unlocked. He tried the door handle, then reset himself and gripped it with both hands, giving it a good yank. It wanted to open, the glazed snow around the doorframe cracking slightly. "Watch out," said Roy, Banka giving him room, as he jerked at the handle with his boot braced against the body of the vehicle.

The wide door pulled open. The frigid temperatures had slowed putrefaction. The corpse had been stabbed repeatedly. Its torso had been sliced open with a blade, maybe a Sawzall, the victim disemboweled.

But not burned. Its decaying face held a look of stupefied somnolence.

Roy said, "Goddamn Jesus Christ."

Banka, standing back at an angle from the released odor, put a name to the frozen face.

"Paré," he said.

"What?" said Roy, his arm across his nose.

"Didi Paré," said Banka. "Strong-arm thief. I arrested this guy before. Ninety percent sure it's him."

Roy started to stick his head inside to look at the rest of the car, but the smell was gaseous, too much. He backed off with Banka, looking at the naked corpse behind the wheel.

"Feliks," said Agent Roy, "I think we got something here."

T he *Edge of Night* was a late-afternoon television soap opera, also a crime series, and only a half hour long. There was a matriarch, as well as a whole thing with her family and multiple untimely deaths, and vendettas and affairs and endless amnesia cases, but there was the cop story too, set in the fictional city of Monticello. It was jarring to see stories about drug shipments and gangsters and district attorneys on television at four in the afternoon, when that primary audience was mothers cleaning up the house around their children after school. It was difficult to know who this show was aimed at, aside from Nicky Pins.

One day recently, a new police chief named Derek Mallory came to Monticello. He was tall and trim, clean cut except for a broad mustache. He was smooth moving, poised, a good talker. Nicky watched him with growing fascination for maybe two months before it clicked: he had seen this actor before. One stag night, the group he was with had taken over a hotel suite downtown and run a 16 mm porno that someone in the projectionists' union had brought, titled *Punk Rock*. In it was a cop character played by the very same actor who played Monticello police chief Derek Mallory. In the bachelor-party porno, Derek Mallory got it on with women, of course—and maybe this was wishful thinking, but—

The guy in that porno, in turn, had reminded Nicky of the one and only time he'd been to New York City, on a bag job that had to be handled personally. That night, after he'd had a few, which was a bigger problem with him then than it was now, Nicky wound up in a back-of-the-store booth in Times Square, watching what were known as "loops." Short porno movies, no plot or story, one encounter running over and over. Unless Nicky's memory was playing tricks on him, the guy playing Police Chief Derek Mallory definitely didn't perform with a woman in the loop. He got it on with a bearded stud in a cowboy hat in a lounge chair by a pool. The actor was younger then, with shorter, more conservative hair, but he'd had the same mustache, the same hairy chest, the same California blue eyes.

Sure, Nicky could have conflated the performers from the gay loop, the straight porno, and the soap opera. Short of tracking down the other movies, how was he ever to know for sure?

But the other thing about all this was—and on this point, there was no mystery—it struck Nicky how much Monticello police chief Derek Mallory resembled Chicago FBI special agent Gerald Roy. Not dead ringers, but cut from the same cloth, right down to the mustache and the body type.

Nicky usually watched *Edge* on the thirteen-inch Trinitron television behind the counter while spraying disinfectant into rental shoes or doing some other busy work, as he was trying to do on this quiet Tuesday afternoon, while Detective Kevin Quiston insisted on regaling him with a cop yarn from the other side of the counter.

"The captain gives us our marching orders, and the riot squad goes into the movie theater. Me, I'm up front. First thing I see is a woman behind the register who's not a woman but a cross-dresser, right, wig, makeup, and skirt, though I'll be honest with you, he didn't put much effort into it. Three days without a shave and sideburns poking through. He screamed like a girl, though, and we shoved through a couple of raincoat homos waiting to pay their money, through the curtain next to a poster advertising *All-Male Cast*. It's another world in there. Two guys up on the screen in mid-assfuck, guys all over each other in the seats, smells like you'd expect but also worse. We go down the aisle, banging on seatbacks to rile them up, as the house lights come on. Like roaches in your kitchen, these queens zipping up and skipping down to the exit. What is this shit you're watching here?"

Nicky set aside a shoe with a ripped seam over the toe cap. "The cops have a hunch the Red-Head Killer might be one of their own. That means Deborah could be next."

"Red-Head Killer, huh?" said Quiston, leaning over the counter to see. "Deborah, there, she's a fine piece of work, but these cops look like the queens we clubbed coming out of the Bijou."

Nicky ignored that. "So the Bijou's shut down."

"Nah, civil rights, freedom of whatever. We were there to harass them. Neighborhood complaints. You walk down the sidewalk that part of town after dark, Nicky, you get whistled up. Fuckin' meat market. But they really are roaches. You scare 'em out of one place, they pop up somewhere else a month later. Better to let them have their little ghetto, I say. Keep them out of proper neighborhoods. That way we know where they all are."

Nicky turned to Quiston as the soap opera went to commercial. He looked at this eager-faced adjudicator on men and morality. "You probably have an eye for them. Ever see any in here?"

"In here, Nicky? You kidding or what?"

"Well, if you ever do, you let me know."

Chuckie walked over with a second man. "Nicky, this is Gerry. He's here to fix the pinball machine."

The repairman wore a denim work shirt with a patch bearing the brand name Bally stitched over the breast pocket. He wore tortoise-shell eyeglasses, which threw off Nicky only for a moment.

The man standing on the other side of the counter was Gerald Roy.

He carried a tool belt in one hand and a toolbox in the other, setting down the toolbox and offering his free hand to shake. "Hiya."

Nicky looked at the hand. He gripped it and shook it, slow to play along.

Repairman Roy said, "You got a pinball machine out of order?"

Nicky barely understood the words he was saying.

Chuckie said, "The Evel Knievel game, right, Nicky?"

"Evel Knievel," said Detective Quiston. "There's a crazy son of a bitch."

Nicky looked at Quiston and suddenly woke up to the moment.

"The arcade's back there," he said, and thumbed at the glass door.

"Got it," said Roy, who picked up his toolbox and started toward it.

Nicky did not watch him go. He remained looking at the space the FBI agent had occupied.

Detective Quiston said, "My kids emulate the guy. Jumpin' bikes off my garage roof. How he doesn't get sued coast to coast, I don't know."

"Seriously," said Chuckie. "He's gonna kill himself getting rich."

Nicky pulled himself into the present. "No, yeah," he said. "I just..." He was mumbling. Nicky looked at Quiston again, then at Chuckie. Nicky said, "I'm gonna go keep an eye on this guy."

Nicky stepped out from the counter, leaving the two men behind. The closer he got to the arcade room, the angrier he became, and by the time he reached the glass door, he was furious.

Along the row of pinball machines, Roy stood before the fully electric Evel Knievel game, which stood out because it was trimmed in white with a blue ribbon of stars on the side of the machine, along with a sketch of Knievel riding his motorbike, cape flying. The backglass featured an action image of Knievel riding out of the game at the player, next to a sexy woman wearing jean shorts.

Roy already had the metal-sided play surface propped open, like the hood of a car, exposing complicated MPU wiring beneath the playfield. He had buckled on his tool belt and held an electrician's screwdriver in one hand.

Nicky went two-thirds of the way toward him before stopping, making sure the door was shut behind him. He said quietly, "Are you out of your fucking mind?"

Roy looked back at him, unfazed, matching Nicky's intensity, though not his rage. "You should have returned my messages, Passero," he said. He pointed the long-bladed screwdriver at Nicky. "*You* answer to *me*."

Roy's pale blue eyes were penetrating, and the pushback startled Nicky. How was this happening in his own place? "What the fuck are you doing here?"

Roy started to reply, then the door behind Nicky opened. Nicky whirled.

Two teenagers, one wearing a Bears parka, the other Levi's with faded knees, entered the arcade laughing. Nicky waved them back. "Arcade's closed right now."

The boys looked at the lone machine being repaired. One said, "Can't we just play the others—"

"Get the fuck out," said Nicky.

The teenagers' faces fell, chins tucked in like they'd been slapped. But they didn't move.

"I said fuck off!" said Nicky, and the boys turned and walked right out. Nicky turned back to Roy after the door closed again. "Are you trying to get me killed?"

"Tired of chasing you, Nicky. I need to be your first call, not your last."

"I have a fucking life here—"

"I am not interested in your life. I'm not interested in anything else except these thieves turning up across town, tortured and executed."

Nicky looked back at the closed door. "Keep it the fuck down."

"I will once you start talking."

Nicky took a few steps toward him so they could speak more measuredly. "I don't know. I just started hearing things. Score settling, I assume. Happens all the time."

"Faces burned off? Does that happen all the time?"

"Faces—what?"

"Burned off. As in, with a torch. News to you?"

"They didn't put that in the paper," said Nicky. "But you really think I'm like a clearinghouse here? Guys check in and confess their crimes to me and their motives too? I run a bowling alley, not a church, for Christ's sake."

"And I'm a pinball-machine repairman," said Roy.

"What do you care, some guys in the game get knocked out of the game?"

"The *degree*," said Roy. "You are such a bullshitter. You're shameless, Passero. You know these guys."

"I know these guys?" Nicky scoffed. "I know *of* them, maybe."

"Vin Labotta was in on the race-fixing thing that brought you down."

"Vin, I knew. Vin was a screwup. Fuck him."

Roy tapped his screwdriver against the machine, open like a patient on an operating table. "You want me to leave this the same way or make it broken worse?"

Nicky felt the lanes at his back—and Chuckie and Quiston—and knew he had to give Roy something to get him out of the building. "Listen, my guess? And I don't know, so take it for what it's worth. Is the Levinson heist."

Roy's eyebrows went up. His shoulders appeared to relax. He wanted more.

"Common sense," said Nicky. "Every thief who disappears before the split, everybody *else's* percentage goes up."

Roy thought about that. "They haven't split it up yet?"

"I don't know. How would I know? I don't even know how long these guys been trunked. Do you?"

Roy nodded. "Killings happened a while ago now."

"Okay," said Nicky. "So maybe."

This made sense to Roy. "The jewelry heist."

"Again, I'm guessing—I don't fucking know. You must have considered it. It's a theory. You need a mind reader—you don't need me."

Roy stared at him, processing this. Things had relaxed between them. Nicky thought again about Derek Mallory on *Edge* as he looked at Roy here in disguise, acting. Playing a part.

Nicky said, pointing at the machine, "Don't you think you should've unplugged that thing first?"

"I don't know what the fuck I'm doing," Roy said. "Now talk to me about Accardo."

Too much going on—Nicky had to work to keep things straight. He didn't know what Roy knew. "What does he have to do with any of this?"

"He flew out of Palm Springs earlier this month. We picked him up talking to his wife long-distance. From here."

Nicky wondered if anybody might have seen him at Accardo's home on Ashland Avenue—so his reaction to Roy's revelation was delayed. He said, "You got authority to tap the Man?"

Nicky's legitimate surprise sold his innocence to Roy. Roy didn't confirm or deny, didn't shrug it off. Nothing.

Now Nicky was really worried. He made it sound like curiosity when he said, "Shit, what do you have?"

Roy said, "Never mind that. It must be related to this. Him coming back unannounced, unexpected, without Mrs. Accardo?"

"I don't know how it would."

"It doesn't seem like word has gotten around that he's back. Which itself is odd. Like he's hiding—or at least hiding something."

Nicky was spooked. Roy was on the right track for once.

"Look," said Nicky, "I gotta get back out there before people wonder. You need to close that thing and get the fuck out."

Roy said, "*You* look. There's murder—and there's *murder*. Guys turning up in trunks isn't anything fresh and new around here. Guys turning up in trunks looking like they've been worked over by the Viet Cong? Something's up."

"So? Something's up."

"I need to know what. I want to know why Joe Batters is back in town suddenly, and why thieves are getting hacked up. And by who."

"You're giving me lists now? Assignments? Do I get a fucking badge too?"

"I'm telling you something serious is going down inside the Outfit. And you don't seem all that impressed or interested."

"What do you want me to do about it?"

"You're Nicky Pins," said Roy. "So ask around."

Roy's words followed Nicky out of the game room, putting him in a daze. *The FBI on Accardo's phones?* That was bad for Joe, and not particularly good for Nicky either.

He walked toward Chuckie, who was smoking at the counter. "Everything okay in there?" said Chuckie.

"Oh, yeah," said Nicky. "I'm working on getting more video games, thought maybe Gerry there would know something. But he was totally useless. Quiston gone?"

"He's gone. That cop, he's a yo-yo."

"Tell me about it," said Nicky. He looked around like he didn't know what to do. Because he didn't. Except that he couldn't stay there with Roy in his place—he just couldn't.

"I'm running out for a bite," said Nicky, reaching over the counter for his heavy coat.

N icky came in too hot, still keyed up from his encounter with Roy inside Ten Pin. And a little puffed up, full of himself for being the one to break the news to the Chairman of the Outfit that his phones were being tapped or bugged.

He regretted it now, Accardo hovering over his shoulder, questioning everything.

"Maybe Salita brought the Feds in here with him when he broke in," Accardo said.

Nicky carefully lifted the top plate off the telephone, setting it next to the disassembled receiver. The kitchen phone was the last one in the house Nicky had to check. He had to talk the old man down. Nicky told him, "No sign of that whatsoever."

There were three possibilities. The first was straight-up illegal, but also the most common, and favored by police detectives looking to poach some incriminating evidence that could then be turned around and used to procure a legal, court-ordered wiretap. All it took was screwing a pair of wires from a basement telephone box to a voice-activated tape recorder. This required access inside the home, obviously, and at least two breaking and enterings, one to set the tap and one to take it away. Accardo's alarm, which had been repaired, made this option highly unlikely.

The second also involved direct access: installing a tiny recording device in the telephone unit itself. Nicky had taken apart all six phones at 1407 Ashland Avenue—and each one was clean.

That left the third, and most worrisome: a Title III wiretap intercept.

Nicky reassembled the telephone. "They're not on you here," he said. "Palm Springs—maybe. I don't know. That wouldn't be too hard, since you're away most of the year. Worst-case scenario, it's not a hard tap. It's the wires."

Accardo said, "That means a court order. Over what?"

"We don't know what we don't know. That's the problem."

Accardo looked around the room at the light fixtures, the walls. "Who says it's gotta be in the phones?"

"You could get your place swept, right?" said Nicky. But that would mean coming clean about his home being broken into, which was unlikely.

Accardo said, "And you got on to this how?"

"Detective I know, property-crimes guy, completely unrelated, overheard it from a Fed, saying they knew you were here in the city."

"Then you can find out more."

Nicky shook his head. "I said he overheard it on another thing. Brought it up to me offhandedly, random. He's a dead end. But that's how lucky we got, knowing this now."

Accardo walked away from him, then stopped, hands on hips. He came back with something to say.

"Cops talked to Doves," he said.

"What?"

"Two badges in Palm Springs. Asking where I was."

"Local or federal?"

"Local."

"And?"

"And Doves talked to me. I hadda tell him. Most of it, anyway. I put it on Levinson, the jewelry thing."

"Saying what?"

"Saying those thieves are no fucking good, and it's being settled. Nothing about my house here."

Nicky rubbed the back of his neck. "Oh, fuck."

"No, see, actually it's paying off," said Accardo. "Doves put some feelers out on the street. He got a tip about those last two thieves— the ones with the stupid names."

"But, Joe . . . *they talked to Doves.*"

"So?"

"So? It means you're next."

"Ah. Let 'em come."

"Let them come? You wanna talk to them about this? Be involved?"

"Fuck 'em. We can take care of it."

Nicky put his palms out like it wasn't his business. But it was. "Hear me out? Okay?"

Accardo shrugged grudgingly.

"The answer to this is easy. Go back to Palm Springs."

Accardo immediately shook his head. "No."

"Let this all cool down. Let it settle. You don't need any of it. I can handle things here for you."

Accardo said, "Out of the question."

Nicky pressed him. This was about Nicky's well-being too. "Listen. The cops, the thieves. Everybody's getting spun up. Nobody knows what's happening—or why. You just parachute out. Why do you need this?" Nicky went full car salesman on him. "Sit in the sun—you earned it. I'll mop up here. Maybe a lull will even cause these thieves to poke their heads out, think the coast is clear. And then we move in and finish it . . ."

Nicky's voice trailed off as Accardo stepped away again, thinking it over. Nicky felt a lift, like he had gotten through to him. Nicky already felt the pressure easing.

Accardo sighed heavily, his back to Nicky. "There's something else," Accardo said.

"Something else?" said Nicky. "Okay. What?"

"The cuff links? That wasn't the only thing Salita took."

Nicky's relief at having convinced Accardo to pull back on his vendetta dropped right out of him, onto the floor. Accardo was still facing away from him.

"A pair of notebooks," said Accardo. "Taken from my office in the basement. Transaction records."

Dread settled over Nicky like a cloak. "Of what?"

"Everything," Accardo said. "Everything from Vegas."

"Everything, meaning...?"

"From the beginning. Going back years. Everything, all of it." Accardo's voice became defiant suddenly—before Nicky could ask him why he put incriminating evidence down on paper. "It's all in code! You gotta keep a ledger somewhere..."

Nicky said nothing. You don't castigate the boss. Even when he tells you he didn't tell you everything you needed to know. Even when he puts you in further danger. Even as you're watching a bad thing get worse and worse and worse.

Nicky said, "Is there anything—*any little thing*—else I need to know about all this?"

Accardo picked at a dry stain on the kitchen counter with his fingernail. "The books also got names. Judges. Politicians. Cops."

Accardo turned back to Nicky then, fully, his beagle eyes glaring.

"I need Salita, Nicky," he said. "I need those notebooks."

Pino's Lighting and Fixtures had been a landmark on West Armitage Avenue for more than three decades, its ornate storefront chandeliers glowing brightly in the windows after dark. Across the street was a barbershop that closed at six, and next to the barbershop, a small, underlit parking lot with a clear view diagonally across at Pino's.

A white-on-tan box truck was parked in the lot, some unintelligible graffiti marking its roll-up back. Two men sat in the front cab with the engine off. Cue Stick Pino, whose uncle had owned the lighting store for the past thirty-eight years, was fidgeting in the passenger seat. He'd been on edge for weeks, but right now he had an acute case of the nerves. Rhino Guarino was annoyed, impatient, cold. It was quarter to midnight, the arbitrary hour they had set for their burglary.

"Let's just go," Rhino said, wanting to be done with this already.

Headlights preceded a vehicle rolling east on West Armitage, toward North California, a green Volaré station wagon.

Cue Stick sat forward and pointed. "Didn't that green Volaré pass by ten minutes ago?"

"And if it did? Who do you think is driving around looking for us in a green Volaré wagon? What kind of gunman is that?"

"Did you see who was driving?"

"No, and neither did you. Cue, it's not enough to be scared all the time, asshole. That's not being careful—that's being a jumpy priss. Use your eyes, use your fuckin' brain."

"*Two* green Volarés, Rhino?" said Cue Stick. "We should wait a while longer."

"I am not waiting," said Rhino, bolstered by Cue Stick's stupidity, tugging his gloves on more tightly and pulling his knit cap down low to his eyebrows. "You wanna wait, wait. But you wait alone."

Rhino opened the door and climbed out. They had already switched off the interior light, so there was only the noise of the door, open and shut.

Cue Stick called after him, which was dumb. He looked around the parking lot and decided he was better off not staying behind. "Son of a—" He jumped out, boot treads hitting a plane of ice, Cue Stick almost falling on his ass. He closed the truck door, short-stepped over the patch of ice, then hustled to catch up with Rhino at the sidewalk.

Rhino looked both ways, traffic lights stretching into the distance in either direction, west and east down the avenue. The coast was clear. He tucked his hands into his pouch pockets and hurried across the mostly cleared street to the low bank of frozen snow on the opposite sidewalk.

With short, careful steps, they approached the bright entrance. A few of the fixtures inside flashed on and off, trying to catch passing customers' eyes. Still no traffic behind them—they were lucky. Rhino pulled out the ring of three keys. The first one he tried fit perfectly in the lock and turned. The door opened. They were in.

Cue Stick bounced on his heels as Rhino locked the door behind them. His uncle's store didn't have an alarm, because the bright lights dissuaded thieves, and because he operated on a safe block. His uncle felt secure enough to leave a spare ring of backup store keys with his sister, Cue Stick's mother, for safekeeping at her house in case of emergency.

This was an emergency, all right, just not the kind his uncle had anticipated. The emergency was that somebody from the Outfit was killing thieves. Vin, Gonzo, Didi, Joey the Jew. Tortured and trunked. Cue Stick and Rhino had driven down to Saint Louis for New Year's to see some girls Rhino knew, stayed there a few weeks, partying until their money ran out. They returned to town, looking to get back into something, but nobody answered the phone. Pretty soon they figured out something was wrong. Since then, they'd been hiding out like refugees, sleeping nights in the van around the outskirts of the city. They were cooped up for a few days in a house in Beach Park they broke into, until a neighbor spotted them, asked who they were. Rhino was leaning on a hooker he knew, the two of them sleeping on her floor between tricks, but that couldn't last. They needed money to stake themselves a big move, to get out of town, probably for good.

They moved away from the bright windows fast, deeper into the store, under dangling price tags, fluttering in the breeze from a display ceiling fan. The store darkened toward the back, their shadows disappearing. Rhino used a penlight to lead them behind the special-order counter, looking for Cue Stick's uncle's office.

A key opened that door too. Cue Stick entered behind Rhino and saw his uncle standing to the side and almost screamed.

It was a cardboard cutout, an advertisement, his uncle with one hand on his hip, the other holding a lit light bulb above his head. *Get Bright Ideas at Pino's Lighting and Fixtures!*

"Fucking Jesus, Mary, and Joseph," said Cue Stick. Heart pounding so hard he heard it in his ears now, he wanted out of there as soon as possible. Stealing from family was a cardinal sin. Even if he paid it back someday, as he intended, his uncle, his mother, everybody would never look him in the eye again. He was despondent over it, but his back was against the wall. Rhino had convinced him it was their only chance.

Cue Stick took over the search, pulling open drawers in his uncle's desk, rifling through them until finding a black lockbox in the rear of the bottom right drawer.

He pulled it out, set it on top of the desk. Heavy but not solid. Penetrable. Rhino looked it over with his penlight beam. A simple enough three-dial combination lock. Cue Stick partly hoped it held only papers and documents, for the salvation of his own soul. But they needed money. They could get inside easily with a mail opener or even a good nail file.

"Not here," said Cue Stick, his imagination running wild. "Come on."

Rhino said, "Open it here. We can take what we need and put it back. He might not notice it gone for days."

Cue Stick shook his head, tucking the lockbox under his arm as if he were running a quarterback sneak. "The deed is done. We're gonna be three states away from here this time tomorrow night."

He made for the door, leaving Rhino no choice but to follow.

Cue Stick swatted dangling price tags out of his face like a treasure-hunting grave robber escaping under jungle foliage. He was almost at the front display lights when he stopped dead.

A young couple, strolling arm in arm, crossed the exterior of the store from the left. They stopped, drawn by the light display, stepping up to the windows. Cue Stick saw them plainly, but they couldn't see him behind the bright lights—though it felt like they could. It felt like they were looking right at him instead of the fixtures.

The female reached for the male's chin and pulled his face to hers. They kissed and started really making out. Rhino stood next to Cue Stick, watching.

"That's tongue," said Cue Stick.

The guy started feeling her up over her red cloth coat.

"Look at these two," said Rhino.

"She fuckin' wants it," said Cue Stick.

"He's gonna get laid right here in the street," said Rhino.

She pulled her mouth away from his, hungrily, pulling on his elbow, towing her man away from the storefront and toward home.

"Fuckin', I hate that guy," said Rhino.

Cue Stick's anxiety returned immediately. "Let's go."

They went to the doors, turned the lock, and exited fast, Rhino relocking the door from the outside. But Cue Stick didn't wait for him, just like Rhino didn't wait for him to leave the truck. He hopped the snowbank and jogged across the avenue to the parking lot with the lockbox like a loaf of bread under his arm.

The hooker, Roxie, stood by her kitchen stove, wearing a hip-length silver silk robe that was loosely tied and falling open over a lace camisole and white cotton panties, arms crossed, smoking. Black hair to her shoulders, green eyes, a bit of a belly, wide hips. A Portuguese girl who could easily be mistaken for Italian. The piece that didn't match was her moccasin slippers.

Nicky, seated at the table with his back to the wall separating the rooms, could not be seen from the apartment door. She had fixed him a *francesinha*—she had offered to make sandwiches when it was clear they'd be there awhile, waiting—bread, ham, and linguiça. Nicky was certain Rhino wasn't cooped up there because of Roxie's kitchen talents, though he might as well have been. She wasn't smart enough to steer clear of Rhino, yet she had the savvy survival skills to prepare a small meal for the three guys who had forced their way into her apartment, keeping them happy and occupied. Not that she had anything to fear from Nicky, Sally Brags, and Crease Man, but she didn't know that. Nicky was impressed.

Footsteps came up the stairs. Nicky gave Roxie a reassuring nod, and she stood very still. A key turned in the lock and the door opened. "We're back," called out a man's voice.

Roxie didn't move from her spot by the stove. The door closed and two pairs of footsteps approached. Rhino was the first one through the door—and the first to see Nicky sitting at the table, Sally Brags standing by the fridge.

Rhino froze. Before he could say anything, Cue Stick bumped into him from behind, then saw their unexpected visitors. He turned fast—but Crease Man was behind him, ushering the two into the small, crowded kitchen.

"Welcome home, fellas," said Nicky. The hooker eased her hip off the oven, arms down at her sides. Nicky nodded to her. "Thanks, honey, you can clean this up later."

She didn't wait for anything else, no word or look from Rhino, slinking behind him and Cue Stick, Crease Man turning to let her through. Nicky waited until he heard her bedroom door shut. They had already disconnected her phone.

Nicky pointed to the lockbox under Cue Stick's arm. "What's in the box?"

Cue Stick looked like he was going to start sobbing. "We shouldn't of come back. I told you—"

Rhino whipped his head around and spat a reply at him. "Shut up!"

"We could of driven away if you had your stuff—"

"Shut up!" Rhino was thinking about how to handle this, gears turning, his attention going back to Nicky and Sally Brags. "Is it you guys?" he said.

"Is what us?" said Nicky, picking up his sandwich, taking another bite.

Rhino watched Nicky chew, trying to figure it out. "She dime us?"

Nicky wiped his lips with a paper napkin. "Roxie?" he said. "Does it matter?"

Cue Stick, having lost all hope, said again, "We could of driven away…"

Nicky picked up the knife the hooker had sliced his sandwich with and offered it to Rhino, handle first.

"Here. Open it."

Rhino looked like he wasn't sure he should accept the knife, confused.

Nicky said, "The box. Open it."

Rhino accepted the knife, taking the lockbox from Cue Stick's grip, Cue Stick offering no resistance. Rhino set the box on the table, combination facing up, eyeing Nicky across from him. He slipped the sharp edge of the blade under the lid, sliding it along until it met resistance over the numeric dials.

Nicky sat not three feet away from the knife—almost daring Rhino to try something. Easy to do with Sally Brags at Rhino's back, and Crease Man at Cue Stick's.

"Careful of your hand there," said Nicky. "Don't slip." He was leaning hard on these two. He wanted this to work.

Rhino regripped the handle and applied force against the inside latch. The blade bent a little, Rhino twisting it, his grip firm. The lock popped without too much effort.

Rhino set the bent knife down on the table. Nicky smiled and drew the knife toward him, away from temptation. Rhino righted the box. He opened the lid, which blocked Nicky's view.

Rhino straightened. Cue Stick peeked over into the box.

"Well?" said Nicky. "The suspense is killin' me."

Rhino pulled out three bundles of cash, a half inch thick each, used twenties bound tightly with twin elastic bands. Then a silver Rolex wristwatch with a gold face and a metal band. Then a folded bindle of paper. Nicky thought it might be blow, but when uncreased, it revealed a men's inlaid diamond ring and two loose stones, an emerald and a ruby.

There were also some papers and an insurance-company packet.

Nicky said, "Nice Rolex. Your uncle's lighting store, huh? The one on Armitage? Nice family. Nice nephew."

Tears sprang from Cue Stick's eyes, streaming down his pie face.

Nicky went on, "Enough here to get you two on your way outta town, I'd say. If you'd planned it better. Cue Stick was right, Rhino. You shoulda kept on driving."

Rhino stared straight down like he was going to be sick. He didn't like Cue Stick being right about anything.

Cue Stick said, "Green Volaré?"

Nicky said, "What's that now?"

"Green Volaré wagon—right?"

Nicky looked at Rhino. "What the fuck's he talking about?"

"He's an idiot," said Rhino, as much an admission to himself as to Nicky. Rhino raised his gaze to look at Nicky, man to man. "You're behind all this, Passero?"

"Me?" said Nicky. "Whoa, whoa, no. I'm trying to *stop* it, Rhino. You know who's behind it. We all know the answer to that. This thing starts and ends with Johnny Salita."

Rhino looked back at the bundles of cash that couldn't help him now. "We don't know where he is," he said.

Nicky shrugged and said, "I didn't even ask."

Rhino looked at Cue Stick, and Cue Stick looked at Rhino. Neither thief said anything.

Nicky smiled. "Okay," he said. "Now I'm asking."

Nicky stepped away from the tension in the garage, to the entrance where what used to be the front counter was bare and the no-brand soda machine was empty and unplugged.

Nicky looked out at the dark street. He rubbed some heat into his cheeks. Then he heard the phone ring.

He hurried back inside the garage. One telephone was set on a tool cart next to Rhino's chair. Nicky had left him sitting with elbows on knees, head down, almost in prayer. Now Rhino stared at the phone as Nicky approached.

Cue Stick sat in another chair a few feet away, both thieves under the watchful eyes of Sally Brags and Crease Man. The second phone ran off a long extension cord to the padded folding table he and Sally Brags and Crease Man used to play cards on, when the garage was a place of leisure and fun.

Nicky grasped the receiver without picking it up yet and looked to Rhino, who did the same on the dingy garage phone.

"Okay," said Nicky.

They lifted their receivers off the cradles at the same time. Nicky listened. Rhino said into his, "Hello?"

"Who's this?" said the voice. "Somebody called me from this number."

"It's Rhino, Johnny. It's Dom."

"Dom?" said Johnny Salita, talking into a pay phone somewhere, Nicky was certain. "Where are you? What's this number?"

Rhino answered as Nicky had coached him. "I'm at a hotel outside the city. I'm near O'Hare. Wondering what to do. I hadda call you, Johnny."

"Dom, you're lucky to be alive. I wasn't expecting any more calls."

"I don't know what to do here."

"About what? They're whacking us out. Everyone. Get on a plane."

"I don't have money for that." Rhino glanced at Nicky, who nodded encouragingly, wanting Rhino to draw out Salita. "I'm stuck here. Where are you?"

"Where am I?" said Salita. "I'm where I should be. Anybody with you?"

"With me now?" said Rhino. "Yeah." He looked over at Cue Stick leaning forward, hanging on Rhino's side of the conversation. "Cue Stick's here. Say hi."

Cue Stick leaned even farther forward, saying meekly, but with forced enthusiasm, "Hi! Hi, Johnny!"

"I can't believe you two made it, of all of 'em. Where you been hiding?"

"We were outta town for a while, came back. Walked right into this."

"You better walk back out again," said Salita.

Rhino pressed him. "What's your plan? Can't we get together? What are you doing?"

Salita said, "They tried to trunk me, Dom. They tried to trunk me like the others, and they missed."

"They who?" said Rhino.

"It was Vin, but somebody put him up to it. My money's on Nicky Pins, his dipshit crew. Those two retards he rides with."

Rhino closed his eyes and shook his head fast. Cue Stick's head fell almost into his lap.

Crease Man and Sally Brags glanced at each other, then back at Rhino on the phone.

Rhino looked across at Nicky, who shook his head. Meaning *Not us*.

But Rhino knew. He knew as soon as he'd walked into his hooker's kitchen the night before. He knew he had to produce here—and even if he did, it still might go bad for him. But he had to try. His hand relaxed around the receiver, shoulders loosening. He went off Nicky's suggested script, speaking plainly.

"We shouldn't've done it, Johnny. You got us loaded and talked us into it. Breaking into the Man's house…Suicide. Why did you make us do it?"

"You wanna know why?" said Salita. "Fuck him, that's why."

"But, Johnny," continued Rhino. "You brung the whole city down on us."

After a moment's silence, Salita said, "I know. You're right. We fucked it up. I know we did. What can I tell you?"

"Maybe we can fix it," said Rhino, sitting forward. "Can we at least get together? Figure out a way?"

More silence. Nicky held his breath so as not to be heard on the extension.

"There's no fixing it, Dom," said Salita. "There ain't no way back. Only forward."

"But, Johnny—"

"Only forward, Dom. That's it. Tell that to whoever's listening. And they should know this also. I got what I got—what I got from the Man's house. They should know that I know what it is. *I know*, you motherfuckers. Codes are nothing to me. They're gonna have to deal with me now. On *my* terms."

The line went dead.

Rhino pulled the receiver away from his ear, confused, having no idea what Salita was talking about. Cue Stick sat near him, understanding only that Salita had hung up on Rhino.

"Aw, fuck," said Cue Stick.

Rhino said, "He said he took something from the house. Something about codes? What did he take?"

Cue Stick was crying again and shaking his head.

Rhino looked over at Nicky, phone receivers still in their hands.

Nicky hung up his extension, looking at the two thieves.

Banka caught another corpse, this one jammed into the trunk of a dark blue Lincoln Continental with a cream vinyl top, a stolen vehicle, parked in a corner space on the third level of the parking structure at O'Hare. It was early evening, two patrol-car searchlights lighting up the vehicle and the bloody, naked corpse curled up on the blue carpeted interior of the open trunk.

Detective Banka and Agent Roy stood at angles to the car so as not to block the light. The overweight corpse's face was burned, its hair singed, eyes melted. The corpse's clothes were in a bundle near its wire-bound feet.

"Overkill again," said Banka, "but a little different. No torch this time. They dowsed the body and the clothes with lighter fluid and lit the guy on fire in the car. But the geniuses shut the trunk and didn't open any windows. No air flow, so the fire died out. We don't have to wait for dental on this one."

Banka used a handkerchief to show Roy the dead man's wallet, flopping it open with an expert hand, sliding out an Illinois driver's license without his finger skin touching it.

"Berardi, Carmen," read Roy.

"We ran the name. Two-time loser. Truck hijacking."

Roy squinted at the photo, a guy with double chins. Birth date said he was in his fifties. "Older than the others."

"Not older than Labotta, the first one."

"Any connection to him?"

"I don't put him with any of the others, but you know, things overlap." Banka slid the license back into its slot in the wallet, then tossed it onto the dead man's clothes. "All I know for sure is that this is still ongoing."

Roy nodded. "I think right now the most dangerous occupation in America is being an Outfit thief."

Banka said, "Why there aren't many left in this city, so I'm told. They got out while they could. Scattered to the wind."

"Mob guys scared," said Roy. "That tells you something."

"It docs," said Banka, turning toward him. "But what?"

Roy walked out of the patrol lights' glare to a four-foot-high wall of cement. A half mile beyond, aircraft lifted off and landed under the watchful view of the air traffic control tower.

Roy said, "I believe we're seeing another Saint Valentine's Day Massacre, Feliks. Only this time, in slow motion. Back then it was seven North Siders lined up in a garage and gunned down by assassins dressed in police uniforms, right?"

"Two in uniform, two in overcoats big enough to hide tommy guns. One of whom, they say . . ."

"The Big Tuna himself. Joe Batters when he graduated up from a bat to a submachine gun. True or not, it tells me this. That Tony Accardo learned to eliminate his enemies with brute force and great speed from none other than Alphonse Capone himself."

"Enemies?" said Banka. "Fat thief Berardi there?"

"I can only read the parts that are clear," said Roy. "And everything I'm seeing only makes sense if you postulate that somebody here in Chicago is taking a run at the Man."

Two afternoons a week, Helena volunteered at the parochial school or the church rectory and dropped Nicholas off at the Lanes after school. Nicky tried to find things for him to do, but sometimes the best days were when they just hung around. Like this day, Nicholas sitting on a wooden stool next to Nicky behind the rental counter, drinking a root beer float with a straw and a spoon. Making a mess and making his father smile.

"You like the foam part best?" said Nicky.

Nicholas spooned the brown froth into his upturned mouth.

"That's crazy," said Nicky. "It's the ice cream part that's best. And who put that together, anyway? Who thought root beer with vanilla ice cream could go so good?" Off Nicholas's shrug, Nicky said, "Mr. Float, obviously," and Nicholas giggled.

A wrench dropped with a clatter onto the polished maple wood of lane seventeen, and Nicky grimaced. Sally Brags was on top of a ladder straddling the center two lanes. "Sorry, Nicky," he said. "It slipped."

Crease Man let go of the ladder to retrieve the wrench. They were hanging a new mirror ball Nicky had purchased, installing a brace in the dropped ceiling.

"Looking good," said Nicky. "Just be careful."

Crease Man handed the wrench back up to Brags. The AMF trade magazine had run an article saying that disco dance nights in bowling alleys were becoming a thing. A revolving mirror globe and four spotlights created a swirling starlight nightclub effect.

Nicky nudged Nicholas, speaking quietly, indicating Uncle Sally and Uncle Frankie. "Ever see *Heckle and Jeckle?*"

Nicholas nodded. "The cartoon."

"Your Uncle Sally and Uncle Frankie sometimes. Don't tell 'em I said so."

"I won't," said Nicholas with a smile.

Nicky looked out at the two guys and said, "Nicholas says you two remind him of Heckle and Jeckle."

Nicholas quickly said, "I didn't—he did!"

Nicholas liked his fake uncles, but he was a little intimidated by them too. Nicky swiped the counter around his fountain glass with a bar rag and looked at his boy's soft nose, his bright eyes and dark lashes, the ten-year-old's features starting to come into definition like a once-distant signal getting tuned.

"How's your mother doing?" asked Nicky.

"Fine," said Nicholas. With a shrug he said, "We go to church every day."

"Every day?"

"Every day except when I come here."

"Well, that's good. That's good for you. You know that's where your mother and I met? In church, in our church. You know she was the most beautiful singer in the choir? Beautiful looks but also her voice. First time I saw her, she was wearing a doily-veil thing over her hair in the back, like an angel, like a bride. I said to myself, 'I'm gonna have to marry her.'" Nicholas made a face, allergic to the romantic stuff. "She was shy like you," said Nicky. "Who knows, maybe you'll meet your wife in church tomorrow."

Nicholas stuck out his tongue and pulled a face that Nicky had never seen, so sour that Nicky laughed out loud.

"Just you wait," said Nicky. "You wait."

He glanced up, scanning the lanes. Only eight or so were active. League players didn't start coming in until six. Chuckie had just gone off to take a late lunch.

When Nicky asked Sally Brags and Crease Man for their help mounting the mirror ball, he'd forgotten he had Nicholas that day. He was going to surprise them with a steak dinner after this, his thanks. But also to keep them close, keep his eye on them. Get them through this.

"What was jail like?" asked Nicholas.

Nicky looked at his son, who was digging at a lump of ice cream at the bottom of the glass.

"Huh," said Nicky. "Your mother bring that up?"

Nicholas shook his head unconvincingly.

"Well, first of all, it wasn't jail. It was prison. Which is the big kind of jail, where you go for months at a time. You were young. I can tell you it wasn't much fun, and I missed you every hour of every day. How about that?"

Nicholas looked concerned. "What'd you do to go there?"

"What did I do?" said Nicky. "You watch TV, right? Bad guys do bad things, they get thrown in the slammer. The big house, right? Alcatraz. Am I a big, bad guy? What do you think?"

The boy shook his head. "No."

"What I did was, I made a mistake," Nicky said. "I trusted the wrong people, I did something I shouldn't of, and I had to pay the price. You know, that's a good lesson for you. Don't ever trust the wrong people. Friends and family only."

Nicholas nodded. "But... what did you *do*?"

"The truth?" said Nicky. He leaned closer, making a big secret out of it. "I stole candy. Don't never, ever steal candy."

Nicholas looked up at him doubtfully, but Nicky held his expression, and the answer was within the boy's realm of experience. He believed his father, for now, and that was good enough.

A flashing red light in the ceiling over lane one gave Nicky a convenient way out.

"See that?" said Nicky. "Stuck ball on lane one. Chuckie's on break. C'mon, you can help me."

Nicky held his arm as Nicholas hopped down from the stool. Father and son Passero stepped out from the counter, walking down the two steps toward the leftward-most bowling lane. A father there was keeping score for two little kids, a boy and a girl who didn't look much alike, the gate down in front of the pins at the end of their alley.

Nicky stepped into the well around the scorer's table, playing it up a bit for Nicholas. "Hi, what seems to be the problem here?"

The father turned, a Ten Pin Lanes golf sized pencil behind his ear. He smiled at Nicky and then at Nicky's son.

Nicky's mood flattened. The father—the man—was Agent Gerald Roy.

"The pins didn't reset," said Roy, in blue jeans and an olive turtleneck, dressed like a father of two.

Nicky glared, unbelieving, then looked at the children with him. Nicky glanced at Sally Brags and Crease Man, halfway across the lanes, hoisting the mirror ball up to the brace, steadying it, not paying attention to him at the moment.

Nicky remembered Nicholas at his side. Protectively, he stepped in front of his son.

Roy said genially, "These two are slow bowlers. The heavy balls, I think one got stuck in there."

Nicky turned angrily and started down the narrow walkway running along the first lane to the rear. At the end was an employees-only door, and he walked through it and down four steps to the working area behind the lanes. The automatic pinsetter machines worked noisily, thirty-six of them, and on busy weekends the cacophony back there was deafening, with all thirty-six of them going.

"I always wondered what it looked like back here."

Nicky turned. Roy was at the open door, standing right behind Nicholas, both of them having followed Nicky down the walkway.

Nicky shot a stern look at Nicholas. "Go wait with those other kids, okay?"

"Daddy, you said I should help—"

"Just go, Nicholas. Go."

Nicholas closed his mouth, something in his father's face telling him not to press it. He turned and started back past Roy down the walkway with his arms straight and tight at his side.

Roy watched the boy go, then descended the four steps, the door behind him closing most of the way shut. "So that's your boy, huh—"

With a hand on Roy's chest and his forearm up on his throat, Nicky drove the FBI agent backward against the wall. Roy hit it hard, surprised at first.

"What the fuck are you doing here?" said Nicky, his voice just below the clatter of the pinsetting machines, his forearm forcing Roy's chin toward the ceiling.

Roy's eyes stayed fixed on Nicky, angry but also darkly cocky. "Really?" he said, half-choked.

Nicky didn't let up. "I should take you apart right here."

"Go ahead," said Roy.

Nicky hated the agent, never more than at this moment. The door was still open a foot or so above them. Anyone could walk through.

Nicky let up with his forearm, releasing Roy, backing off. Roy straightened out the fold of his turtleneck collar, glaring at Nicky.

Nicky turned away. He looked at the pinsetter. He saw the pinhead trapped under the belt and pressed the kill button, reaching in for it.

Roy said, behind him, "This couldn't wait."

"*Fuck you*," hissed Nicky over his shoulder. "It's *gonna* wait."

"You basically *live* here, Passero. There's no place else I can find you."

Nicky freed the pin and fed it back into its basket.

Roy said, "Forget about that thing. Look at me."

Nicky kept working.

Roy said, "We found two more trunked thieves."

Nicky fed the pin and released the kill button. The sweep bar engaged and the conveyor belt resumed, feeding the freed pin into the elevator, carrying it upward.

Roy said, "Total's up to eight."

Only when Nicky backed out did Roy's words hit him. *Eight?* There weren't eight. Eight was two too many. Roy was trying something here, tricking him.

Nicky turned to Roy with a sneer. "You deliver traffic and weather too?"

"Two thieves, Berardi and McClean. You know them? Can you place them with the others from Levinson's?"

"Who?"

"Berardi, fat guy, truck hijacker? McClean, German-Irish pickpocket, also high-end home burglaries."

Nicky's confusion was legitimate. "I don't know these guys, or what the fuck you're talking about. Fuck off. I'm going."

"It's Accardo," said Roy. "Enough with the bullshit, the tap dancing. Something went down. Somebody took a shot at him? What?"

"You got the wiretaps. You tell me."

"Yeah, about that," said Roy. "Mysteriously, the phone chatter's gone dry."

Nicky held his gaze, not letting Roy read anything in his face. "Are you saying that's on me now?"

"Thieves are turning up dead all over town—but I notice at Ten Pin Lanes it's business as usual."

"What the fuck does any of this have to do with me?"

"You don't even care. You're untouched."

"I should worry? I'm a thief?"

"What *are* you, Nicky Pins?"

Nicky didn't like the look Roy was giving him—and definitely not the insinuation. "I gotta get back to my kid. You don't too?"

Roy flashed a smile. "I borrowed two other agents' kids."

"You're a fucking master of disguise, you are."

"I got the full weight and force of the bureau behind me now, Nicky. And if I find out you know more than you've been telling me—"

"You'll do what? Lean on me some more? Twist the knife deeper? Stop by more fuckin' often? How 'bout I put you on weekends, you like it here so much?"

Nicky started up the stairs, done here, getting only as far as the second step before Roy grabbed his right elbow, stopping him.

Nicky looked back at his arm, then down at Roy's face, furious. They were close. Nicky had never been so near Roy's eyes.

Roy said, "I'm tired of the attitude. You thinking you're in charge here. One call from me. One insinuation. You're tough behind closed doors here, but how tough would you be if the guys hanging around this place knew what I knew about Nicky Pins, and his separation from his wife, and his taste for scotch and men."

Nicky stared at Roy's eyes, the lips these words came out of, face-to-face, a matter of inches between them—and had a revelation. "You *like* coming in here," said Nicky. "You like fucking with me."

Roy smiled, his face inching closer, Nicky smelling his menthol and mint aftershave. "You know, Nicky Pins?" said Roy. "You're right. I kind of do."

Nicky jerked backward, ripping his arm free of Roy's grip. He shoved the FBI agent in the chest, setting him back several steps.

Roy took it, regaining his balance, still grinning.

Nicky had seen that look before. Guys in prison, at the top of the pecking order, had that look. They lived to fuck with people. Roy had that dark joy in his eyes, a combination of lascivious smile—and hard-core mocking. He held Nicky's life in his hands, and he liked it that way.

Nicky turned and went up the steps and quickly through the door, out into the lanes. Nicholas was there, halfway up the walkway ahead, and Nicky marched over and scooped him up, something he hadn't done in a couple of years, the boy almost too big to carry. But Nicky wanted him close and safely in his arms.

Roy's voice came from behind. "Thank you, sir!" he said, jubilant, performing. "That was really interesting!"

Nicky didn't look back. He couldn't get away fast enough.

"Nicky!"

Sally Brags called to him, stopping Nicky short. Nicky turned toward the ladder at the center lanes.

The four spotlights came on, each aimed at the hanging mirror ball, which started to turn. Hundreds of rays of light shone out from the slowly rotating orb, exploring the lanes like probing eyes, giving the wide room the sensation of spinning.

icky left his car at the corner of Lathrop and Le Moyne and ducked between two homes like a prowler. He made his way across the yards of back-to-back houses, working his way up the street unseen on this moonless night. He banged his knee on the angled strut of a metal jungle gym, set off a barking dog, waited behind a shed until a neighbor finished his cigarette on his back deck. He ducked tree branches and clambered onto a garbage can to get up and over a wobbly picket fence. He saw families watching television, a woman drinking alone at her kitchen table, a couple eating ice cream out of a carton in silence. Squeezing through a privet hedge, he crossed the last backyard to a row of eight-foot pines spaced for privacy, standing before a sturdy iron fence.

Nicky climbed through branches of prickly needles, swinging a leg over the top spikes and dropping into the yard on the other side. A man stood there in the shadows. *"Shit!"* Nicky jumped back.

Michael Volpe was bundled in a dark wool coat, waiting for him. "Sorry, Mr. Passero."

"I made it, Michael." Nicky shook needles out of his coat collar and kicked his boots against an exposed flagstone, knocking some grime and slush off the treads. "That's all that counts."

They walked around the covered pool, up to the patio and the sliding door. Opening the door revealed music playing, loud, eerie. Volpe shut and locked the door behind them, Nicky shedding his coat. "What's with the music?"

Volpe shrugged pleasantly, pulling off his gloves. Nicky recognized it now, Bobby Vinton's doleful falsetto crooning "Mr. Lonely."

He walked through to the living room, where Tony Accardo stood in his evening robe over shirt and pants, peering through heavy sun-flower-gold curtains drawn across the street-facing picture window. The record album played in the cabinet stereo system, speakers blasting, and now Nicky understood why. The Polish Prince's haunt-ing voice was turned all the way up in order to baffle any listening devices that might be planted inside 1407 Ashland Avenue.

Accardo sensed his presence and turned from the curtains. He was eager to speak, coming up close, hands in his robe pockets. "Anybody see you?"

"A couple of squirrels," said Nicky, still feeling pine needles tickling his back.

"I sent Michael out to take a little walk earlier," Accardo said, his mouth close enough to Nicky that Nicky could smell stewed toma-toes. "Up and down the block. The parked cars were all empty."

"That's good," said Nicky, nodding. Maybe coming in through the backyards was a wasted adventure, but probably not. The last thing he wanted to do now was get made by the FBI at Accardo's front door, ringing his bell. He had called Michael Volpe on the house-man's own home telephone the night before, setting this meet.

"*Not* good," said Accardo, contradicting him. "I think maybe they moved in across the street."

"Across the street?" said Nicky. "In your neighbor's house?"

"Assume it," said Accardo, nodding with certainty. "Assume everything."

Nicky wasn't about to question it, but this was a strange thing to say. The Feds could have guys in the park that was diagonal to the house, long-range binoculars. Simpler than displacing a family and much less noticeable.

Someone, not Volpe, entered the room from the study across the hall. He wasn't more than a kid, twenty-two, maybe twenty-three, trim with crow-black hair falling over small eyes, the flared-out collar of his black polyester shirt laid over the lapels of his flint-colored leather jacket like he'd dressed up for the occasion. Behind him, a second guy, same age, softer, bigger-armed, squinting like a poser.

Nicky said, "What the fuck is this?"

Accardo put one hand on Nicky's shoulder, introducing him under the music. "This is Stingy, one of Doves's grandnephews. Him and his friend are spendin' some time with me. Some protection around the place."

"*They're* your protection?" said Nicky. "What are they protecting you from?"

"We'll see," said Accardo. "Whatever comes, Stingy here can take care of it."

Nicky didn't like this at all. Here he was working overtime to make things right for Accardo, and now there were two interlopers, young guys eager to prove their mettle with guns. Maybe Accardo actually needed some backup, like he knew something Nicky didn't, or maybe he was giving in to paranoia. From the sound of Mrs. Accardo's favorite Polish performer's wailing carrying through the house like a keening animal, Nicky guessed it was the latter.

He turned Accardo away from the two young hoods. "You got a whole phone book of guys, trusted guys, steady guys. Why the Mickey Mouse Club?"

"I wanna keep this in-house," Accardo said. "Small circle. These boys don't talk to no one, because they don't know no one, and they follow orders."

Nicky indicated the end of the room farthest from the stereo speakers and from Stingy and his pal. Accardo walked with Nicky, standing beside a three-headed floor lamp with shades of different-colored glass. Nicky spoke confidentially. "You're sure you're doing okay here?"

Accardo said, "What does that mean?"

"You look like you haven't slept much. Haven't shaved. Haven't left the house in a while. Maybe take these two mutts for a walk or something, get some air."

"My air's fine. What is this?"

Nicky let it go. "A couple more thieves turned up, I heard," he said.

"Yeah," said Accardo.

"Two more thieves, both in trunks."

"Yeah."

Nicky looked at Accardo, waiting for an explanation. "What is that?"

"Bad news, sounds like."

Maybe Accardo was being cagey for the presumed microphones. Or maybe now he was being cagey specifically with Nicky.

"Two thieves that I didn't do," said Nicky. "What the fuck's going on?"

"Sounds like someone's sending a message."

"Wait, another message?" said Nicky. "Or the same one again and again? Because I'm losing track. That message was sent."

"Don't worry about that now," Accardo said.

"Don't worry about it?" Nicky glanced over at Stingy and No-Name. It had to be them. "If the somebodies who did it fucked it up, that could impact me. That could very much come back on me, for the original messages I sent, special delivery, that were sent for you. How many messengers you got here?"

"Nicky, settle down. I said don't worry about it."

Accardo was getting stern with him, but Nicky already had a head of steam. "I think I will worry about it."

"The messages sent before didn't get much response."

Nicky's smile was knife sharp. "Really."

"Not much I saw, and I still got a problem. But forget about that right now. There's another thing. Somebody's talking."

Accardo's eyes stayed on Nicky.

"Talking, what?" said Nicky. "Somebody who?"

"That, I would like to find out."

"Okay, back up for me here. You *think* this—or you *know* this?"

Accardo said, "What about your two guys? Your crew?"

Nicky's mouth fell open. "What are you talking about, my guys?"

"I don't know. Tell me more about them."

"No," said Nicky. Very simply, he said again, "No." He looked straight into Accardo's eyes, not answering his question, telling him he was wrong about this, maybe wrong about everything. Once more, firmly, Nicky said, "No."

"I'm not askin' you to vouch for them. I just wanna know—"

"I'm vouching for them," said Nicky. "Okay? They're vouched."

"You're getting upset."

"One hundred percent vouched," said Nicky. "I'm getting upset? I claw my way through backyards to get here to help you, I find two kids playing soldiers, you question my guys." Nicky took a breath and reset. "I think you're thinking about this too hard. Okay? You're working too hard on this. My guys've done everything you've asked—*everything*. These aren't brutal guys by nature. I told you that. But you wanted it done a certain way—and they did it a certain way. For you. Because you ordered it."

"I don't want nothing links to me."

"Nothing links to you!" said Nicky. "You are clear."

"I'm clear," said Accardo, thinking it over. "Am I, though? It's best to be sure."

"What do they know?" said Nicky. "They don't know anything."

"They know about me," said Accardo. "They're with you, right? And you know things."

Nicky stepped back. Was he hearing this right? Was he on the hot seat suddenly?

"*I* know things?" Nicky said, repeating Accardo's words.

"Do they know about the break-in?" asked Accardo. "Simple question."

"Simple answer," said Nicky. "No. I didn't tell them. I didn't tell anybody. That's it. *No.*"

Accardo said, "I'm not questioning *you*, Nicky. You understand? I'm just questioning you."

"That makes me feel better not at all." Nicky tried to find a way to take the reins. "When does Mrs. Accardo come home?"

"When I feel it's right," said Accardo. "Soon."

"You should have family with you now. Someone to take your mind off these things. Which daughter do I call?"

"You're gonna call my daughter?" said Accardo, eyes hardening.

Nicky held up one hand. "You're holed up in here, peeking out curtains, taking on two popgun guys? You're bringing more heat on yourself needlessly."

"I need Salita, Nicky."

"You'll get Salita."

"This has gone on a long fuckin' time, too long."

"You gotta stop with the trunks," said Nicky. "No more thieves, no more trunks."

Accardo glared at him. Nobody spoke to him like this, Nicky knew. But he had to drive this home. It was Nicky's ass on the line as much or more than the Man's.

"Bring me Salita," Accardo said.

Nicky said, "If I had a magic wand..."

"Then get one!" Accardo nodded and looked at the lamp, the stereo. He seemed to relax a bit. "Okay, no more trunks. So you think disappearing's better?"

"I think anything's better."

"Okay." Accardo stepped back. "Well, maybe that's good advice." He laid a hand on his gut over his dinner jacket. "I gotta eat something."

With that, Accardo stepped away, walking right out of the room, calling for Michael Volpe, leaving Nicky standing there alone with the lamp and *The Many Moods of Bobby Vinton*, wondering what the hell had just happened, and what was coming next.

S ally Brags and his wife Trixie's new place was on Sunnyside Avenue in West Ravenswood, minutes from Nicky and Helena's house in Avondale. Like Nicky's house, Sally Brags's had a patch of yard in back leading to a garage off an alleyway running parallel to the next street over.

Nicky came from the bathroom inside, stopping on the brick steps in the rear, able to see in through the window at the women sitting together in the living room. Trixie was opening presents, holding a onesie over her pregnant belly to the delight of Crease Man's fiancée, Debra, and Helena, who sat with a teacup and saucer on her knees. It made Nicky smile to see Helena looking happy and carefree.

He continued out to Sally Brags and Crease Man, the two of them standing around the basin grill, stoking charcoal with a wooden stake to release some much-needed heat. "This winter's gotta end sometime," said Sally Brags, shoulders hunched under his army jacket.

"Winter never ends," said Crease Man, bouncing boot to boot. "It only pauses in May, then resumes again in October."

"I just saw the ladies opening presents in there," said Nicky, pulling a crumpled paper lunch bag from his coat pocket. "I thought we should do the same."

His two guys looked at the bag, then at each other.

Nicky unrolled the top, reaching in, distributing the contents by the light of the orange embers. He handed Sally Brags the ring and loose gems from the lighting-store strongbox.

"Shit, Nicky," said Sally Brags, examining the stones.

"I figure you can do something for Trixie with that, get them reset."

"Aces," said Sally Brags.

Nicky pulled out the Rolex, handing it to Crease Man.

"Are you fuckin' kidding me right now?" said Crease Man. He shook off his gloves, pulling the watch band on over the three fingers on his left hand, to his wrist.

Nicky said, "I saw your eyes go blooey when the strongbox was opened." Nicky also pulled out the three banded bundles of cash, handing those to Sally Brags. "And these. I'm making it as even as possible, factoring in the watch."

Sally Brags accepted the cash happily.

Crease Man admired his watch by the light of the coals. "What about you, Nicky?"

"You guys did the lifting," said Nicky. "You know I appreciate you. Gotta make sure my guys are cut in and taken care of. Cheers, right?"

They grabbed their beers and drank. Both guys were blown away by their gifts.

Nicky said, "And by the way, you should know the Man sends his respect as well. He's in on these too—his thanks for all your dirty work. Which he greatly appreciates. He knows what it took to do what you did, and he's grateful."

The guys nodded solemnly, though it reminded them of the deeds they'd done.

"Speaking of which," said Nicky, "any concerns? Any anything?"

Sally Brags shook his head. "None."

"Everything good?" said Nicky, checking on Crease Man.

Crease Man said, "Is it done, Nicky? Not gonna lie to you…This shit keeps me up at night."

Nicky nodded quickly. "Just Salita, I think. We gotta find him. We do, and we never have to speak of this again. Keep asking around, but smartly. I don't think he's gone for good—I think he's around town somewhere. We can end this."

"Good," said Crease Man.

Sally Brags said, "You talk to the Man about the video game thing? We anywhere on that?"

"I saw him just a couple of days ago and I meant to bring it up, but you know, the timing's never right on that with me and him. Once we get done crawling through all this shit. But I'm working on it—I haven't forgotten."

"That's big for us, I think," said Sally Brags. "That'll set us up good."

Crease Man raised his bottle. "One day these three kids from the neighborhood will have their own pieces of Palm Springs—and fuck winter."

Nicky clinked each guy's bottle. "Here's to."

Helena had drunk a glass of wine at dinner; she'd had a good time. But alone now with Nicky, driving her home after, she was quiet. There were things outside her window more interesting than him.

"Trixie's ready to drop, huh?"

"I can't believe it," Helena said. "Twins."

"Two more Bragses. That's a double yikes. Hope they're girls, for their sakes. She's happy, though."

"Very."

"Yeah," said Nicky. "It's a happy time."

He turned onto Milwaukee Avenue, passing through Chicago's Polonia, the three baroque towers of the Basilica of Saint Hyacinth coming into view, almost home.

"We're doing a new thing at the Lanes this Saturday night," he said. "I hired a disc jockey, we're doing radio ads, everything. There'll be dancing, new lights. Trying to get some adults in with money to spend, instead of them going to the movies or a regular nightclub. I know you don't love it there, the Lanes, but—you should come. You and Nicholas."

Helena looked at him and nodded, her way of politely saying no. Nicky looped around, coming down one-way Wisner.

"You have enough for the sitter?" he said.

"Sure," said Helena, her purse on her lap.

Nicky pulled up outside their front steps, put it in park, and turned her way. "Thanks," he said. "For coming. It was fun. Like old times."

"It was fun," she said. "Good night, Nicky."

Helena got out of the Satellite. Nicky leaned over to look at their front stoop. He would have walked her to the door if he'd thought she wanted him to.

"Good night," he said, and Helena nodded and closed the car door, walking up the steps.

B owling Fever" sounded like a disease. "Saturday Night Bowling" didn't quite do it either, and ripping off *Saturday Night Fever* might have drawn a legal claim. So "Boogie Bowling" it was.

The radio station DJ, a drug-skinny dude wearing a Chewbacca iron-on ringer T-shirt and earphones the size of salad bowls, set up his equipment at the lanes end of the lounge. With the disco lights adding to the outer-space feel, the DJ's *Star Wars* T-shirt—reflecting the other movie craze of the moment—added to the spirit of the event.

There were more teens in attendance than actual adults, but the place was packed, and with a two-dollar cover charge, which included rental shoes, that was what counted. Low-cut dresses and low-buttoned polyester shirts, everyone grooving to the beat, strutting, flirting, and yes, bowling. The counter was three deep all the way along, with the new kid, Danny, enjoying lots of attention from the girls with his bare, noodly arms and his Travolta hair.

Boogie Bowling was a success by any measure, so Nicky didn't know why, after being the one to catch the trend and put the whole thing together, he felt lost in the middle of it all. Perhaps he was at a place in his mind where he just couldn't enjoy anything. He felt old, for the first time ever, throwing a party featuring music he didn't know how to dance to. Even Chuckie was walking around with a few shirt buttons undone, but Nicky couldn't get into it.

He was checking on bar stock when Detective Kevin Quiston appeared, having stopped by for a quick one, not knowing what he was walking into. "What is this?" he said.

"This is the future," Nicky told him.

"Not my future," said Quiston.

"You got kids?"

"My kids aren't into this disco shit," he said.

"Too young, then. Hey." Nicky got closer so he could be heard over the music. "What are you doing betting the Bulls?" said Nicky. "The *Chicago* Bulls?"

"I gotta bet underdogs, Nicky. I gotta get even."

"Okay, Kevin. You got a serious fuckin' problem. You're betting scared—trying to 'get even'? I'm not a bank, nor a casino. You think I'm waiting for you to strike it lucky? Do you know how much you're into me?"

Quiston nodded quickly. "I know."

"I wonder if you do. You keep digging, you're gonna get to China, and then what? We need to talk about what we're gonna do to solve this."

"You know I'm good for it—"

"Yeah, see, I *don't* know that. Four kids and a house mortgage? And me—I'm your fifth kid."

"Would I come in here, stop by, if I was ducking you?"

"It's because of that badge you wear. Weren't for your shield, you'd be in the hospital with two broken legs. I don't think it's stupidity—I think you got a sickness."

The way Quiston was looking at him in the whirling lights, Nicky understood his words had come out more harshly than intended. Nicky was in a weird place. But it was true; the detective was hooked, no different than a junkie. Betting games with no excitement in it for him, no sporting fun. A mental disease. Nicky wasn't a shark like

Dimes—he didn't want a customer for life at 20 percent. He'd meant what he'd said: being a cop protected Quiston. Conversely, carrying a detective who owed him was the only good part of this for Nicky.

"C'mere," Nicky said, turning to the bar. He signaled Leo the bartender to get Quiston one on the house. "Will you please do me a favor?" Nicky said, laying one hand on Quiston's shoulder, the other over his own heart. "For me? Please? And for the last time? Don't bet Chicago."

Quiston smiled flatly at the floor. It looked like all was forgiven. "You got it."

"Drink up and go home to your kids before they fall prey to disco, all right?"

Nicky patted him on the back and moved along, determined to better manage his short fuse. He considered stepping behind the bar to help out Leo, but his disposition wasn't right. Ahead of him at the bar, a guy weighing barely a hundred pounds, dressed in bell-bottoms and heeled shoes and an open shirt, chatted up a Latin girl in a leotard top under a bunched-sleeve blouse and a nearly see-through skirt. It seemed all you had to do to play the disco game was look the part.

Helena was a no-show. He wished Nicholas could see the place rocking like this. At the same time, Nicky wished he were home with them instead of here.

Farther down the bar, Nicky viewed a sight that brought out his first smile of the night. Connected guys and the usual wannabes gathered in a tight circle, outnumbered by the new generation—but, as Nicky saw, even they were sporting gold medallion chains all of a sudden, wearing open shirts, flared slacks. The disco craze was spreading like a virus. You had to respect it.

Belts, a small-timer, one of those guys who were in although you never really knew what they did, a short guy who was always trying to buddy up with Nicky, stepped out to intercept him.

"Nicky, my girl's here. She just got offered blow in the ladies' room."

"Okay," said Nicky. "Is that good or bad?"

"Good for her, which is good for me, I guess," said Belts. "I just thought you oughta know."

"I don't wanna know," said Nicky with a small smile. "I don't wanna know nothing."

"Understood. Join us here."

Nicky pushed in. There was Dimes Forbstein with his thin mustache and his thick smile. "Gangbusters, Nicky," said Dimes.

"Kids seem to like it."

"That one," said Dimes, pointing toward two young women on lane twelve, either the one that was all cleavage, no bra, or her friend in a bright blue tube top.

"I'm gonna sign you up for dance lessons," said Nicky, drawing a laugh from the group, Dimes chuckling and patting his huge belly. A tray of shots arrived at the bar. "What's this?"

Leo said "A dozen Wild Turkeys" and went to take another order.

"Plenty to go around," said Dimes, handing them out. Nicky got one. "What's your detective friend's name?"

"Quiston," said Nicky, turning and beckoning the off-duty detective, who joined them and was handed a shot along with Belts and everybody else.

"What's the toast?" Quiston asked Nicky, who didn't know.

Dimes said, "Another drink for the dead."

"Another trunker?" said Quiston, over the music. "Sheesh. Anybody I know?"

"Not a thief," Dimes corrected him. "Not another trunk job. No, this is somebody none of us seen for a while, and won't see again until we're all reunited. Clams Cassino. In Joliet. The fuck was his real name...?"

Belts said, "I think Christopher?"

"Right. Found in his cell, two plastic laundry bags over his head, elastic bands around his neck. Poor kid suffocated himself, and here's the real tragedy. He only had a couple of weeks left before getting out."

Belts said, "You musta known him, Nicky. You and him woulda been in Joliet same time."

Nicky was barely aware of the conversation, the bowling alley, the disco music, the spinning lights. All he really knew right then was the sound of his own breath.

The others raised their shot glasses, spilling a bit.

"To Clams, huh?"

"To Clams."

Everybody threw back.

"Clams!"

"*Salut!*"

After closing, once the place was finally empty and mostly cleaned up, and the music stopped—everything dark except for the mirror ball slowly revolving in silence—Nicky didn't even count the money. He put it in one of his cloth bags from the bank and shoved it in the back of the file cabinet in his office. He sat in his office chair for a while. Then he went under his cot and dug around the clothes and things he kept there, finding the letters.

Nicky carried the letters across to the lounge, going around the bar to pour himself another drink. He swallowed it down and poured half as much again, then stood blankly staring at the white disco lights swimming around his bowling alley. When the Lanes began to spin, he refocused, carrying his glass to a barstool and sitting in front of the letters.

The return addresses were all the same, a red stamp, *Joliet Correctional Center*, with Christopher's name, prisoner number, and cell block written in the spaces provided below it. The letters themselves, written in slanted, all-capitals penmanship, were not very remarkable. He never put down anything on paper that could come back on him; two of the twelve letters Nicky received had been opened and taped shut again by someone in the warden's office. Nicky only kept them, well—because.

From one envelope, Nicky pulled out a photograph of a smiling, skinny-armed, then-nineteen-year-old Christopher Cassino leaning against a '69 Mustang Mach 1 that had belonged to his uncle, the kind of car Christopher had dreamed about owning himself. The kind of car that put him in prison, because he boosted one similar, and because the elderly man whom Christopher ran off the road in the ensuing police chase suffered a heart attack and died. They added murder counts to his case, and though Christopher beat that piece of the rap, his lawyers weren't very good anyway, and he got whacked with a stiffer sentence than he would have for grand theft: ten years with minimum seven to be served.

They got paired up as cellmates six months into Nicky's bid, Nicky having known him in passing on the outside through his older brother, the late "Chips" Cassino. Christopher looked and acted younger than he was, which made him a mark inside Joliet, so Nicky watched out for him on the cell block. In private, Christopher had a bad prison habit of talking himself sick—homesick, going on and on about people and things he missed on the outside. Ulcers limited his eating. Some nights after lights out, Nicky would hear Christopher crying himself to sleep—softly, almost silently, the top bunk creaking faintly from his shuddering shoulders. At first, this enraged Nicky. He wanted either to toughen up the kid, who wasn't a kid, or else to put him out of his misery. But after weeks and months, Christopher's vulnerability rubbed off on Nicky, who found himself trying to make Christopher feel better in order that Nicky could feel better.

Something happens over time when you're confined with someone, anyone, in any close situation, be it in a marriage or on a life raft. A piece of one becomes a part of the other and vice versa, and that was one way Nicky looked at what happened. Another was that the emotional connection he developed with Christopher was the kind of thing Nicky had resisted most of his life.

One night, consoling Christopher crossed a line. The next morning, nothing was said. It seemed never to have happened and, as such, could never happen again. And then, two or three more times later, suddenly you are the line that you crossed. And then you have something: you have a secret. A hidden path. But you're not alone on it: the journey is shared. The secret is forbidden and sacred at the same time, going against everything you have ever known. Something private to protect, something you control and something that controls you. You don't have to call it love. You can call it anything. Call it hope.

When Nicky got out, he was conflicted, naturally. He had always been one person; was he now another? The problems with Helena were immediate, and at first, she was patient. Soon she became nervous and worried. Then she blamed herself, and Nicky let her.

One drunken night, he did try to tell her. It was a mistake to do so.

He wasn't sure how much he'd said. But if she didn't know it, she maybe guessed it. She definitely feared it. She had been raised the same way he had been.

Eventually Nicky put Joliet behind him and returned to himself, essentially. But too late for Helena, as the distance had spread to every other thing in their life. She was the wife of a convicted criminal now, and that didn't go over well with her parents, nor at church. After months of pushing her away, Nicky found himself trying to cling to her, because she helped keep him who he wanted to be. Kept him from what he was.

Nicky slid over a tin ashtray and stacked the letters on it. He struck a match off a matchbook—*Ten Pin Lanes—36 Lanes—Strike HERE*— and lit the lower corner of the bottom envelope until the stack of paper caught fire.

Once it got going, he laid the photograph on top of the pile and crossed himself, offering a whispered one-word eulogy: "Christopher."

The flames worked upward along the edges of the paper, the corners of the photograph blackening, curling back. The swirling lights animated the rising black smoke. For all his despair, Nicky couldn't help thinking that a problem had solved itself today. Facing Christopher on the outside would have meant having to confront this thing inside him. He accepted that he was a terrible person for thinking this.

The room brightened from an outside light source, shadows lengthening and angling toward Nicky. A car had pulled into the lot, parking out front under the dark sign. Nicky had forgotten about his meeting with Roy—an even bigger problem for him, one that wasn't going away. But why was Roy parking out front?

Nicky grabbed a damp bar rag, used it to wipe his face, then dropped it over the ashtray, smothering the flames. The headlights stayed on the doors, and Nicky was angry, Roy knowing better than to risk being seen out front. He stood, steadying himself on the back of the barstool, feeling the booze, and went toward the door to point him around to the rear.

Halfway there, Nicky heard a *tap-tap-tap* at the door glass and made out the shadow of a man silhouetted by the headlights, wearing a cap of some kind, a beret—and holding a rifle.

The car headlights went out, revealing the glass tapper to be a young Black guy, his beret having military styling. The guy was pointing at the locked door handle.

It's a robbery, thought Nicky, with confused detachment.

Then, behind the Black guy, a second man stood out of the vehicle, this one wearing a three-quarters coat, walking toward the door.

Nicky made the mustache before he could see the face. It was Johnny Salita.

Nicky understood then that he was dead. He had gotten distracted over Christopher, and Salita had him lined up here, and Nicky deserved to go.

Even more surprising: Nicky thinking, *I'm ready.*

Salita stopped outside the door, waiting. His gunman rapped on the glass again—harder this time—and Nicky noticed that a third man, another Black guy with a beret and an assault rifle, was standing outside the car.

Nicky had no choice. He twisted the lock and pushed open the door. The first gunman backed Nicky inside, smiling behind his weapon. Salita entered behind him. The second gunman slid inside the closing door and moved to one side, just out of sight of the parking lot and the street.

Salita's hands were in his coat pockets. He might have had a gun. Nicky couldn't tell. Salita shrugged grandly.

"Nicky Pins," he said.

The contempt on Salita's face roused Nicky from his stupor. "We closed an hour or so ago," said Nicky. "But what the hell." Nicky pointed to the gunmen. "What're you guys, size twelves? You, Johnny, size nine, maybe?"

Nicky had been backpedaling as he spoke, and now turned, getting halfway to the shoe-rental counter, where he kept a .25 handgun taped under a drawer—before Salita said, "That's far enough."

Nicky stopped, sighing. He looked at the revolving mirror ball, trying to focus his thoughts. He weighed his options before realizing he didn't have any. He turned.

"Well," he said, "if you don't want to bowl a few, what do you want?"

Salita stepped forward, coming abreast of his gunman. "You enjoy burning off faces, Passero?" he asked. "Strangling guys, guys you know? Castrating them? That your thing? Something you do for Old Man Accardo?" Salita took another step forward, hands lifting out of his pockets, empty. He extended them toward Nicky. "You like these?"

Salita's hands were ringless and uninteresting—but then Nicky saw the cuff links on his shirt cuffs at the end of his coat sleeves. Nicky made out little gold figures seated around an onyx craps table. A gift from the Stardust Hotel—stolen from Tony Accardo's nightstand.

Salita smiled brightly, savoring the moment, and Nicky also noticed, in the starry light of the mirror ball, a sheen over Salita's bright eyes. His tight smile, jaw muscles flexing, teeth bared.

Salita showing up here high on cocaine meant one of two things.

Either he had tooted up to get the guts to massacre Nicky, revenge for Accardo ordering the gutting of his crew. Or—even with two hired gunmen, he didn't have the courage to walk into Ten Pin Lanes sober to confront Nicky face-to-face.

"I gotta know," said Nicky, ignoring the flashy cuff links, "exactly what were you hoping to accomplish by breaking into the Man's home? Besides everything that has happened since. You're the one got your friends slaughtered. Now you're on the run, hiring militants from—you guys Black P. Stone Nation? Latin Kings?—and looking like shit."

Salita nodded fast, angrily. "I wasn't looking for a war. This ain't a war."

"Sure it is."

"All I want is what's mine. And my safety. I think you know what I have. I don't need a gun to take down Accardo, or Joey Doves, all those gargoyles. I don't need judges and cops. I got the books."

"About time you came forward."

"Says the Man's errand boy. No way I can come back and be left alone, I know that. I need to be bought off. And the price is two million dollars. One million each for the notebooks. That look you're givin' me—you wouldn't be if you saw the books."

The gunman standing beside the front door said, harshly, "Car."

Salita turned to see a pair of headlights turn into the parking lot. Nicky's gut clenched. It was Roy, had to be. Nicky thought fast—was there a way Roy could get Nicky out of this jam?—but saw that there wasn't. He could only make things worse.

Salita stepped to the side, out of sight from the lot. The car stopped, then started forward again—Nicky's heart dropping—but then the headlights turned, the car swinging around in a U-turn, exiting the lot back onto the street. Gone.

Salita's guys relaxed, easing off their rifles. Salita was spooked now, and in a hurry to finish. He looked back at Nicky, pulling out a card from his coat pocket, tossing it to the floor between them.

"That's how you reach me," Salita said. "*You*, Passero—you. You get the honor, nobody else. Tell Accardo not to bargain or stall. If he stalls me, I start ripping out pages and mailing them to the FBI, one at a time. Or the *Tribune*." Salita backed to the door with his gunmen. "Do you know what happens then, Passero? If the Outfit's secrets get told?" Salita stopped to smile. "It'll be Tony Accardo's turn inside a trunk. And probably yours."

He backed out through the door, both gunmen following him, one watching Nicky, the other jogging to the car, starting it up. Nicky didn't move, watching them climb in, back up fast, and drive away.

Nicky went to the door and locked it again. Turning back toward his place, he saw the lights swimming around the inside. The emptiness.

He had thought he was done for. "Jesus," he said.

He picked the card up off the floor. Seven digits, a local Illinois exchange. Probably another beeper, though. Nicky slid the card into his left pocket, his head spinning like the lights. He returned to the bar, seeing the rag over the ashtray. He dumped the works into a trash barrel.

Salita must have been watching the Lanes, to know Nicky was there. Nicky had to be even more careful now. He was a sitting duck here. He could have gone off locked in the trunk of Salita's car, and that would have been it. No goodbye to Helena or Nicholas. No nothing.

Nicky poured himself another scotch, saying the word "fuck" to himself in rapid succession, many times. He switched off the spotlights and the mirror ball, turning on bar lights only. He grew angry at himself. He could have died. He had to be smarter.

Headlights again. He turned fast, watching the vehicle pass the front this time, driving around to the rear. Nicky finished his drink and rubbed vigorously at his eyes. "All right," he said, coaching himself. "All right. Fuck this." He walked around the rental counter so that he was between it and the lanes and couldn't be seen through the front door.

The rear fire door opened, grating, shoved from the outside, Agent Roy poking his head in first. He saw Nicky in the low light and entered cautiously, letting the door slam shut.

Nicky pointed at him and said, loudly, so he could be heard across the lanes, "You're gonna get me trunked."

Roy stopped a few steps from the door. "What did I do?"

"Fucking *trunked*," said Nicky.

Roy came up the side walkway. "I pulled in, there was a car still. At the meeting time *you* stipulated. So I took off, drove around awhile—"

"Shut up. Just shut the fuck up."

Roy crossed in front of the rightmost lanes, walking up two steps to Nicky. "What happened? Who was here?"

"Never mind. Who else knows about this?"

"About what? About our arrangement?"

"Our 'arrangement'? This *extortion*. Of me, by you. Who else knows?"

"You're drunk. Tell me what happened."

Nicky shook his head and sneered. "What protects me? When I tell you things?"

Roy set his hands on his hips. "Me. I protect you."

Nicky laughed. "That's not good enough. Not by a fucking mile, baby."

"Well, that's too goddamned bad—"

"ACCARDO'S GOT PEOPLE ALL OVER!" Nicky was losing it. He pulled back a little, getting his breath. "*All* over. I could be talking my way into the trunk of a car here!"

"If you're in trouble, tell me. We can figure it out."

"Fuck you. You don't give a shit about me. You're the fucking devil. There is nothing you can do to me that is *worse* than what I got coming my way anyhow. So threat nullified. I'm through. Get the fuck outta here and do whatever you have to do."

Roy frowned, staring at Nicky, as if trying to figure him out here, seeing a side of him he'd never met before. Roy decided something and started talking.

"You are classified a 'top-echelon informant.' That means high value. Now, I had to push for that. Normally it's reserved for the Accardos and the Giancanas of the world. Your existence, meaning the existence of an informant who is cooperating with me, is known only to the head of the Chicago field office—and even then, only by a code name. No identifying details. I never have to divulge your identity to him, unless you start taking payments from us."

"Never gonna happen." Nicky studied Roy's face, needing the truth. "*Nobody* else?"

"Nobody else but me. You have my word."

"Your word." Nicky walked away a few steps, stopped. He looked at the ceiling and blinked his eyes. He turned back. "What's my code name?"

"Your code name?"

"My secret FBI code name, what is it?"

Roy looked confused. "Why do you want to know that?"

"*Who the fuck wouldn't want to know their fucking code name?*" said Nicky in disbelief. "Are you kidding me here?"

Roy looked confused, as though this was a trivial matter. Not to Nicky, it wasn't.

"Scotch Mist," he said.

It was Nicky's turn to be confused. Was he ordering a drink? "What?"

"Your code name. 'Scotch Mist.'"

Then Nicky remembered: *That fucking night at Merle's.* The drink Roy brought him at the booth. Which might as well have been a cup of poison.

Nicky seethed at this unhappy memory. "Hands down, worst fuckin' code name, all time—really, the fuckin' worst. And this is whose hands my life is in. Jesus Christ."

Nicky went for a walk again, back and forth—buying time, unsure what to do.

Roy said, "Something happened. There's something you want to tell me."

Nicky turned, came back. "Other than 'Fuck you'?" Nicky bit down on his thumbnail, then stopped. "One condition."

Roy shook his head. "There are no conditions."

"You *never* set foot in here again. I mean—*ever*. We'll figure something else out, I don't give a shit—*anywhere* but here."

Roy didn't want to give Nicky anything, but Nicky could see he was eager to hear what Nicky had to say. "Fine. Deal. Now talk."

Nicky took a breath. Doing this went against every instinct he had.

"See, I'm loyal," he said. *"Loyal."* He directed this at Roy, but he was really talking to himself.

Roy said, confusedly, "Okay...?"

"Levinson's," said Nicky. "The jewel thing. This all goes back to Levinson's. The crew that did it, they never cleared the job. Never cleared it, got called in, hadda give it all back. Everything—per Accardo's orders. Okay? But they didn't like that. He went out to Palm Springs... and a few of them, not all, broke into his house early this year to take back the jewels."

Roy looked at him. "Broke into—"

"I know. It sounds crazy because it is crazy. These guys beat the alarm at Accardo's house—what I hear—and broke in while he was gone. I guess to get the jewels. Which they didn't end up finding, by the way."

Roy slowly said, "They broke into Tony Accardo's house?"

Nicky spread his arms like he had completed a magic trick.

Roy held up one hand, a player asking for a time-out. "How many thieves?"

"What I think is, for Accardo, what started out as revenge against these fools—getting the thieves who crossed him?—has, since then, gotten outta hand."

One hand on his hip, Roy turned half away from Nicky, processing this. "Okay," he said. "This is bananas, but okay. Who's doing the street work for Accardo?"

"I don't know that, but recently somebody said he's got two young guns with him all the time now. So assume what you assume."

Roy smoothed out his mustache a few times, spreading it more broadly across his upper lip. "I don't know if any of this makes sense," he said. "Why are you laying all this out for me now?"

"Dribs and drabs, you know? Took me a while to put it all together. And like you, I couldn't believe it either, at first. The Man's house? That's fuckin' crazy. If I had it sooner, you'd have had it sooner. But it's all kind of blowing over now—with most of the thieves dead, plus some others besides."

"What's blowing over?"

"The thing. There's only so many thieves to be snuffed. I think things're settling back to normal again."

"Oh," said Roy, with a small smile, "I doubt that."

Nicky looked at him. "What does that mean?"

"It means things you don't need to know about," said Roy, smiling fully now. "What I will tell you? And only because you came through for me here, just now. We got a grand jury convened."

Nicky said, "A what?"

"A grand jury looking into the thief murders."

Nicky opened his mouth, then he shut it again.

"We figured Accardo was involved—we just couldn't for the life of us figure out exactly why. But now? Ordering multiple murders as revenge for a break-in?" Roy nodded to himself, pleased. "I was hoping to hand Tony Accardo his very first night in prison. But now? *Now?* Accardo could be looking at his very last night *outside* one."

Nicky drove north out of Chicago into horse country. No leaves yet, but the cold snap had long since broken, and the unrelenting snow was like a traumatic memory the city was trying to move on from.

He passed the sign for Barrington Hills and drove with the map on the seat beside him, looking for the street and the house: a brown-brick Tudor with castle-like turret roofs and latticed windows. The driveway was paved in geometric cobbles and lined on both sides with bare trees ready to bloom. Three cars were parked near the garage, only one of which, Accardo's black Caddy, he recognized. But Nicky could guess whose car the black Pontiac Trans Am with gold rims was.

Nicky waited while the doorbell chimes rang. The woman in her late thirties who answered, Marie Accardo Kumerow, was attractive like her mother.

"I'm Nicky Passero. We've spoken on the phone."

"Of course, Dad said you were coming. Come in. Long drive?"

"Thank you, not too bad." The foyer inside was grand, a stairway curling up to the second floor, a chandelier hanging from the high ceiling on a long chain that centered it in the window. A table near

Nicky held photographs of Tony and Clarice Accardo and other relatives.

"He's in the back room—you just go straight through," she said, heading the other way. "I've got one in a high chair. Get you anything?"

"Very kind, all set," Nicky called after her, but she was already gone. Accardo's daughter was married to a union boss, but even that didn't explain this house, halfway between a church and a mansion. In Nicky's Wisner Avenue three-bedroom, the windows on either side looked ten feet across at his neighbors' moldy siding.

He walked where she indicated, up two steps and along a honey-walled hallway, down two steps again, into a perpendicular hallway. Two young children went racing past him, one on each side, chased by a familiar growl, which said, "Don't run!"

Nicky walked into an airy sunroom. A low sofa ran the length of one side, a few toys and an indoor tricycle on the floor, *Time* and *Newsweek* magazines fanned out on the table. Through the windows, a yard of gray grass and knotty trees ran back to a pond with a short dock.

Tony Accardo stood before the windows, wearing a cable-knit cardigan, hands deep in the pockets of his baggy pants. "Shakes," he said with a shrug. "Gramma's making ice cream shakes. They love shakes."

Nicky nodded, looking around for Stingy and his pal. "Nice back here."

"Have a seat, sit. Marie getting you something?"

Nicky chose a cushioned rattan chair rather than the sofa. "No, I'm fine, all good."

Accardo nodded, approaching him. "You, eh, check out the phone number? Anything?"

"What we thought. Beeper service. Forwards to a service in Dallas, Texas. That one forwards to a service in Delaware—which forwards to another in Newark—on and on."

"Son of a bitch. You can't trace it?"

"Electronics is his strength. Knowing how to use technology and how to defeat it. I thought *maybe* if somebody flew out to these places, traced the billing, and *maybe* if Salita made a mistake and didn't prepay with a money order..." But Nicky shook his head.

"There's gotta be a way. Something."

Nicky checked the open doorway to make sure they were alone. "There is," he said. "Pay him."

Accardo shook his head. Nicky went on anyway.

"Buy back the books, be done with all this. Fuck him. Send him packing, and life goes on."

Accardo looked down at his slippers, still shaking his head.

Nicky said, "Salita's a thief—that's who he is, right? I bet he's pulled a couple of small things around town to pay for his two henchmen and the beepers. He'll crop up somewhere else, pulling other jobs. Some other city where you know people. Put the word out, keep an ear to the ground—then get him. Matter of time."

Accardo shook it off. "What, he's gonna give the books to the Feds? For free? Then what? What's he got? He's got nothing. He goes into witness protection?"

"He's already in witness protection, the do-it-yourself kind. He's sitting on these books, and it's his only hand to play. What if he does?"

"If he does, I'm a dead man. Just—dead."

"Then buy him off."

"It's funny how, after all the looking for him you been doing, Salita finds you first."

Nicky bristled at the insinuation. "Me? I'm easy to find. Thirty-six lanes, open late weekends. What's that supposed to mean?"

"What about the Negro gunmen?"

Nicky took a breath. "Working on that, but I don't have a lot of connections on that side of town. The Black P. Stone Nation, I hear their leader went Muslim and's talking about building a mosque now? Some of his guys shook out, broke off. Not what they got in for. It could be two of them. But even if—what does that get us?"

"Bribe 'em. Buy 'em off. Keep trying. The only reason he bought Negro guns is because nobody else would touch him. He's desperate, like all rats. He's scrambling."

"That, I believe," said Nicky. They heard a blender running somewhere in the house, mixing ice cream shakes. "You're stayin' out here awhile?"

"Nah. Yes and no, back and forth. I don't like to leave Michael all alone." Accardo looked up, reminded of something. "They served him, you know. You believe that? Sons of bitches served Michael a subpoena at the house. Clarice too, along with me, through our lawyer. You know what that means."

Nicky shook his head. "What?"

"I gotta get Clarice a new dress for court."

Nicky smiled. Accardo wasn't too worried about the grand jury—so why was Nicky?

"And get Michael a lawyer," continued Accardo. "You didn't get a letter, did you?"

"Me?" said Nicky. "A letter? Fuck no. Why would I get subpoenaed?"

Accardo shrugged. "You like these slippers?"

Nicky looked at them. Coffee-colored suede moccasins. "They look nice."

"They are nice. I'm never takin' them off."

Nicky nodded. He waited for more.

Accardo looked around. "Michael doesn't know nothin'."

"Right," said Nicky. "So now we just, what? Circle the wagons? Lie low, right?"

Accardo looked confused. "What for? Business as usual, so far as anyone else knows."

"You're not concerned at all."

"We have plenty of friends." He stepped up in front of Nicky, looking down at him through his eyeglasses. "I do think, though, maybe somebody should look into the grand jury."

Nicky said, "Look into it?"

"The jurors. Sometimes they get led astray by ambitious prosecutors. Get overzealous. Start discovering things they didn't know were there to begin with."

Nicky said, "I'm not following you."

"It should be somebody who ain't been implicated. Somebody with a deft touch. You got a deft touch, Nicky."

"Me?"

"Better to know what's coming than to get a bad surprise—don't you think?"

R eturn from Witch Mountain was a movie about a brother and a sister who were space-traveling aliens, but who looked exactly like humans and not only could communicate by reading each other's minds but also could move things with their minds. That it was a sequel to a previous movie made sense to Nicky, because almost nothing else about the movie did. But the crowd of kids and parents at the well-attended matinee performance ate it up.

Especially Nicholas, who no doubt wished he had the power to control adults and the world around him. Nicky cheated looks at him throughout the movie and twice caught Helena doing the same, seated on the other side of their son, smiling at his expression of wonderment. Nicky felt he and Helena had connected on this point, and in that regard, it was the best moviegoing experience Nicky had ever had.

After, Nicholas chose deep dish, and they ate at a pizza parlor with red-and-white checkered plastic tablecloths and jukeboxes at the tables. Three songs for a quarter, and all three times, Nicholas chose to play "Rock and Roll All Nite" by Kiss, a makeup-wearing hard-rock group Helena strongly disapproved of, but for which she made a special exception that afternoon. Nicky pressed his finger to his temple, à la the *Witch Mountain* kids, and pretended to levitate a slice of cheese pizza into his mouth, and even Helena laughed. Outside the old trap of bad memories that was their house, when the three of them were together, she wanted things to be good, the way they used to be.

Nicholas walked ahead of them on the sidewalk after, as bouncy as the restaurant balloon floating on the ribbon in his hand. Nicky walked next to Helena, whose handbag dangled from her crossed arms.

"Movies, pizza, balloons?" said Nicky. "This kid hit the trifecta today."

"He sure did."

"Love seeing him like this, right?"

"It's nice, Nicky," Helena said. "Real nice."

They shared another smile. The moment felt right.

"What do you think about me coming home more often?" said Nicky. "For Nicky Jr.'s sake, you know."

"Nicholas," she corrected him.

Her preference was that the boy be called by his full name. Nicky still took it as a slight, but he let it go. "For *our son's* sake—how's that? And mine."

She looked at him, pushing a lock of black hair back from her eye so she could see him better. She knew the request was full of meaning. It seemed like she wanted him to—and it also seemed like she didn't.

"How about Sunday dinner?" he said, downshifting smoothly. "We can go to church, then have a meal at home? If it's nice enough, like this, we can go for a walk outside after. How about if we start there?"

Helena looked ahead at Nicholas waiting for them at the curb, the blue balloon floating over his head. A junior version of Nicky.

"We can do that," said Helena, and then she hurried ahead to catch up with Nicholas, taking his hand before crossing the street.

I f he'd been quicker or cannier, he could have gotten out of it, like the others who had been dismissed. Hardship. Sick child. Didn't speak English. A few obviously and shamelessly lied, saying whatever it took to get out of there. The court officer spoke to their civic duty, which Paul Rutledge found inspiring, and yet it still felt to everyone in the room that they had lost some sort of contest and sitting on a grand jury was their penalty.

Six months. A long time to be away from his desk. Would he come back to stacks and stacks of work waiting for him? Or, worse, no work stacked up—someone else having taken on his responsibilities—the office having gotten used to him not being around?

At least his job was safe. Job security was the best thing about working for a utility like ComEd. As the manager of customer service, Rutledge would never get rich, but he drove a company car and had a secure pension plan, and he could plan safely and assuredly for his future.

Now, thirteen weeks in, Rutledge found he didn't miss the office as much as he had thought he would. Sitting on the grand jury started out interesting, because it was new, but soon became routine. Civil cases were notably uninteresting. Then the Outfit case started.

Going into this, friends had ribbed him about getting a mob murder trial, something long and drawn out. He was glad he was forbidden from discussing the case with anyone, because his wife would be terrified of him having anything to do with the broken-nose crowd—even being in the same room with them. But Rutledge found it intriguing, certainly more exciting than dealing with disgruntled electricity customers and downed power lines.

He was almost home, humming along to Dolly Parton on the car radio, when he saw the blue police light in his rearview mirror. He checked the speedometer, but he hadn't been speeding, then signaled right and pulled over to let the patrol car pass.

But it didn't pass. It pulled in behind him, headlights bright on his mirrors now, blue light illuminating the residential neighborhood. Paul Rutledge hadn't been pulled over since he was a teenager. He opened his glove compartment, finding the plastic sleeve containing the registration he'd gotten with the company car. He pulled his eyeglasses out of the soft case clipped to his front shirt pocket so he could scan the document. His name wasn't on it, of course. The 1975 Malibu was registered to Commonwealth Edison. But that shouldn't present a problem.

The officer came up behind a flashlight beam. Rutledge rolled down the window, his registration at the ready. He couldn't see much behind the bright light, only that the officer strangely wasn't in uniform.

"Evening, sir. License and registration?"

Official sounding, not unfriendly. "Right here." Rutledge tipped up his hip to get at his wallet underneath, fumbling it open, sliding out his identification. "The car is a company car, not mine. I work for ComEd. I'm on my way home."

"Yes, sir."

"You are a police officer?" said Rutledge. "I wasn't speeding, was I?"

The officer produced his own identification, flashing his beam on his badge barely long enough for Rutledge to see it. He was a detective, and his last name was something like "Question."

Rutledge handed over his license and registration, and after a moment of scrutinizing both under the flashlight beam, the detective turned and walked back to his vehicle.

Squinting to keep the reflected headlights out of his eyes, Rutledge looked straight ahead up the road. Thank God he hadn't been pulled over on his own street; he'd never be able to live it down. The neighbors would talk for days. A detective? It was only one blue light behind him—not two like the patrol-car racks. It must have been those magnetized ones like on the cop shows. He wondered if a speeding ticket would get back to his company, and if it impacted his insurance policy or theirs—then realized it didn't matter. Perhaps he had made a bad turn or rolled through a stop sign at some point in the past mile or so.

Rutledge heard his rear door open and felt the car suspension sink an inch or more, somebody climbing inside behind him. The door closed again. Rutledge was startled. He hadn't seen the detective's flashlight returning. He turned to look over his right shoulder.

"Face forward," said the voice—different from the detective's voice, a local accent, but deeper. All Rutledge could see through his rearview mirror now, other than a portion of the shadow of the man's face and shoulder behind him, was the silhouette of a wide-brimmed, rather ill-fitting hat.

"Are you sure you really want to identify me?" the man said.

Rutledge looked away, then down. This wasn't cop-speak. This was something else. Someone he didn't know was sitting in the back of his car.

"Who are you?" said Rutledge.

"Don't worry about it. On your way home?"

It sounded like gangster-speak. The accent and the tone. Where was the detective?

"Yes," said Rutledge, then wondered if it would have been smarter to lie.

"That's nice," said the man. "Going home for the night."

Rutledge didn't say anything after that. He had started to tremble.

"Western Springs," said the voice. "Nice safe suburb."

He felt a tap on his shoulder, something sharp. He didn't know what to do.

"Take these," the voice told him.

Rutledge reached up and took them. His driver's license and the vehicle registration in its plastic sleeve. Why did this man have them and not the detective?

This man knew his home address now.

"What is this?" Rutledge asked, his voice close to a whisper.

"I'm here to say thank you," said the man. "Thank you for doing your civic duty, serving on this grand jury."

Rutledge stopped breathing for a moment. He was going to be sick.

"Also, I want to tell you what a lovely family you have."

Another tap on Rutledge's shoulder. He stiffened, then reached up and accepted what was handed him.

In the light from the headlamps behind him, he saw they were photographs, glossies, white-bordered snapshots.

Cathy leaving the house with the baby in her arms.

The twins playing in the front yard, wearing matching rompers under matching red velvet coats, plastic barrettes holding back their unruly brown hair.

Rutledge himself, putting the twins in the back seat of their VW hatchback.

The photographs had been taken right across the street from Rutledge's brick three-bedroom on Claire Avenue. From a car, apparently. The picture of him had been taken the previous weekend.

"I think you got a good shot at making foreman on this jury. I really do."

Rutledge was having trouble breathing. He didn't know if the man wanted the photographs back or not.

"You keep those for your scrapbook. Beautiful young family. Mr. Rutledge, you don't have to do much. It's really simple. You just let us know, end of every day, how the day's testimony went and where it seems like things are going. You'll call from a phone booth away from the courthouse—that's very important, Paul—every day without fail. Do you have any problem with that?"

Another tap on his shoulder. Rutledge didn't hesitate this time; he reached up and took it.

A card. With a phone number written on it.

Then the hand gripped Rutledge's shoulder, making him jump.

"Your girls with their pretty hair. Your wife home alone with them all day. Just keep thinking of them, and this'll be the easiest thing you ever did. And the smartest."

After another hard squeeze and a sharp pat on the trapezius that set Rutledge wincing, the door behind him opened and closed again, and the car's suspension lifted. Rutledge waited until the headlights behind him backed away and turned, the detective's car driving off in the other direction. Paul Rutledge opened up his door and leaned out onto the road and vomited.

Nicky worked the electric polisher on lane twenty-three, twin rotary brushes gliding over the finished maple. Annual spring cleaning. One job that one-armed Chuckie couldn't do, but Nicky didn't mind; he was looking for something mindless—anything that didn't involve him bouncing back and forth between Tony Accardo and Gerald Roy like that digital square in the *Pong* game.

The day before, he had taken Nicholas to high mass at the basilica, where Helena's choir group sang. That meant a longer mass than usual, but Nicky liked it. Afterward, Helena braised a lamb while Nicky played the Slime Monster board game with Nicholas, the Don Knotts half-animated fish movie playing on TV. They laughed during dinner, Nicholas in the best mood of all three of them, which Helena surely noticed.

Coming back to the Lanes that night and closing up and bunking down in the tiny back room was another low point for Nicky, but also catalyzing. He had resisted getting a place of his own after separating from Helena, telling himself that it was only temporary and wanting back into his own house. Then letting go of things week over week, having to put in the shower, adapting to a new routine, and he had gotten used to it. He had let it become him. Now he saw himself for what he was: a guy who lived in a bowling alley. What a lonely, terrifying prospect. No kind of life.

Nicky looked at the clock above the rental counter. He had plenty of time. Around five, he'd leave and head over to the Conrad Hilton, the bank of pay phones off the lobby, setting up shop in booth number one and waiting for the ComEd manager Rutledge to call. Nicky would then relay the day's developments—if any—to Accardo and get a bite to eat in the coffee shop there or somewhere downtown. Then maybe call Helena and swing by the house to help Nicholas with the math fractions he'd been having trouble with, making his presence there more normal.

As Nicky finished on twenty-three, Chuckie called to him from the register. "Phone for you," he said. "A lady."

"A lady?" said Nicky. "Helena?"

Chuckie shook his head. Nicky stood the polisher at the head of the lane and stepped over the long cord, walking to the phone on the counter.

"This is Nicky."

"Nicky? It's Trixie." Sally Brags's wife.

"Hey, Trixie, how you feeling?"

"I'm okay, Nicky. Nicky—is Sal with you?"

"With me? Here at the Lanes? No."

"What happened last night? He never came home. I figured he went straight to work—that's what he does sometimes. His car's gone. But he was supposed to take me to the doctor's at three, and I called down to his supervisor, and they haven't seen him all day."

As she spoke, Nicky's neck and face went cold. He struggled to find his voice. "Trixie?" he said. "Hey, listen to me. What do you mean, he never came home? Never came home from where?"

"He was with you, Nicky. Wasn't he?"

Inside phone booth number one off the lobby at the Conrad Hilton, Nicky stared intently at the floor. Tony Accardo was on the other end of the line, set up at a drugstore pay phone across town.

"My two guys," said Nicky. "Nobody can find them."

Customers made noise in the background on Accardo's end. "What's this now?"

"My guys, *both* guys. The ones who..." Nicky frowned—Accardo knew who he was talking about. "My *guys*, Joe."

"Yeah, I don't know, Nicky. They're your guys—I don't know. I got a grand jury on my mind. I sleep either no good or too good."

"I need to know. I *need* to know. You don't know who it was? Was it Salita?" Nicky meant *Was it you?*

Accardo said, "How would I know who it was?"

"You might know because..." Nicky closed his eyes, not wanting to think it. "Look, they did everything you needed done. Exactly the *way* you wanted it done. These're my guys, guys I known since third grade..."

"Look, this isn't what this call is for. I don't know what this is. I'm goin'."

Accardo hung up. Leaving Nicky staring at a taxi-service sticker on the booth wall, a dead connection in his ear. Nicky hung up, thinking what to do next.

No more trunks, Nicky had warned Accardo—who had disagreed.

Disappearing is better, Accardo had said.

Nicky refused to consider it. Salita had bad-talked the guys too. It had to be him—not him, but his militant goons. If that was true, then Nicky was next. Nicky looked out the booth window at the hotel guests passing back and forth from the lobby. It would be a simple thing to watch him there. Easy for anyone to follow Nicky around.

They met at Sally Brags's house in West Ravenswood, Helena sitting with very pregnant Trixie and Crease Man's distraught fiancée, Debra. Nicky, the only guy in the room, sat on a chair at an angle to the three women, feeling sick. Nicky was in shock. He sympathized with their misery, completely. He shared it.

The women went over their stories again, same as they'd told the police, and Nicky learned nothing more from what they said. Only Sally Brags had said explicitly that he was going to meet up with Nicky—though Trixie wasn't sure that he hadn't also said something about having to be somewhere else first. Debra had been out with salon friends from work celebrating someone's birthday, and Crease Man hadn't left her a note or anything, which wasn't unusual. In fact, she hadn't even known he was missing until Trixie called her looking for Sally Brags.

Debra was the one who brought up the murdered thieves. She had read the newspaper articles about guys being found in automobile trunks—and both Sally Brags's and Crease Man's cars were gone.

Nicky reassured them it was nothing like that. Probably a bender, the two of them—though no one in the room believed that, only wanted to. Debra had her own car, but Trixie didn't have a ride now, eight months pregnant. Nicky promised to get her a car the next day.

"I'm gonna figure this out," he told them.

"But what's going to happen, Nicky?" asked Trixie, her hand on her swollen belly. She and Debra both turned to him for answers, just like their men always did.

The only thing Nicky knew for sure was that with every hour that went by, the chance of them walking through the door again got smaller and smaller.

"I don't know," said Nicky, feeling Helena's eyes on him too. "I'm sorry. I really don't know."

He got away when he could, to the bathroom, where he ran water and looked at himself in the mirror, trying to think of whom they would have gone out to see who might have used Nicky's name in order to throw a rope over them. Then he went to the kitchen and opened the refrigerator, seeing the Michelobs on a low shelf, but couldn't bring himself to drink one. He saw a photograph on a magnet of the three of them at a Cubs game, maybe three years before—good seats, all smiles. He looked out the back door to the yard and the black drum grill they'd gathered around just a couple of weeks ago, where Nicky had handed out the take from the lockbox and they'd talked about the future.

Helena found him there, looking out the window. She laid her hand on his back, startling him, and he turned. "You look terrible," she said.

Nicky nodded. "I gotta go," he told her. "Let's go."

Helena was teary in the passenger seat of Nicky's Satellite, after being strong for her girlfriends, dabbing at her eyes with an embroidered handkerchief. Nicky drove in silence, gut churning, keeping his focus on the road ahead. Passing lines of parked cars, wondering where Sally Brags's and Crease Man's cars were.

He felt something on his knuckles as his hand rested on the gear shift. It was his wife's hand. A gesture of comfort. Nicky was grateful—and torn.

"Do you want to go say a prayer?" she asked. Nicky nodded quickly, realizing that was exactly what he wanted to do.

The basilica was open all hours. They went in together, crossing themselves at the entrance. They walked to the white candles, dipping a taper into the flame and lighting new ones. Heads down, silent with their thoughts. When they were finished, they walked together to the front of the church, crossing themselves again before the altar upon which they had been married, then stepping to the side, kneeling at the rail. Elbow to elbow, Helena prayed over her handkerchief and her rosary while Nicky held his head in his hands, asking for guidance, praying for a miracle.

Taped over the front of a blackboard on wheels was an organization chart drawn on poster paper, arranged in the form of a broad pyramid. "Associates" were named in long lists along the bottom, under each low branch at the base of the chart. Above them were "Lieutenants," their street names in quotes, accompanied by photographs, mostly booking mug shots. Above those were "Area Bosses," also with photographs, one each for the West Side ("DuPage County"), the South Side ("South of Eisenhower, NW Indiana"), and the North Side ("Elmwood Park, Lake County"), each area boss's last name running more than ten letters in length. Above that, narrowing toward the top, were "Advisers," of which there were two. Above those was the "Underboss," whose name was Jackie "the Lackey" Cerone. Above him was the "Boss," Joseph "Joey Doves" Aiuppa.

On the first day of testimony, one of the lead prosecutors made a show of taping another name and photograph above "Boss" at the very top of the chart. That was Anthony Joseph Accardo, legal name Antonino Leonardo Accardo. His nicknames were listed as "Joe," "Joe Batters," "Big Tuna," "The Man," "Chairman," and "King."

That was the same day they started displaying transparencies via overhead projector, each showing the corpse of a gangland figure, many of them trussed up in car trunks, some unearthed from shallow graves, a few mercifully shot multiple times at close range.

Paul Rutledge did not squirm in his seat that day. He sat rigidly at attention. He had taken an oath, having pledged to weigh the evidence objectively, and that pledge still held. He had also sworn to keep confidential the facts revealed in that room as well as the testimony offered as evidence. That pledge he had no choice but to break.

Every afternoon after the jury's session was called for the day, Rutledge walked to his ComEd company car and drove three blocks to a pay phone outside a tobacconist, where he called the number he had memorized from the card he had been given, a second pay phone somewhere else in the city. He spoke to the man who had entered his car that night and threatened him and his family, the man who appeared suddenly behind him nightly in dreams, whose voice called to him as he sat straight up in bed. The man for whom Rutledge looked out his windows late at night, parting the curtain ever so slightly, watching the street for the man who was watching him.

After the phone call, Rutledge drove straight home, and every evening he walked in the door and kissed Cathy and hugged the twins and held baby Suzy and reminded and consoled himself that he had no choice in the matter. All he was doing was providing information. For the souls of his family, he would continue to carry out his duty exactly as expected.

Every morning on his long, lonely drive from Western Springs to the block-long Everett McKinley Dirksen United States Courthouse, Rutledge wished he were driving to his own office instead, to the drab desk where he addressed the needs of Chicago's three million residential electricity customers. Most days, he felt as though he were moving in a dream state. He would look at the fifteen other impaneled jurors, representing a cross section of the city of Chicago, all listening attentively, and speculate how many of them had been compromised as well. Not all? Perhaps some? Believing that he was not the only one suborned absolved him, in a way.

On this particular morning, Rutledge was aware of extra court officers in the hallway—not security, necessarily, more like they were there as spectators. Curiosity seekers. After the usual good mornings with his fellow jurists, and a cigarette and a half cup of burnt coffee from the jurists' room's four-gallon percolator, Rutledge, along with the others, was escorted by the bailiff through a side door into the grand jury room, which resembled a courtroom, with attendant prosecutors, bailiffs, court officers, a stenographer, and, eventually, the judge. Missing were a gallery of benches for spectators and members of the defense. Testifying witnesses were admitted one at a time and were not permitted to have legal counsel present.

When Tony Accardo entered, Rutledge recognized him immediately from the newspapers. He shed a heavy coat and removed his tweed hat inside the door, the room silent as he walked to the witness box. A stocky man, not tall, practically rectangular. He looked relaxed and not at all concerned as he laid a hand on the Bible and declared and affirmed that the testimony he was about to give was the truth, the whole truth, and nothing but the truth, before taking his seat and refusing to answer any of the prosecutor's questions.

PROSECUTOR: Mr. Accardo, where were you on the night of January 8, 1978?

ACCARDO: I decline to answer on the grounds it might incriminate me.

PROSECUTOR: Mr. Accardo, your home address is 1407 Ashland Avenue in River Forest, is that correct?

ACCARDO: I decline to answer on the grounds it might incriminate me.

PROSECUTOR: Mr. Accardo, I am simply asking you to confirm your legal address.

ACCARDO: I decline to answer on the grounds it might incriminate me.

PROSECUTOR: Mr. Accardo, do you also own a condominium residence in Palm Springs, California, on Roadrunner Drive, adjacent to the Indian Wells Country Club?

ACCARDO: Making me say this again? I decline to answer on the grounds that it might incriminate me.

Tony Accardo had an unassertive, hangdog face, not unlike that of an aging bus driver. But his eyes, quick and curious, stood out. His voice was a low growl. Paul Rutledge did not think he was looking at a murderer, not at the moment. But he would not have liked to have encountered this man fifty years ago.

Twice, Rutledge felt that the septuagenarian mob boss was looking directly at him. Each time, Rutledge fought back an attack of anxiety, an unreasonable fear that he would leap to his feet and decry the criminal exaction being committed against him. His tortured mind kept his anxiety in check by countering with images of Rutledge discovering the corpses of his wife and daughters.

Mrs. Clarice Accardo presented herself very favorably.

PROSECUTOR: Mrs. Accardo, were you in Palm Springs on the night of January 8, 1978?

MRS. ACCARDO: I decline to answer on the grounds that it might incriminate me.

PROSECUTOR: That's your answer, Mrs. Accardo? To a simple question like that?

MRS. ACCARDO: That's my answer. To everything.

The look she gave to the prosecutor was an expression of toughness mixed with disgust. But when she turned to the jurors, her eyes seeking out each one individually—especially the females, Rutledge noted—her smile was grandmotherly. The prosecutor, sensing his dead-end questioning of this kind-looking woman was losing favor with the jury, abandoned his interrogation of Mrs. Accardo after a matter of minutes.

The next day, a tall, distinguished man with white hair and wide eyeglasses entered the courtroom, laying his topcoat neatly over the back of an empty bench. After the hostile silence of the aging gangsters who had been subpoenaed to appear, this man, Michael Volpe, exuded the deference and modesty of a different subset of the same generation.

He sat erect in the witness chair, necktie knotted tight and held fast with a pin. He appeared nervous and a little bewildered behind his huge eyeglass frames. Rutledge was not surprised when Volpe, a naturalized citizen of the United States for forty years, spoke with a faded but distinct Italian accent.

PROSECUTOR: Mr. Volpe, how long have you been employed by Mr. Tony Accardo as his housekeeper at 1407 Ashland Avenue in River Forest?

VOLPE: I...I decline to answer on the grounds of intimida of incrimination.

PROSECUTOR: More than forty years, Mr. Volpe?

VOLPE: I decline to answer on the grounds of the incrimination.

PROSECUTOR: Or are you no longer in the employ of Mr. Tony Accardo?

VOLPE: I...I decline to answer that, sir.

PROSECUTOR: You decline to answer because it is not true? Or because it is? Don't you work for Tony Accardo, Mr. Volpe?

Right here Paul Rutledge saw a man torn between continued willful obstinance and helpful deference, as was his wont as a lifelong house servant.

VOLPE: Yes. Yes, a *great* man.

That was all it took. The prosecutor turned from the witness, in the general direction of the jury, sharing an expression of surprise and delight at Mr. Volpe's response with his prosecutorial colleague.

PROSECUTOR: Thank you, Mr. Volpe. Directing your attention to the morning of January 9, 1978. Will you please describe what you discovered when you arrived at the Accardo house that day?

VOLPE: I decline to answer on the grounds of incrimination.

PROSECUTOR: Your Honor, the witness has opened the door to further testimony.

JUDGE SAMUELS: Mr. Volpe, I want to remind you that you are under oath. You will answer the question.

It was warmer in the backyards this time, with more hazards like toys and dog pens and sprinkler hoses to avoid, but at least Nicky knew the way, moving quickly along at this late hour toward Accardo's property.

He landed in the yard and made his way to the patio slider, knocking gently. Michael Volpe came to see who it was, recognizing Nicky, and after drying his hands on a dish towel, opened the door. He had a vacant expression, his eyes ringed red.

"Evening, Mr. Passero," he said quietly.

"Good evening, Michael," said Nicky, though it certainly wasn't.

Nicky left him working in the kitchen and found Accardo—no haunting Polish pop music this time—sitting at the head of the table in his formal dining room, a napkin tucked into his collar.

Accardo nodded at Nicky when he entered. "Sit," he said.

The table was set for two on a sunflower-yellow tablecloth. Nicky's place was across from Accardo. He sat, watching the Man, wondering why he was here, saying nothing.

Presently, Volpe entered the room, shoe soles silent on the firm carpeting. He held two plates, a thin dish towel protecting his hands from the heat, serving Accardo and Nicky each a steak fillet with julienne potatoes and boiled onions and beets.

Volpe was intensely nervous in a way that made him appear unsteady. Nicky knew what Michael Volpe meant to Accardo, how many years they had been together. Nicky sensed that not many words had passed between them that evening, contributing to Volpe's distress.

Accardo did not pick up his fork. After standing to the side for a moment, Volpe withdrew and turned to leave the room.

"Michael."

Volpe stopped. He turned back toward his employer of forty years.

Accardo said, without expression, "How did it go today?"

Volpe nodded, looking down. "I don't think it went very good."

After a moment of steely silence, Accardo said, "Can you elaborate about that?"

Volpe said, "They ask me questions . . . They try to make you out in a bad way . . ."

"Sure," said Accardo, not interested in that. "But can you elaborate on what *you* said?"

Volpe was an old man making confession. "I say that I call you at the golf club that morning. I say I no report to police because . . . because you say not to."

Accardo said, "Did you say there was a break-in?"

Volpe nodded. "I say there was a break-in."

Accardo said, "Anything about the house?"

Volpe said, still looking down, "They ask about the basement. They show me blueprints from the builder. They want to know what down there."

"And what did you tell them?"

"Meeting room. Office. Burner, heater. Pantry room. Vault."

Accardo was very still. "Michael," he said. "You were carefully instructed. You were coached."

Volpe, teary, nodded. "I know."

"You were told what to say every time, to every question. Over and over."

"They press me," said Volpe, suddenly looking up.

"You were told to expect that. To stand your ground."

"I never want to hurt you."

Nicky couldn't help him; he didn't dare jump in.

"Michael," said Accardo. He pulled out the empty chair next to him. "Come here."

Accardo motioned to Volpe to sit, which he did. Accardo gave him his linen napkin so that Volpe could wipe his tears. Accardo watched him do so. Accardo looked tired.

"Michael, you've been loyal to me and a friend for many, many years," said Accardo. "I see now, I shoulda fought your subpoena. I was selfish—I wanted you here. I shoulda sent you home to Palermo."

Volpe said, "I just want to keep house here."

Accardo nodded. He patted Volpe's knee reassuringly.

"Okay," said Accardo. "Okay, Michael. I understand. It's over. You can go now."

Volpe looked to make sure he had heard him correctly. He didn't know what to do with the napkin, now a handkerchief, so he left it on the tablecloth, standing and walking out of the room, back to the kitchen.

Accardo looked at his meal. He pushed his plate back an inch and rested both forearms on the table, looking straight ahead, though not at Nicky.

"Fuckers," he said.

Nicky didn't speak. Accardo had pardoned Volpe, to Nicky's great relief. Now that Nicky didn't have to worry about the old Sicilian, he was worried for Accardo. Nicky didn't see how he could make this grand jury go away now.

Accardo said, "I'm tired, Nicky."

Nicky nodded. "I can bet."

"Tired of all this. They're gonna call Michael into open court, swear him out."

Nicky nodded. It was bad.

"My lawyers say this break-in motive, it bumps up charges to a capital offense. Opens the door to all sorts of things."

"You'll find a way through."

Accardo shook his head, downcast. "I dunno," he said. He looked defeated. "Maybe it's time. Maybe this thing has gone on long enough."

Nicky wasn't sure exactly what he meant, but it sounded like Accardo was pulling back, which was a good thing, good for them both. Nicky said, gently, "You are in a tough spot here."

Accardo nodded, resigned, looking as though he'd reached the end of something, a journey, like there was nothing left to do on the train once it stopped but climb down off it.

E very time the door to the Lanes opened, Nicky looked over. Every ring of the phone set his heart pumping.

He'd had nightmares about Sally Brags and Crease Man where he found them at the body shop, all cut up and burned, but still alive, waiting for him—trunking *him*. Nicky brought groceries to Trixie Bragotti, who had started smoking again after giving it up for the first two trimesters. In going around their house, looking for money Sally might have stashed, she came up with a roll of ones stashed in one of his shoes along with a short list of telephone numbers—which she proceeded to call, hoping for some clue about his disappearance, only to find herself speaking to waitresses and dancers. Not good. Crease Man's Debra punched an aunt of hers in the face who asked for the return of an engagement gift, and Nicky'd had to go to the police station to get her out of it. He was concerned about Debra telling Helena some things about Crease Man's illicit sources of income that might lead Helena to speculate about how Nicky earned the money he gave her. For her part, Helena had gone from worrying about Sally Brags and Crease Man to being afraid for Nicky.

The phone rang. Nicky picked it up quick. "This is Nicky."

A female voice he did not recognize said, "Your jacket is pressed and ready."

After a moment and a swallow, Nicky said, "Okay, thank you."

He hung up. Chuckie was looking at him, hopeful for news about Sally Brags and Crease Man, and also dreading it. Nicky shook his head. Chuckie nodded and went back to leafing through his car magazine.

"I gotta go to the bank," Nicky said.

Nicky pulled into the parking lot of River City Dry Cleaners, wheeling into an empty space farthest from the entrance. He got out quickly, scanning the premises as he walked to a Mercury Bobcat parked nearby, climbing inside the front passenger seat next to Agent Gerald Roy.

Roy surveilled the parking lot from behind a pair of mirrored Ray-Bans. He wore a tan leather jacket and faded blue jeans. A mesh bag of clothes lay in a laundry basket in the back seat. Did the FBI agent not own a washing machine? Roy turned his attention to Nicky. "Why didn't you tell me about your missing guys?"

Nicky wasted only a few seconds wondering how he'd heard. "They're good guys, friends of mine. Not thieves. Not mixed up in the thing you're interested in. I thought they'd turn up. Why?"

"When I heard they were friends of yours, I went down to the transit authority, asking about Bragotti. They didn't know anything. Santangelo, I guess he was a longshoreman in name only. A no-show union job. But you knew that."

"These guys aren't heavy hitters. They're like me. Trying to make a living. You find out anything?"

"Nothing. So you're saying that the odds are I pop open a trunk someday soon and they're in it are ...?"

Nicky said, "Zero."

"Really?"

"There'd be no reason."

Roy took a good look at him. "Your best friends are gone, Nicky.

You know they got iced. You live in this world. Why you acting like it's some other mystery?"

Nicky had to get him off this. "You wouldn't believe what I'm dealing with. Their ladies, one pregnant wife—twins—one fiancée. Both losing their minds. I got a lot going on."

"Tell me why you don't automatically think it's Accardo."

"Accardo? Why? That's because. What would he care?"

"Michael Volpe," said Roy. "Know that name?"

"Uh," said Nicky, as if he were thinking. "Accardo's houseman, old guy?"

"Got called before the grand jury couple of days ago." Roy visually swept the parking lot again, looked back. "He confirmed the break-in of Accardo's house."

"Ah, okay," said Nicky, playing that this confirmed his earlier tip. "So there you go."

"And now he's disappeared too."

Nicky stared at Roy. He saw the reflection of his face doubled in Roy's lenses—and saw his own shocked reaction.

"Disappeared how?" said Nicky, numb.

"We found his Toyota Cressida parked at a shopping center in Englewood, locked, keys inside. This is a seventy-five-year-old man, Nicky. Been with Accardo since the thirties. Think about that."

Nicky was thinking about that. He was also thinking about how he had left Accardo's house a few nights ago certain that all had been forgiven between the two.

"By the way," continued Roy, "Accardo never reported him missing. Forty years in his employ, he doesn't call a friend at district headquarters, do a wellness check? Nothing."

Nicky just shook his head. Could this be?

"A grand jury witness gives damaging insider testimony against Tony Accardo—then vanishes a few days later. The noose is closing tighter and tighter, Nicky."

Nicky didn't want to believe it. He was figuring out his next move when Roy said something he didn't catch.

"I said look at me," said Roy, getting his attention. Nicky did look at him. The sunglasses, the mustache, the brushed-back amber hair. "Tell me your two guys Bragotti and Santangelo had nothing at all to do with Tony Accardo."

Nicky's face in the twin reflections allowed Nicky to see himself as Roy saw him. This smartened Nicky up. All he had to do was get out of this car. "This is what you called me out here for?" he said, turning indignant. "Telling me some old guy fucked up and got whacked? Throw around blame and accusations under the guise of 'I'm trying to help you'? Your noose is tightening? Beautiful. Go with God. But leave me out of it." Nicky threw open his door. "I got enough I'm dealing with here."

Nicky bailed out and slammed the door before Roy could stop him. He walked fast to his Satellite, Roy rolling down the window and calling after him once—"Nicky!"—but more hissed than spoken, unable to make a scene. Nicky flipped him off and got into his car, speeding away.

Nicky knew he had to be patient. But it wasn't just Michael Volpe he needed answers for now; it was Sally Brags and Crease Man. He couldn't go to Ashland Avenue. He doubted he could ever go there again. There was only one thing he could do. He waited as long as he could bear, until later in the afternoon, then drove out to Barrington Hills, back to Accardo's daughter's house.

He remembered that look of resignation on Accardo's face at the dining table. Of defeat. Did Accardo change his mind the next morning? Or was the resignation from knowing what had to be done?

Nicky pulled in over the patterned cobbles, parking near the garage. No other cars in the driveway, not Accardo's black Caddy, though the garage was windowless, and anybody could have been parked in there. He rang the bell at the front door, hearing church-like chimes inside.

After a peek through the spyglass, Marie Kumerow answered. She was wearing pants and a blouse, but her hair was still wet, done up in a towel. "Nicky," she said. "Hi. Dad's not here."

"He's not?"

She let him inside, closing the door on the cool air outside. "He and Mom left for Palm Springs," she said. "On short notice. You know how Dad is. I'm surprised he didn't tell you."

"Palm Springs," said Nicky, wondering if this was the truth, then deciding it probably was. "I guess I'm out of the loop." He felt relief, both that Accardo was gone and that now Nicky didn't have to confront him. "Which is actually fine," he added. This was the best possible outcome for both of them, for the time being.

"You okay?" she asked him. "You look gray."

"Me? No, yeah, I think I'm fighting something off."

"Want a drink of milk, something?"

"Don't bother, no. You're kind." Nicky sighed, not knowing what to do next. "All the way out here for nothin'." He smiled. "Always call first, right? That's on me."

Over their small talk, Nicky heard the sound of cars pulling in. One after another—and car doors opening and closing.

Marie heard it too. "You come with someone?"

"Not me," said Nicky.

Marie went to look out a side window, Nicky following.

Police vehicles, two marked and three unmarked, filled her driveway. Uniforms and plainclothes cops assembled at the end of the walkway, starting toward the door.

Marie said, "What the fuck is this?"

The window glass was opaque, his view distorted, so Nicky couldn't make out faces—but he thought he recognized Gerry Roy's tan Bobcat out there.

"I can't be here," he said, half-apologetically, backing away, "so if it's okay with you, I'm gonna..."

Marie said, "Yeah, yeah—go."

He went. The doorbell chimes rang—church bells—and Nicky saw her tug the towel down off her wet hair as he hustled down the honey-yellow hallway, turning out of sight from the foyer, stopping there to listen.

The door was pulled open. Marie's voice was angry, offended. "What's this?"

A voice said, "Mrs. Marie Kumerow?"

Marie said, "I just got out of the shower. What do you want?"

Roy's voice. "Special Agent Gerald Roy, FBI, Mrs. Kumerow."

"Okay, and?" she said.

Another voice. "Detective Feliks Banka, ma'am. Chicago PD."

Nicky was trapped. He stood with his shoulder to the wall, next to a framed keepsake invitation to the Kumerow-Accardo wedding. *Mr. and Mrs. Anthony Accardo request the honor of your presence...*

Roy's voice. "Pleasure to make your acquaintance, Mrs. Kumerow. We have a search warrant here—"

Marie said, "Gimme a fucking break—I have two young kids in the house."

Roy's voice. "Mrs. Kumerow, the warrant is for this house and for your father's residence on Ashland Avenue. We've already been there, and there was no answer. We thought you might have a key, and if so, your father might like his front door not broken down."

Nicky heard cops moving inside. He retreated farther, to the sunroom where he'd met with Accardo the last time, but stopped there, seeing a uniformed cop walking around the backyard. Nicky didn't know the layout well enough to find another way out, if there was one. And hiding there and waiting like a sitting duck until he was found would make things a hundred times worse.

On impulse, he strode back into the hallway leading to the front foyer—rubbing his hands like he'd just come from the john. A uniform saw him first, holding up a hand to stop him. "Who's this?"

Marie turned in surprise. Nicky stopped at the edge of the foyer with a *What's this?* expression, recognizing Banka the Polish detective, not looking at Agent Roy.

"Passero?" Banka said. A confused smile formed. "What the hell are you doing here?"

Managing his own surprise, playing his part, Roy said, "Who's this?"

"This is Nicky Passero," said Banka, introducing him like a curiosity. "Nicky Pins. Runs the bowling alley on West Grand." Banka looked back and forth between Nicky and Marie, trying to figure this out. "This your babysitter, Mrs. Kumerow?"

Nicky said, "We're setting up a birthday party for her little boy at the Lanes."

Marie said, without missing a beat, "He loves bowling. And I love planning ahead."

She was good. Her father's daughter.

Nicky said, "What'd I walk into here?"

Banka said, "We're having a party too. A search party."

Nicky said, "That's not my kind of party."

Roy, staring at Nicky—who knew what he was thinking?—said, "Get his ID."

"No need," said Banka. "Nicky Pins is known."

Roy said, "Convenient, him being here in Accardo's daughter's home."

Banka looked back and forth from Marie to Nicky. "Bowling alley owners make house calls forty-five minutes outside the city?"

All the cops around insulated Nicky from Roy for the time being, but Nicky knew this mishap was going to fuck up his game in the long run. "Can I go?" said Nicky.

Banka said, "You *should* go."

Nicky said to Marie, "Thank you, Mrs. Kumerow, and I'll be in touch."

Roy, ignoring Nicky now, turned to Marie, warrant in hand. "Mrs. Kumerow, we're paying your father a courtesy here."

Marie snarled, "Yeah—right."

Nicky stepped out the open front door onto the walkway. Behind him, Banka said, "Do you have a key or don't you?"

"What I have," said Marie, "is my father's lawyer's phone number. I'm gonna need all your names and badge numbers..."

Banka walked through the rooms of the home of the boss of the Outfit, marveling at his unprecedented access, of which other law enforcement organizations could only dream. He stood in the Chairman's bedroom while his men searched closets and drawers. Banka thought about the thieves who had broken in there, and shook his head. Even if the lion is out of his cage, don't you still think twice before stepping inside? It wasn't the lack of respect that shocked him most—it was the lack of fear. Why let the lion get the scent of you?

Banka left the bedroom and was running his gloved hand over the ornately carved railing along the upstairs hallway when he heard a discussion on the first floor below him.

Roy said, "You're telling me you don't know what's down there."

Accardo's daughter Marie, who had driven herself over from Barrington Hills after getting a sitter for her two children on short notice, said, "I have never been in the basement."

"Never?" said Roy, in disbelief. "You grew up in this house."

"You obviously don't understand, so I won't waste my time trying to explain it to you," she told him. "But when Dad says it's not allowed—that's it. It's not allowed."

Banka joined them downstairs. The police locksmith was on one knee in front of the secret basement door. Marie Kumerow, arms crossed, hair covered comically by a soft-brimmed gardening hat, stood next to Accardo's lawyer, Bernard. When Bernard had offered Agent Roy his business card upon arriving, Roy had snatched it and tucked it into his jacket pocket with such contempt, he might as well have put it in his mouth, chewed, and swallowed. Roy had no qualms about strutting around inside the lion's cage.

The door opened and the locksmith stepped back, his job done. Roy, wearing gloves and paper booties over his shoes like Banka, went right down the revealed stairs. Lawyer Bernard followed.

Banka, pausing at the door, said to Marie Kumerow, "If you ever wondered what's down there, now's your chance."

She followed him down into the cool, dry air. Banka wasn't as roughshod as Roy. He poked his head into the conference room, stepped inside the office, looked at the hunting trophies—but treated things respectfully, the way you would upon entering a dead man's house. Roy went from room to room like the unloved nephew looking for mattress money.

Roy was arguing with Bernard in the pantry. Behind another fake door there was the very real door of a sealed vault with a dial lock. "You're his lawyer, and you're telling me you can't get him on the phone to give us the combination?"

"Mr. Accardo is not reachable by telephone," said Bernard, in his sixties, dressed in a European-tailored suit, briefcase in hand.

Roy shook the warrant pages at him. "This says we can take as long as we need to. You want us here all night? It's gonna happen. We can get real comfortable. How would he like a crew of guys burning their way into his vault, like Levinson's again, because I'm getting inside, one way or another."

Bernard sighed. He set down his briefcase on a countertop and clicked open both locks, raising the cover just enough to insert his hand, pulling out a piece of paper and closing and relatching the briefcase.

Bernard handed Roy the paper, which contained the vault's combination.

"Look at that," said Roy flatly. "What do you know."

He went to work on the dial, left, right, left. He pulled the lever, and the lock disengaged with a sound like a piston firing dully. The heavy vault door opened, Roy pulling it wide.

Roy entered the strong room, roughly eight by fifteen by ten feet. Some shelves to the left contained revolvers, boxes of ammunition, and a few antique pistols. Roy found no jewelry whatsoever, only cash, and lots of it—all neatly wrapped in paper bands bearing the names and insignia of three different Las Vegas banks.

Roy flipped through a few packets of currency and did some rough math. "Could be a quarter million dollars here." He stepped out and showed one of the packets to Bernard. "Do you have receipts for any of this?"

Bernard said, "Of course not."

Roy summoned the police photographer. "Take pictures of every-thing inside," he said. "Then confiscate it. We're seizing it all."

Bernard said, "I object absolutely, Agent. You have neither claim nor right to my client's money."

"These are ill-gotten gains, unless you can prove differently."

"I must contradict you, Agent. The burden of proof is on you."

Roy smiled again. "Not on me," he said, lobbing the bundle of Las Vegas cash back onto a shelf inside the vault. "It's on government lawyers."

"This is blatant harassment," said Bernard.

"Tell your client, Mr. Tony Accardo, that if he wants his money back, and his toy guns too, he can file a claim just like any other taxpayer."

Roy looked to Banka for his approval. Banka was leery of any lawman acting too overconfidently. Hubris, like bad luck, had a way of finding you.

"Feliks!"

Banka recognized the voice and went back down the hall to a utility room where a cop he liked, named Donnelly, had pulled open a steel panel in the stone wall. Donnelly was shining his flashlight inside.

"Incinerator," said Donnelly back over his shoulder. "Ever seen one in a private home?"

"Never," said Banka.

"Got something?" asked Roy, coming up behind Banka.

"Take a look," said Donnelly, turning his flashlight over to Banka.

Inside the burn space, among a landscape of soft ash and charred debris, was a partially melted pair of eyeglasses. The specs were upside down in the cinders. The lens frames were extra wide.

Roy called for a folder to be brought over to him. After flipping through various long-lens surveillance photographs of the exterior of the Ashland Avenue house, he pulled out a blown-up exposure of Michael Volpe locking the front door.

"What do you think?" he asked, handing the photograph to Banka.

Banka, after a good look at the photo, which showed Accardo's missing houseman wearing the very same eyeglasses, nodded in agreement.

Nicky pulled Chuckie into his office with him when, as he expected, Detective Banka came by to follow up. He was alone, no Agent Roy—whom Nicky had barred from coming inside again, and anyway, having visited twice before in different guises, Roy's third visit would not have been a charm.

The aging Polish detective stood in the open doorway, wearing a decade-old wool sport coat and a necktie so wide the knot was the size of a child's fist. Nicky leaned back in his chair, its creaking springs punctuating his answers, his half-eaten roast beef sandwich waiting on a paper plate on the blotter. Chuckie leaned against the counter to Nicky's right, smoking.

"How well you know Accardo's daughter?" said Banka. "And how well does her husband know *you*?"

"Nothing like that," said Nicky, scowling it away. "Joe Batters's daughter calls about renting the Lanes for her kids' party, it makes good sense to go personally."

"Does it, though? After two of your guys go missing?" Banka shrugged. "You didn't think it might be a trap?"

"Never occurred to me."

"Really." Banka believed none of this but couldn't come up with a reason for Nicky's visit that fit. "By the way," he said, thumbing back at the lounge, "how is it a felon like you has a liquor license?"

"I don't," said Nicky. He stuck his own thumb out, at Chuckie. "He does."

"Convenient," said Banka, the brim of his hat in his hands. "What do you know about Accardo flying out to Palm Springs?"

Nicky said, "What do I make of it? This is a bowling alley, not a travel agency."

Banka processed the answer, suspicious of the quickness of Nicky's response. "Who do you think offed your friends?"

Nicky said, "Solving crimes is your job," remembering now why he didn't like Banka.

"Last time Bragotti and Santangelo were in here, anything stand out?" said Banka. "They talk about meeting anyone, going anyplace?"

Nicky said, "*Now* you're interested in what happened to them?"

Banka said, "Well, now I'm interested in you."

Nicky didn't like that. "There wasn't anything they said or did that stood out, no."

Chuckie said, "Except the Rolex."

Banka looked at Chuckie. "How's that?"

Chuckie said, "Crease had a Rolex watch he was showing off."

Banka straightened, his shoulder coming off the doorframe. "A Rolex watch? Any idea where he would have picked that up?"

Chuckie shrugged.

Nicky thought fast and said, "He said he got it secondhand off some guy in from Rockford, I think."

The detective smiled widely. "Secondhand, you *think*," said Banka. "A guy on your crew shows up with the cost equivalent of a new car on his wrist—and you *think* he got it off some guy in Rockford, but you don't care to know how?" Banka added a nod to his smile, fiddling with his hat brim again. "Let's try this. Either of you two know Johnny Salita?"

Banka was coming down harder than Nicky expected. Nicky wondered if Roy knew that Banka was here now—or if Banka was doing this on his own.

Chuckie answered, "Nope."

Nicky said, "I know his father-in-law, runs a tool and die. I've seen Salita around, never in here. But I don't know him. Why?"

Banka said, "Bragotti and Crease Man, they know him?"

"Not that I know," said Nicky.

Banka nodded, his reaction difficult for Nicky to read. "Bragotti told his wife he was heading to see you, last time she saw him."

"I know that very well. She told me. But he wasn't."

"And you have an alibi for that night?"

Nicky said, "That's really fuckin' cold, but yeah. I was with my wife and son at home."

The detective smiled, but again it was impossible to read. "Let's be honest here? Whether I end up pulling them out of the trunk of a car or up from the bottom of the river, or dragging their bones out of a shallow grave, Sal Bragotti and Frank Santangelo are never walking in that door again. And if you ain't personally worried, Passero—I don't know, maybe you should be."

Nicky took Nicholas to a batting cage since he didn't want him hanging around the Lanes with everything going on. Nicholas had a good stance and a solid swing, but he was still a little afraid of the ball, understandable because the cage machine was pretty fast and more than a little wild. But when he made contact, he drove the ball, which put a big smile on his face, and therefore his father's face too.

Nicky found an ice cream parlor that sold malteds and old-fashioned candies, all in the 1950s style. Nicholas ordered a triple-scoop dish—vanilla, chocolate, strawberry—which he attacked with a long sundae spoon. Nicky had a root beer float, which he drank through a stiff red-and-white-striped paper straw, and they sat in the front corner window emblazoned with old-timey shop lettering. That was when the argument started.

"It's just not done," Nicky told his son. "This is a real problem."

Nicholas said, "Why not?"

"You have to choose. This is basically against the law."

"Why do I have to?"

"Because! You gotta!"

"No, I don't." The boy was laughing.

"This is serious business," said Nicky. He pointed to the sweat-bands on the boy's slender wrists. All the kids wore them, emulating big leaguers. Nicholas wore a blue Cubs-branded sweatband on his left wrist and a white White Sox sweatband on his right.

Nicky said, "They take kids away from their parents over stuff like this."

Nicholas shook his head willfully and ate another spoonful.

"You pick one team," said Nicky, "and that's your team. You don't put money on the red *and* the black. You gotta make a choice. Let's start with who's your favorite player? Chet Lemon? Manny Trillo?"

"Reggie Jackson." Who slugged for neither the Cubs nor the White Sox, but for the New York Yankees.

"Okay, I'm losing my mind here. Let's do this," said Nicky. "Say tomorrow, the Cubs are playing the White Sox. Say it's the World Series—which of course will never happen, not in a million, million years, these being professional sport teams that play in Chicago, but say it. Then what? Who are you rooting for? And don't say both."

Nicholas twisted his mouth, which he did when he was deliberating. "Who's pitching?" he said.

"Oh boy," said Nicky, enchanted by his boy's stubbornness but playing the opposite. "I give up."

"What about you? Your team?"

"You know the answer. Cubbies all the way."

"Was that your dad's favorite team?"

"No, see, he grew up in Battle Creek, on the other side of the lake, so he was a Detroit fan, the Tigers. The Old English D. I had actually forgotten that about him."

Nicholas stirred the chocolate and vanilla together in his dish. "What happened to him?"

"I told you this—you know what happened. He left. He went out one day, driving his truck, like any other day, to hear my mother tell it. Never came home. That was it."

"You think he got lost?"

"No, I don't think he got lost. I like that, though. You know what I used to think? I thought maybe he got a new family somewhere."

Nicholas said, "Why would he want a new family?"

"I don't know that he did. I just thought for a long time—assumed, after he never came back—that he didn't like the family he had. In the absence of any evidence to the contrary, as they say." Nicky smiled. "I blamed myself for a while. Maybe it was something I did. But then—then I grew up, I got my own family, and I'm like, that's impossible. It's completely impossible—it don't compute. To go away and never look back? Seriously, I know now, he must have got into some trouble, something he couldn't fix or get out of."

"Like what?"

Nicky sighed and took a better look at his son. The boy wasn't fishing for information; he was looking for reassurance. "Let me guess," Nicky said. "Your mom tell you about Uncle Sal and Frankie?"

Nicholas nodded.

"I see," said Nicky. "Okay. That explains it. Look. Me? I'm going nowhere. You couldn't get rid of me if you tried."

"Are you going to move in back home?"

"That's a separate question, and a very good one. You ask your mom that?"

Nicholas nodded.

"And?"

Nicholas shrugged.

"It would be pretty good, wouldn't it? I think so."

Nicholas nodded.

"Tell you what. Here's what I do when I got a decision to make or I want to know what's gonna happen in my future. You and I will get Polynesian food later, a pupu platter, with the blue flame you like, but really what we're doing is, we're going for the fortune cookies so we can crack 'em open and see what they say."

Nicky sat back from the table, excited by this idea. As he did, he scanned the street through the window and noticed a black Trans Am with gold rims parked a few stores down. A truck passed before he could make the driver, who was doing something in the front seat, not looking Nicky's way.

For sure, it was Stingy. Accardo's young gun.

Everything changed in that moment. Nicky stood up so fast, his iron-legged chair fell backward, clattering, startling Nicholas.

"Wait here," Nicky said.

He pushed out the double doors catty-corner to the street, crossing traffic to the Trans Am's driver's-side window—reaching in and grabbing the kid by his collar.

Stingy's mouth was full, a half-eaten sandwich on butcher paper in his lap. In the passenger seat, his no-name buddy nearly spilled his soda cup out of fright.

His head in the window, Nicky said, "What the fuck is this?"

Stingy's buddy was reaching for something under his seat.

Nicky told him, "Don't."

Stingy choked down his food. "The fuck—?"

Nicky shook him. "What are you tailing me for?"

Stingy looked at him, outraged. He held up his sandwich. "I'm eating my lunch!"

"Bullshit." Nicky shook him again, wanting to smack the kid's pretty little pout. He glanced back at the ice cream shop window, Nicholas sitting alone, watching him. Nicky turned back. "I'm with my son, you piece of shit!"

Nicky released Stingy's collar with a shove.

"Where is he?" said Nicky. "The Man. Is he here? I wanna know."

"Huh?"

"*Where is he?*"

Stingy said, "Palm Springs, right?"

His buddy said to Nicky, "Jesus, man, get a hold of yourself."

They had the dumb act down. They excelled at idiocy. A coincidence this was not.

Nicky said, "I want a number I can reach him at. Not at his house—a number he can talk from. I need to talk to him." Nicky pulled his head out of the window. "And you two fucking stay away from me."

How's the weather there?" came the growl.

It was raining when Nicky finally connected with Accardo, coins spilled over the metal shelf beneath the street-corner pay phone. The rapping of the raindrops against the booth made reading Accardo's voice even more difficult over the long-distance connection.

"'The actual weather?" said Nicky, looking for meaning. "Or like— 'the weather'?"

"I dunno," said Accardo. "Both?"

Nicky shook his head to clear his mind. The handgun from behind the counter at Ten Pin sat heavy between his belt and his lower back. "The weather is shitty," answered Nicky. "Like everything."

"Tell me about it," said Accardo. "I can't set foot inside my own home again. The thought of those pricks in there. Probably didn't even wipe their fuckin' feet. It's ruined for me. My *home*."

Nicky was in no mood to hear his complaints. "What happened to Michael Volpe?"

"It's very worrying," said Accardo. "Clarice is a wreck over it."

Nicky saw a distorted reflection of his face in the telephone's chrome plating, lit sickly yellow from the weak light overhead. "You didn't hear what they found in your basement incinerator?"

"He must've thrown an old pair in there," said Accardo.

Nicky mashed his palm into his eyes, running it down over his mouth. He watched cars sluicing past on the slick road. "Why am I being followed by your pet cat, Stingy?"

"Ah, that." Nicky could envision Accardo waving it off. "He told me about that lunch misunderstanding when he called to set this up. He's all right, he's just green."

"*I was with my son*," said Nicky, too fast. He collected himself and repeated it, slow. "I was with my son."

"Your son. Getting big, huh?"

"You're following me now? Am I not loyal?"

"That was just a misunderstanding. Listen to me now. You done a lot for me, Nicky. I don't forget that. Okay? Your loyalty's been a blessing."

"I *am* loyal," said Nicky, near his breaking point. "It isn't fuckin' right."

"I have two sons, Nicky, you know that. Both adopted. You, Nicky—you're like my third adopted son. I mean that now."

Nicky was suddenly, shudderingly, overcome by emotion. Almost gasping, breathing carefully to keep from breaking into tears. But deeply, strangely moved. "Thank you," he said with no voice, mostly breath.

"I gotta go, Nicky. I got tails too, here, I'm watched all the time. They're in my house, Nicky. I feel it. Could really use you out here. Grand jury's coming up with racketeering now. Stacking all the trunk hits up, like a pattern. I gotta ask you for one more thing. You're the only one who can do it, why I'm coming back to you. I want you to talk to Salita, Nicky. I want you to reach out to him, tell him I'm ready to make a deal."

Nicky said, "Are you? Ready to deal?"

"No. But you tell him I am. You talk to Salita and deliver him to me, Nicky. I gotta go."

The line went dead. Nicky hung up the receiver, his hand shaking, still stunned by Accardo's affection for him. So unusual. So out of character. It was almost like—a goodbye.

"Oh shit," Nicky said aloud. "Oh shit!"

Nicky went out the folding door into the rain, leaving all his coins behind.

Nicky cleared off his office desk, sweeping a bunch of things—purchase orders, old inventory lists, receipts he didn't need—into the trash can. He surveyed the office again, having already junked a third of what was in his files, getting things in order.

Chuckie stood inside the door, wearing his custom two-tone Ten Pin Lanes bowling shirt with *Chuckie* in script on a patch over his breast and the unneeded left sleeve sewn shut. "Is this about that detective who was here?"

Nicky was in perpetual motion, pulling down a couple of notes tacked up to the wall and trashing them too. The only thing slowing him down was the gun in his belt, keeping it from falling out. His energy was off the charts. "Just overdue. I been meaning to take you through this for a while." He pointed to the file cabinet. "Packet of papers, back of the bottom drawer. Everything you need for the premises, the AMF certification, all that. And a few grand loose, just in case, smooth over anything might come up."

Chuckie nodded warily. "Okay."

"You're cut in on the Lanes—your piece is set. It's one-third you, one-third me, one-third Helena."

"One-third me?"

"You're in for a third. That wasn't always clear?"

"Nicky, I never put anything in. A stake."

"You carried this place when I was away. You were already on paper as a partner for the liquor license, but I fixed it a year and a half ago, made it real. You're good."

"Nicky, I . . ."

"Pay attention now. So, that's the business itself. Ten Pin Lanes. The real estate, this property, anything happens to me, the physical building and the whole lot flows directly to Helena. You don't have to do nothing, just—just make sure you don't let her sign anything anyone might put in front of her, right? She's not a fan of the Lanes— she doesn't know or care about the business—but this is her nut, her nest egg, and Nicky Jr.'s, anything happens. You make sure no one tries to move in on her claim. Got it?"

"Nicky . . ."

"Chuckie." Nicky put his palms together in prayer. "Tell me you got it."

"I got it."

"Thank you." Chuckie wasn't much, but he was solid. "There's also a paper in there, outlines my arrangement with Darryl and his group who owns Clyde's. It's a small piece, five percent. Let 'em buy you out, okay? Put that money into the Lanes here."

"Who's gonna run the place?"

Nicky stopped and looked at him. "You, Chuckie. You would run it. It would be yours. A third yours, two-thirds Helena. That's another reason why I'm putting up your stake. I trust you and I'm counting on you. To take care of things—if and only if."

Chuckie rubbed his unshaven chin. "Jesus, Nicky. Okay. Don't worry about nothing."

Nicky said, "Everything's good. This is all just in case."

"Nicky—I don't know what you got going, but you need a one-armed soldier, just say the word."

"I don't need a one-armed soldier. I need a one-armed friend."

Chuckie nodded, eyes a little bugged out from the talk. "This is a lot to take in, you giving me a piece of this."

"You're a fuckin' war hero, Chuckie." Nicky patted Chuckie on his good shoulder. "Who deserves it more?"

Nicky went out past him but didn't get five steps before a long-faced man he didn't recognize, looking like an undertaker but wearing a khaki jacket and casual pants, stopped him. "Nicholas Passero?"

Nicky saw the envelope in his hand. "Hey, I'm in a rush, envelopes go to Chuckie here—"

The guy pressed the envelope into Nicky's hand, too thin for a payoff. He showed Nicky his billfold, which contained credentials and a badge.

"FBI," said the agent. "This is a grand jury subpoena. You've been served."

Roy said, "Are you a subject or a witness?"

"I don't know," said Nicky. "It was all legalese. But what the fuck?"

"There's two kinds of grand jury subpoenas. Subpoena ad testificandum is to bring people in to testify. Subpoena duces tecum is to have evidence brought in. Did it ask for anything like photographs, phone records?"

"No."

"Okay. So you have three choices but really only one. You comply, you petition a court that you don't have to comply, or you refuse to comply and get held in contempt. So you'll comply."

"I gotta fuckin' show up and talk under oath? Why me?"

"You had two friends go missing, Nicky," said Roy. "They're looking into all the trunk jobs and disappearances. And there is nothing I can do for you about that."

They were sitting in the parking lot of another dry cleaner's, Rocket Cleaners, a spaceship blasting off on the road sign.

Nicky said, "I just want to know, you know—what the fuck?"

"Pretty simple. You'll get a lawyer, you'll show up. You have nothing to hide, right? Maybe you'll even tell them the truth—who knows? I'd like to get you under oath myself."

"You're so fuckin' glib. There's nothing you can do? And what about Banka leaning all over me?"

"Look, if I tell Banka to lay off you," said Roy, "he'll know."

"Know about this?" said Nicky, meaning them talking. "He don't already?"

"I told you, nobody does."

"It better stay that way. He asked a lotta fucking questions."

"That's his job, you know."

"I don't like him."

"It would break his heart if I told him that."

"Banka's been around a long time," said Nicky.

"That's why I brought him on. He's got a solid reputation."

"So don't I," said Nicky. "And look at me here."

"Sitting in a parked car with another adult male," said Roy.

Nicky's ears burned. "Fuck off."

Roy said, "You're just trying to get me off the subject of Accardo. By the way, it was nice running into you at his daughter's house."

"Come on," said Nicky.

"You sure do get around. You know what? I'm not even mad. Seriously. Know why? Because I got him on the run. Joe Batters is holed up back out there in Palm Springs—and he may never set foot in Chicago again, not until a trial. I got him on the ropes and no way I'm letting up."

Nicky said, "You been here three years, right? This system, the way things go here, has been in place for fifty. Ask your good pal Banka."

Roy shook his head. "Accardo went out too far this time. He lost his way. Now he's scared, thinking he can climb out of this, trying to pull the ladder up after him. His man Volpe being the prime example. He'll do whatever it takes, but he's running out of people to eat bullets for him. Tell me I'm wrong."

"You got all the answers. You don't need me."

Roy said, "I got a call last night, late, to come into Central Precinct. A hooker got picked up, priors. She was trying to trade out, said she had information on the trunk murders. Why Banka called me in. This young lady described for me an incident involving three guys confronting two of the murdered thieves, Rhino Guarino and Cue Stick Pino, last time she saw them."

Nicky remembered the hooker whose apartment they'd taken over before Rhino arrived with the lockbox. Roxie, her name was. Made a good sandwich. Nicky went on the attack.

"Whores sell anything to anyone to deal them out of trouble."

Roy nodded. "That's why you nail down details, and she had some. She was pretty specific. Most compelling part was about a Rolex wristwatch."

Nicky frowned, fighting to remain relaxed. "Yeah. Right. How soft do you think I am?"

Roy smiled. "You think I'm playing you here?"

"You're trying to link my guys to those guys. There are a lot of Rolexes around."

"Maybe in your world. She was locked in a bedroom the whole time, but she heard it. I didn't say 'Rolex.' She did."

Nicky nodded, saying, "Right, sure." Fearing retaliation, she had wisely taken herself out of the story, unable to identify anyone. Smart girl. Good survival instincts.

Roy said, "I could also tell you that somebody else saw someone drive Vin Labotta's car out of his parking spot at the tile store, early in the morning after he went missing. Someone who wasn't Vin Labotta, but who fits Frankie Santangelo's description pretty good."

Nicky said, "Somebody saw somebody who looked like they might be somebody else? Forget about holding up in court, that doesn't even hold up in this car."

"Non-denial denial," said Roy. He slid a piece of paper out of his inside jacket pocket, unfolded it. "Any idea what this is?"

He handed it to Nicky: a photostat copy of a smaller page of handwritten notes and a bunch of crossed-out words, torn out of a wire-bound notebook.

Roy said, "We received it in the mail. No note, no return address. Ran it by our handwriting experts. They did some comparison tests. They say one hundred percent certainty, that's Tony Accardo's handwriting."

Nicky was looking at a copy of a page torn out of Accardo's stolen notebook. Salita, tired of being stalled, had followed through on his threat. The words didn't make sense, random letters interspersed with geometric symbols, such as triangles and squares. Maybe—probably—the one-page sample wasn't enough for them to be able to figure it out.

Nicky said, "What is all this? What's it mean?"

Roy said, "I'm asking you."

"You need me to tell you this is some kinda code?" Nicky handed it back.

Roy looked it over before refolding it, tucking it away. "The numbers could be bribe amounts. This confounded us until I remembered—all this started with a burglary where nothing was stolen."

Roy was watching Nicky for his reaction. Nicky had walked into something here. Roy wanted to see him squirm. "Why are you telling me all this?" he said.

"Because," said Roy. "Because I've got a pair of bowling shoes I want you to try on for size."

Roy had the upper hand now, and his eyes shone. Nicky played like he was curious. "I'm listening."

"No bullshit, no half-truths. It's time. You're gonna help me get Accardo. I've already stuck multiple arrows in him—so this is almost humane. There's a few ways to do this, but only one way that benefits us both."

Nicky said, "Both?"

"Salita's sitting on something. That's clear. He's hiding out somewhere, and he must have help. We like him for a couple of minor break-ins on the North Side, staying-alive money. But I'm guessing he's taken this about as far as it can go. You don't have to deliver me Accardo personally, stick your neck out that far. If you can get me to Salita, I'll do the rest. And if it goes the way I think it goes, all the dominoes fall. Accardo, sure. Doves Aiuppa and Jackie Cerone after him. Other area bosses. On and on. You with me so far?"

Nicky said, "So far? There's more?"

"A power vacuum forms. Picture it. You talked about the system in place—you're exactly right: there's an organization, a structure. It needs someone to step in, to run it. I'm saying, with a little cunning on your part, and with a lot of behind-the-scenes pull from me—here and in Vegas—Nicky Passero, a.k.a. Nicky Pins, rises to the top."

Nicky laughed out loud. He prided himself on seeing angles. This was one he did not see coming. "That's fucking crazy."

"You can't see it because you're too close to it. You are perfectly placed. You know everybody and you have few or no beefs. If you went after it, if you chased the top spot, it wouldn't be characteristic—it would be a disaster. People would look at you twice. But if it gets suggested—right? If the house is burning down and people look around for somebody who's good with a hose? Then you're in. Somebody's got to be the Man. That's how the Outfit is built."

Nicky couldn't get his arms around it. The whole thing was beyond consideration, but the fascination for Nicky was in the design. Because maybe Roy was right: maybe it could work. This was like looking at your hand in hearts, holding the queen of spades and high cards in every suit, and seeing that by dumping your low cards early, *maybe* the round could end up playing itself out with you controlling the hands, taking every trick. Shooting the moon, turning a bad hand into a big win.

Throwing over everybody at the top was a great way to get

killed—but those notebooks held more firepower than any gun. Nicky said, "When did you come up with this?"

Roy smiled. "Okay. That's not a no. Think of what would fall to you. The city of Chicago and the Vegas skim. Nicky Pins, the next capo."

Nicky wasn't smiling anymore. If anything, he was short of breath. Whether it could work or not was almost beside the point. If a thing is possible—well, then the thought of trying it was temptation itself. He looked at Roy with amazement. But the hungry look in his FBI handler's eyes brought Nicky crashing back to earth.

"You're the devil," Nicky said. "You'd love this whole thing, of course. Because then you'd have the boss of the Outfit by the short hairs."

"I have you by the short hairs now, Passero. You're a midlevel guy at best, a worker, an earner, somebody who maybe had the boss's ear. You run book out of a bowling alley, and you're an FBI informant and at least a part-time queer. Where's that going? Sideways at the *very* best. I am offering you the keys to the kingdom. A partnership."

Nicky's face flushed. He hated Roy, almost as much as he hated himself.

"Or . . ." said Roy, "or you can go down with the rest of them. You're already holding a grand jury subpoena. Nothing else you can give me could save you from what is to come. If you even live that long— the way things are going." Roy laid his hand on Nicky's shoulder. His pale blue eyes held Nicky, his voice softer. "Or we can flip this and both come out on top. This is it, Nicky. Time to decide. Do you want to go down with Accardo—or ride to the top with me?"

Nicky couldn't go back to the Lanes after that. He couldn't think of what to do. He drove around awhile, trying to get his focus back, while also on the lookout for tails.

Weighing his options meant thinking about Roy. Hating the man, but also imagining a scenario where they combined forces, effectively running the city. An alliance more secretive than the one they already had. He couldn't stop himself from thinking about it. The audacity of this daydream union held great appeal for him.

But it was just that, wasn't it? A daydream. It was the *Edge of Night* fantasy version of their relationship: cop and criminal working together secretly as power brokers. Nicky needed to get away from Agent Roy, not closer, not enter into a bond with him more inextricable than the one they had now. His very life was in the guy's hands as it was.

No. More than anything, Nicky wanted to kill the past. Forgive himself of all the mistakes. Dry-clean himself. Get free.

His drive took him northwest to Dunning, to the body shop that, in the good times, had been their hangout. Nicky parked around the side, out of sight. It was colder inside than out. The garage was home to ghosts now, of killers and the thieves they'd killed. Nicky could feel Sally Brags and Crease Man watching him, their presence. He thought of the kids they had been, the plans they had made. How Nicky had let them down.

He tried to envision, for the umpteenth time, what his guys had walked into. The moment they knew that they were going to get what they had been giving. He made himself sick picturing it, which was the point.

Nicky had stopped pretending it wasn't Accardo who had ordered it. Accardo, who had once stood right there, in the very spot Nicky stood now, facing Labotta in the chair, at the start of it all. If Accardo did go down, that would mean no protection for those other two: Doves's grandnephew Stingy and his moronic friend. They would be dog food with Nicky as boss.

Nicky found three gasoline cans, each less than half-full. He dipped in rags to soak, laying them around the garage like wet socks. When he ran out of rags, he splashed the contents of the cans on every surface until they were empty, careful not to douse himself.

He ripped off the covers of the dozen or so Ten Pin Lanes matchbooks from his glove compartment—igniting each tuft of cheap phosphorus-and-carbon-tipped paper, setting multiple small fires. Then he went to his car, pulling out of the lot, across the street to watch and think.

Sam Giancana had warned him. Tony Accardo's apparent fondness for Nicky meant nothing. How far would Tony Accardo go to avoid prison? As far as he had to. As far as he *could* go.

If Nicky told Roy no, Nicky would be useless to him, and most likely Roy would let Nicky go down. Prison meant being pulled away from Helena and Nicholas, maybe forever. Prison meant other things too. Being owned by Agent Roy would be no worse than the extortive hold the bastard had on Nicky right now.

Wisps of dark smoke squeezed out from under the bottom and low sides of the closed garage doors first. The smoke grew faint, and for a minute Nicky feared the fire had gone out. Then it picked up again, angrily, billowing, the garage acquiring an orange glow. A window exploded, fire escaping, licking at the exterior walls, air being sucked in. Then flames started eating through the roof.

A funeral pyre for Sally Brags and Crease Man. Nicky took one long, last look, then drove away. Ten blocks later, he found a pay phone. Not an enclosed booth, but a freestanding Bell System phone mounted outside a closed sandwich shop.

Nicky emptied his pockets, dumping all the matchbook covers he found there, finding the card Johnny Salita had given him.

Nicky Pins. Loyal snitch. Truehearted fink.

His hands smelled of gasoline. Nicky played a dime and dialed the number.

A recorded voice said, "This is the answering service. Please leave your message."

Nicky said, "This is for Johnny Salita. Tell him Nicky Pins is ready to talk."

They folded their hands and bowed their heads, Helena saying grace before dinner. Nicky, at the head of the table, opened his eyes to watch his wife speak to God on their behalf, asking him to bless the food before them and to keep them healthy. He glanced at Nicholas, small hands dutifully bundled, ball-club sweatbands on his wrists. Then the moment broke. They opened their eyes as though waking.

"Amen," Nicky said.

They passed bowls of green beans and mashed potatoes, everything moving slowly for Nicky. He was trying to lock in this moment, forge memories of his wife and son in this place in time. But his brain kept crossing him up, taking him away from where he wanted to be—here—to the dangerous plan he had initiated, like a strong current pushing him out to sea.

Earlier, he had gone upstairs alone and pulled down a vinyl bag from the top shelf of the hall closet, where it had sat untouched for almost a decade. He had carried it to his bedroom bureau and lifted out the ball inside—a nicked-up urethane house ball, fourteen pounds, swirled blue and white like a marble version of Earth—stored along with the rental shoes he'd worn on the day, gifted to him by the bowling alley owner, and the signed and authorized score sheet. Inside a velvet clam box was the commemorative *300* ring he had been sent when the score was certified.

A perfect game in bowling meant throwing twelve balls for twelve consecutive strikes. One strike over each of the ten frames, then two more to pick up points on the bonus rolls. Three hundred points total.

For the first eight frames, Nicky remembered, he had been his usual self. He strutted up to the line each time, confident, focused. Bowling came easily to him; it always had. Until he reached that ninth frame. He balked; he hesitated. A moment of self-doubt. He shook it off and rolled the ball confidently. Another crashing strike.

But now, after putting up nine Xs in a row—neat across the scoring sheet—that empty box for the tenth, with the extra spaces next to it for the possible triple strike, loomed large. Perfection within reach.

The entire bowling alley had become aware of what was happening, and the place was quiet, which was unsettling, every eye turned his way. He went through his motions, and the ball rolled away down the lane and the pins fell. He hit the tenth. He had no memory of it now. Only that he had become acutely aware of what was at stake—and that his palm had begun to sweat. This had never happened before. He switched the ball from hand to hand, standing before the blower vent on the pin return, drying his right palm and fingers. When he gripped the ball and stepped to the back line for the eleventh time, setting himself, the pins seemed very far away and small.

He muttered something to himself, probably a curse. He shook off the tension, regripped the ball, shut out everything else, and went into his stride. Four paces, his arm rearing back, swinging forth, the ball spilling out onto the right edge of the lane.

At first, he thought he'd missed it. Not by much, but you get to know the rotation of your ball as it spins and glides and starts to catch the polished wood by friction, and Nicky thought it was off. The ball went into its hook at absolutely the last possible moment for success, coming back leftward across the lane, curling into the head pin, smashing through. A fraction of an inch too short, but luck was on his side, and the front pins fell away with enough force to bring down all ten.

There was no sigh of relief. Missing that ball would have freed him, he realized. Now he was closer still—not to perfection any longer, but to failure. It should have been the best he'd ever felt, but it was the worst he'd ever felt. He didn't want to throw the last ball. The pins listed in the distance, as though he were bowling on a boat. He couldn't get saliva to swallow. This was all interior. No one else had any idea he was melting down, having to force himself to throw one more ten ball.

At the time, Nicky didn't know he'd never bowl again—that this would be the last ball he'd ever throw. He loved the sport; that hadn't changed—but the nightmares of that game, of facing that last roll, everything on the line, never went away. That feeling of collapse from within. It was ridiculous, waking up feeling that same panic weeks, months later. But he came to realize that it wasn't about that one game. People are made for certain moments. He had thought he knew his world and his place in it, and then he stood on the line and realized he didn't. He dreaded being tested like that again, having to throw that twelfth perfect ball with everything on the line.

"Where are you?" asked Helena.

"I'm here," he said, resuming eating. "I'm very much here. Thinking."

"What about?"

"The future," he said, which was a lie, but also the truth.

Helena smiled. Things were good between them, cordial and easy, which gave him hope and made him nervous. Because Nicky also knew what every good bowler knows: rolling a strike is actually easier than having to pick up that one last pin sitting out there all alone.

Later, after cleaning up, Nicky stayed longer than normal, reluctant to leave. He worried that the world of this house and his family might go on without him, and what that would be like, all the things he would miss. Thoughts like that threatened to put him into a tailspin. Everything was going to work out, he told himself. But the clock on the wall said it was time to go.

Nicholas was watching the Harlem Globetrotters on *Wide World of Sports*, smiling at their basketball gags and stunts, and Nicky sat with him as long as he could. He would share the story of his perfect game with Nicholas someday soon, and the lessons of his imperfect life. The boy was almost old enough. Nicky reached over to tousle his sandy hair, and Nicholas looked up in a way that made Nicky realize their family didn't show enough physical affection. He bent down and kissed the boy's warm, smooth forehead, his son reacting with surprise.

"Gotta go," said Nicky. "I'll see ya."

Helena was standing by the kitchen sink window wearing a grass-green top and yellow slacks, smoking, traditional Polish music playing on the crackly AM radio station. Nicky wanted to watch her a moment as she looked pensively into their backyard, but she sensed him there and turned.

"You're leaving?" she said.

"I got a thing," said Nicky, moving through the room. "That was really perfect today."

"Perfect?" she said, with a laugh. "You want to take some with you?"

He pulled on his shop jacket, the straight-fitting blue windbreaker. "I'm full. It won't keep."

Helena nodded, stubbing out her cigarette. "I'll walk you out."

She followed him down the short, dark entrance hallway to the front door, out onto the stoop. The coolness of the late hour hit him, the stairs lying below, the sidewalk and the evening beyond. He wished he could stay, thinking of all the wasted days they had spent apart. He stalled awkwardly, swiping his hand through his hair, rubbing his face, nervous tics, looking back at her with a guilty smile.

"What's wrong, Nicky?" she asked.

Nicky reached for her suddenly, her bare biceps, giving her arm a squeeze. He kissed her on the lips, sweetly. Then he went down the steps, stopping on the bottom one, turning, looking back up at her.

She was concerned. Nicky started back up toward her, his hand on the cool iron railing, but stopped, unable to go all the way.

They had never talked about it. Nicky had never known how to, or what to say. Now a flock of words flew out of him.

"It was never you," he said. "Okay? It wasn't you."

Her confusion was silent. All in her face. She started to ask but didn't.

Nicky backed off, digging his hands deep into his pockets, and walked on.

Nicky waited, alone and at the arranged time, just back of the intersection of Clinton and Roosevelt on the edge of Little Italy, standing between a NO PARKING sign and a wire trash can. The decent weather and fading hours of the weekend brought out more foot traffic than usual for a Sunday evening. He looked over everybody who passed and didn't see anyone watching him particularly or looking suspicious. He didn't have his handgun   he knew he would be frisked. A lot of things could go wrong here, the vast majority of which he was helpless to prevent.

A squash-orange four-door Dodge Dart pulled to the curb directly in front of him. The passenger door was pushed open by the driver. Nicky bent down to look inside.

The driver was one of Salita's bodyguards, dressed in a black denim jacket, pressed black pants, and sunglasses. He opened his jacket, showing Nicky the gun in his belt. This didn't look promising. He pushed a few newspapers from the empty passenger seat onto the floor. "Let's go," he said.

Nicky climbed inside, closing the door, smelling aftershave warmed by the circulating heat. "Where to?" Nicky asked.

"Don't worry about it," said the bodyguard. With a hard spin of the steering wheel, he pulled away recklessly from the curb. There was a nasty *thud*, and Nicky saw, in his side mirror, a pedestrian in a navy-blue trench coat tumble over the back fender, sprawling on his back in the road.

The bodyguard slowed long enough to understand what had happened, not long enough to care. "Asshole," he said, and the engine lifted as he sped away.

The setting sun squeezed behind two skyscrapers, wind whipping off Lake Michigan as Nicky stood on a high rooftop in the middle of downtown Chicago. The bodyguard had let them in from the parking garage below, walked Nicky up three flights to a low-level floor, then to an elevator—Nicky seeing a directory listing law firms and insurance agencies—which took them to the top.

The roof door had been latched from the inside and was presently propped open by a bucket of roofing nails at the far corner of the tar-paper roof. The bodyguard sat on the edge of a wide vent fan grate, twenty feet away from Nicky, one hand warm in his pocket, the other holding the gun. Nicky was terrified of the height, the roof edged only by a low three-foot wall, not ten feet away. With the wind, just standing too near to the lip could be fatal. The only other way off this roof was through the propped-open door.

Johnny Salita stepped through that door, his hands buried deep in the pockets of a penny-colored parka that had seen better days. No hat, which wouldn't have lasted with the wind anyway, his untrimmed hair swirling around. His other bodyguard exited behind him, remaining near the open door.

The seated bodyguard stood as Salita walked past him. Salita scanned nearby roofs as he came, as though he might spot a sniper. Closer, Nicky saw that he was strung out, haggard, his skin patchy and unshaven. The earnest bullshitter Nicky had confronted inside Child World before Christmas was gone, maybe forever. Salita hunched his shoulders against the wind.

"I don't see a bag of money," he said. "Gimme one good reason my friends here don't throw you off this roof right now."

"Well, for one," Nicky said, "it would hurt me, badly."

"This guy," Salita said, directing his remarks to his bodyguard. "Nicky Pins, he plays like he's a scrounger. A nobody. He looks like one thing…but he's another. What you see ain't what you get."

"Get it all off your chest," said Nicky. "You'll feel better."

"Piped in straight to the top," said Salita. He scowled, turned his head to the left, spit. "How's your boss? How's Tony Accardo doing? Good?"

"Better than you, I'd say," said Nicky. "You're a bit of a mess, Johnny. You're shaky."

Salita laughed it off. "I'm up here with two guns," he said. "You're a piece-of-shit gofer. We'll see who's shaky. I guess he heard about my letters?" Salita's smile disappeared. "Maybe he's through stalling me now."

"I'm here to get assurance—your word, on your baby girl's life—that the notebooks are complete, nothing missing except the page you mailed out, no copies or photographs, and that this ends it, once and for all."

"I wanna know—what took you so long for you to come here and say that?"

Nicky shrugged. "It's not up to me. I'm just a piece-of-shit gofer."

"It's because Accardo thought he could top me. Hunt me down and rub me out. Probably you were behind it. Tried and failed. Hell, I'm surprised you're still here. Surprised you're alive to play along tonight. I thought for sure you were gonna pull something with your guys."

Nicky angled his head. "My guys?"

"The ones that shot at me at the tile shop. I didn't think you'd have the onions to come here alone."

It wasn't Salita, but Nicky already knew that.

The silence went on long enough that Salita angled his head as well. Realizing—smiling. "You don't got your guys no more. How about that."

Nicky said, "You've had too much time to think. Hide-and-seek is a tough game when played for real. Remember when I asked you for your word about the notebooks? Am I wasting my time here?"

Salita stepped closer, still six feet away, Nicky wary of getting rushed, thrown over the roof's edge. The man he saw before him was scattered and mentally starved, washed out, ragged. Playing this game of chicken was his only way out. Salita thumped his own chest. "I am a man of my word, Passero. What about you?"

Nicky nodded. "You're getting your money. Noon tomorrow."

Salita's eyes narrowed in doubt. He was riding a seesaw mentally, up and down. "All of it?" he said.

"You said two million. It's a lot of paper, by the way. Do I need to be the one to deliver?"

Salita nodded fast. "And nobody else."

The way he answered told Nicky something he had already assumed: that Nicky was going to be murdered at noon tomorrow. At least it wouldn't be tonight.

"It's a lot of work for me," said Nicky. "I don't know what I'm gonna carry it in yet. The sheer bulk. But we can't do it on a rooftop, for sure. Gotta be a car swap. Have you considered any of this logistically?"

Salita smiled, but the answer was no. "Car swap, huh?"

"I drive up, pop the trunk. You see it's good, everything there. I toss you the keys, you toss me the notebooks, and we're gone. It'll be a hot car—you ditch it wherever, make your own swap."

"No tricks."

"You choose the place and let me know. How about I phone your magic pager around eleven or so? You give me an address, and be real specific and clear. I don't want anything to go wrong."

Salita glanced at his nearest bodyguard, as though soliciting his opinion. The bodyguard gave no indication of what he was thinking. Salita said, "You'll come alone."

"I told you, if I can drive your money in, then I can do it alone. The only way. It's a shitload of paper."

Salita ran both hands back through his hair a few times, thinking. "He got it from the bank already?"

"Presumably. He ain't getting it from me."

"And nobody comes after me."

"Johnny, what do you want me to say? Take the money and fucking run. You named the price. This is what you wanted."

"Shut the fuck up."

"These are your terms. You'll be a rich man who ripped off the Outfit—that's your play."

"That's enough," said Salita, backing off, the skyline getting dark. "Fuck you."

"Fuck me," said Nicky. "Okay."

Salita backed off further, motioning for the bodyguard to retreat with him. "It goes down noon tomorrow!"

"High noon," called Nicky after him, not moving. "And hey—don't shoot the messenger, right?"

Salita turned and disappeared inside the roof door, followed by both bodyguards. Sweating, Nicky didn't wait long before jogging, then running to the door, for fear the wind would grab it somehow and slam it shut on him, trapping him up there all night. He got inside okay, hearing a door close below him, so he stood still, waiting for the footfalls to fade away. He turned back and looked out at the darkening cityscape under a sky made of pewter, scored by clouds.

Ninety minutes later, Nicky was still waiting in one of the corner phone booths he liked, his back and shoulders against the closed door, arms folded, dreading the ring of the phone.

Accardo had had Sally Brags and Crease Man clipped in order to save himself. He was going to clip Nicky too, if he had to—and face it, he had to. Salita thought he was the one holding Nicky's fate in his hands, and he was, but not in the way he understood. The only thing keeping Nicky upright and breathing right now was his link to Salita. Once he delivered the meet location to Accardo and Salita was wiped out, Nicky was through. And if by some miracle Nicky did survive, he would have to walk into the grand jury and take his oath. That was dead end number one.

Turning in Salita to Roy was another option, taking his chances with the notebooks, bringing down Accardo and all the top guys and hoping he didn't catch the hell that would follow. But if Salita and the notebooks did go to the FBI, the legal maneuvering would take months, even years, giving Accardo plenty of time to suss out who it was that knifed him. And then Nicky would see his family murdered before him. That was dead end number two.

Was there an option number three? Run, like Salita had? With both the Outfit and the FBI on his tail? Winding up shivering in a rathole like Salita, a hunted animal, waiting to be put down? Dead end number three.

He looks like one thing ... but he's another.

If only Nicky had listened to Sam Giancana. How had he not seen that this would all come back around on him?

All it takes to knock down the top boss is one fuckin' fink.

In a way, it was like killing Giancana had set free a curse, allowing it to come into Nicky. The hit that had married him to Accardo that night had also opened the door for Roy to walk into his life.

The problem was Nicky. Not wanting to believe or understand or acknowledge what he was. Was he blindly loyal or consciously deceitful?

He looks like one thing ... but he's another.

What was he?

And then the phone rang, as though with the answer. Nicky straightened so quickly, the booth shook and the pale light above flickered. He gripped the receiver handle—holding it for one more ring, feeling it vibrate—then picked up.

"Yeah?"

"Nicky?" Detective Kevin Quiston's heavy, soft voice. "It's me."

"I know it's you," said Nicky. "So?"

"I got it."

"You got it?" These words sent a surge of adrenaline through Nicky. "I didn't see anybody there. Who was it? The guy who got hit by the car? Blue trench coat?"

"That was my guy," said Quiston. "He didn't get hit—he walked into the car himself, stuck a bumper tracker under the fender, rolled off."

"Jesus," said Nicky. "That guy was fuckin' good."

"We retrieved it off the vehicle a couple of minutes ago. Nobody saw us."

"Did you see Salita?"

"No, I didn't see him."

"Okay," said Nicky. "But you're sure Salita is there?"

"He has to be, right? I did all I could without being made."

"I got it, good. What's the address?"

"North Halsted near Roscoe. Place called Anita's."

Nicky pulled out a pencil and was scribbling this down on a piece of paper. "Anita's?"

"Disco spot—your favorite music. A nightclub. Mostly Negro. Partly fag."

Nicky shut his eyes a second, then shook his head and opened them again. "Awright, good."

"You want me to report it in?"

"No, no. It can't come from you. Let me worry about that."

"Nicky," said Quiston, and Nicky was expecting this. "This is serious stuff."

"C'mon, Quiston," said Nicky. "We discussed this."

"Seriously. I'm outta my league here. This'll square us up, right? All the way?"

Nicky said, "Squared up for good. I told you."

"Okay," said Quiston. "*Fuck*. Okay."

"Okay," said Nicky, and hung up.

He flipped over the piece of paper on which he'd scribbled the address. On the other side was Accardo's lawyer's number, the one Accardo had told Nicky to use if he needed to set a call with him in Palm Springs. Next to that scrap of paper was a blank business card, the one Roy had given him, with his secure number written on it.

Between each piece of paper lay a single dime, heads up.

Nicky gripped his forehead and a lock of hair. He slid the dime off the tray and pinched it between his thumb and forefinger, tapping it on the metal, looking again at each phone number.

He could be feeding a dime into his own electric chair if he made the wrong move here. He picked up the receiver, put it to his ear. Then he plugged the dime into the slot.

The coin hit. A dial tone started. Nicky punched seven silver numbers on the keypad and waited for the connection to take.

A woman's voice answered. "Hello?"

Nicky swallowed. "Yeah, uh...it's the dry cleaner's. We found that lost garment."

"Hold please."

A soft *click*, followed by hold music, soft and inoffensive. Nicky leaned his elbow on the tray, the phone holding up his head. He heard himself breathing into the receiver.

The line picked up faster than he had expected. He stood upright.

"Yeah?" said Roy's voice.

"I got him. Salita. He's holed up in a nightclub near Wrigley. Could be he has more than one place, but he's there now, and he's strung out and twitchy. Time is of the essence. You need to go tonight—now."

"We can do that. You're sure? How do you know?"

"I know because I know. That's what you want from me, right?"

"Okay. Give me the address."

"Yeah." Nicky nodded, needing a moment. "So...I'm calling you with this."

"I know," said Roy. Nicky could hear him out of his seat and moving around his office, getting things together. "You made the right decision, Nicky."

"Maybe."

"Absolutely you did."

"Look—I'm being straight with you. Now I want you to be straight with me."

Roy said, "What are you talking about?"

"That night," said Nicky. The words didn't come easily. "That night at Merle's. What did you...Did you follow me in there?"

The sound of Roy moving around stopped. "What?" he said. "This is what you want to know right now?"

"That night," said Nicky, his breath hot suddenly, fogging the chrome-plated keypad. "You weren't following me." Nicky realized this because if Roy had been, he would have seen him at Accardo's beforehand—or Giancana's before that. "So you were watching Merle's?"

"I don't get this," said Roy.

"How did you know I was going there?" said Nicky, too loudly. "I didn't know I was going there—how did you?"

"What the fuck does any of this matter now?"

"It matters," said Nicky. "It fucking matters to me. Matters if... if we're gonna be working together. If Accardo goes down."

"Matters to you whether I was on the job that night... or ducking into a gay bar for a drink on my own time?" Roy was sounding out the words in order to figure out Nicky's intent. "Is that it?"

Nicky swallowed. He hated this. *Hated* it. But he needed to know.

Roy said, "Am I a part-time queer too?" His voice was incredulous. "After all this time, is this what you're asking me?"

Nicky closed his eyes. "That is what I am asking you."

After a moment, Roy laughed. "Jesus Christ, Nicky. Are you a full-time queer now? What is this? Just give me the fucking address, will you?"

"Were you watching that place... or did it happen?"

"Did *what* happen?"

"Why were you there?" said Nicky. "I need to know."

"I don't..." Roy wasn't laughing anymore, his voice having turned taunting. "Do you want to suck my dick? Is that what this is? This whole time?"

The pay-phone receiver trembled in Nicky's hand so hard he could barely hold it to his ear. Roy was mocking him now.

Roy said, "Nicky, give me the goddamn address!"

Nicky could not speak.

"What do you want me to say?" said Roy. "We can hold hands? Kiss but no tongue? You are a fucked-up piece of work, Passero."

"You were watching that place. Hoping to recognize somebody on your mug-shot list." Nicky was saying this mostly to himself, figuring it out. "Somebody you could trap and use."

"Passero, stop fucking around and *give me that goddamn address!*"

Nicky's face went cold. He picked up the paper with the address on it. He blinked away tears in order to read what he had written.

"North Halsted near Roscoe," he said. "Anita's."

"Anita's," repeated Roy, writing it down. "What is that, a nightclub?"

Nicky did not answer him.

"You better be right with this, Passero. You fuck with me here, I will end you."

Nicky hung up. His head rested on his hand holding the cradled receiver for a moment, then he crumpled both the torn piece of paper and the business card, stuffing them in his pocket.

He couldn't think about what was going to happen now. He had just released his twelfth and final ball. It was out of his hands. Let the falling pins do the work.

Banka had to pause his speech for an L train above them along the elevated tracks astride North Clark Street, a long city block west of Anita's, to rumble past. The staging area was a closed-off event parking lot across the intersection from a Cubs bar, just north of where the Red and Brown Lines diverged.

Banka had a hand-drawn map of the club's interior—dictated to him over the phone by the only person working in licensing and permits on a Sunday night—spread out on the hood of his Olds 88. A blown-up copy of John Salita's driver's license photograph was being circulated among the dozen cops in riot gear, who were under the command of two members of the Special Weapons and Tactics team.

"There's a maze of private rooms in the back," said Banka, resuming. "Offices too, storage and supply closets. Lots of doors. We don't know which one Salita might be behind. We don't know how much protection he might have."

Banka lifted the map, scrawled on four pieces of typewriter paper taped together, walking it over to the FBI detachment gearing up near Agent Roy's subcompact Bobcat. Four special agents, including Roy, strapped on and buckled up bulletproof vests, exuding their usual studied confidence, giving the map a glance and a nod. Roy slid his sidearm into a holster strapped over the right leg of his jeans.

Banka said, "You feel good about the quality of this information?"

Roy nodded with a small smile. He never shared information about his contacts, but they were well placed. Banka liked to play a guessing game in his own mind, and this particular tip narrowed down the list of possible candidates considerably.

"Guy we sent in earlier to scope out the place said it's a pretty full house for a Sunday night," Banka told him. "You're sure we need to go in strong now?"

Roy said, "Gotta be now. Like right now—let's go. I want this guy. We close in on him, front and back, he's got nowhere to go."

Banka nodded, returning to his contingent of riot cops. "For your information, Salita is a material witness and we want him in one piece, okay? To reiterate—no gas, no riot shields, batons only. This'll be mostly crowd control. Entry and extraction."

The cops grunted their acknowledgment. Banka looked to the SWAT guys, who each gave him a gloved thumbs-up. Banka checked the stragglers behind them, who nodded, geared up. He recognized a few familiar faces, including Kevin Quiston, among them. It wasn't unusual for guys already on the clock to want in on a tac raid, and the more the merrier. What Banka wondered was, what was a plainclothes property-crimes detective doing working on a Sunday night?

The FBI agents loaded into their vehicles. The riot cops boarded two SWAT trucks, going first, Banka falling in behind them. Roscoe was a one-way, so they diverted north, turning right under the L tracks, down a residential side street that dumped them onto North Halsted. One SWAT truck turned left, the rest of the vehicles rolling up across the street from the sign reading ANITA's in a thin, angled font, the *T* fashioned in the shape of a cocktail glass.

There was no line to get inside. Two Black bouncers in wide-collared shirts stood at attention as the cops emptied out and advanced. Banka badged them and did the announcement, one of them hurrying inside the club, the other coming at them, looking for an explanation. He was taken down hard on the sidewalk, thick arms wrenched behind his back. Banka pointed a pair of riot cops inside after the other one.

Banka followed them in, holding up his badge to a young woman with large, fake eyelashes behind the glass teller's window. She slammed the cash register shut and yelled to someone nearby, maybe in the coatroom. Banka stepped past the second bouncer, already on the floor. Two more riot cops rushed past him through a heavy curtain leading to a wide club space with a crowded dance floor and pumping disco music.

Inside the fortified office that used to be the money room—Anita's previous incarnation had hosted after-hours dice and card games in the back rooms—Johnny Salita slid a baggie of cocaine out from the top drawer and did two more small bumps off the desk. Merc was getting some shut-eye in the easy chair that folded out into the lumpy bed where Salita slept. The Carter brothers, Merc and J. B., were taking a grand a week to keep Salita hidden here, while their cousin, the manager of Anita's, rated half as much again for the back room and for his silence.

Salita tipped back his head, letting his nasal juices flow the coke back to his sinuses and his brain beyond, nostrils raw from sniffling. During club hours, six nights a week until two a.m., Salita lived like a deaf man underwater, foam rubber plugs wedged into his ears, which filtered but did not completely mute the pulsating disco beat. The cocaine didn't make things much better, only different; if he did too much, it turned him into an animal stalking around in its cage.

But this was it. The last night of torture, the end in sight. Salita was working on every possible angle for the exchange tomorrow but thinking mostly defensively: above all else, he could not bear the thought of being double-crossed by Old Man Accardo and Bowling-Ball Passero. He had an old taxi map book open on the desk next to his vodka tonic, circling potential locations for the swap. Someplace busy enough that he wouldn't be ambushed, someplace with exit options so he couldn't get bottled in, someplace near roads that could get him away as fast as possible. He thought about bringing more guys in to help him last minute, but that was problematic too. The Carter brothers were counting on a bonus at the end of this, which they had earned. But they knew a big payday was coming. Salita needed to keep half an eye on them as well.

He was running all this double-time through his over-cranked brain when the red light bulb high on the wall near the door started flashing. All these weeks, Salita had never seen it light up before. He called to Merc, who also wore earplugs and couldn't hear him. Salita got up and shook the young militant for hire, who jerked straight up out of a dream, reaching for his assault rifle.

He saw the raid signal flashing, triggered from the booth up front. Merc got to his feet and grabbed the weapon leaning against the wall, unlocking the barricade lock bar across the door, pulling it open.

Two people ran past, fleeing the dance-floor area, moving deeper into the VIP area. J. B. came running up, handgun drawn. He was yelling at them to go, and Salita couldn't hear his voice over the music but read his expression just fine.

Salita turned back to gather the things in his desk, but a hand on his shirt collar yanked him back. He fought Merc's grip, yelling that he couldn't leave without his things, but the bodyguard couldn't hear him and didn't care, hauling him out of the office into the dark warren of hallways.

They moved past curtained doorways and around stacked cases of Smirnoff and Hennessy, club patrons running both ways. They turned the corner to the rear exit, only to see—the door to the alley lot open, two barbacks fighting uniformed riot cops pushing inside.

The dance floor was flanked on both sides by lounge tables with high-backed rattan chairs. The disc jockey's booth was in the far-right corner, now vacated, music still pumping.

With the high, swirling lights, the funky, bumping bass, and the

Mylar-covered walls, Banka had been plunged into sensory overload. The Black patrons on the dance floor regarded Banka and the other white cops first with disgust, then with fear. There was a panic of swiveling hips in short dresses and long, flared slacks running for cover. Someone—not a cop, though they never figured out who— fired two gunshots into the ceiling from the right-side lounge area, and that started everyone screaming.

Riot cops rushed toward the sound of the gunshots, a fight having broken out. Banka saw Roy with his badge held aloft, bulldozing his way through the swarming crowd toward the rear. Banka tried to follow but was pushed sideways by exiting dancers. Banka fought his way along the far-left edge of the dance floor, moving toward the back, where a velvet rope had been trampled.

No house lights yet. Past the restrooms, Banka entered a darker, smaller space, with no idea where he was or where he was going. Ahead, he recognized a uniform, saw a riot cop swing his baton at panicked clubgoers, lit by a flashing red light—then lost track of him. A big woman with a purse in one hand and her wig in the other came out of nowhere, shoving Banka against the wall, running on past him.

In the midst of this pandemonium, Banka heard the unmistakable sound of gunfire. Two quick shots—*crack-crack*—which were answered immediately by a different-caliber *pop*.

Banka drew his weapon. Many of those trying to shove past him now hit the floor. Banka moved in what he perceived to be the direction of the firefight, coming to a blind corner, going low, gun in both hands out in front of him. He rounded it, finding nothing.

Two more shots from the first weapon—*crack-crack*—and Banka sprang ahead, throwing caution aside. He turned another dark corner, gun out protectively.

Body on the floor. A man knelt over it, wearing a riot vest over plainclothes. A cop kneeling over a Black guy with a chest wound.

The Black guy was dead. The plainclothes cop wasn't offering first aid. In fact, Banka was unclear what he was doing.

The cop saw Banka and straightened fast, hands empty. It was Detective Kevin Quiston. Banka straightened too. Quiston was looking Banka's way, but not at him—past him.

Banka turned. Another man lay at the opposite end of the hall. He also wore a vest, but a different model. He was FBI.

He was on his back, legs moving, blood spurting out of the side of his neck in high, pulsing arcs.

Banka rushed to his side. It was Gerald Roy. His gun was still in his hand, moving at his side.

Banka looked into his eyes, which stared at the ceiling but saw something else.

Banka reached across with his off hand and clamped it over the spritzing neck wound, Roy's pulse pushing against his palm.

Banka looked back, down the length of Roy's body to where Quiston stood near the dead man. It had been a shoot-out.

"TEN-ONE, MAN DOWN, MAN DOWN! TEN-ONE!"

It was Quiston yelling into his radio, trying to be heard over the music and the chaos—Banka not ten feet away and barely able to make it out.

Banka leaned over Roy's face again, getting in his gaze. Roy's eyes found him. Roy was trying to speak. He was speaking. But Banka couldn't hear what he said.

Roy's pulse weakened against Banka's palm. Banka looked around for something to help him, medically, but there was nothing. Nothing he could do.

Roy's jaw stopped moving. His gaze went wide, then long. His irises became fixed, Banka feeling the agent's body settle against the floor.

Banka kept his grip on Roy's neck, unreasonably afraid to let go at first. When he did, and gradually, his hand came away a gooey, dripping mess.

Banka sat back on the floor. He looked around, trying to under-stand what had transpired.

Two widely spaced bullet holes in the wall behind where Roy had stood before he fell. Two shots that had missed.

He saw a tear in Roy's vest now, just below his shoulder. A shot deflected.

Quiston's radio hand fell when he saw that Banka had given up on Roy. Quiston's service piece remained holstered, Banka noted.

Banka got to his feet using his gun hand, not the one drenched in Agent Roy's blood. When he had first come upon the scene, Quiston had been kneeling over the arm of the other dead man.

Banka crossed the short distance to the other dead man's splayed shoes. The corpse wore black pants and a black shirt, a military-style beret fallen from its head. A gun was in its hand, lying against its side, where Quiston had been kneeling. A smaller-caliber weapon than Roy's. The dead man's grip on the weapon was loose.

Banka reviewed the math in an instant.

Heard two shots—then one answering shot—then a pause.

The first two must have missed Roy, fired in the dark.

Roy fired back on instinct; that was the answering *pop*. That one struck the Black militant in the chest. He fell.

And then—after the pause—the militant fired two more shots at Roy? From the floor? Without Roy firing back at him?

Banka looked at Quiston. Quiston's eyes went to Banka's, the property-crimes detective looking sick and in shock.

But there was something else in his eyes. Banka saw it sometimes in suspects he questioned. That thing when a person is trying to read your reaction to the story they are telling. Gauging if you're buying it or not.

Another FBI agent rushed into the hallway, gun up. Banka pointed him to Roy. The agent's mouth fell open, and after a moment he brought his walkie-talkie to it.

One of the SWAT team leaders ran in, a flashlight on the top of his long weapon. He pulled on Banka's shoulder, yelling into his ear.

"SALITA!"

Banka looked at him dumbly, then turned his ear to the SWAT leader's mouth again.

"DEAD!"

Banka followed the man's flashlight beam deeper into the rear of the club. Past a woman on her knees, covering her head with her hands, too scared to stand. Past a dazed man sitting against a wall with his legs straight out, bleeding from his scalp. Stopping at a body sprawled atop overturned cartons of liquor.

The SWAT team leader's flashlight beam lit up Salita's face, his eyes terrified in death, mustache fringed with blood where he'd coughed out his final breath. A pool of alcohol from the broken bottles darkened the threadbare carpet.

A few feet away lay another Black man dressed similarly to the dead militant. These men could have been brothers. Salita's muscle, maybe.

It was a total fucking disaster.

Banka felt stickiness on his hand and remembered Roy's blood. The SWAT team leader illuminated it.

"YOU HIT?"

Banka shook his head. He found his holster and jammed his sidearm into it.

And then—suddenly, blessedly—the music stopped. A ringing noise pealed in Banka's head, with voices yelling under it, and the sound of someone moaning nearby.

A commotion down the hall. The SWAT team leader rushed to it.

Banka stayed where he was, his head swimming as he sought to right his thoughts. A shit show. He was going to catch hell. They all were.

Near him, he saw a flashing red light. This one was inside a room. That brought him back. Focused him.

He commandeered a passing riot cop, grabbed him by his vest. Banka pointed to the doorway of the room with the flashing light.

"Stay right here!" Banka yelled, unable to hear his own voice.

The young cop nodded, taking up a position by the door, facing out.

Banka entered the room, which was vacant. With his elbow he closed the door almost all the way—noting a barricade lock. It was a windowless office stripped bare: desk, beat-up easy chair, corner floor lamp, clothes on the floor. An odd built-in sideboard contained a hot plate, foam take-out cartons, an oversized bottle of Russian vodka.

Atop the desk was a drink in a rocks glass, half gone. A ripped-open roll of Certs mints. A Chicago taxi map book opened to a South Side neighborhood. And, in a black glass ashtray, a pair of gold-and-black cuff links from the Stardust Hotel in Las Vegas.

With his clean hand, Banka reached into his rear left pocket and pulled out a handkerchief. He used it to pull open the central drawer, finding two more rolls of Certs mints there and a baggie of white powder.

In the next drawer down on the left side, he found cash, loose, stacked, and rolled. He touched none of it.

The second drawer down was empty.

The bottom drawer held two identical steno pad notebooks, paired with an elastic band.

Using his handkerchief, Banka picked up the notebooks. The cover of the top one contained scratched notes and a few telephone numbers written at odd angles and later crossed out.

Banka didn't think about it too long. He sucked in his gut and slipped the twin notebooks up underneath his bulletproof vest.

He closed the bottom drawer with the toe of his shoe, plucked the cuff links from the ashtray, wrapped them in the handkerchief, which he pocketed, then moved back to the door to bring the riot cop inside.

At the Lanes that night, after closing, Nicky sat alone at the lounge bar, the mirror ball rotating. The only other light in the place was the television over the bar behind him. Nicky had poured himself a drink some time ago and was still working on it, pacing himself. He liked watching the lights swirl over the empty lanes and the walls. It made him feel as if he were hurtling through space.

After a commercial for a local technical trade school ended, there was a station identification at the top of the hour. Then the news he had been waiting for came on.

He didn't move, didn't turn and watch. He just listened to the musical theme over the opening.

"Good evening, thanks for joining us. Tonight—mayhem at a North Halsted discotheque, as a botched police raid leaves four dead, including an FBI agent..."

Nicky's brain blocked out the rest. He closed his eyes and let his head dip forward. Not in prayer, though that was what it looked like. Nor in regret. Certainly not in triumph.

His greatest problem had been resolved in one bold stroke—but all he could think was that it didn't have to be this way. Nothing did.

Eventually he turned to the bar. He pulled over an ashtray and a book of matches—*Ten Pin Lanes—36 Lanes—Strike HERE*—and fished the card with Roy's private phone number out of his pocket. Nicky lit the card and watched it burn, laying it in the ashtray before the flame touched his fingers.

Breakfast didn't sit right with him. Lately, nothing he ate did.

Tony Accardo roamed the rooms of the first floor. He liked Palm Springs, but it wasn't home. He had already given the word to sell Ashland. Clarice was busted over it, but Accardo had decided he could never set foot inside that house again.

Clarice was also worried about him. He didn't like that.

Salita was dead; that was the good news. A stroke of luck. Gunned down in a cop raid on a Black discotheque, along with the strike-force FBI agent Accardo had heard about.

It didn't make total sense how it had happened, but it was good for him. With one big piece still missing.

His lawyer, Bernard, had called to say he was coming in on the earliest flight. Lawyers didn't travel to deliver good news. But talking on the phone wasn't safe now, even with the attorney-client privilege.

He stood in front of the open fridge, trying to remember what he went there looking for. He poured himself a glass of lemonade from the Tupperware pitcher and carried the drink into the backyard.

From his chair at the patio table, he could see golfers hitting. He heard the whine of electric carts in the distance. White sun visors over the crest of the green slope.

The sun was strong and bright. He closed his eyes and dozed for a while.

A flurry of movement in the house behind him opened his eyes. Bernard had arrived with his briefcase. He came out and sat in a chair. "I brought you some mail," he said.

Bernard was a tough read. Normally Accardo liked that about him but not today. Bernard put a stack of mail from Ashland Avenue on the table. On top of the stack, he laid a padded brown envelope, addressed to Bernard at his office. Bernard set a leather-handled letter opener down next to the mail stack.

Accardo looked at Bernard, who nodded at the opener. Accardo cut open the top package. A pair of gold-and-black cuff links tumbled out onto the table like dice.

His stolen cuff links.

Bernard sorted through some files in his briefcase, not looking.

Accardo reached into the envelope and pulled out two steno pad notebooks. He recognized them and the elastic band around them. He snapped it off, leafing through.

He closed the notebooks and set them down on the table. He placed his hand upon them. After a few moments, he drummed his fingers softly.

Accardo stood and walked back inside the house with the notebooks. The best part about his Palm Springs house was the fireplace. He flipped the switch and, an airless second later, *fwooomph*! Accardo tossed the notebooks into the fire. He watched them burn.

Clarice came downstairs, having heard the gas come on. She went to his side.

"Everything okay, Joe?" she asked.

He told her, "We can go back to Chicago now, whenever you like."

Clarice turned him to her, looking in his eyes, making sure he was sure. She kissed his cheek and gave his arm a good squeeze. Then she went off and called Marie.

Accardo's mind wandered sometimes, and he didn't like it. Memories intruded, and once in a while he became distracted by the voices of people who weren't there.

He thought of Frank Nitti in the rail yard in 1943, stumbling drunk, shooting himself in the face three times until he collapsed dead.

Capone with the mind of a child in 1947, tearing apart a room in a lunatic rage.

Sam Giancana shot six times in the face in his basement kitchen in 1975, food sizzling on the stove.

Accardo looked into the flames. He switched off the gas, and the fire went out with a sigh. "Michael?" he said. He looked around, calling out for Michael Volpe one more time before he remembered. Only Bernard was near enough to hear him. Bernard wouldn't react.

Bernard came inside, said he had a flight to catch, and left.

Accardo went back to the patio and collected his cuff links, dropping them into his pants pocket. The mail could wait. When Clarice was done, Accardo picked up the telephone. He dialed Doves, who owned a house a few streets over. Let the FBI listen in on him now.

"I changed my mind," said Accardo. "Let's tee off at one thirty."

A week passed.

Nicky stayed clear of the Lanes as much as he could, letting things settle. If he had to go in but saw a car in the parking lot he didn't like, he kept driving. The first five nights he stayed at five different hotels, food ordered in.

Salita was dead. A bonus. Nicky held his breath about the notebooks, hoping Salita had at least been smart enough to keep them not on his person, but someplace hidden and remote. When they didn't turn up by week's end, he allowed himself to believe that the secret had died with Salita. Nicky had thought the notebooks might mysteriously disappear anyway.

In the aftermath, it occurred to Nicky how wrong things could have gone, how much he had needed a Hail Mary and it had come through. He didn't want to jinx it. Why he stayed scarce. He didn't even eat Polynesian for fear of what a fortune cookie might tell him.

He'd had no contact with Quiston; that was the plan. Let him lose money betting on Chicago teams with someone else. A good deal, wiping his slate clean. And good riddance.

He begged off going home to Helena and Nicholas, because what

311

if somebody was watching for him there? He couldn't even think of who, but just the thought of bringing trouble to their doorstep was reason enough to steer clear.

End of the week, he started feeling much better. Lighter, freer. Like new, in a way. He was getting that second chance he'd always dreamed of.

No more half measures, no more distractions. He would move back home, establish himself there. Cut back the drinking to two a night, max. Run his schemes, sure, but be smart about it, staying small. Keep Helena smiling, keep hearing that laugh. Do more things with Nicholas—more ball games, more treats. Maybe even teach him bowling. Pick up a ball again. See if he still had the touch.

After the following weekend, Nicky returned to the Lanes full days again. Business was down, the nice weather making the day-time hours go slow, but that was expected. Even the Lanes looked different to Nicky now. While he was away, he had started thinking—blue sky, maybe it was crazy—about turning the Lanes into a full-time discotheque. Updating the lounge, taking out the alleys, and putting in a dance floor, ceiling lights, sound system. He envisioned his entire life being halfway legit; maybe there'd be multiple night-clubs and, separately, a string of video arcades—something he could cut Trixie and Debra in on. Get ahead of trends, set himself up big for the 1980s and beyond. It was something to think about anyway.

The Edge of Night came on. Nicky had missed a week of episodes, so he was curious to catch up, but when the show opened on Police Chief Derek Mallory, the character who reminded him so much of Gerald Roy, Nicky didn't feel right. It was like watching Roy live on in the city of Monticello, handsomely pursuing justice on the trail of the Red-Head Killer. Nicky didn't make it to the first commercial before switching it off.

Chuckie noticed. "Your soap," he said.

Nicky shook his head. "It's stupid."

"Here he is," said Dimes Forbstein, waddling in, big, gap-toothed smile. "Feeling better? I came by twice last week, no Nicky Pins."

"Little under the weather."

"Glad you're back. I missed you. I like stability."

"Nobody," said Nicky, "and I mean nobody, likes stability more than me."

"We should drink to that," said Dimes. "Nicky Pins is back, the Man is back. Things getting back to normal."

Nicky said, "What's that?"

"The Man is back. Back in town. Back in all ways, I presume."

Nicky looked at him. "Accardo's back in town?"

"What I heard. Nice to be feeding you some bit of news for a change."

Good or bad news, Nicky wasn't sure. His grand jury date was coming up still—one more thing to deal with. But with no button men, no Michael Volpe, no Johnny Salita, and no notebooks, what did they have?

Chuckie came over laughing with some other guy. A repairman in his thirties wearing a rayon crewneck jersey, holding the grip handles of a canvas tool bag.

"Nicky, this is Patrick," said Chuckie. "Stuck machine I told you about. That game, the new one. *Space Defenders.*"

"*Space INVADERS,*" Nicky said. "Yeah, thanks for coming so quick. We're losing customers to the pizza joint over on Rutherford, because their game works." Nicky started across toward the arcade room with him. Over his shoulder, Nicky said, "Chuckie, get Dimes a drink. I'll join in a bit." Nicky shook the repairman's hand as they moved. "I actually have a few questions for you. About the business."

The repairman said, "Happy to answer if I can."

Nicky opened the door for him and followed inside, showing him to the new *Space Invaders* video game console.

"This is my workhorse, my golden goose," said Nicky. "Coin jam,

I think, but Chuckie was afraid he'd break it trying to get in there. You see the screen works fine."

The demo screen showed rows and columns of descending aliens, the sound effect a thudding, staccato bass-line march: *DUH-DUH. DUH-DUH*.

"Let's take a look," said Patrick, setting down his tool bag.

Nicky said, "I'd love another one of these units if I could get my hands on it. I need more games, as many as I can get. What's the wait time currently?"

"Well, I just repair them. I can give you the sales department's number."

"No, I have that," said Nicky. He watched Patrick kneel and inspect the coin slot. "Would just love to get somebody with contacts on the inside."

"I don't really know that part of the business."

Nicky nodded. It was worth a try. He got a weird echo, subtly, of the time he was in here with Roy, fooling with the Evel Knievel pinball machine. Which was still busted. Nicky backed off. "Anything you need, just holler."

Nicky was almost back at the double glass doors when Patrick the repairman said, "There is one thing."

Nicky stopped and turned. Patrick was still on one knee, his tool bag open before him. "Yeah?" Nicky said.

"Maybe something to drink?"

"Sure, like a water? You want a Pepsi?"

"How about a scotch mist?"

Nicky thought he had imagined the guy saying that. He thought for a moment he was in a nightmare.

"What'd you say?" said Nicky.

Patrick the repairman pulled, from his tool bag, a billfold, and stood to full height. He showed Nicky his credentials, his badge and photo card with the blue block letters *FBI*.

"Special Agent Patrick Greavey," he said. "I'm taking over for Gerald Roy."

Nicky stared. He could barely push the word out. *"Who?"*

"I think you know, Mr. Passero."

Greavey pocketed his credentials. Nicky stood there staring.

Roy had lied to him. He hadn't been the only one who knew about Nicky.

Nicky had to assume this guy knew everything.

Every last thing.

The sound of the action on the lanes outside faded, and the only sound Nicky could hear was like a beating heart or a ticking clock—

DUH-DUH. DUH-DUH.

Special Agent Patrick Greavey said, "I'm your new handler, Nicky Pins."

There was nothing for Nicky to say. He turned slowly and pushed through the double doors of the arcade, back into the main bowling alley.

Chuckie was on the phone, cigarette dancing on his lips. Dimes sat wide-legged at the bar, waiting for him. A ball rolled down an alley, struck pins falling.

1984

HOTEL EMPLOYEES & RESTAURANT EMPLOYEES INTERNATIONAL UNION

Hearings Before the
PERMANENT SUBCOMMITTEE ON INVESTIGATIONS
of the
COMMITTEE ON GOVERNMENTAL AFFAIRS
UNITED STATES SENATE

Ninety-Eight Congress
Washington, DC
Thursday, June 21, 1984

The subcommittee met, at 10 a.m., in room SD-342, Dirksen Senate Office Building, under authority of Senate Resolution 354, agreed to March 2, 1984, Hon. William V. Roth, Jr. (chairman of the subcommittee) presiding.

OPENING REMARKS

This morning, the Permanent Subcommittee on Investigations will receive the testimony of the reputed "Godfather" of Chicago Organized Crime for many years, Mr. Anthony J. Accardo. He is a legend in his own time, an heir to Mr. Alphonse Capone, the founder of the Chicago syndicate. It is fitting that Mr. Accardo appears here today, because it was Congress that passed the prohibition legislation which gave birth to organized crime as we know it today in the United States.

Although organized crime has at times been glamorized, its day-to-day operations are violent and murderous. It rules by fear. It punishes without judge, jury, or trial. It shakes down the public every day.

It is interesting to note that while these criminals flagrantly violate local, state, and federal law, they ruthlessly enforce their own form of justice. For instance, published reports stated that a number of burglars suspected of breaking into the home of Mr. Accardo were murdered in cold blood.

Perhaps, then, Mr. Accardo can understand why we in Congress are so fed up with the continued lawlessness demonstrated by the Chicago syndicate.

While organized crime can intimidate individuals against testifying in criminal trials, it can never intimidate Congress.

I have asked Patrick Greavey, a staff investigator on special detail from the FBI, to present a brief introductory statement concerning Mr. Accardo's background, and the subcommittee's attempts to secure his testimony.

TESTIMONY OF PATRICK GREAVEY, STAFF INVESTIGATOR

I am Patrick Greavey, a staff investigator with the Permanent Subcommittee on Investigations. I have been asked to summarize events leading to today's hearing.

Anthony Joseph Accardo was born in Chicago in 1906. His involvement in organized criminal activities has been well documented by law enforcement authorities and widely reported by the media. Many of his alleged associates are well-known organized crime figures, including notorious gangsters such as Al Capone, Murray "the Camel" Humphreys, and Jack "Greasy Thumb" Guzik, all publicly linked with Mr. Accardo during the 1930s and 1940s. Accardo was reputed to have been Capone's bodyguard and chauffeur, and his initial notoriety stemmed from his alleged role in the St. Valentine's Day massacre in 1929. When he was twenty-five years old, Tony Accardo was named in the "Public Enemy" list of prominent underworld figures published by the Chicago Crime Commission. More than five decades later, the name "Tony Accardo" is still listed among the power brokers of organized crime as the top adviser in the Chicago mob.

Although Accardo has been arrested numerous times, he has often boasted of not spending a single night in jail. In the early 1960s, he was convicted of filing false income tax returns and sentenced to six years in prison, but this conviction was overturned on appeal and his retrial resulted in an acquittal. Accardo was cited for criminal contempt by both the McClellan and Kefauver committees for his refusal to answer their questions, but he was never successfully prosecuted. More recently, in 1981, he was indicted in Florida with fifteen other persons for his participation in a scheme designed to defraud the welfare fund of the Laborers' International Union. Accardo was also acquitted in that case.

In these hearings, as in the past, congressional committees have been told of organized crime's influence within the Hotel Employees and Restaurant Employees International Union, and Accardo's name has repeatedly surfaced. This subcommittee recently heard specific testimony attesting to Accardo's great power and influence.

On November 17, 1983, Accardo appeared before this subcommittee. He was immunized pursuant to court order, preventing him from invoking his fifth amendment privilege. Still, he refused to answer the subcommittee's questions, claiming they were derived from illegal electronic surveillance. The Committee on Governmental Affairs and the full Senate subsequently passed Senate Resolution 293, which authorized the institution of a civil contempt action against Accardo. This was only the second time in history that such an action had been instituted.

Mr. Accardo's testimony today is particularly important to our ongoing investigation of the influence of Chicago's organized crime family in the Hotel Workers Union and in the city of Chicago generally...

S even weeks after the raid at Anita's, Feliks Banka retired from the Chicago Police Department. He and his wife sold their brick bungalow in Montclare to their daughter, Renata, and retired to Key Biscayne, the barrier island off the coast of Miami on Florida's southern Atlantic coast. Banka bought property there in the late 1960s, before Richard Nixon did and put it on the map. In fifteen years, Key Biscayne had gone from a quaint, quiet fishing community to a warm-weather playground for the wealthy. Banka's neighbors wore polo shirts and boat shoes and played a lot of tennis, but he had a few friends down at the marina. He fished a bit and for a while even hired himself out as a boatmate on charters, thinking it would be fun, though the rich assholes made sure that it wasn't.

Six years had passed, and he did not miss the Chicago winters, nor the traffic, nor the murders. His wife was happy with her small circle of friends, and the sunrises—viewed most mornings from the Crandon Park beach parking lot, his newspaper spread open over the dash while he drank his coffee—rarely disappointed.

Only his conscience bothered him. He'd been following the Las Vegas hotel employees labor racketeering and union corruption case in the *Miami Herald*, with occasional rides into downtown Miami to pick up day-old *Chicago Tribunes*. It troubled Banka that Tony Accardo was still active in the life, still living like the laws of the land didn't apply to him.

The buildup to Accardo's court appearance saw a fair amount of suspense, his testimony having been delayed a number of times. In his first appearance before the subcommittee in November of the prior year, he had refused to answer any questions, even under a grant of immunity, taking the fifth more than fifty times. That led to a contempt-of-Congress resolution, followed by a federal district judge's order compelling him to appear a second time and answer questions in depth. That appearance was delayed when Accardo checked himself into the Mayo Clinic for an undisclosed illness. His appearance was scheduled again for May, but a fall at his daughter's home the day before resulted in further hospitalization and eight stitches in his scalp.

His testimony was rescheduled again for June 21. It had been a long time coming with delays and continuances. Was it all stall tactics, or had the Man finally lost a step or two? Banka felt he had to know. As the day approached, it was all he could think about. Thoughts of Accardo consumed him. It felt like unfinished business. Unfinished business for his soul.

He told his wife he had to go, and after years of being a detective's wife, she didn't question it. Banka phoned up a contact at the Chicago Crime Commission, who got him on the list for a pass. The proceeding was to be held in the Dirksen Senate Office Building, named for the same late senator from Illinois as the Dirksen Federal Building in Chicago, where the FBI field office was located. Banka visited AAA and picked out maps to plot his trip, heading up on the day of the twentieth when it seemed that Accardo finally would appear and actually testify under oath.

Banka had personally met Tony Accardo twice, and never in

Chicago. The first time was in April of 1973. Paul Ricca, born Felice De Lucia, a.k.a. "Paul the Waiter," had died the previous autumn from a heart attack. Ricca had been Accardo's most trusted confidant and consigliere, and there was concern among law enforcement that his death could destabilize the Outfit if Joe Batters, a.k.a. "the Big Tuna," was left to his own devices. There were also whispers, at the federal level, that Sam Giancana might be returning to the US from his exile in Mexico; Paul Ricca had been a mediating force between the two headstrong former capos.

Banka didn't care much about the goombah family drama. He went to see Accardo that afternoon in Key Biscayne because it was neutral territory, and because he'd been invited and he was curious to know why. Banka arrived at the tuna boat to find Accardo dressed in Bermuda shorts, a Havana-style linen shirt, dark, horn-rimmed sunglasses, and a straw hat. Banka never forgot the crime boss's reply after he offered Accardo condolences for Ricca's death.

"I already lived too long myself," Accardo had said. That was ten years ago now.

Accardo had offered Banka a cold Żywiec, a Polish lager, showing he had done some homework. It was a talk, just a sit-down, not a chess match as far as conversations went. Eventually Accardo got around to saying what he wanted to say, how he'd been able to befriend—that is, co-opt—most men, meaning judges and politicians but especially cops, yet he had never succeeded in befriending Banka. He respected that, he claimed, and Banka said that he respected the fact that he was being respected. Accardo offered to pay Banka a retainer on the order of fifty dollars a month, further to that respect, at which Banka laughed and turned him down.

"You're here, though," said Accardo. "You took the meeting."

And so he had.

The second meeting, in the spring of 1976, took place on a different boat. Banka was down on vacation, and somehow

Accardo knew this and invited him fishing. Doves Aiuppa was there also, sitting with them for a while before going to the front of the boat. Accardo offered Banka the name and number of his lawyer, Bernard, in case Banka ever wanted to get in touch, and vice versa. "You seem like a reasonable person," said Accardo. "Who knows? Maybe you'd like a nicer retirement down here than you're in for, a soft landing like you deserve."

Banka didn't say yes at the time. He didn't say no. He didn't discard the lawyer's phone number either.

By then it was late in Banka's career. He'd had a minor health scare the summer before, his kidney, which turned out to be no big thing, but enough to make him think. *A soft landing like you deserve.* It was puffery—Banka deserved no more or less than anyone—but the point Accardo made stayed with Banka. How short was life?

Going by the book had seen Banka through. Sleeping at night was worth it. But he was getting toward the end, and that was when he thought about hedging his bet. By 1978, Accardo was semiretired, it seemed, taking sun out west in Palm Springs, not dealing with things in Chicago day-to-day. Banka knew Accardo was careful about getting tripped up in his sunset years, after running the table for so long. So feeding him information—such as the fact that there was *apparently* an inside informant talking to the FBI about the break-in at Accardo's house and the subsequent purge of thieves—felt like a safe play. Banka had no specifics to give. And he never did learn who the informant was, though he had some suspects.

And then the notebook page came into the strike force by mail, matching Accardo's handwriting on file. Sharing a photostat of it with Accardo's lawyer resulted in a request from Bernard, with a large reward offered.

Accardo already had both feet out the door. He was all but through. Everything was winding down. That was what Banka believed at the time.

The disastrous raid at Anita's sealed it for him. Roy's death was a harsh reminder that it could all end just like that, and that it was time for Banka to get out. And land softly.

Banka was not concerned about any of that coming out today. Fear wasn't what drew him to these proceedings. Guilt did. Banka wanted to see Joe Batters one more time. Accardo had slipped the noose again in 1978, a grand jury ultimately never bringing charges in the slayings that followed his home burglary. After a career spent fighting Accardo and his Outfit to keep his home city safe, Banka prayed that by giving the Man a lifeline near the end, he hadn't abetted any real harm.

When the committee-room doors opened, all heads turned. Tony Accardo entered slowly, walking with the assistance of a cane. Now seventy-eight, he hobbled through the gallery, moving to the central table where his name card and a microphone waited.

Banka was shocked at Joe Batters's appearance. The intervening six years had not been kind. Banka had heard cancer; others said heart disease. It was probably both. Accardo looked shrunken inside his suit, a shadow of his former broad-shouldered self. There were medical personnel seated along the side wall, including, apparently, a cardiologist with a heart monitor, on hand for Accardo.

The reclusive capo lowered himself unsteadily into a chair, assisted by his lawyer—not Bernard now, but a new, criminal lawyer in a pin-striped suit with widely padded shoulders.

Banka couldn't help but think of Joe Batters as a symbol of Chicago itself, part of the mosaic of the city—and it was a blow to see it looking so feeble and worn.

After Accardo was seated, Banka was surprised to see Pat Greavey, an agent he remembered from Gerry Roy's strike force, get up to read a statement. Roy's murder inside Anita's had been laid off on Salita's dead bodyguard at the inquest. Banka returned to Chicago some months after the raid to testify as to what he'd witnessed on that night. In court, you say what you *saw* happen, not what you *think* happened. Detective Kevin Quiston testified at the same inquest, and everything he said held. Banka didn't speak to him. He'd heard Quiston got deeply into debt a few years later, gambling trouble, and stole some narcotics from the property room, which he got caught dealing to a snitch. He was in the process of being fired when he shot himself with his service weapon in his car outside Arlington Park in 1981 or early 1982.

Accardo was asked to stand again, and they administered the oath. He raised his right hand, answered in the affirmative, and sat. Three senators faced him, but only Roth, the chairman, asked questions.

"Mr. Accardo, you have been granted immunity from prosecution for your testimony. Would you care to make any comment on Mr. Greavey's introductory statement?"

Accardo said something inaudible.

"Please get the microphone right before you so we can hear you, Mr. Accardo."

Accardo's lawyer did it for him. Accardo said gruffly, "No, sir."

His voice was raspy and thin. Banka was rocked by how gravelly he sounded. The pugnacious Joe Batters was no more, and a frail old man had taken his place.

"Mr. Accardo, you were head of the Chicago organized crime syndicate for many years, isn't that true?"

"No, sir."

"That is *not* true?"

"No, sir."

"Are you familiar with the organized crime syndicate known as the Outfit?"

"No, sir."

"Did you not, at one time, work for Al Capone?"

"Sir?"

"Al Capone, did you ever work for him?"

"I knew him socially, Senator."

The senators looked at each other.

"Mr. Accardo, are you asserting under oath that you've never associated with organized crime in any way?"

"No, sir. Never."

"You've never associated in any way with illegal activities?"

"No, sir."

Accardo's lawyer covered the microphone and spoke into his ear. When the lawyer removed his hand, Accardo corrected himself.

"I've gambled."

The senators were already exasperated. It went on like that for a while. They tried to make headway with some tax questions, but that went nowhere. Accardo claimed he was a retired beer salesman.

"Do you recall the FBI agents, some FBI agents raiding your home at River Forest?"

"Yes, sir."

"Do you still own a home there?"

"No, sir."

"Did the FBI find money in your home? In a vault in your home?"

"Yes, sir."

"How much?"

After conferring with his lawyer, he answered, "It was $275,000."

"And they seized that money?"

"Yes, sir."

"And did you bring suit against them in court?"

"I did, yes, sir."

"And you recovered the money?"

"Yes, sir."

"And where did that great sum of money come from?"

"From gambling."

By this point, the frustrated senators saw how this was going to go. They brought out organizational charts and photographs.

Accardo identified Doves Aiuppa and Jackie "the Lackey" Cerone as golfing partners but denied knowing either man professionally or even knowing what they did for a living.

"Mr. Accardo, do you really expect us to believe you had no knowledge of any kind that these individuals were reputed mobsters?"

"Yes, sir."

"Don't you think that's a little incredulous?"

"I think I answered the question."

It was laughable, but nobody in the gallery made a sound. The few names Accardo did offer up were those of men long dead. The mood inside the room grew tense once a projector was turned on and slides were displayed on a screen at the side of the chamber, one after the other. Murdered gangsters, starting with Sam Giancana.

"You knew Sam Giancana, Mr. Accardo?"

"He gave me some car rides."

"What can you tell us about Mr. Giancana's murder?"

"I have no knowledge about it."

"You have no knowledge, direct or indirect?"

"None whatsoever."

"Did you have anything to do with it?"

"No, sir."

"Have you ever directed anybody to commit murder?"

"No, sir."

"Mr. Accardo, I want to show you the victims who were murdered or disappeared during the Chicago gangland purge of 1978, following a reputed break-in at your house in River Forest. Please direct your attention to the screen."

Banka recognized Vin Labotta in the next photograph, an old mug shot. Underneath it was the word MURDERED.

"Vincent Labotta. Did you know this man?"

"I don't remember."

They cycled through photographs of the trunked thieves. Gonzo

Forte. Didi Paré. Joey "the Jew" Lemmelman. Rhino Guarino. Cue Stick Pino. Most of them were mug shots, all with the label MURDERED in bold black underneath.

"You don't remember any of these murdered felons?"

"No, sir."

Sal "Brags" Bragotti's mug shot came up. His caption read, DIS-APPEARED, PRESUMED MURDERED.

"Salvatore Bragotti?"

"No, sir."

Frankie "Crease Man" Santangelo. DISAPPEARED, PRESUMED MUR-DERED.

"Francis Santangelo?"

Accardo said, "No, sir."

Michael Volpe. DISAPPEARED, PRESUMED MURDERED.

"Michael Volpe's remains were never found—however, his eyeglasses were recovered from an incinerator inside your home."

Accardo hesitated. His lawyer conferred with him.

"Michael worked for me for many years."

Johnny Salita's driver's license photograph, the same one Banka had distributed the night of the raid on Anita's. DECEASED.

"This man, John Salita?"

"No, sir."

"Mr. Salita was killed along with two other men in the botched raid that resulted in the murder of FBI agent Gerald Roy."

"I didn't know him."

Then a mug shot of Nicky "Pins" Passero, from his pinch for the race-fixing scheme. DISAPPEARED, PRESUMED MURDERED.

"And this man, Nicholas Passero?"

Accardo was slower to answer this time. His lawyer interrupted the silence by conferring with him, but Accardo seemed not to listen. He was looking at the photograph on the screen.

The senator said, "Mr. Accardo?"

Banka watched as Accardo appeared to struggle. With memory, maybe, or speech. Maybe with sorrow. Maybe something had finally broken through Accardo's shroud of willful ignorance.

"I think..." said Accardo, still looking at the projected photograph of Nicky Pins's face, "I think he ran a bowling alley."

They called a recess soon after, with an afternoon session to follow, but Banka had seen enough. For him, it was over. He had a long drive home.

1992

The video store on Noe Street, a block off Market, was called Mission Video, though it was in the Castro. A corner location, deeper than it was wide, roughly half the size of a typical retail space, paired with a gourmet cookie shop next door named Chocolate Ginger. Four narrow aisles of VHS tapes on wire racks, arranged in categories, with "New Releases," "Staff Picks," "Cult," and "Queer Interests" up front. The posters on the walls, such as *The Presidio* and *Pacific Heights*, highlighted the store's San Francisco location. The rearmost section of the store was curtained off, porn kept separate from the mainstream titles.

Mission Video's owner, Nino Porchera, had gotten into the industry early, working at a store named Action Video in 1983. Action Video started as a boutique in the Tenderloin for cineastes and hobbyists interested in the emerging new home-video industry, but very quickly its owners realized that half their profit came from renting pornographic movies. Action Video soon moved to a larger space, still renting traditional feature films, but the inventory was 90 percent gay smut. As such, and with home video contributing to the closure of many porn theaters, the location became a pickup scene.

When the owners had a personal and professional falling-out,

Nino jumped to another outlet, one of a chain of six local shops named Treasure Video, which balanced mainstream Hollywood fare with top-shelf raunch. Nino was promoted and later asked to open a seventh location for them, which was so successful he was hired away to perform the same function for a bookstore chain that wanted to branch into video rentals.

That was Mission Books, which spun off Mission Video, a family-friendly store that kept the artwork for "adult titles" in binders at a discreet counter for twenty-one-plus customers to flip through. Spooked by the influx of the national Blockbuster Video chain at the end of the decade, Mission had decided to shutter its video stores and return its focus exclusively to books. Nino had set aside some money by that time and struck a deal with the company to purchase the "Mission Video" name as well as its inventory, which he moved into his current location. Nino didn't own the building, so he was never going to get rich, but the home-video rental market turned a reliable profit. As long as you kept up with each week's new releases, the business basically ran itself.

Nino worked mostly days, the slow hours, sitting on a stool behind the counter by the store's front window, overlooking the street he shared with boutiques and brownstone condominiums. He ran movies constantly on two twenty-seven-inch televisions in the store, while a small television set behind the counter was reserved for his afternoon soaps. Customers brought their movie selections up to the register, showed their club cards, paid a two-night fee of $3.15, and went home happy. All the regulars knew Nino by name. At fifty-three, stout and garrulous with a distinctive Chicago accent, his dark hair fading on top but long on the sides and in back, Nino stood out in a city of young, upwardly mobile professionals.

The big new release that week in May was the movie *JFK*, which, because of its three-hour running time, was packaged as a double VHS cassette and was therefore a pain in the ass to rent. Nino had to

Velcro two plastic clamshell cases together and hope one of the tapes didn't get lost in the first few weeks of rentals, rendering the unit useless. Shift manager Heather, a terrifically skinny San Francisco State grad with a butch haircut and six piercings in one ear, walked in at five o'clock on the dot, wearing a Jane's Addiction T-shirt with the sleeves artfully snipped away.

"How was your Wednesday, Heather?" Nino asked as she joined him behind the counter.

"Hell," Heather replied, with a blazingly cheery smile, ruby red lipstick being the only makeup she ever wore.

"They brought over some cookies from next door," he told her. "Eat some, awright?"

She gave his arm a friendly squeeze and hopped up onto the counter itself, heavy boots dangling.

"If you get bored," Nino told her, pulling on his faded leather jacket, "there's a couple of defective tapes to check there."

"My pleasure!" said Heather, with hyper-arch enthusiasm, saluting him sharply. Nino smiled, her attitude incomprehensible to him—but it was her generation's world now, and he was just passing through.

"I think I like you because you scare me," he said on his way to the door.

Nino picked up Chinese takeout on his way home, his apartment a second-story walk-up in the Castro. He opened the door, and his roommate, a West Highland white terrier, came scampering over the scuffed maple floor to meet him.

Nino lifted up the dog, which licked him through its stringy white beard. "Hello, Shithead," he said. "Who wants a walk?"

After a quick lap around the block, Nino fixed the dog's meal, then pulled his own dinner out of its plastic bag. Crispy beef and pork fried rice, because fuck vegetables. He cracked open a Miller Lite and took his seat in the kitchen nook, flipping on the television to watch the news, his nightly routine.

"Tony Accardo, the reputed longtime head of the Chicago mob, died today. He was eighty-six years old."

Over the news reader's shoulder, a photograph of Accardo walking down a sidewalk wearing a fedora, over the dates *1906–1992*.

A video segment began. The visuals distracted Nino from the reporter's narration.

Photographs of an almost unrecognizable young Accardo with Al Capone.

Film of him and Clarice outside a church at one of their daughters' weddings.

Accardo in sunglasses, seated before a microphone, testifying before the Kefauver Committee in '51.

Accardo testifying again in 1984, looking frail.

Video of Saint Mary of Nazareth Hospital on West Division Street on the West Side. The low-voiced reporter stepped into the camera angle outside the hospital. The cause of death was heart failure.

"Recent successful prosecutions of gangland leaders across the country indicate that the days of the crime bosses are over. In that respect, Tony Accardo is the last remnant of a bygone era in this country, one that the American people may be grateful to leave behind."

The news went on after that. Nino sat in stunned silence as memories came flooding into his mind, memories he had worked hard to forget.

The dog's barking brought him back. A dog-food commercial had come on the television.

Nino had to get moving. It was a nice enough night. He needed to mark this passing.

He leashed the dog and walked to a café on Gough Street, next to a thrift-shop boutique that sold vintage clothes—from the 1970s. The café had tables outside where you could sit and watch the city pass. At night there was just enough light from the interior that you could see but not really be seen. He sat before an ACT UP sticker and a men's health clinic flyer in the window, the dog at his feet. A server came out to see him, young guy, white towel tucked into the front of his apron.

Nino said, "Would you bring me a scotch? A good one, just make it a double, neat."

"Any food tonight?"

"Just the drink. I'm toasting a friend who passed today."

The young guy dipped his head, looking stricken. "I am so sorry."

"Oh no, not that," said Nino, realizing he had been misconstrued. "Old guy. Eighty-six. Long, full life. Too full, maybe."

The server went inside to get his order, and Nino felt a tug on the leash. Two young men strolling past on a date stooped to pet the dog.

"Who's this little fella?" asked one.

Nino said, "This is Shithead."

After giving the dog the attention he craved, the couple walked off into the night hand in hand. Nino watched them go. It was a different world now. It had all passed him by, like the Pride parade they put on every summer. He had come late and reluctantly to the festival and because of that, and his own solitary disposition, he felt mostly like a spectator. Maybe there was still time for that to change. He looked out into the evening and thought about everything that had brought him here.

In 1978 Chicago, it was easy to vanish if you were a gangster. You walked away, and everyone assumed the worst. Especially if you went somewhere no one would ever think to look for you, got a new name, and kept your life so small that there was no chance of anyone from your old life crossing your path.

Once he left Chicago, it was like a dream he'd once had. All gone.

Nino didn't hate who he was anymore, so there was that. You can punch yourself in the face only so many times. He hated some of the things he had done in Chicago. What he'd had to do. Things he'd tried to forget.

His drink arrived, and Nino raised it to Tony Accardo, who had died in the city he owned, with this family at his bedside, as every man wishes to go. His funeral would be a small one because he had outlived them all. His passing marked the end of an age. The old ways—everything—died with him.

Nino sipped his drink, the booze hitting, but he remained wistful. When he was finished, he lowered the glass so that Shithead could lick out whatever was left. In doing so, the dog's nose nudged Nino's hand, what passed for physical affection these days.

Even the good memories hurt. A woman standing on a stoop on a Sunday afternoon in 1978. A boy sitting in an ice cream shop with a triple scoop in a tin dish, a different sweatband on each wrist.

They were better off without him. It hurt most of all knowing that this was true.

Nino Porchera left a good tip, took up Shithead's leash, and found his way home.

Acknowledgments

This novel would not exist if not for authors James L. Swanson and Gus Russo, who introduced me to the incredible true story of the home burglary of the last great crime boss, Tony Accardo. Great thanks also to Richard Abate and Johnny Lin, my editor Wes Miller, and, of course, my own crime family, Charlotte, Melanie, Declan, Colin, and Lila.

About the Author

Chuck Hogan is the author of several acclaimed *New York Times* best-sellers, including *The Town*, for which he was awarded the Hammett Prize. He lives with his family outside Boston.